A

RIVER

DIVIDED

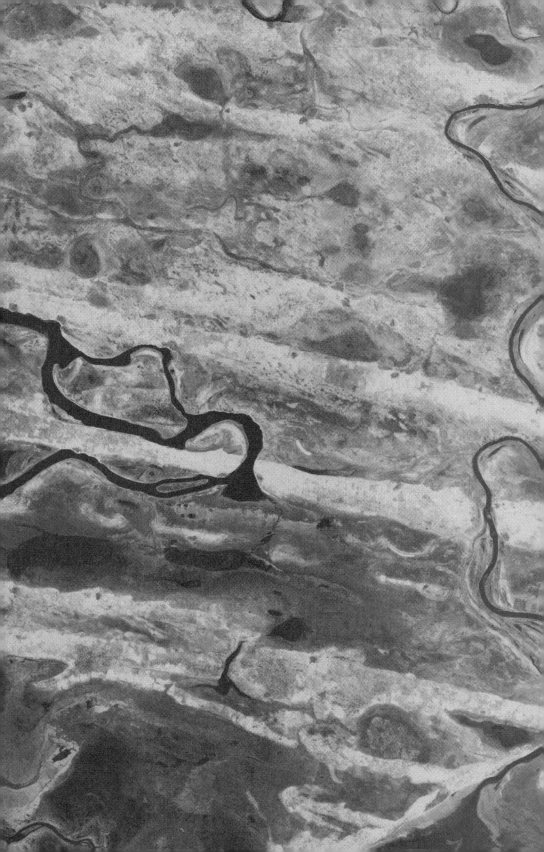

A RIVER DIVIDED

GEORGE PAXINOS

HEADS & TALES

Published in 2021 by Heads and Tales an imprint of
Hardie Grant Media

Heads and Tales (Melbourne)
Ground Floor, Building 1, 658 Church Street
Richmond VIC 3121, Australia

headsandtales.agency

Heads and Tales acknowledges the Traditional Owners of the
country on which we work, the Wurundjeri people of the Kulin
nation and the Gadigal people of the Eora nation, and recognises
their continuing connection to the land, waters and culture. We
pay our respects to their Elders past, present and emerging.

A catalogue record of this book is available from the
National Library of Australia.

A River Divided
ISBN 9780646846651

To Melpo Lekatsa

I praise the scoring drought, the flying dust,
the drying creek, the furious animal,
that they oppose us still;
that we are ruined by the thing we kill

From "Australia 1970" by Judith Wright

Prologue

DEAD SEA SHORE, AD 75

"With love eternal," said the woman as she kissed her gold bangle and placed it on the top of the bones. She saw it slide between the human remains to rest at the bottom, where they had earlier placed the cylinder and the sphere.

The three men sealed the ossuary with its stone lid, before lowering it to the depths of the pit they had dug.

All four of them tore their clothes in grief as they sang—

In the splendor of His glory,
He shall give life to the dead,
And rebuild the city of Jerusalem,
And complete His temple there.

Shreds of their clothing fluttered in gusts of wind. In the distance, they could still make out Masada through the sand storm that veiled it.

"The nine hundred and sixty died free," said the woman, tears filling her big brown eyes. "You are now near the bones of our brothers."

One by one they knelt and kissed the lid that sealed the ossuary. They piled earth on top. Each of them placed a rock for remembrance.

Book One

EVELYN

Chapter 1

DEAD SEA SHORE, JANUARY 10, 1997

The skull stared back at Evelyn through its empty eye sockets.
She could see that its dome, the calvarium, had been removed. Clearly visible were also a pelvis, a femur and what seemed to be a clavicle. The bones were human.

Feeling like a fugitive, Evelyn stood up to look around. She was on the cusp of a shallow depression, surrounded by lifeless earth, flat and gray. The sky was not graced by a bird, the earth not by a tree. Even the mountains beyond were devoid of vegetation. Marching beside the road were pylons bearing powerlines, oddly juxtaposed against Masada, which resembled a volcano with a flattened top. On the horizon to the south, erosion had sculpted the earth into low-lying profiles, like barges stranded on a dry lake. A few kilometers to the east, Evelyn could make out the shimmering Dead Sea.

Though she was only about a hundred meters from the road, the desert had the silence of a cemetery. Just then she became aware of the fortress-like security station at the Masada foothill. *If I can see them, they can see me*, she thought.

She went down on her knees to look again into the ossuary. It was about a meter deep and there were other things in it besides the bones. Pushing herself back, she sat on her heels and put her hand on her chest. Her heart was racing and she paused before reaching for the camera.

This had once been a person who breathed, who played, who loved, she thought.

The camera felt heavy and getting the settings right took time. Activating the flash, she captured images from as far into the ossuary as possible without touching the bones. It was a reburial. Was it recent or ancient? Could there be an engraving?

She started removing the soft earth around the ossuary. The earth was easy to shift, but kept falling back into the area she had cleared. Sweat was running down her face and between her shoulders. The sun was getting to her. It would make sense to return when it was cooler. Repositioning the lid, she concealed the ossuary with earth.

Earlier, on her way back to Jerusalem after visiting Masada, she had left the road to get a good photograph of the mountain. Visiting the place where nine hundred and sixty people chose death over slavery had been an emotional experience. But this was eclipsed by the discovery of the ossuary.

Now, the rugged landscape unfolded around her as she drove through the Judean Desert following Route 90 along the coastline of the Dead Sea. She felt like a schoolgirl dazzled by her first crush. *It is illegal to dig, but I have to,* she thought. *Once I tell them, the authorities would never let an amateur like me anywhere near this place again.*

She passed the sign for the Qumran Caves—the Dead Sea Scrolls. A shepherd had stumbled across them. *The soil here is full of history,* she thought. *This person might have died recently or thousands of years ago.*

❧

In the King David Hotel, Michael was just reaching for his shirt when Evelyn burst through the door of their room saying, "I found a skeleton near Masada!"

"A skeleton near Masada," he repeated. "Was he crossing the road?"

"I'm serious. It was in a stone ossuary." She sketched the shape of a rectangle with her hands. "I was photographing Masada when the rock I was standing on slipped from under me and rolled into a trough. When I looked down, I saw a straight edge. Nature doesn't have straight edges, so I brushed the earth aside. It was a lid. I tried to remove it, but it was stuck. I got the crowbar from the car."

"How come nobody had seen it before you?" he asked.

"There might have been more soil on it. Wind erosion? Rains? And mini earthquakes happen here all the time, you know—the Masada Fault Zone."

"And you're sure it's human."

"Look at these." She scrolled through the images on her camera. "The calvarium has been sawn off. It must be human. And the orbits—the eye sockets can't be anything else."

Michael zoomed in. "Alas, poor Yorick." He frowned and shook his head. "I should've come with you. The gynecologists' brunch was a dead affair—more dead than your skeleton."

"I'm going back this afternoon," she said, looking at him in what could only mean invitation.

"You might get me interested in archeology, after all." He kept scrolling through the images. "They must have taken out the brain," he said. "Otherwise why remove the calvarium?"

"It could've been somebody important."

"Well, darling, there was a massacre at Masada."

"But this is a reburial. It's not just a body dumped in a shallow grave."

"How do you know about reburials?"

"My Greek grandfather. He would have been an archeologist had he had the chance. And, you know, he was the one who taught me Greek."

How beautiful and full of life she is, he thought as she paced the room. Beyond her, outside the window, the midday sun was illuminating every corner of Jerusalem. "So, when are you going to report it?" he asked.

"I want to examine it before the authorities tie me up in red tape. I won't contaminate it. I just want to document it."

"Cheer up … It only took them twenty years to release the Dead Sea Scrolls. At that rate, you'll still be this side of sixty-five."

"Why wait for twenty years for something you can do this afternoon?"

Michael noticed Evelyn's eyes were not focusing on him. She was consumed by her find. He watched her sink into the armchair, her arms draped over the sides of the chair, her long legs on the footrest. He forced his eyes up to her face. Her mixed Greek–Maltese ancestry had produced light olive skin and green–brown eyes under long brows that almost met above a Grecian nose. But it was not only her appearance that enchanted him. It was how she tilted her head when listening, how she raised her shoulders when uncertain, how she bit her lip when in suspense. A simple flick of her wrist as she dismissed something could set his heart racing. *If I don't help her, she will do it alone,* he thought.

"Michael, this could be the find of my life."

"Evelyn, I thought that was *me*."

꙳

Warm air coming through the car window caressed Evelyn's face as they headed back to the site that afternoon. She glanced at Michael as he was driving, his blue eyes fixed on the road. His hair, once blond, was increasingly white, but his toned body suggested a younger man.

Why remove the calvarium unless you want to extract the brain? she kept thinking. "I can't take my mind off that skull," she said. "Do you think they preserved the brain?"

"I can be certain of only one thing, Evelyn—it wasn't the Egyptians who buried him. They heedlessly discarded the brain and sent millennia of pharaohs brainless to the afterlife."

"And there wasn't much love lost for the brain amongst the Jews either." She looked at her GPS. "Slow down; we need to stop in five hundred meters. We really have no idea how old it might be."

"Just as well you took the coordinates. It all looks the same around here."

Evelyn did not respond and simply led the way to the depression, following the rocks she had noted before. Crouching down, she swept away the earth with her hands, revealing the lid of the ossuary.

Michael glanced over at the security station. "Are you sure we're allowed here?"

"We're certainly not supposed to be doing this." Using her hand as a visor, she also looked across at the station. From this distance, it seemed innocuous, a toy house. Even when she had visited Masada, the guards were nowhere to be seen, but they were no doubt observing everybody.

"Good idea to pretend we're here for something else." Michael opened his arms. "Evelyn Camilleri, kiss me, darling."

She let him pull her into an embrace and kissed him on the cheek. "Look at all the blue tents over there. If they allow campers, this can't be such a sensitive area. Besides, this depression is deep enough to hide us."

"Yes, but is there a depression to hide the car?"

"I just hope they don't think it has broken down. Last thing we need is help."

They spread out a sheet, weighting down its corners with rocks. "Ready?" She lifted the lid of the ossuary, this time with Michael's help.

Michael leaned over the opening and, motionless, stared inside. Watching him, it became real for her. She had discovered a skeleton, from who knows how long ago. She had brought the past into the twentieth century.

Evelyn recorded the length and width of the ossuary in her notebook. Slipping on gloves, she reached in and gently pulled out the skull. The calvarium was just underneath it. After showing Michael how to dislodge dust from the bones, they started arranging them in rough anatomical order on the sheet.

Something glittered among the small bones at the bottom of the ossuary near two clay containers, but the assembling of the skeleton had to come first.

There was no thickening of the skull or joints and the dentition was nearly intact, indicating the skeleton belonged to a young person. She picked up the pelvis. It was small and heart shaped. "This is male, isn't it, Mr. Gynecologist?"

"There is no way a baby could've come out of that."

Something caught her eye. She picked up another bone and showed it to him. "Look. There's a scratch on this one. It has to be a metacarpal, right?"

"It's been a mighty long time since I did anatomy, but, yes, it looks like it."

On close inspection, the size and curved prismoid form of the shaft confirmed it. Despite the dust and age, the abrasion was clear.

Evelyn glanced at Michael, who had stood up and was stretching as if to touch the Judean sky. She watched him squat once more and resume ordering the bones on the sheet, as if he were assembling the pieces of a puzzle. This time, he was examining each bone to determine if it belonged to the left or right side of the body and then matching it to the joints it should have formed. After he finished ordering the major bones, he started inserting the smaller ones.

"Here he is," he said. "We've built a man from a pile of bones."

She took a big breath. "He's coming together. Good height, broad shoulders, long tibia and femur. Good size skull, too."

"He is taller than you, Evelyn." He showed her a small bone. "Look. This tarsal has an abrasion too."

She took it from him. "Abrasions on the hands and feet?" she murmured.

"I haven't checked every bone. There could be more with marks."

"The ones we've checked so far seem clean," she said.

"This could go back to the battle of Masada. Maybe a Roman officer was given a second burial."

"He must have been *somebody* to remove his brain and rebury him. But Romans didn't rebury. They usually crem—"

A roar drowned her voice. Two low-flying military planes were disappearing into the distance, outpacing the noise they were making. Evelyn threw her arms around Michael who said, "Evelyn, we've got to put him back. They were above us. If they saw us, we'll be surrounded in minutes."

Grabbing the sheet by its corners, they brought it close to the ossuary, returned the bones, replaced the lid and covered it with earth. They hastened to the car.

"Do we drive off?" he asked.

"I've never been more scared in my life," Evelyn said. She grabbed his hand and placed it on her chest. "Can you feel my heart? You look troubled, too."

"Well, this is a lot more exciting than you promised, Evelyn."

He added, "Anyway, how can you expect me to be calm when you put my hand on your breast?" He stroked her hair. Reclining his seat, he said, "The removal of the calvarium must have been postmortem."

Realizing what he had just said, she asked, "Why so?"

"Because there is no evidence of fracture. It was done with precision."

"Oh, of course. But the fractures to the hands and feet? They may not be postmortem."

"What are you thinking?"

"Michael, could it be crucifixion?"

"Perhaps you have discovered a criminal."

"But why would a criminal be reburied? Remember, this is a *reburial.*"

"This proves the money and the power was in the hands of the criminals even then."

"Shouldn't crucifixion have left more marked bones, though? Perhaps I'm wrong. So few skeletons have been found with signs of crucifixion. This is very confusing."

"Who knows, Evelyn. Perhaps the bones scratched one another."

They sat in the car, letting the desert consolidate its silence.

※

"Can you stand some more excitement?" she asked.

With no sign they were being watched, they had retraced their steps and the skeleton was once again taking shape before them.

Evelyn noticed another marked bone. Its length and thickness indicated it was one of the true ribs. It did not have the sharp angle of the first rib, or the thickness of the second. There was a blemish on its inferior surface, on the sternal side, as though a sharp object had nicked it. "Michael, I wonder what this is."

"It's a fractured middle rib from the right cage."

"Yes, but do you think it has any significance?"

"It could have been an old fracture, darling. Who knows?"

"I have to read up. It could be someone known to history—a general, a governor, a high priest."

"Carbon dating would narrow the window."

"It's probably from the Roman occupation," she said. "Crucifixions were not popular before or after."

"Let's arrive at the data before we arrive at the conclusions, if you will."

"Yes, but indulge me for a moment," said Evelyn. "We know of someone who was crucified and was speared at the side. Perhaps ..." She trailed off, hoping he would complete her thought.

"Oh, come now!"

"You're right," she said feeling deflated. "Of the thousands of crucifixions, what are the chances?"

"You know, darling, one of the most common injuries to the thorax is a rib fracture. Really, even a strong cough can do it."

"Yes. I'm getting ahead of myself."

"Overinterpreting data is not your style, Madam DNA. And the marks on the hands and feet may also be nothing sinister."

Evelyn was handing him small bones, which he was inserting into the skeleton, when she found buried in the dust an ornate bangle with little pendants. It was heavy—possibly solid gold. "Michael, look," she said, handing it to him.

"Let's grab this and forget about the skeleton, Evelyn."

"Yeah, right, Mr. Graverobber."

"It's a well-to-do skeleton, though the bling could have been ill-gotten."

"Don't condemn my skeleton. He's innocent until proven—"

"Evelyn, a car!"

She dropped the bangle and thrust the camera at him. "Quick, take my photo!" She stood on a rock and posed with Masada as the backdrop, while the car took forever to pass by and disappear down the gently sloping road.

She picked up the bangle again. It formed almost a full circle, its ends ballooning as they confronted each other. Using a tissue she gingerly removed the dust and then held it up to the light. It was bright yellow, its five little pendants catching the sun. One of them bore an engraving. "MM," she muttered. *Is this whispering a story or am I making it up?*

Showing it to Michael, she said, "It's Greek, or maybe Latin. Look, what do you think it stands for?"

"Michael of Masada," he said. She did not respond. "Come on, Evelyn, even prisoners of war have humor."

"You don't think this is serious? It could be an offering from His lover."

"Whose lover?"

"Could be from Mary of Magdala."

"Evelyn, sorry to say, amateur archeologists have also discovered Noah's Ark—in a few places."

"Inexperienced I am, but I am not fabricating anything."

"I thought we dismissed that hypothesis."

"I know. I know. Science is doubt in the face of evidence." Feeling light-headed, she sat down and tried to think of all possibilities. But her mind was stuck on one.

Michael sat next to her. "Jesus was supposed to have been resurrected in body and spirit. His followers would have left not a skerrick for you to find."

She nodded. "More to the point, Jesus would have been buried in Jerusalem. According to custom, there would have been a secondary burial—His bones would have been reburied in a limestone ossuary a year later."

"This is not a limestone ossuary, Evelyn. So, our friend was not even Jewish then."

"No. But it is stone. Anyway, we can philosophize later. For now, let's see if the ossuary is marked."

She reached for the crowbar and loosened the earth.

Michael scooped it away with his hands. "You know, if it wasn't for the salt, this would have been good soil for the garden."

Eventually they freed most of the ossuary. Circles with radii resembling daisy petals adorned the sides. There was no writing.

She wiped sweat from under her nose and over her eyebrows. "That was a waste of time." As she returned to the assembled skeleton, she noticed a tiny plant with a solitary yellow blossom. "You're a flower in the desert," she whispered.

"Evelyn, that is the nicest thing you've said to me all day."

She smiled at him. *Everything is barren here,* she thought. *Where did it find the colors to bloom?*

⁊⸜

With the sun now dipping toward Masada, Evelyn cast a long shadow on the desert floor as she stood up to stretch. *I'd better duck back down before my luck runs out with the security station.*

"Look at this." Michael showed her a piece of wood he had taken out of the ossuary earlier. "There may be a carving here."

Evelyn took the roughly hewn block in her hands. It was the size of a book. As she dusted it off, a letter that resembled an "R" emerged amongst what seemed to be fragments of other letters carved superficially into the desiccated wood. "Iēsus Nazarēnus, Rēx Iūdaeōrum," she said and breathed in sharply. "Michael, it must be. Look where the 'R' is." Her mind raced back two thousand years, to when Jesus attempted to kindle love in the minds of people. "The Titulus," she whispered.

"The what?"

"Titulus Crucis. Remember, the piece of wood the Romans put on the cross; we saw it depicted at the Church of the Holy Sepulcher."

"Wait … This is moving too fast."

Evelyn took the camera and began photographing the bones, zooming in to capture the blemishes.

The sun was now resting on Masada.

"Darling, it's getting dark. We should put all this stuff back."

"We will, but I'm going to take a bone."

"You're going to take a bone … You're not going to take a bone."

"Yes, and a piece of the wood. For carbon dating. It could be a hoax, like the Shroud of Turin."

"I know I suggested that, but it won't confirm anything, even if the dates matched. Evelyn, there were so many crucifixions back then."

Using her Swiss Army knife, she carved out a tiny fragment of wood from the block. Wrapping it and a small bone in tissue, she placed them into her backpack. All that she could think about was that it could be Him. *Unless it is a fraud, but, if so, what would have been in it for the fraudsters?*

She gave a quick wipe to the two clay vessels they had set aside earlier when they were concentrating on the bones. They were both dark orange, one cylindrical the other spherical, both sealed.

As the dust lifted off the sphere, an engraving appeared. On closer examination, she could make out curved lines, like a diagram. *Could this contain the brain?* The cylinder seemed unmarked. "I'm going to take the pots. They may hold the key."

"You're crazy. This is … you're really crazy. Do you know how risky it is to smuggle them out of Israel, let alone into Australia?"

"Michael, I have to know what's inside," she said, placing them in her backpack.

"This is the best way to extend our holiday here indefinitely."

They returned everything else to the ossuary. In the fading light, they reburied it, heaping earth over it and placing two rocks on top.

The desert that kept the secret for so long will do the rest, she thought.

As they were walking away, she turned her head to look back one last time.

Chapter 2

THE GEMS OF HIS MIND

C arpets in shades of red, cream and blue felt soft underfoot.
Evelyn was waiting in the hotel lobby, surrounded by rectangular pillars with palm tree motifs that supported a ceiling displaying ancient fertility symbols in various metallic colors punctuated with gold. In glass-fronted octagonal recesses set into the walls, sapphire earrings and various pendants, bracelets and bangles glinted under the display lights. One bangle resembled the one from her ossuary. She went for a closer look, reflecting on how the new art borrowed from the old.

"Her ossuary;" the words felt unreal. So much had happened since the morning. She had disturbed the remains of a man. But who was this man? The contents indicated he had been someone important. His skeleton suggested someone young and strong. Taller than her. And the cranial dome; why remove that? It was not common posthumous practice in the land of Judea as far as she knew. But what did she really know? She could not even say what era he came from. Had he been crucified? It surely looked like it. So, perhaps during the time of the Roman occupation.

The Titulus was another clue, as was the engraving "MM." And the bangle—the "bling" as Michael called it. The delicate piece would be priceless today and must have been valuable even then. There would be answers somewhere. *I had thought my DNA research was important. But what could be more important than this?*

As Michael crossed the lobby, a few women glanced at him, some half his age. Seemingly oblivious to their attention, he took Evelyn's arm more forcefully than usual as they entered King's Garden Restaurant. It occurred to her that her lips would be in line with his if she wore high heels.

If only I wanted a kiss.

The outdoor restaurant overlooked the garden and pool, its backdrop the illuminated stone walls and alcoves of the hotel. As requested, the waiter took them to a corner, but to Evelyn the table seemed totally exposed. Thanking him for reciting the specials, they ordered quickly.

She scanned Michael's face as they sat opposite each other—the blue eyes, the high forehead, the small bump on his nose level with his eyes. His jaw was square and his neck thick, like that of the rugby player he had been.

As soon as they were alone, he began softly, "I put a do-not-disturb sign on our door, not that it makes me feel much safer."

"Good idea."

"You know, it's possible you have found His bones."

Evelyn leaned toward him. "They found me, more like it."

"Either way—but now what?"

"We announce the find. Let the chips fall where they may."

"Evelyn, blind Freddy can see where they'll fall—on your head."

"No, no. Christians will welcome proof He existed."

Michael shifted position in his chair. "How naïve can you be! If He has mortal remains, He is no God."

"They'll find a way to accommodate it. Religious beliefs are irrational, anyway."

"I'll tell you what's irrational—to think the Church will tolerate this. They'll say you tampered with the evidence."

"I'll say *you* did it."

He exhaled, more than laughed. "I'm telling you it's dangerous. To *you*. At the very least they'll discredit you. Not that geneticists have credentials in archeology anyway. Not every academic is an Indiana Jones."

"You don't need to be an archeologist to find something in the ground. A shepherd found the Dead Sea Scrolls."

"Yes, and he got seven pounds for them. But, really, what do you expect the Israelis to do? Can't you see? They hope the Pope will come here to apologize for what the Christians have done to the Jews. The Israelis are not going to risk that. They'll rebury the relics in another desert."

His arguments made sense, but, like a hound on the scent, she could not let go. "Let's be positive, Michael," she said, tracing the edge of the table with her fingertip. "This is an entirely different situation."

"I can't think of a bigger provocation. And you want me to be 'positive.' Just as well your evidence is so skimpy."

"I feel positive about the discovery and it is 1997. Queen Isabella is not around to throw me to the Inquisition."

"Can't you lower your voice?"

"I'm not shouting," she said, but then she realized she had been and apologized.

"When the dust settles," she whispered, "there'll still be just as many Christians."

"No. There won't. It renders the Resurrection a lie."

"You keep your voice down too," she said, adding, "anyway, I've always thought the Resurrection is a metaphor for the rising of the soul. I mean, who needs a body in Heaven?"

She felt his foot on hers and kept quiet. The waiter was approaching, bringing a bottle of white wine, San Pellegrino water and a tasting plate of dips with warm pita bread. He unfolded the embroidered serviettes across their laps as though they could not do it themselves. Worse yet, he poured the sparkling water without tilting the glasses. Evelyn watched the bubbles escape. In the pause in conversation, her mind turned to the night she met Michael at a friend's New Year's Eve party two years earlier. It was on a balcony at Circular Quay in full view of the fireworks that burst into colorful bouquets over Sydney Harbour. Light had fallen on his face and she had fantasized being with him, being challenged by him, being swept up by him, loving him.

He was fifteen years older, but that did not matter. The dry spells in her emotional life were as big as the Australian deserts. So, when a chance for love arrived, she reached for it. But she was too damaged from her first love; the pain inside her was alive. She could not make it work. In the end, it was—

"All right then," said Michael when the waiter left. "I guess if Adam and Eve can be taken metaphorically, why not the Resurrection?"

"Finally, we agree on something." Her eyes met his. Their stare held a moment too long for her. Dropping her gaze, she focused on the food, the olive dip a reminder of her time on the island of Ithaca.

"They might even canonize you for streamlining the dogma. "St. Evelyn" has a nice ring to it."

"I'm not trying to streamline anything. I just want the truth. He should be acknowledged for what He was. One of us," she said, pointing to herself. "Someone with love and courage. We need Him as a *human* role model."

The waiter approached again, this time with the seafood platter. Michael seemed to dither over whether to take a bite of octopus or say something. Eventually he took a bite and asked with his mouth full, "Since when have you been so enamored of Jesus? You're lionizing Him because you think you've found His bones."

"No. I've always admired Him. He told the truth and accepted the consequences."

The couple sitting at the table closest to them departed.

"Let's return to the point. Assume we manage to smuggle the artifacts into Australia and dating is consistent with your hypothesis. Then what?"

"I don't know. I really need more evidence. Perhaps the clay pots have the answer." She looked at the illuminated wall and then back at Michael. "And another thing. You know, it's like that old question—whom would you invite to dinner, dead or alive? For me it is Jesus, the greatest moral innovator of all time."

"Others had suggested many of those ideas before, Evelyn. But, indeed, He did pull it all together."

"And was ready to die for it."

"He must have had a special combination of genes," said Michael, adding a moment later, "Someone like Him is not born every minute."

᠅

Michael's reference to genes still resonated with Evelyn two days later, when, from the back seat of their taxi, she watched the familiar streets of Sydney's Eastern Suburbs go by.

All was quiet, bottlebrush trees with red flowers, willow myrtles and paperbarks the only sentinels to the early morning.

It had been an exhausting twenty-four hours—a sleepless night on a crowded flight and encounters with immigration and customs at both ends of the journey. Her precious cargo was in the middle of her suitcase, inside layers of bubble wrap and clothing.

When the sniffer dog had approached as she wheeled the trolley through arrivals, she was certain the game was up. It kept wagging its tail while sniffing her belongings. The beagle became a menacing tiger, but then it moved on to another passenger.

Michael carried her suitcase into the house. The taxi was waiting, yet she kept him just inside the front door in a tight hug.

He slowly pulled away. "I'll be back tomorrow."

"Come back. Without you, none of this would have happened." She stood on her toes to reach his lips.

Rays of the morning sun, filtered by the Sydney blue gum, followed a slanted path through the windows. She crossed the open-plan kitchen and went directly to her room. Resting the parcel on the bed, she lay down curling her body around it.

Serendipity favors the prepared mind, she thought. *And mine is totally unprepared.*

❦

Evelyn was only half listening to the discussion on molecular mechanisms involved in the initiation and timing of cell development.

Every Monday morning she met with her postdoctoral fellows and PhD students. Just as a postdoc was asking her to explain something, her phone rang. For the first time she had left it on during a meeting. It had been nearly a week since she sent away the bone and wood sample for carbon dating and the results were expected. She excused herself and stepped out.

"Have they called yet?"

"No, Michael. Not yet. I thought you were them."

"Well, keep me posted."

After the meeting, she returned to her office and forced herself to write an ethics application for work with transgenic mice constructed to spontaneously develop neuronal plaques, the hallmark of Alzheimer's disease. She was distractible, pouncing on new emails and glancing at the telephone in case it flashed before it rang. Although she had been back for almost a week, there was still a lot of paperwork and unanswered emails.

The phone rang. *It is the carbon dating lab.*

Both artifacts were from between 30 BC and AD 50.

She thanked the technician and quickly hung up, worried they might ask where she got them from.

After a few minutes, she settled down. It was encouraging they were from the right period, but it still didn't *prove* anything. She ached to tell Michael, but she wanted to work on the other two pieces of the puzzle first.

It was hard to keep from running as she headed home, straight to her garage.

She unpacked the two containers and laid them on her carpenter's bench, having first covered it with clean plastic. Over the previous week, she had procured a high-speed dental drill and other instruments to work on the specimens.

She felt like a child at Christmas—the buildup of excitement as she waited to open the gifts. With dates confirmed, she could proceed. Snapping on a surgical mask, she investigated the cylinder first. "Twenty-five and a half centimeters in length and nine centimeters in diameter," she wrote in her notebook. Under the white light of the fiber optic cables, it had the waxy color of the skin of a butternut pumpkin. She could feel a rough texture through her gloves; the surface of the clay was pockmarked where tiny areas had disintegrated.

She fitted her reading glasses with loupe six-times magnifier lenses. Placing the cylinder in a padded vise, she took a deep breath to allow her hands to steady, then started to drill. She scored the baked clay a few centimeters from one end. The drilling produced a small cloud of dust. Despite the mask, she could feel dust in her throat. Turning her head to one side, she took another deep breath and then returned to her position, hunched over the vise.

Before long, she needed to pause and clean her glasses, which had fogged up from her breath. She stopped drilling when the circumference was almost completely scored. With a tap, the end fell off, revealing the dark brown edge of a papyrus. It was stuck to the internal wall on one side. She stared for a little while at the ancient document nesting in the cylinder.

This scroll could hold all the answers.

❧

Evelyn's hands shook as she nudged the papyrus free with a thin spatula. She was desperate to read it, but, as though paralyzed, could not unfurl it. Orthogonal arrays of papyrus strips had been woven together. Clay dust had accumulated in patches on the document, especially at its edges. The scroll was thick, but black ink had seeped through to the reverse side.

All of a sudden, she could hear the sound of raindrops drumming against her roller door. Aware of the rain now, she could even smell the wet earth. There were sheets and towels on the clothesline, effort now wasted by a Sydney downpour. *Could the humidity affect the document?*

With the aid of the loupe lenses and dissecting forceps, she slowly unfurled the fragile papyrus. Her heart fluttered like a trapped butterfly when the scroll cracked. It had broken into four pieces by the time she flattened it between two glass plates.

She feared it was in danger of disintegration. *What am I doing? I don't have the training for this; I cannot protect it; I cannot preserve it.*

However, the find was hers; the opportunity was hers too.

Slowly she traced the letters on the glass with her finger. They were Greek. Many of them were legible; the symbols were exactly those her grandfather had taught her. But there were no spaces between words—it was all one continuous flow and all in upper case.

She jotted down the letters, guessing where she could, using "x" where illegible, consulting her dictionary when she could not understand a word. It took hours to decipher something of what was written.

Thou art gone silence has fallen upon our ears xxxxxxxxxxxxx minds xxxxxxxx Thy bones to speak xxxxxxxxxx lift the darkness that has xxxxxxxxx spirit May the cross xxxxxxxxxxxxxxxx the symbol xxxxxxxxxx blood that flowed xxxxxxxxxxxxxxxx fountain of redemption xxxxxxxx Rest here Righteous One xxxxxxxxx splendor xxxxxxxxxxxxxx to rebuild xxxxxxxxxxxxxxxxxxxxxxxxxxxxxxx dead The prophecy xxxxxxxxxxxxxx for the day xxxxxxxxxxx Thou shall be xxxxxxxxxxxxxxxxx not by two not by xxxxxxxx.

The papyrus was speaking to her after two millennia of silence.

As a scientist she wanted more evidence, much more, but her instinct told her she was right. It mentioned rebuilding—this had to refer to the Temple in Jerusalem. Therefore, the reburial in the desert must have taken place after the destruction of the Temple by the Romans, after AD 70. It mentioned the cross and blood. This was real evidence. *This and the piece of wood. Who else could it be?*

On the other hand, not all the script was legible. The "x" was everywhere. All this indecipherable text could spell out precisely who it was—and it could have nothing to do with Him. Hyperspectral imaging could help decipher the rest.

She started photographing the papyrus. *Would the photos be good enough if the original is damaged?*

She picked up the other container, the sphere. It was heavy for a small object, 3.23 kilograms on her set of kitchen scales. As she cleaned the surface with a brush, an elaborate diagram began to emerge. The carving showed the right brain hemisphere as it would appear to an observer positioned above the brain.

When she finished, there it was, a detailed and accurate representation of a hemisphere. The tracing depicted the sulci, the grooves that give the surface of the brain its wrinkled appearance. The lateral sulcus, the Grand Canyon of the brain, was appropriately the deepest carving. To her surprise, other common sulci were also represented. The diagram could have been used in a modern neuroanatomy tutorial. She marveled at it as she had at the Leonardo da Vinci tracings many years earlier when studying anatomy.

The sphere has to contain the brain.

What if she ruined it by exposing it to the atmosphere? She did not have the right equipment. She did not have the right training. She did not have qualifications to dig a hole in her own backyard. Even professional archeologists would tremble at the idea of tampering with this. And then, what exactly could she do with the evidence? She had already broken the law to get it. Michael's concerns about the Church were the least of her worries.

She could not open it. She should not open it. A find of this magnitude, if it were Him, was not hers to tamper with.

If I compromise the evidence, I will destroy a part of human heritage and become the laughing stock of science.

❧

Exam results were due the next day, but Evelyn could not concentrate, losing track of whether an idea had come from an earlier paper or the one she was currently marking. Words kept blending with one another. It was futile to continue.

Sleep was not possible either. She wanted to share her find; but, strangely, she was also content to keep it hidden. Sipping chamomile tea, she mulled over whether to call Michael. She was dying to talk to him, to show him there were real data consistent with her hypothesis, but this did not feel like the right moment. They had dinner plans for the following evening, so she would be seeing him soon anyway. *But what if he does not agree with my inference? If he derides me, I have no one to turn to.*

As it stood, the totality of evidence was weighty—a skeleton from the appropriate period, marked with injuries consistent with crucifixion and buried together with relevant artifacts. But *none* of this was conclusive. The papyrus supported the hypothesis, but it was not enough. Michael, or anyone else, could argue she was proving preconceptions.

There is no way the sphere does not contain the brain. But what would that prove? On the other hand, there was the piece of wood. "INRI" was as close as you can get to a nametag. But it did not say *INRI*—only one letter remained. *I have to talk to Michael.*

She had slipped into considering him just a friend, a brother. When he had first come into her life, it felt she had finally found the person she had been waiting for. Everything about him fascinated her—love had colored it all. But after only three months she was bereft of feelings for him. Nothing he did had caused it. It was just that love had left. He wanted commitment, and, although he never intentionally pressured her, it was so obvious he adored her that it became pressure in itself. His very happiness seemed to depend on her. It was too much. She felt trapped. The rest of her life was being mapped out for her—marriage, kids, old age—and all of this with someone she did not love. Logically, he was the perfect man, but love was never—

Lightning illuminated the windows and was almost instantly followed by deafening thunder. It must have struck something very close. Might it have been the tallest tree in the block, her beautiful Sydney blue gum?

Evelyn did not want to lose Michael altogether. It had been selfish to offer only friendship when it was so obvious he wanted more. She knew how he felt, having suffered a similar rejection after falling in love in first-year university. Her boyfriend had moved on following their breakup, but she had remained fixated on him. No one else had his eyes, his smile, his humor. If only she could hate him instead of love him, she would have found the right person by now. About a decade after their breakup, he invited her to his wedding. It was torture to see him marry another woman. Yes, love was made in heaven; but hers, in hell.

And now, the ghost of an old love was killing all future ones. Since that breakup, Evelyn was even more afraid of intimacy. But what could she do? Unlike her sister Kathryn, she had always been reserved. Human relationships were such a hard task. Even Kathryn's once beautiful marriage had ended in bitter divorce. *It is so much simpler to be on your own.*

She was lying in bed—lying in bed while the sphere was concealing its secret.

Kicking away the covers, Evelyn put on her track suit and headed back to the garage. She had to know what was inside. *This is a step I have to take, whether Michael supports me or not. I will just have to do my best to protect the integrity of the brain—if that is what is in there.*

Switching on the fluorescent lights, she went straight back to her workbench. Avoiding the carving, she weakened the structure of the sphere by drilling along its equator, where the two halves had been joined. With a screwdriver, she split the vessel in two.

An exquisitely preserved brain appeared. It looked like a cauliflower.

Evelyn put on a fresh pair of gloves and gently eased it from its resting place.

She held the brain in her palms.

The meninges had been removed, rendering the cortical mantle visible. The ancient artist must have drawn that very brain because the carving on the sphere surface corresponded to the groove pattern of the right hemisphere. The lateral sulcus was so deep that it made the temporal lobe look like the thumb of a boxer's glove. Modern plastination methods could not have produced a better preservation of structure. *What chemicals did they use to preserve the tissue?*

The brain was a dull brown, like the clay that had protected it all this time. As people age, brain matter wastes and grooves passively expand. Here, however, the sulci were thin, indicating it belonged to a young adult, in agreement with evidence from the skeleton.

Whoever preserved the brain must have had a sense of its importance. The papyrus was in Greek, consistent with the Hellenistic influence in that period. She thought of the ancient Greek physician Hippocrates. He was the first to conclude that from the brain, and from the brain alone, arise our pleasures, joys, laughter and jests, as well as our sorrows, pain, grief and tears.

I am getting ahead of myself again, she thought. *The only scientific evidence I have is that the carbon dating matches.*

The brain was flexible and, to her relief, it did not crumble. It was much firmer than jelly, nearly as stiff as rubber. Of the twelve cranial nerves, only the olfactory was missing, as were parts of the olfactory bulb. She took photographs from all angles and then weighed the brain—1.403 kilograms she recorded in her notebook. This was about 100 grams above average, but the method of preservation could have altered the weight.

Driving rain was again drumming the garage door.

Using a scalpel, Evelyn cut out a block of approximately one gram from the primary motor cortex of the right hemisphere and placed it in a vial. The structure of cells in the different layers of this part of the cortex was well known and she was familiar with the normal morphology.

I need to get to my lab. If only the ancients have used a process that preserves neuronal integrity!

⁂

There was more lightning, followed immediately by thunder. The dangerous thing to do was to point an umbrella to that sky.

Evelyn endured the rain as she hurried to the campus of The University of New South Wales, the vial with the tissue firmly in her hand. Following the steps on the slope south of the library, she reached the Biological Sciences Building through the wind tunnel created by the tall buildings of the upper campus.

Once in her laboratory, she released her vise-like grip on the vial and tried to dry her hair with a towel. Pushing back her wet fringe, she began to work.

Finally, she was back in her area of expertise. Amateur archeologist she was, but she was also a professional geneticist. She snap-froze the tissue on dry ice and positioned it on the stage of a cryotome, a sophisticated salami-slicer used to cut frozen tissue into serial sections. She obtained 40-micrometer thick sections and placed them on a gelatin-coated glass slide.

The unstained tissue looked amorphous, revealing virtually none of its secrets. After drying the sections on a hot plate, Evelyn advanced the slide through baths containing xylene to remove the fat, then progressively through decreasing concentrations of alcohol to rehydrate the tissue in preparation for staining for Nissl substance to reveal the neurons.

Impatiently she waited the five minutes for the uptake of stain into neurons. She looked at her nails—they needed painting too. After washing off the excess stain, she passed the tissue through an ascending series of alcohols and then into xylene, in preparation for cover-slipping with another piece of glass for permanent preservation.

She placed the tissue slide on the stage of her Olympus microscope and turned on the light that shone through a condenser onto the undersurface of the slide. She closed her eyes for a moment, knowing the evidence was already there.

After a few seconds of tense immobility, she opened her eyes. The cells were shining bright blue and were arranged like stars in constellations.

When she moved the stage of her microscope to different fields of view, she was an astronomer training a telescope on unexplored sky. The cells were beautiful and their arrangement a work of art. She was the sole witness of a spectacular pyrotechnic show.

Using the forty-times lens objective, she zoomed in on one neuron, a giant pyramidal cell, a Betz cell, located in the fifth layer of the cortex. She could see the structure of the neuron, including its nucleus, where the genetic information was stored.

It was a flower whose closed petals kept the secrets of how to construct a life.

The stain was taken up not only by the cell body, but also by the closest parts of the dendrites, tentacles with which neurons communicate—exchange protoplasmic kisses in an epic love journey.

The cell looked as though it had been obtained from an on-the-spot biopsy during surgery, rather than from 2,000-year-old tissue.

She zoomed out and looked at the distribution of the cells again. This was not just any brain. These were not just any cells. These were the neurons responsible for a historic change in civilization.

All the ideas came from here. All the courage was generated here. All the suffering was endured here.

Bent over the microscope, Evelyn closed her eyes again as she recalled the discovery of the ossuary and the stigmata on the skeleton.

She opened her eyes. Arranged in six neat layers were giant pyramidal cells, granule cells, spindle cells, stellate cells, chandelier cells.

These are the gems of His mind.

۶€

Dawn found her at the microscope.

It had been a sleepless night, like those she had spent earlier in her career. Evelyn was then extracting fragments of DNA from a preserved specimen of the thylacine, the beautiful Tasmanian tiger, a species that became extinct in the 1930s. She had never worked harder in her life, clocking over a hundred hours a week for seven months straight.

Two of her articles were published in *Science* and became citation classics. She had developed the theoretical framework for a novel approach to cloning and had been on the verge of proving its success through experimentation with the tiger.

She was shattered when her director ordered the project be abandoned because of funding shortfalls. The dream was lost and all the effort behind it.

And yet, now nothing seemed lost. From the literature and more so from her own attempts to resurrect the Tasmanian tiger, she knew the principles of how to produce a clone. She wondered whether there was viable DNA in the neurons in front of her.

If there were viable DNA, an extractable nucleus, it might be possible to clone. *It might be possible to clone* Him.

She buried her face in her hands.

Chapter 3

HYPOTHETICAL

She has been up to something with those artifacts, but she hasn't kept me in the loop.

He had helped her dig them up; he had helped her bring them home. He had shared the risk. But not a word. Maybe the dates didn't match and she was lying low. Even if she had disconfirming evidence, she should have told him.

Michael had arrived early for dinner with Evelyn and chosen a table in the outdoor section of the Barzura restaurant, on the footpath with sweeping views of Coogee Bay. The sun was retreating from the beach, but was still illuminating Wedding Cake Island, a small outcrop of rocks on which waves broke, frothing like frosting on a cake. It had been a humid summer day, but now a refreshing landward wind brought relief and the faint scent of seaweed.

He could not keep his eyes on the crossword puzzle. A four-wheel drive slowly cruised by, the driver searching for parking. After it passed, he saw Evelyn striding toward him from halfway down the beach, her long white skirt wrapping around her legs, her brown hair whipped into a frenzy by the breeze. *Is that triumph in her walk?*

He folded the paper when she arrived. He was taking no prisoners. "What was in the containers?" he asked as she bent down to kiss him.

"Hello to you too," she said, handing him her notebook. "A scroll. There was a scroll in the cylinder."

"Was it legible?"

She sat opposite him. "Some of it. And it's not inconsistent with the hypothesis."

"The hypothesis," he repeated as he scanned the page. There were notes on the artifacts, and the translation of sections of the papyrus. As he read the scattered words, he felt a sense of vertigo. "It's not inconsistent. But are you sure this is what it says?"

"I checked it time and again. It's Greek of the post-Hellenistic period."

He looked at her. "And the other one?"

"The carbon dating is consistent too."

Her voice was velvet, but her words were missiles. "And now what?" he asked. "What will you do?"

She changed seats and sat next to him. Her hair was unkempt and she wore no make-up. "I don't know. I don't know where to go from here. I surely need more evidence."

He took a sip of his wine. "You are in a bind. And you look it. How can you have these relics in your garage and keep quiet?"

"But how can I publish anything without incriminating myself?"

"You don't have to say you took anything. You just reveal the location. There is so much there. It's still possible to make it all legitimate, if that's what you want."

She leaned toward him. "The other one—at first, I couldn't bring myself to open the sphere, but then I couldn't resist... The brain was inside. The brain. So well preserved. And do you remember those carved lines? They depict the sulci of that very brain."

She was really close to him. "Your hair is all over the place," he said as he reached to push it back. "It hides your pretty face."

She caught his hand and held it. "Michael, I might be able to extract viable DNA from a brain cell."

"DNA?" he echoed. "What for? What could you do with it?"

Evelyn was biting her lip.

"You said 'viable,' didn't you?" She remained silent. Silence to Michael meant only one thing. "What? No ... No," he said and took his hand back. "If we suppose you're right about the skeleton, you have made a discovery, a discovery without precedent." He shook his head. "And you're throwing it all away. And to chase ... what?"

"Michael, it's just speaking hypothetically."

"Rubbish. You are not speaking hypothetically." He recalled the way she had worked at the ossuary—the squint of her eyes against the rosy desert light, the furrowing of her brow as she focused the camera; the graceful, easy movements of her long slim legs, bending and extending as she crouched over the relics to photograph them. The little flower, the yellow flower she found and talked to. *How could it all have come to this?*

"Forget about it," he said. "This is risible. You couldn't even do it with the tiger."

"It probably wouldn't work, even if I wanted to ..."

He had heard her, but he wanted to hear her say it again. "Even if you wanted to do what? *Clone?* I don't believe you mean that."

Thoughts of cloning were quickly elbowed away by thoughts of his personal loss.

Halfway through his meal, Michael could no longer endure the uncertainty. Surely what she was thinking could not be as bad as what he was imagining. "Evelyn, nobody has cloned a human. This is not the Tasmanian tiger. This isn't an experiment, you know. And what about the risks? The obstetric complications? Besides, who's going to bear the child? If it ever came to that."

"Me. I would."

Her words made him feel ill. "You would do *what*? Put yourself at huge risk? ... And you know very well human cloning is banned."

"If I didn't believe it was Him, I never would have thought of it."

He could not hold back. "Too bad you're not a virgin ..."

She leaned back and looked at the ocean. He continued, "Do you even know what you're talking about? If you fail you die, and if you succeed there goes the Messiah."

She turned sharply to face him. "Oh, come on, Michael."

He was caught out. He was exaggerating, but there was nothing to hold on to. Evelyn was deaf to all but her own arguments. The loss of hope felt like a physical blow. He could no longer hope for a child with her. *What is the meaning of life if the person you love poisons you?*

Mechanically he took a bite of bread dipped in olive oil; it moved down his throat, heavy and tasteless. The idea of cloning was revolting enough, but this was nothing compared to the bitterness of his personal loss. She was rejecting him in the most fundamental way.

When she was still in love with him, they had talked about having a child. Then she lost her way. This further rejection should not have come as a surprise. Yet, she had not moved on to someone else, not even for sex. So, hope had remained, hidden somewhere deep inside. He was the only man in her life—until now that this *skeleton* came between them.

"Anyway, it's going to be impossible. I might not even try," he heard her say.

He knew she was just saying that. In reality, she had already decided. Fatherhood would have been the consolation. With Evelyn in her mid-forties, this would have been his last chance for a child with her.

His last hope had just turned to despair.

The more she thought about it, the more conflicted she became.

Evelyn wove her way through the Saturday crowd on The Corso at Manly, the birthday gift for her six-year-old niece in her hand. She was confused, plagued by unanswerable questions, but the allure of cloning would not go away. *What about impregnation? What if I succeed?*

Michael was never far from her thoughts. She would need his help, but how could she ask knowing how much he wanted his own child with her? When she had broken it off, she had emphasized her desire to remain friends, but he had made it clear she was the only one for him. She hid her jealousy when he dated other women. The last thing she wanted was to see him alone and unhappy just because it could not work between them. A part of her still wondered if anything could rekindle her love for him—presumably the same part that kept jealousy alive. Perhaps having his baby would be the way to bond again; perhaps raising a child together might be enough.

Not really, she thought, as she recalled that her father had had no regrets about abandoning them. *A child is not enough. It is not enough to create love; it is not enough to sustain it.*

With thinking no more lucid than before, she arrived at the ocean beach her sister had chosen for her daughter's party. The greasy smell of takeaway food was replaced by the fresh breeze of the Pacific. Blue waves curled before breaking into white froth and pounding the shore. There was a sheltered cove at the southern end, safe enough for children.

Evelyn spotted her niece making a sandcastle at water's edge with her friends. Dripping wet sand through their fingers, the children were building towers with tall spires. They had dug a hole large enough for two of them to shore up the walls from inside the castle, while the other two worked on the moat around it. She stood back and watched.

If I really wanted a child, I could have one with Michael. Discovering the bones is more than enough for anyone.

What right did she have to recreate a person, especially when there was no way of foreseeing how it would impact the baby? The science was too limited. She could not predict the genetic implications, let alone the behavioral ones. In worst-case scenario, she would bring into the world a child with DNA so damaged he would not enjoy a decent life. *What mother would knowingly inflict that on her child?*

When lunch was announced, the girls abandoned the castle, squealing as they ran to their towels. Kathryn was shepherding the children, fussing over them, loving them.

This was what was missing in Evelyn's life. She walked over and gave her niece her present. "Happy birthday, Leanne."

"Aunty Evelyn!"

She lifted her niece in her arms. The girl was very much like Kathryn around the nose and eyes. As they hugged, Evelyn could feel sticky sunscreen smearing across her face and onto her clothes.

Her niece tore the paper to uncover a palette and a box of paints. "It'll soon be Monet, Modigliani, Picasso and Leanne," said Evelyn.

Leanne looked puzzled and Kathryn said, "She hasn't heard of all these guys."

"I know who Picasso is," said Leanne. "Come on, Aunty, tell my friends about the tortoise and the hare."

After lunch, Evelyn went to swim with the children in the shallows.

Later she watched Kathryn teach her daughter how to hold out her arms, timing her dive so she entered the water head first, the wave washing over her. *A child is what remains after romance evaporates.*

A cool southerly change cut the party short. Evelyn helped her sister load food, toys and fractious children into the car. She then walked back toward the harbor ferry, passing through the greasy food smells again before arriving at the welcome scent of freshly ground coffee at The Corso.

She began noticing children everywhere. Their presence was so intense that it felt as if previously they had not existed. They were strong, healthy and happy. Seeing the kids play reminded her of games she had played with her sister. Kathryn had always wanted to be the mother, forcing Evelyn into various other roles—baby, milkman, gardener, husband. When she was older, Evelyn had insisted on playing the doctor and even the scientist after they were given a microscope for Christmas.

Most of her university friends had drifted out of her life after they married. She had gone to their weddings and christenings, dutifully happy for them. She sensed they were secretly sorry for her for being childless, but she had rarely felt the lack. Children were something to be put off until some distant date. Unlike Kathryn, she had never felt the burning desire to be a mother.

Babies never settled quietly in her arms. They seemed to sense she was anxious holding them. She didn't understand them and was intimidated by their vulnerability—their soft skulls and tiny bodies. She had been unwilling to hold even her niece when she visited Kathryn at the maternity hospital. But her sister had insisted, and she remembered the feeling of cradling Leanne and how she snuggled against her chest—it had been beautiful, but uncomfortable. When inevitably Leanne cried and Kathryn expertly calmed her, Evelyn felt inadequate.

On The Corso, there was a young street singer, his skateboard resting against a palm tree, his amplifier and speakers behind him, the case of his guitar with its rich red interior open in front of him. He was singing an old tune, *The House of the Rising Sun*. Two girls were sitting cross-legged on a bench behind him, their bodies moving in synch with the rhythm. Two other girls stopped, one of them bending to leave a coin. Everything was moving slowly, except her thoughts.

If she were to go through with her plan, she would have to commit to being a mother. If the cloning worked, it would mean looking after a child, a *real* baby, not some ephemeral experiment. This was something that would go on forever—for the rest of her life. This was not a job where she could close the lab and go home. And unlike Kathryn, unlike most women, she would be setting out to do this without a partner. All alone. *Is this what I really want?*

On the other hand, Kathryn had what *she* wanted—a child, someone to love and to be loved by. Evelyn reflected on things her sister had exulted over—the first word, the first step, the first day at school. She started feeling something that was more than just emotional; it was *physical*. It was as though her body had awakened and was demanding a child. *And I could raise a child who might make a difference.*

Drops of rain started to fall. Her eternal optimism about the weather did not serve her well—she was without umbrella. Neither was her thinking on cloning anything rational. She was jumping the gun on every occasion. First of all, she had to extract viable DNA—a huge ask. There were hardly any animal studies to use as a guide, let alone human data. *And then who knows what the consequences would be for the child?*

She shivered. What if cloning shortened telomeres and the child aged prematurely? There could be other genetic defects. It was impossible to know. What would it be like raising a child with a disability?

Kathryn was always anxious about health issues with Leanne. Imagine a child who would need constant care for the rest of his life. It dawned on her she was not sure she was willing to sacrifice her science, her lifestyle, herself for a hypothetical child, especially given the risk of things going wrong, horribly wrong—*for the baby, for me.*

She had now reached the middle of The Corso—the halfway point between a turbulent ocean and a safe harbor. *If I am serious about having a baby, then I need to think like a mother. I need to decide what is best for my baby. In that case, I should not clone. End of story.*

And, besides, she would be suppressing the data. She would be depriving the scientific community of the discovery of His remains and herself the pleasure of publishing it. If she followed one road, the other would be forever forfeited.

But not quite, she thought. *Not forever. If cloning failed, I would still have the chance to publish the find.*

The display board at the terminal showed the ferry departing in three minutes and she quickened her pace to catch it.

She sat on the outdoor section that would give her views of the North and South Heads and, between them, the Pacific Ocean. At the end of the journey, she would pass meters west of the Opera House.

But I was so close with the thylacine, she reflected. *So close. I could have corrected a human error—the extinction of a species. The tiger would have graced again the Tasmanian landscape.*

If I give myself a chance, I might correct a far greater injustice. If ever there were a reason for cloning …

ৰ

Out of habit, Michael tapped out a tune on Evelyn's red front door, feeling anything but jaunty.

Three weeks had passed since she had mentioned the possibility of cloning and they had not spoken of it again. Standing on her steps, his mind ran through possible variations of the impending conversation. He was not yet sure how he would react if she persisted with the cloning idea. Was it an idea or had it become a plan? He wanted to be prepared, but anxiety prevented him from thinking clearly. He had even tried to talk himself out of going altogether.

In the end, something she had said weakened his resolve to distance himself. On the phone, when inviting him to dinner, she had mentioned how the sight of her sister with little Leanne had triggered a yearning for a child of her own. She had said it in passing, but it set off bells in his head. *I need to know what she wants from me,* he thought.

Although he was trying to keep his mind free of expectations, his hopes were soaring—perhaps now the time was right for them to start a family together, couple or not.

"Finally, you are here," Evelyn said with excitement, but he could see the smile did not reach her eyes.

They both went for the same side for a kiss on the cheek, and, without meaning to, they kissed on the lips.

"Are you hungry? Shall we eat straight away or would you like some wine first?"

"It smells nice." It was his favorite of Evelyn's dishes, roasted rack of lamb with vegetables. "We can drink with dinner."

He sat opposite her at the oval table, served the food and poured the red shiraz. "You know, you'll have to give up the wine if you get pregnant."

Evelyn smiled in a way that revealed nothing. She kept talking about her lab, her niece, the construction delays for the upcoming Sydney Olympics, and kept asking about his work—everything but the reason he was there. He responded automatically as he glanced around the room. It was familiar, cozy. He had to remind himself he was just a guest. The creaky velvet couch, so inviting and soft, was draped with the batik she had bought on a trip to Indonesia. Her niece's paintings were stuck on the walls and on the fridge. Even the off-white walls seemed warm. He had hired an interior designer for his own house, but it always felt far from the home he envisioned sharing with her one day.

Right here was what he wanted, but it could just as well have been in another world. *If only she would give in to her feelings ... I know she loves me. If I believed she didn't, I would be able to let go.*

He cut her off mid-sentence. "Let's not beat around the bush, Evelyn. We might be many things, but not hypocrites. Tell me straight. What's going on?"

She repositioned the salt and pepper grinders and smoothed a nonexistent crease on the tablecloth. "Michael, honestly, what do you think? Am I dreaming or could it really be Him?"

"There are alternative explanations."

"But the scroll and the dates?"

"You still can't be certain. You only know of one crucifixion and you think it must be Him. What about the thousands of others?" He saw her take a deep breath. Was that a sign of doubt or frustration?

"I understand that rationally, logically, what you say is right. But I know, I *know*, even without hard evidence, this skeleton belongs to Him."

"Evelyn, that's hardly science."

"What can I say? All the circumstantial evidence is consistent. I haven't fabricated anything. I've exaggerated nothing."

"You have joined the dots and ignored the gaps. You cannot be certain, even if you feel you are."

"But what more should I expect? Some sort of death certificate? I mean, this isn't a mathematical proof. The scroll and the—"

"What you're saying might make gut sense to you, Evelyn, but to someone else ..."

"Yes, well, I believe it. I think I've found Him."

"You have a hypothesis looking for evidence."

"For me, it's the *only* hypothesis that fits the evidence."

They stared at each other. Confronted with her certainty, he tapped her glass with his. "You certainly found *somebody*."

"Michael, we were in love with each other once and now you're my best friend. There is no one as close to me as you." She paused, biting her lip.

Her words made him uneasy—compliments laid to soften a blow. He recalled the magic dusks they had spent on Maroubra Beach and thought of the photo on his bedroom dresser—the two of them embracing in front of rolling waves. A relic of a romance lost.

"I want to have a child, but …"

Perhaps she just wants my technical help, he thought. *Maybe she wants me to be the father; could I hope?* He tried to meet her eyes again, but her gaze kept roaming around the room. "Evelyn, you're stubborn and as distant as the dark side of the moon. But I'd like to know if I can help."

She was now looking at him intensely. It seemed this was exactly what she was hoping to hear. "I know you objected when I mentioned it," she said. "But I want to produce a clone and impregnate myself with the embryo."

The words streamed from her mouth in perfect diction, but they were not what he wanted to hear. Her eyes were still fixed on him. He cursed his own naïveté. What did he think she was going to say? *How could I have been so unprepared?*

"I know you will not like me for this," she continued. "But this is my plan, my hope. I need to have my eggs harvested so I can combine them with the nuclei from the cells of—"

He couldn't listen anymore. "That's where I come in, right?" he interrupted. "Technical gynecological support."

"I know I'm asking for too much. It's unlikely I'll succeed anyway …" her voice trailed off.

He stared at her. Her face had gone white. *She knows she needs me,* he thought. *Nobody else will help her. But what about* me? *Maybe I am mistaken. She can't be saying this is all I am to her.*

He took a big breath. "So, what then?" he prompted. "I imagine you have some sort of back-up plan involving me."

"I was thinking, if I fail," she said, as though weighing her words, "I would still be able to go through with IVF and sperm donation. I haven't really planned that far ahead. Maybe I would just give up."

She stopped, but only for a moment. "I know it's a lot to ask, but will you help me? I need an obstetrician and I can't go to anyone but you."

"It *is* 'a lot to ask,' Evelyn."

His worst fear was confirmed. If only he could go and leave it all behind.

"How do you think I feel?" he finally asked. "Have you any idea? Do you really think you have good enough reasons to justify this? You're doing all this, you're rejecting me, on the slimmest of evidence."

She was silent. He agitated his glass of wine, watching the red fluid swirl. She was obsessed with the idea. He felt weighed down by anger. In silence, he tried to reason—*she is a clever scientist, but she can also be so naive. I loved that about her, but not in* this *way. Not now.*

He made an effort to control his voice. "You're putting yourself in danger. Too many unknowns. A prion could be spliced in that DNA. How can I know I will do no harm, to you ... to the child? Not to mention it's illegal. You're asking me to risk your health and my career."

"I've been agonizing over the ethics as—"

"Ethics," he interrupted. "You can't weigh anything up because you're blinded by your obsession."

"Michael, at the end of the day, trying to bring life into this world cannot be immoral."

Of course, she would rationalize anything as long as it meant she could have her way. "Evelyn, this isn't the only way to bring life. All of a sudden you're *desperate* for a child."

"You know, I always wanted to have a child at some point in my life," she said. "And now, seeing my sister with my niece ... I started thinking. They were together, so close to each other. I mean really seeing their bond ... I felt ..."

Michael sensed there was more to come.

"For the first time in my life I felt so close to what might be the maternal instinct. Michael, if there ever were a reason to do it, *this* is it."

"Plenty of women go for sperm donation long before they discover a skeleton. At least be honest with yourself—do you want a child or an experiment?"

She remained silent in front of the protea that was standing tall in a white vase, silver petals reflecting the ceiling downlights. *She has to answer this. Does she want to be a mother or is this just part of her obsession?*

"I am sorry I placed you in this position, Michael. Perhaps I want both."

Maybe she is devout after all, he thought. *She never showed it. But why else risk her life?*

"Evelyn, am I missing something? Could it be you are a believer?"

"Not since primary school. But I've always been an admirer. His ideas placed Him on the cross—and they concentrate the meaning of life for me."

He let his hands rest limply on the table and bowed his head. "This is mystifying," he said. "It's distressing. What's ethical about it? And what about the child? Have you spared a thought for what he will think when he grows up? What kind of mother are you going to be if all you want is an experiment?" He pushed his plate away. "The truth is, as you admitted yourself, if cloning fails you're not even sure you will go through with IVF."

He paused, waiting for her to respond. There was no response. "It's always going to be about *you*. Isn't it? Always *you*," he continued. His words were barely audible, but she recoiled.

"I know I am mixing science with my personal life. I know it's selfish. I know it's my curiosity, my 'obsession' as you say. But I wouldn't be so determined if there wasn't more to it. Having a chance, even the slightest chance … How can I turn my back on this?"

"I exist too, Evelyn, I'm not here just for *support*. You know I have feelings—real feelings."

A storm was rising inside him; something he could no longer suppress. He had had enough.

He stood up. She would not have her way this time. He did not even look at her as he walked out. She was calling his name, but he refused to give in to melodrama.

Slamming the door behind him, he stood in the street trying to pull himself together for the drive home.

Suddenly, unexpectedly, a totally different thought crossed his mind—

If this is what she *wants, I will find a way to get what* I *want out of it.*

Chapter 4

BORROWING THE CODE

The lab coat felt comfortable, the original starchy texture of the fabric having softened and molded to Evelyn's frame from wear. Her fringe, poorly held back by bobby pins, kept falling down, limiting her view. She pushed her hair back and rolled her head and shoulders before starting work.

It was Sunday morning and the lab was deserted. The beach, not the bench, had won the students. Far from being in the lab on weekends, most left at 5 pm on weekdays, as though hearing the bell for end of class. None showed her dedication when she was at their level working on her tiger. She had slaved over the microscope as a student, as a postdoc and even now.

It was, however, a slavery she loved. There was nothing she enjoyed more than noticing something unknown to science, no matter how seemingly insignificant. She would have persisted with science even if she never saw her name in the authorship of a publication. It was clear to her from early on, science was not for external rewards, not for glory, not even for suffering humanity. She was a scientist to satisfy her curiosity, for the pleasure of doing something thoroughly, carefully, analytically, and in the hope it would reveal some of life's secrets.

She was now focusing all her energies on the extraction of the genetic material, trying to convince herself this was like any other procedure she had done countless times. *After all, He was human— twenty-three pairs of chromosomes, just like everybody else.*

But as she began her efforts to isolate the nucleus of a brain cell, the envelope containing the genes, her pretenses collapsed. *I am extracting the code of His life without His consent.*

Her gloved hands were unsteady and her effort was a failure.

She wondered again whether she should do hyperspectral imaging on the papyrus. This method had the potential to reveal the hidden words. *Why am I loath to search for something that might reject my hypothesis? Even if the hypothesis is wrong, there would be a silver lining—I will be able to return to normality. Let go of my obsession.*

Right now it felt like she was back in her undergraduate years, when virtually nothing she tried worked. She took deep breaths to bring her emotions under control and sort through the confusion of her feelings. But her hands would not steady. It suddenly felt hot in the air-conditioned lab, but the windows were stuck. She cast off her lab coat, but it was still too hot so, she paced up and down the corridor, her sneakers squeaking on the linoleum floor.

In the ladies' room, everything seemed ugly—the off-white walls, the taps with their black base of verdigris, the chipped washbasin, the scratched paper dispenser, the toilet bowl. *Why am I doing this?* she asked, looking at herself in the mirror. *I don't even know what I'll get out of it. Michael is right. I am ditching a discovery to chase a chimera.*

And I am throwing him away too—the only man who ever loved me.

She recalled their last dinner. He hadn't called since, nor had he responded to her emails or texts. His absence served to highlight his presence in her life.

In the end, if she were to take the IVF option, who better to be the father than Michael? Imagine a child with his intelligence and sensitivity—a miniature version of Michael she could truly love. Even if romantic love never arrived, she would love her child, clone or not. This is what she wanted in life—to love. She had been damaged, but she wanted to heal. A child would be a way to heal, and a lot more besides.

She could find nothing appealing about her reflection in the mirror. *I want to extract this nucleus, but what am I going to do with it without his help? I can't even publish any of it. I have broken the law every step of the way.*

But that is not what this is about. I just want to prove it can be done. Even if no one else ever knows but Michael and me.

She wondered if he would rethink and help her bring up a child anyway. *No. I have to stop hoping he will do what I want.*

If he did not help her, that would be the end—there would be no chance that extracting the nucleus could lead to a clone. So, this would just be an academic exercise—just testing to see if she could extract the nucleus with the DNA.

Feeling less agitated, she took a last look at her face in the mirror and walked back to the lab. Her hands were steady and her mind was clear of everything but the cells before her.

It did not happen with that pyramidal cell; it did not happen with the next, or with the one after. But Evelyn persevered.

⁂

How can I turn back time?

A magazine sat open but unread on Evelyn's lap as she waited for her appointment. The room was full of pregnant women. Comparing herself to the others around her, she guessed she was about ten years older than the oldest.

With egg donation she could get around this obstacle. She remembered what Michael had said about that. "The uterus is the physiological example of a good husband—it does what it's told, regardless of age." It was the eggs that could become problematic.

She had staged a daring visit three nights before. It could have gone either way. She had driven over to Michael's house after midnight, the first time she had ever done that. Earlier that night, her efforts had finally borne fruit—she had successfully extracted a nucleus. And the hours working on the brain cells had activated enough of her own. She remembered, she reflected, and saw things more clearly.

The more she looked back on it, the more she cringed at the recognition of how selfish her request for Michael's help to clone had been. It must have felt like the ultimate rejection, when his hope had been to have a child with her. What it had come down to was that she was rejecting his sperm, preferring another way to fall pregnant. Even if Michael did believe the DNA came from Jesus, it would have been cold comfort. In fact, his doubts about the authenticity of the remains might have had more to do with jealousy than lack of evidence.

Yes, she thought, *he is jealous because he has feelings for me. Ancient skeleton or not, for Michael, it is still another man. I am the one who is taking advantage of his good heart. I asked for help for an idea he was never convinced about, while at the same time denying him a chance to be a father. If he had refused to help, it would not have meant he did not love me.*

It had taken a few days for the enormity of what she had done to sink in, and by then she worried a late apology would reopen the wound. Michael was the most precious person to her, but she still wanted to go through with her plan. He was right, she was obsessed. Obsession was part of her character and she knew it. Even at school, she would read science books in the playground and, as a student, all she cared about was work, until the shattering love affair with … and even that was now a chronic pain. Michael was an important part of her life, but she simply did not want to have his child—not now when the alternative seemed possible.

Straight across from her, a mother lowered her bra to feed her baby. It was so natural, so beautiful.

She knew that, even after successful nuclear extraction, nothing could happen without his help. So... what if she had extracted a nucleus from a brain cell? She had no eggs. She could hardly go to another obstetrician. It would be impossible to explain, and even if they believed her, who would help her—and who could be trusted to keep the secret? It had to be Michael. So, she had come up with a compromise she hoped he would not reject. Knocking on his door in the middle of the night, she could read the surprise on his face, but also his pleasure.

She had apologized for being insensitive and laid out her cards. They had talked for hours and he fully accepted her offer.

It was what she had hoped, but she was still wrenched by bouts of guilt, all too aware she had used Michael's love to get what she wanted. At best, he would receive but a shadow of what he desired. Still, he was going ...

"Evelyn Camilleri," the receptionist called out. "Dr. Adamec is ready for you."

Feet heavy, she walked through to Michael's office. He greeted her warmly, but she felt the absence of a hug or a kiss. Perhaps he was treating her like all his patients.

"These are fine, Evelyn." Her results were in front of him. "You're definitely not peri-menopausal. We should start routine procedures like organizing folate supplements to prevent neural tube defects, but everything looks good."

As Michael continued, presumably with the sort of thing he said to other patients, she felt the tension in her muscles ease and became oblivious to everything but the idea she was now one step closer. Finally, she could breathe a sigh of relief.

"I know you're pleased, Evelyn, but I want you to understand these results. You need to know what is under control and what still needs to be done."

She nodded and tried to concentrate.

"With all women your age, there is increased risk of fetal abnormalities. So, you might want to consider pre-implantation genetic testing."

He paused. "Evelyn, the next step is sensitive, given our history ..."

He led her to the examination bed.

A bed of nails would have been more comfortable. Her mind went back to a different bed they had shared. Contact that once had given meaning to life was now a clinical procedure. He drew the curtain and asked her to cover herself with a sheet. She lay on her back, legs bent at the knees, arms behind her head. She felt his eyes on her and turned her head to face the wall as he drew up the hem of the sheet to take a Pap smear. She pressed her lips together at the touch of the cold speculum and could only wonder what Michael was thinking. She saw his shadow move on the wall. He worked without speaking, as if she were a stranger.

"The red flowers suit you," he said, after she got dressed and sat opposite him at his desk. "You could play Carmen in that dress."

It was a compliment, but any comment would have been helpful to backward mask what they had just experienced.

"I know there's a lot to absorb, but it's all written here for you," he continued. "I'll get the rubella vaccine organized and, when you're ready, we can start the fertility treatment."

Just before he opened the door to see her out, he kissed her on the cheek. "You don't need to hurry," he whispered. "Think a bit more before you decide which road to follow."

Which road to follow, she repeated to herself as she turned to look at the door that closed behind her. *I am simply going where my steps are taking me.*

⚜

Why can't I concentrate?

Evelyn had to comment on the innovation and feasibility of the fourth-year-honors thesis proposals she was reading, but her mind was lost on the question of whether a clone could be the opposite of its original.

No, if you clone yeast, you get yeast—you don't get drosophila.

But how much of the emotional self was inherited? How much was due to upbringing? She put down the proposal she was reading and settled her head on the backrest of the couch. "Michael, is it nature or nurture that's stronger?"

He was sitting in the rocking chair opposite her, sifting through the Saturday *Sydney Morning Herald*. "Come on, Evelyn, you won't be *that* bad of a mother. Giving you a baby is better than giving it to the wolves."

"No, seriously, there is always a chance we will succeed. I'm thinking ahead and I have no idea how he might turn out."

"Well, you're in good company. You see, no parent knows."

She stretched her arms and closed her eyes. "This is different."

"You'll have to ask an expert. Have you heard of this Professor Fred Eastbrook?"

"Yeah, come to think of it, I saw him on a panel not long ago. On preimplantation genetic testing."

"He might be good."

"I'll email him." She wondered what to say next. Could she ask him to see the professor with her without offending him? Eventually, she said softly, "Want to come along?"

"I'll come," he said without hesitation. He got up and massaged her neck. "Now, about tomorrow. Are you nervous?"

The tension in her neck was melting away. She turned to look at him. "Should I be?"

"No, it's a simple procedure. I do it all the time. As I said, the complication rate is extremely low."

"Yes, you've said all that. I'm not nervous about the procedure, but about the whole plan. We are following a path that abandons the option of publishing the find. I don't think I made a mistake. I followed my footsteps; but publishing the find now will be the road not taken."

He bent and kissed her hair. "There have been other roads you have not taken. Roads lost forever. But roads can appear when you least expect them. Wide boulevards that take you precisely where you want to go."

ॐ

Michael picked up his regular afternoon order, a cappuccino without chocolate, from Windscreens Café on the ground floor of the Royal Hospital for Women.

The first sip of the warm frothy milk gave him a buzz. He thanked providence for the placebo effect and strode past the gift shop and the wall of portraits of previous administrators. He shared the elevator with a white-haired man who, bouquet of red roses in hand, stepped out at the level of the postnatal ward. Was he the father or the grandfather? *People would wonder that about me too,* he thought.

The nurses acknowledged him as he walked through the post-op ward. He leaned against the doorjamb of Evelyn's room. Her brown hair was splayed across the white pillow, her body curled up like a comma. He felt a magnetic pull—a desire to curl around her.

It had been devastating walking out on her that night—the night she had asked for help. For days it had tormented him that this could finally mean the end of whatever it was they had between them. He could not bear to tell anyone—not his parents, not his sisters, not his friends. Saying it out loud would have made it real and, besides, he was not ready to hear the truth of what his loved ones thought of this dysfunctional relationship.

His parents lived in a small country town in Victoria and had been happily married since their late teens. Each of his three sisters had married by their mid-twenties and were now scattered between Melbourne and Sydney, juggling children and jobs. He was the only one who could not make it work. Only to him did love owe something.

Until Evelyn, all his relationships had been easy. He had believed he understood women—what they needed, what they wanted, what they thought they wanted. To his frustration, too often he could predict what they were going to say. None of them had Evelyn's intellect and depth. What is more, she was refreshingly unpredictable. He could now see deep inside her. She wanted to be the mother of a child, but not only. She also wanted to be the mother of an idea.

Maybe I should have been more supportive. In a strange way I admire her, even as my own needs are relegated to second—

A nurse approached him and asked if everything was going okay. He told her Evelyn should come out of the anesthetic any minute.

He recalled the sheer relief of seeing her that night—he was alive again. He had opened the door expecting some sort of emergency. Instead, standing disheveled on his doorstep was Evelyn. It was as though *he* had come home. The feelings he had for her were deeper than anything he had ever felt.

She was wild eyed, her words tumbling over themselves as she tried to explain. It reminded him of the time she burst into their hotel room in Jerusalem two months earlier. This time, though, her agitation, her intensity, stemmed from the hurt she had caused him.

He had brushed aside her apology. It was heartfelt and he appreciated the gesture, but it hardly mattered now that he had her back in his life.

She had told him she still wanted to go through with the cloning idea. Uncertain as she was of success, she wanted two things—for him to be the sperm donor for IVF if cloning failed and, either way, to raise the child together, if he wanted.

Even recalling that moment brought a sense of peace. He had felt complete. This was as much as Evelyn could offer anyone and she was offering it to him.

She has limitations as we all do, he reflected. *She fears commitment. But is that any wonder after years in foster care? Do I throw away the one I love for her imperfections?*

As he was watching her now, Evelyn's eyelids fluttered, then opened. She looked about groggily before focusing on him. "When?" she asked. "When is it going to happen?"

"It's done, Evelyn."

Her voice was so sweet. Her eyes so beautiful as they focused on him. She had subjected herself to a lot to get to this point. *It's done; it's all done,* he repeated to himself. *But what comes next? Her plan or mine?*

"I remember the injection. How did it go?"

"Everything went smoothly," he whispered as he caressed her hair. "The eggs have been harvested. You should rest now."

She reached out and pulled him down for a kiss on the lips. Nodding, she fell asleep.

With her ova safely harvested and the nuclei with the DNA from the skeleton extracted, Evelyn now had the option of combining them. However, Michael began contemplating an entirely different combination. Watching her eyes move rapidly under her eyelids, indicating she was dreaming, he considered his own dream—having a child with her.

He thought of *his* old age. He had witnessed the ecstasy of countless couples when delivering their babies. *Why couldn't this be my turn? This could be my chance to have my own baby and, indeed, with Evelyn.*

Just because she could produce a clone, it did not mean he had to use it. He had harvested thirteen eggs. He was the sole custodian of these eggs. She would never know if he kept some.

I can fertilize a few of her eggs with my *sperm. I deserve to be the father. That skeleton has done* nothing *for her.* Evelyn would have a child, but not precisely as she prescribed. And he would be sparing her the risk of contracting something horrible from that skeleton.

It was his best motive to protect her. It was his worst motive to deceive her. At that moment, his best and worst motives coincided.

The only reason Evelyn considered cloning was because she believed the skeleton belonged to Jesus. But her conclusion was an amalgam of evidence and obsession.

He reached over to cover her arm with the sheet.

For every thought, he had a counter-thought. *What about professional ethics? A doctor cannot deceive his patient.* But this case was too extraordinary for normal ethical considerations.

She was going to remove her own genetic material from her ova so the child would carry the genetic information from the person she believes to be Him. She would just be a vessel for cloning. *What perverse thinking she has fallen into—to want to propagate the genes of a skeleton ahead of her own!*

What if she found out I used my sperm? But she would probably never know the difference. He would transfer a *male* embryo. And even if the boy looked like him, she would still love it. And if it looked like her, she would hardly love it any less. And not only that, it would be *her* genes that would be used.

She would go through nine months of pregnancy. She definitely deserved to be the mother—the biological mother. She was not thinking clearly now, but, after birth, oxytocin, the bonding hormone, would be working for him.

It's a bloody nightmare. Can I betray the one I love?

Perhaps I should turn the question on its head and ask—when the one you love is likely to harm herself, isn't deception the only noble course?

⋇

After locking her lab door and closing the shutters, Evelyn switched on the main lights and turned on the fume cupboard, noise from the extractor fan joining the hum of the two $-80°C$ freezers. It was late evening on a Friday and the rest of the Biological Sciences Building was in darkness.

She knew she would need both time and luck for one of the reconstructed eggs to start dividing. She had removed the nuclei from her eggs, replacing them with nuclei from the brain cells. She began treating a reconstructed egg with chemicals to stimulate cell division—to start the clock of life.

My eggs are nothing but empty vessels, she kept reminding herself, *to be filled by an ancient genetic code.*

Virtually all the genes of the child would come from the ancient person. The only genetic information she would be passing down would come from the tiny mitochondrial DNA fraction she received from her mother, who received it from *her* mother and so on. But in appearance, intelligence and emotion, the child would have virtually no genetic contribution from her. Instead, he would be the twin of someone else—*someone far more important than me.*

Nothing happened.

The first egg refused to divide. If she waited a little longer …

She went to the toilet and then to the staff room to make a cup of coffee. She forced herself to sit and flick through a magazine on the table—page after page of celebrities she did not recognize, wearing brands of clothes for which she could not care less. It was what entered the mind that mattered, not what covered the body.

After half an hour, she leapt up from the couch and went straight to the lab. She looked through the microscope, hoping there would be a difference. Still nothing. *When does one give up waiting for the bus?*

Should she wait even longer? Was the problem the process or the ovum? The genes that controlled the first cell division had to be switched on. Evelyn worked on for hours, her neck muscles tense. In the end, she had to abort the trial.

The next egg also failed to divide. She was disappointed, but had the right training for this, having experienced multiple failures in her experiments with the Tasmanian tiger. The real worry was the number of eggs. *Sooner or later I will run out.*

※

Every day I retrace my steps to arrive at the same failure.

It had been a week, but Evelyn's ova were still unresponsive. The only things moving in the lab that night were the test tube shakers as they tilted predictably from side to side to agitate their fluid.

I am a fool to keep trying. Why can't I stop? Am I a free agent or just an actor following a script? Why can't I ditch the bloody script?

The air-conditioning was playing up and it was cold. There was now growing doubt in her mind whether this would work. She had spent the evenings trying to entice reluctant cells to divide.

This night she was employing an alternative method, using electric current rather than chemical catalysts. *I have almost run out of eggs,* she thought, while continuing her struggle to initiate cell division.

It was past midnight when she commenced what was to be her last inspection. Rubbing her eyes with her fingers, she waited for her vision to clear before looking through the microscope.

She thought she saw something and rubbed her eyes again.

Yes—division had commenced. *It is real. The cells are multiplying. It is really happening!*

No scientist had ever gone this far. An elusive dream had come true. Even if the rest of the journey were a failure, she had opened a path for the use of postmortem tissue in cloning.

Do I stop here or do I reach for more?

She looked up from the microscope. The test tube shakers were still tilting from side to side. The cryotome was still telling anyone who cared to look that its temperature was −19°C. The centrifuge was still open, ready to precipitate anything that would settle. The laboratory manual *Molecular Cloning* was still resting open on the lab bench and the deep freezers were still humming as before. All was the same everywhere, except under her microscope. There, the process of mitosis had begun.

She looked through the eyepieces again. The cells were replicating quickly, just copying the genetic material. The embryo was like a budding flower, the number of petals increasing, though the flower was not growing any bigger.

Enchanted by the cell division, it was dawn the next time she took her eyes away. The clock of life had started and she hoped it would not stop. Now she was responsible for the development of a life. She had to act with precision. Her actions had to be timely and flawless.

Life has returned—and I have to synchronize myself precisely with its rhythm.

The Skinner boxes were barren, except for a lever. Rats pressed the levers and were intermittently rewarded with food pellets. Michael reflected as he watched with fascination, *Unlike human relationships, the more the rat works the more the rat gets.*

He and Evelyn found Professor Eastbrook in his office, next to the room containing the boxes where the rats earned their living. The professor was in a white lab coat with yellow stains on it. A rat, fur white, eyes red, poked its head out of a side pocket, giving a clue to the source of the stains.

"Have a seat," he said in a thick Scottish accent. "I hope you're not claustrophobic." His smile produced ripples on his cheeks as it revealed a receding gum line.

Michael had never seen so much stuff crowded into such a small space. The walls were covered with bookshelves and filing cabinets, the desk loaded with scientific articles. He sat with limbs close to his body for fear of disturbing the colorful chaos, which, for the professor, could represent perfect order.

"It's not often I get questions from people working outside my field," the professor continued, his smoker's voice raspy and harsh. "You said, Evelyn, you're a geneticist and that Michael is a gynecologist. I'm keen to see how you'll react to what psychologists have to say. It's Fred, by the way."

Michael pointed to the rat boxes. "You've got some hard workers out there, Fred."

"It's a rat model of anxiety we are studying, but psychologists have used rats to model depression, schizophrenia, Alzheimer's disease, etcetera."

"Fred," said Evelyn, "as I wrote in my email, we would like to ask you your thoughts on the relative contribution of genes and environment to intelligence and emotion."

Michael noticed she was trying not to bite her lip while waiting for the answer. He knew a lot was riding on the professor's response. Given the dangers of cloning, if she became convinced the skeleton's genes were of little value, if she saw a big risk with little gain, she might desist. *She might take the logical option and choose me of her own accord.*

"You mean that old debate—what percentage of IQ is inherited and what is attributable to the environment?" asked the professor.

Of course, if she is not emotionally mature, Michael thought, *there is always Plan B.*

"Yes, please," said Evelyn. "What is the current thinking on that?"

"Well, the best evidence for a genetic contribution to intelligence comes from the study of identical or monozygotic twins, nature's own cloning experiment." The professor filled his pipe as he spoke. "Identical twins have identical DNA. There is no doubt they are very close to each other in IQ, even when raised apart, in different environments, although some concerns have been expressed as to how 'different' the different environments really were in some of the early works." He paused to light his pipe. "One thing is clear—identical twins are far closer to each other in IQ than fraternal twins."

"Nature's own cloning experiment," Evelyn repeated. "That's such an interesting way to look at it."

"I've seen that in my practice," said Michael. "I've delivered a few identical twins. They usually reach developmental milestones together."

"What about mood, emotion and altruism?" asked Evelyn. "Is there a similar contribution of genes?"

Professor Eastbrook leaned back in his armchair, seemingly satisfied he could explain scientific theories to people eager to listen. Michael braced himself for another long explanation with convoluted sentences and unwelcome conclusions.

"The contribution of genes to mood and temperament is again best seen in studies of identical twins. If one of a pair of identical twins suffers from depression, the other twin has a fifty percent chance of also suffering from depression," said the professor, using the mouthpiece of his pipe to "write" the number 50 in the air. "This agreement, this percentage, is ten times higher than the incidence of depression in the population at large, which is five percent. It illustrates the contribution of genes to mood.

"However," he added after inhaling some smoke, "the fact that the agreement among identical twins is not a hundred percent, but only fifty percent, shows at the same time that the environment also plays a crucial role." He took a breath. "Now for altruism. No. It has not been studied in a similar fashion, as far as I know, but I expect such properties of the emotional brain to be as influenced by genes as are IQ and depression."

"But which is stronger in the end?" asked Evelyn. "Nature or nurture?"

"Both genes and the environment are essential for all behavior. It's not nature versus nurture, but nature *via* nurture. Intelligence is the product of two factors—the genetic endowment inherited from parents and the environmental influences on that endowment. The contribution of the two cannot be disambiguated." The professor had interlaced his fingers and was making as if to pull them apart while they refused to oblige. "Nonetheless, given similar socioeconomic backgrounds and schooling, we can assume IQ is principally deter-mined by the genetic make-up and motivation." He quickly added, "Motivation itself has a hereditary and an environmental component."

Michael could see Evelyn was completely absorbed and what the professor was saying would hardly dissuade her from the course she had embarked on. The embryo she had constructed was progressing normally and the intended day of transfer was the following week, to fit in with her natural cycle. "Are there any other factors that influence behavior besides genes and environment?" he asked.

"Nobody has come up with any other credible factor." The professor scratched the back of the rat, which by now had crawled out of his pocket and nestled in his lap. "What is virtually never appreciated is that the environment has an influence on *which* genes are expressed, that is, which genes become active in brain neurons. I'd better stop here before you start mutating before my very eyes," he concluded with a smile.

Evelyn returned the smile. "I've heard behavioral neuroscientists don't leave a crack in the parade of genes and environment for free will to wriggle in, but is there *none* at all? No freedom, no dignity?"

"There is indeed no freedom and no dignity because individuals have no control of either their genetic make-up or the environmental influences on them." The professor seemed to enjoy his theory, his words emerging through the smoke of his pipe. "We are slaves to yesterday. Our brain will make decisions on the basis of our experiences up to today. But here is where psychologists can be of use. Today is the yesterday of tomorrow and our experiences today can change our preferences tomorrow."

Meanwhile the rat had fearlessly moved from the professor's lap to the armrest of his chair, paws bunched together, back humped, long tail counterbalancing the weight of its head, whiskers sweeping rhythmically back and forth as though responding to a melody only it could hear.

Michael realized that the professor was an unalloyed determinist, but while thinking of whether it was worth challenging this, Evelyn rushed in with a question. "Are you saying choices in life are illusions? That everything is determined by genes and the environment?"

"Evelyn, if we could fully predict behavior, then everyone would accept there is no choice. If lack of predictability was proof of free will, then even the weather would have it, because we cannot fully predict that either. With the increasing capacity of psychologists to predict behavior, little room is left for the notion of free will."

The rat was now walking on the table over to a food pellet, which it grabbed with both forepaws and started rotating while chiseling bits off with its large incisors, morsels of food raining down on the professor's diary, a Collins A4 size displaying a week to an opening.

"And let me relate to you a conversation I had with some bright high school students," the professor continued. "All of them were convinced they had free will. I chose one of them, a boy who was the most insistent, and asked him to think of the girl he would most detest being married to. Then, I asked him to change his mind and, instead of detesting this girl, to fall in love with her. The boy replied, 'I don't want to.' This of course means *I cannot*, and indicates there is no free will in the domain of emotion."

"Not to put too fine a point on it," the professor continued after a slight hesitation, "you are as impotent in changing your emotions as you are in changing the color of your eyes. Consider this. Do you know anyone who continued to love a person long after that person ceased loving them?"

Me, Michael thought.

"You might have also witnessed the converse," the professor continued. "A person losing their love for someone, though, logically, they consider them perfect."

There, in two sentences, the professor unwittingly described their own paradox. Michael had made up his mind about what he had to do. The issue was settled—for the moment at least.

❧

How can I open her eyes to the dangers? Surely, she can see there is a safer alternative walking right beside her. Why else ask me to be her back-up?

Michael's strides matched Evelyn's as they made their way through the lower campus, having left the School of Psychology. On the

University Mall, students were marching up to the Scientia Building and down to Anzac Parade, corralled by the short, vertical light posts that lined the path. He wondered if there would ever be anything he could do to change her mind. She might come to love him some day as a father figure to her child. But what if she contracted the human variant of Mad Cow Disease from this cloned embryo?

He grasped her hand as they plowed through the waves of young heads coming toward them. The embryo transfer date was looming, the countdown to the ultimate decision—should he assist her with her crazy plan or should he betray her trust to protect her from herself? He could transfer the embryo from the skeleton, or an embryo that united him with her. The ova he had hidden were in his custody.

In a few days, the decision would literally rest in his hands. *He* would determine which of the two starkly different outcomes became real. Everything was ready and the decision was his alone.

Holding her hand while contemplating deception filled him with guilt, even as he justified it. He watched as their reflected figures moved along the glass walls of the buildings framing the mall. *How can I face her if I deceive her? How can I keep such a secret for a lifetime?*

She only had one embryo from the skeleton; the chances of successful transfer were slim. Perhaps if he waited, he could get what he wanted without deception. *But then again, how could I forgive myself if I helped her and something went horribly wrong?*

He was burdened by feelings he could not command away. It felt so right holding her hand. Even as he tried to explore every alternative rationally, his thoughts ended as a refrain of a sad song, one that concludes on a hopeful note—Evelyn someday reciprocating his feelings. Of course he was much older, but she did not seem to be seeking a younger man, or, for that matter, any man.

They were approaching the western end of the University Mall, but he was no closer to knowing the thoughts behind her green–brown eyes. Whatever these thoughts were, they were not romantic fantasies for him. He felt the wind on his face and, without as much as thinking, he squeezed her hand. "What's on your mind?" he asked.

"That we're all in a checkmate. We're constrained by expectations and taboos. But there was someone who wasn't."

Michael sighed. She was infatuated with the skeleton. *How can I compete with an imaginary idol?*

He had ambushed himself. Why did he have to suggest Professor Eastbrook, a hardnosed determinist who reinforced her conviction of the importance of heredity? He should have suggested a sensitive, soft and cuddly counseling psychologist who would ignore genetics and emphasize the upbringing. Keeping his thoughts private, he said, "If you produce a clone, the child will be identical in appearance to the donor and will have similar IQ and emotions."

"Yes, Eastbrook was emphatic on the importance of genes."

"Evelyn, you know, I've never been convinced the skeleton belongs to Him."

"You wouldn't believe it even if I had double the evidence. But I believe it. And all I've ever asked of you was to believe in me …"

"Even if you're right, don't forget that nobody knows exactly what His make-up was."

"We know one thing. He was an idealist. His principle of mutual love is still the best element of Christianity."

"You've got to look beyond your obsession and consider the worst case." He felt he was shouting into a wild wind, but continued, "He might just have been one of the rabble-rousers who ran afoul of the law. After all, you can't rely on the Gospels; they were written long after His death."

"You're asking me to prove the impossible."

"What if it's a thief you found?"

She turned to look at him. "You know, one more thief wouldn't make a difference. One more Christ would."

There was no hope of reason prevailing. His mind went again to Plan B. There was precedent in nature. The cuckoo—a bird that lays its eggs in the nest of others and makes the other birds hatch its descendants.

Michael had never felt as sympathetically inclined toward the cuckoo as at that moment.

⚘

I only need a few cells to assess the chromosomes.

On Embryonic Day Five, as on every day, Evelyn looked through the microscope at the petri dish holding the life she had created. Concerned the embryo might not be chromosomally intact, she decided to conduct genetic testing.

"Little one, I need some of your cells," she said. "Five-day-olds don't have a nervous system yet. You will not feel any pain."

Holding her breath, she used forceps to immobilize the embryo. The force of her fingers had to be strong enough to arrest it, but not so strong as to damage its cells. She used a micropipette to aspirate a few cells fated to become the placenta.

At that critical moment light from the fiber optic cable shone into her eyes, briefly blinding her.

"No!" she cried. "I've lost him."

What have I done? She had misjudged, grossly misjudged. She had cut the embryo in half. The two pieces floated apart and then drifted close to each other, now standing motionless a few millimeters apart.

She was looking at a wreck. The end of a dream. She had failed to carry out a routine—the simplest of procedures. Incompetence defeated advanced science. Never had she been more disappointed in anyone than now in herself. *What am I going to tell him?*

But after wiping away tears, and still thinking of what to tell Michael, she saw a change in the petri dish. There was activity in both fragments of the embryo. Both halves were dividing. Both were alive and fast multiplying. *It was true,* she thought, as tears filled her eyes again. *This is it. Bisection at early embryonic stages has no ill effect.*

If she had any doubt about her feelings before ... The thought of losing the embryo had made her feel she was losing part of herself.

She now had two embryos. Her chances for a successful transfer to her womb had just doubled. Her only aim now was to protect them, to shepherd them through life's journey.

Hours later, she went to the window and opened the blind. Pressing her face to the glass, she cupped her eyes with her hands and looked up at the sky. Without the moon, the stars were out in force. Most of them were like luminous dust sprinkled on a black dome. But some were bright and stood out, distinguishing themselves like the giant pyramidal cells in the firmament that is the human cerebral cortex.

Hope had returned to the petri dish under her microscope.

After extracting a few cells from one embryo, she placed both of them in liquid nitrogen. Freezing arrested all cellular activity. As butterflies in amber, the embryos were now silent, but with all their cells alive.

Sweet siblings, my beautiful flowers, at $-170°C$ you are as good as immortal.

Chapter 5

A MOMENT LIKE NO OTHER

Is he even growing?

Evelyn stepped off the scales. She should have been heavier by now, but the vomiting was not helping. The nausea ought to have ended weeks earlier. Not wanting to expose the fetus to medication, she had declined drugs for morning sickness. But was that the right decision?

Michael had reassured her some women experienced nausea throughout pregnancy, though he was concerned at the slow weight gain.

In her mind, she would amplify any concern he expressed. What if the fetus was not thriving? Every unexpected change in her body, every delay in the arrival of milestones could be a sign of a fundamental problem with the cloning, with the transfer, with the impregnation. There were so many unknowns in this pregnancy.

Was she carrying a normal fetus, or would her actions come back to haunt her? If ever there were a sacrilege, if ever there were a sin, wouldn't this be it?

No, no, causing suffering is a sin. Creating life cannot be a sin.

She did it because of love. She did it to correct the greatest injustice.

She heard the phone and then the soothing melody of Michael's voice. At least she would have his company that night, the peace his presence brings. When he was not there, the evenings seemed interminable.

⁊

Some of her recollections were fuzzy.

What she remembered clearly was Michael's voice, his hands massaging her lower back, and how it all happened the way he had said it would.

The contractions had started early in the afternoon, while she was alone at home. He had rushed over, helped her into the car and driven the short distance to the hospital. Kathryn met them there. Lying in the birthing suite, Evelyn had clutched their hands as the pain of contractions swept through her with terrifying intensity.

Everything snapped into focus as she recalled the last moments of the delivery—Michael telling her to push, the pain pulsing through her as the baby's head moved down.

The science-fiction scenario of a person inside a person had ended with the miracle of birth.

His first cry was the sweetest sound. Michael had placed him on her chest and she saw her baby—his long body, his shock of wet black hair. The baby looked at her as though he knew her.

Such a moment, there had been no other. This tiny being that was a part of her had just found its own existence.

As she was holding her baby, Michael had embraced them both and kissed her forehead. She looked up at him. At that moment, she was in love with him.

Breathing in Christopher's smell now, a mixture of the scent of milk and baby powder, she could hardly recall the anxiety that had gripped her before and during pregnancy. He was the validation of everything. Far away were the discovery in the desert and the agonizing over cloning.

And far away was Michael's storming out of the house following her insensitive request, when she thought she would never see him again.

She stroked the baby's cheek exactly where the dimple appeared when he cried. His skin was softer than silk. "Your bonsai fingers, your bonsai toes, everything is beautiful about you," she whispered as his eyelids slowly fell shut. Long dark eyelashes matched his plentiful black hair. "I'll sing to you what my grandfather, my *papou*, sang to me.

> Mother, you had two sons
> Two rivers
> And two stars
> Two castles Byzantine
> Two eagles on the wing
> One went west
> The other east
> And alone you pray to the sun.

⁂

How can I find peace while his twin is still frozen?

It was not about having a large family. It was about giving life to a life and giving Christopher his brother.

Evelyn placed the baby on the lambskin in his cot. He stirred without waking. She switched on the monitor and, stretching her back, started making her way to the kitchen, where Michael was preparing dinner. There he was, the perfect friend, and virtually the father to her child.

As though hearing her thoughts, he looked at her quizzically. She shook her head vaguely and sat at the table. "It would be hard to be a vegetarian while smelling your barbecue," she said, helping herself to some chicken.

During dinner, they had an entire conversation in few words—the rhythm of their lives together.

Kathryn had told her not to do anything fancy for Christmas, but when Evelyn found out Leanne would be spending the day with them and not with her father, it became even more important everything was right. The Camilleri family would be celebrating their newest member's first Christmas.

She had already prepared most of the food for the following day, but had yet to wrap the presents. The tree was up, though the old decorations still sat in the storage box waiting for Leanne. The smell of pine took her back to childhood Christmases, when she and Kathryn would pull out the decorations, the silver tinsel, glass icicles and colored baubles—ruby red, emerald green and sapphire. She would pass them one by one to Kathryn, who would stand on a chair to hang them. When they got to the star, they called their father to place it on the top of the tree. Their mother would come too and then they would switch on the lights. Like fireworks, after each flicker there was the anticipation of the next one.

On Christmas Eve, she would sneak into her sister's bed. Every year, they would stay up with renewed determination to catch the old man in the red suit and long white beard in the act of delivering their gifts. They would keep awake by telling stories, eventually resorting to pinching each other's arms until tears, then giggles, then tears again. On Christmas morning, one of them would shake the other awake. They would race to the living room and find the presents and the only traces of Santa—biscuit crumbs on a plate.

Kathryn was one of the few constants in her life. After their father's disappearance, she was her protector, especially when their mother was hospitalized for depression and they were in foster care.

Evelyn had the power to give her son all this and more. If what Professor Eastbrook said about genes were true, the identical twins would be each other's ideal companion.

Michael opened the door to fetch the grilled apples from the barbecue. The air-conditioning kept the temperature comfortable within, but it was hot outside. The weather report said it would be even hotter on Christmas Day.

"I've been thinking about the embryo," she said as he closed the door against the heat.

"Me too. It's incredible to think it's another Christopher." He rested the platter on the table. "Here is the cinnamon. Some honey with the apples, or are you over the cravings?"

She took a spoonful. "The cinnamon smells nice. Michael, tell me, what shall we do?"

"Before we even think about doing anything, you need a break, especially because you're breastfeeding. And at nearly forty-six ..."

"I don't mind. I just don't want any risk to the baby."

"Evelyn, I wouldn't recommend you go through it again. There is a safer option."

"You mean surrogacy."

"Remember the Taplins, darling?"

"I know; they found a surrogate in Buenos Aires, but just because it worked for them ..."

He finished wiping down the bench and sat next to her. "If we find the same woman, we'd know it's someone ..."

"... we can trust," she said.

"The Taplin child is what, about five now?"

"Do you think we could be lucky?"

"Evelyn Camilleri, you have been lucky already. Even when multiple embryos are transferred, the implantation rate is not high. You know, we only have one."

"We have played with probabilities from the start. There is only one way to test them. But, Michael, in another country, how can we protect our embryo?"

He put his hand on her knee. "Don't worry about that. Other people do it too. But there are problems."

"I didn't have any ... or just about didn't. Only mild gestational diabetes."

"Well, no, and hopefully it'll be the same next time—if there is a next time. But what about ethics, Evelyn? The concealment worries me; we can't tell the surrogate what it's really about."

"Michael, let me try. *I* could have this baby."

"I can't advise that. I won't help you do it. If ..." He stopped mid-sentence. "But ... I mean it's one thing to choose it for yourself, and another to exploit someone who is unaware—this woman would have no idea. There's no way she could give informed consent."

"We can be supportive. We can be generous. I know that's not enough, but—"

"Money is no compensation in such a case, darling."

"It'll be so beautiful to give Christopher his brother. Think of your sisters. Imagine if you had grown up an only child."

"The whole of China is growing up like that—one-child policy. It's normal these days. You're emotional. Put yourself in this poor woman's shoes."

"I *do* understand. But when I look at Christopher, I want to savor every moment of his childhood and I want him to share it with someone. I don't know if it's the hormones, but I can't get over the emotional side of this. I can't stop thinking of the other one."

"If all you want is a sibling for Christopher then you could find a surrogate and use an IVF embryo. We can even use your own ova, your genes. You will be the biological mother and there will be no deception."

"No, because there is a life waiting to be born. We *have* the embryo. That changes everything. What are we going to do with it? We cannot possibly harm it."

He stayed silent and she added, "Just now, you convinced me not to have it myself and to go for a surrogate. I agree, but with *this* embryo."

"I know I suggested surrogacy, but we have to think of the exploitation; she will not be making an informed choice."

"Whatever we do, there is huge risk and huge hope. On the other hand, as you say, I'm getting old."

"I didn't exactly say you're getting old. But, anyway, what's the rush? I mean the embryo is frozen."

"You're right. Maybe I'm just being sentimental over Christmas."

"Not to mention the surge of oxytocin you get after birth."

She licked the remaining honey on the spoon. "Michael, I am frightened something bad might happen to the other one. And, like you said, if we want to have the same woman as the Taplins, there isn't much time."

"We can try. But don't get your hopes up. The success rate in IVF is around thirty percent."

Where would I be without my friend? she thought

As though reading her mind again, Michael ran his fingers through her hair and gave her a kiss on the lips. "Even if we find this woman, it probably won't work," he said. "But you're right—we must give the other one a chance to live his life."

❧

In a way, it resembled Paris.

Old buildings with rounded corners flanked wide boulevards that met at busy intersections. But the classic look was spoiled by shabby slabs of concrete and glass. Buenos Aires had fallen on hard times.

Michael was strolling along Avenida 9 de Julio as evening fell. He had to remind himself to keep right to avoid colliding with pedestrians walking toward him. There was continuous car traffic in both directions along the widest avenue in the world. He kept walking south toward the obelisk, which split the night sky in two as it towered above the buildings around it. He had seen it on television during celebrations of Argentina's win of the soccer World Cup.

Earlier in the day, he had cleared the first hurdle, anxiety easing when the airport carousel delivered the Styrofoam box with its precious cargo. Importing the embryo was not a problem because there was no restriction on non-pathogenic, non-infectious human tissue. It was the quantity of dry ice that alarmed the lady at the check-in counter, not the human tissue. He was over the one-kilo limit, but she waved him through anyway. He had tested how long dry ice lasts in ambient temperature and had packed three kilos for the sixteen-hour flight. On arrival, he purchased more to last the next few days.

The taxi ride from the airport was something else. He had given the driver the address of the Aspen Suites Hotel in the upscale Retiro district, only two blocks from where he was now walking. The driver spoke no English and was taking some of the red lights as merely indicative. Michael had searched in vain for a seat belt. He wedged the Styrofoam box between his shins and the front seat, bracing it in case of a crash. "No *buenos aires*," he had said, referring to the supposed City of Good Air. The driver had laughed with him as they traveled behind a car belching dense exhaust fumes.

Now he was walking in the heart of the city and had one night to enjoy it.

Drawn by faint music coming from inside, he stopped at the club El Porteño, a tango venue. It was a rectangular room with a dance floor surrounded by rows of tables and a bar at one end. A few people were eating, most were just having drinks. Searching for a free table, he noticed a woman glancing at him. There was no wedding ring on her fourth finger.

No sooner had he taken a seat next to her than he realized he had made a mistake and was sitting in the women's section. It was as though he had stumbled onto the set of *Westside Story*—men on one side of the dance floor, women on the other. "Sorry, I'm in the wrong place."

"It is fine," she said, brushing his arm with her hand.

Most of the people not dancing were women and the men seemed a lot older. "Men have it easier in tango," he said, leaning toward her to be heard.

"They say when the man starts dancing the tango, he enters a pen of hens."

He watched a tall couple. Their bodies were aligned to one another and to the music. When the man took a step forward, it was a calculated stalking move to capture prey. For the woman, a backward step was seductive, in full expectation her prey would follow.

"How does the Catholic Church allow this?"

She put a finger to her lips. "Shh. We do not tell the Pope."

The singers' resonant voices reminded him of Neapolitan baritones. "I can make out the violins, but is there an accordion?"

"It is the *bandoneon*. It is very much like a small accordion, but has the buttons, no keys."

"It's a beautiful song. What's he saying? He seems about to cry."

"'Historia de un Amor' is the song. The tango is a sad thought that is danced. He is saying, 'Oh, how dark life is, my heart. Without your love, I will not live.'"

That's my story, Michael thought as he stared at the feet of a couple doing syncopated steps in front of him. *The story of a captive.*

⁂

Definitely a captive, he thought. *Last night proved it.*

The whole time Michael had been making love to the tango woman, his mind was on Evelyn—on her face, on her body.

It was now early in the morning and he had just entered the lawyer's office. There was a faint smell of cigar smoke. Señor Luis Guzmán, a lean man in his sixties, wore a black pinstripe suit. "My role is to bring you together with *la Señora* María Olfi," he explained in a deep voice, tongue and lips lazy in the formation of consonants. "I advise that I will not be liable for complications medical."

"You are totally right. We will be responsible for any medical complications."

In his initial email, Michael had described the situation perfunctorily and had since prepared a cover story of why they were seeking gestational surrogacy, but the lawyer did not seem to want explanations.

María was ushered in. Her short hair was blonde, contrasting with her brown eyes. Wrinkled skin covered superficial veins on her robust hands. Her pelvis was well on the generous side. She wore a cream blouse that was tucked into a long gray skirt, suitable for church. She made occasional eye contact with Michael as they chatted through Señor Guzmán about his trip and what he thought of Buenos Aires.

When in Australia, he had requested blood tests. She now gave him the original documents, including her temperature chart. The embryo was to be transferred three days after María's expected date of ovulation. If the procedure were successful, her own egg would be lost and she would become pregnant with the transferred embryo.

"María, I can see you are very healthy. Evelyn and I appreciate your willingness to assist us. As you know, we agreed on an advance of ten thousand dollars, but we are happy to increase this to fifteen. There will be as much to come on first heartbeat and then again after the baby is born. We are here for whatever you need."

"There is no reason. The money is already much more than before." Her voice was soft, contrasting with the baritone voice of the lawyer who was translating her words.

"Your help is crucial. We thought this way you won't have to work hard while you are pregnant and you'll have the things you need."

"Therefore, we are in accord," said the lawyer. "It must be understood. If there is no pregnancy, *la Señora* still satisfies the first part of the contract."

"Of course. There is only one embryo and we understand the transfer may not be successful."

María frowned when she heard the translation. "You help me and I help you, but I do not want the money for nothing."

"No, no. We are very happy with this arrangement."

Señor Guzmán brought forward the contract, placing it in front of the framed photograph of himself with his family. "Good, therefore, we proceed."

She nodded and signed.

"You agree to swear on the Bible you will return the baby?" asked the lawyer in Spanish and English.

"*Sí.*"

Michael still had qualms about the deception. However, he no longer worried the woman might be untrustworthy. In María he saw a decent, honest person. He was usually right in his judgment of people. He winced to himself—even with Evelyn. *She is the right one for me. And one day she will realize she too cannot do without me.*

⁂

"I am Luis Guzmán."

Nearly eight months later, Michael was woken in the middle of the night. As he picked up the phone, he had thought it might be one of his patients. Then he remembered the midnight call from Señor Guzmán announcing María's pregnancy. But what could it be this time?

Señor Guzmán continued, "to have ... to find *la Señora* Olfi ... "

The line was poor and Michael could not understand what he was being told. *Please, please, not a complication,* he kept thinking. "What? What about *la Señora* Olfi? Where did you find her?"

"The Friday she did not go ... the *obstetra* ..."

"Perhaps she just didn't turn up. My patients also—"

"She move from the house. We look ... *La Señora ha desaparecido.*"

"She moved out? Don't you have her new address?"

"We look for her in the weekend ... work ..."

"Are you saying she's disappeared?"

"She take all the things."

"What? How could that be, Señor Guzmán? Have you not been able to contact her?"

"She disappeared. She vanish. Gone."

"What about her family, her friends, her job?"

"If you want to investigate, it is necessary ... the detective private."

"She may have gone to a relative. Could she be in some sort of danger?"

The lawyer said something Michael did not understand. "Can you hear me, Señor Guzmán? Can you hear me? We should go to the police."

"I hear now. *Momento la policía* know there is no crime, they abandon. The courts will not rule for us. We may *recuperar* money, but litigation is expensive."

"Don't worry about the money. Our concern is the safety of our baby. María may be in danger. Wouldn't that be sufficient to involve *la policía*?"

"I can ask questions if you retain me, but if *la Señora* abscond, *la policía* will not do nothing."

"Are you sure? Can you put me in contact with them?"

"I can, but no, they do not listen to you."

"Can you suggest a private detective, Señor Guzmán? I will come to Buenos Aires as soon as possible."

It was just after 3 am. Michael stood up slowly, but then sat down on the bed. *How do I tell her?*

A short while later, he was gazing at Evelyn's red door, his phone to his ear. "It's me; I'm outside."

She was in her pajamas. "What's wrong?"

"María is missing."

"Missing where?"

"She failed to go to her obstetrician. They checked her house. She's gone. She has taken all her belongings."

"Are they sure? There must be a mistake."

"The lawyer just called me."

"What did he say? Michael, what about our baby?"

"We will search. I'll go there straight away. She might have left for just a few days."

"Do you really think so? What are we going to do?"

"The pregnancy should be proceeding normally. If we don't find her now, we will keep searching and we'll find them both after birth."

They stayed silent, looking at each other.

"No, we won't," she whispered. "We won't," she said, covering her mouth with her hand.

"We can put out a reward, Evelyn. Someone would have seen her. We'll hire a private detective."

"Michael, we've lost our other one. Christopher's brother."

"We know exactly what he looks like. He is identical. He has to go to kindergarten. He has to go to school. All kids do. We will keep going to Buenos Aires until we find him."

Holding hands, they went to Christopher's room.

The hours passed, but their fingers remained united as they kept watching him in silence till dawn.

Chapter 6

TO MAKE A RAINBOW

The huge Moreton Bay fig trees of Centennial Park partly shaded the cycle path. Gums and palms could be seen in the distance and there was a faint smell of eucalyptus.

Having cycled twice around the park, Evelyn took Christopher to the café overlooking the rugby fields. As they sat down with their drinks, a flock of rainbow lorikeets took possession of a nearby gum tree. It was a carnival of color—blue heads, red beaks, green wings and tails. A flock of galahs, pink-chested and gray-winged, took possession of another tree.

Evelyn watched Christopher who was observing the birds as they moved incessantly between branches, flowers, leaves and around each other while screeching and squabbling.

"Hey, Mum, the galahs are like the rugby players over there."

"Be careful," she said, half smiling. "Galahs is not something you want to call those big boys."

A stray football came close to the trees and the birds screeched even louder as they rose up en masse and flew south toward the Duck Pond.

With peace returning to the café, Evelyn started thinking about how she was going to broach the subject of his origin. Already when

Christopher was in kindergarten, she had told him he was special, that he had come into this world in an unusual way, different to how most mothers and fathers make babies. Now that Years Five and Six were holding personal development classes, there was an opportunity to expand.

After all, they would have to reveal a lot more to him if they were to use his photo in a missing-persons campaign. They were running out of options in their search for his brother. They had already given photos of Christopher to the private detectives, but with no success. The detectives had located María's sister in Peru, but she claimed to know nothing and there was no evidence the sisters were in contact. Searches for the child in Argentina and Peru had reached an impasse.

"So, Christopher, there's something I want to talk to you about. I want to tell you a little bit about how people make children before you—"

"Aw, Mum!" he said, drawing out the words. "I know all about that."

"There's a lot you *don't* know. While the usual way a man and a woman have children is through sexual inter—"

"Mum! I can't believe you're saying this!"

"My beautiful boy, let me finish. There are things—"

"You're embarrassing. Do we have to talk about this here?"

He was so advanced in cognition that he had been accelerated a year in primary school. But emotional maturity was another matter. "There is nobody around and it's important to know how you were born. It was not in the conventional way and this makes you special."

"Not really—there are other kids at school who don't have dads, you know."

"Let me explain. I conceived you with sperm from a sperm bank." Slowly sipping her coffee, she waited.

After a few moments, he asked, "Sperm bank? How does that work?"

"It does not involve contact between people. It's about getting sperm from an unknown donor. My ova were harvested and fertilized."

"Why somebody unknown? Why not someone you love, like …"

"I didn't want to marry anyone, but I wanted to have a child after I came back from Israel."

"From Israel?"

"Well, no, I mean, yes. Okay, perhaps it was there I decided … But I came back to Australia. It was here really. It was definitely here."

"Evian was from Israel."

"Do you miss him?"

"It was fun when he lived with us."

"One day I will take you to visit him and show you Jerusalem and a few other places."

"But why an unknown donor? Didn't you love Michael?"

"Michael was with me at that time, in Israel."

"He is your friend. He's always with you."

"My beautiful boy, do you love Michael?"

"He's so funny; it's like he's my dad, but not exactly." He slurped the remains of his milkshake, looking away from her.

"He considers you his son. He loves you too."

"Yeah, yeah, but you didn't answer me. Do *you* love Michael?"

"I love him as my best friend."

"I know you do because you cook him his favorite dinners. You always talk about him and you let him choose the movies."

They got up and returned to their bicycles. As they left the café, Christopher stopped to lay leaves on a puddle of water, saying it would make it easier for ants to walk to the other side. Evelyn looked at him. He was tall and slender with broad shoulders and strong arms and legs. There was nothing more beautiful than his face. The dimple on his right cheek, which first appeared when he cried as a baby, now appeared when he smiled.

"When will I meet my real dad?" he asked, looking at the ground.

"I'm sorry, Christopher. We will never meet him; it is not possible to do that." She continued, "But we have Michael and we are a family, even if it's different."

"You always say I'm different. It's because of that, right?"

"Because of that too. Also you aren't baptized. That's something else I wanted to tell you. I didn't baptize you when you were a baby because I wanted it to be your choice."

"But then why did you put that picture of Christ above my bed?"

"I bought your icon in the Grand Bazaar in Istanbul, you know. That's where I got mine too, the one above my bed."

"But you said you're not religious."

"You don't have to be religious to love Christ. We can love Him as a man. He was like us. He was a man who dreamt of people helping one another, loving one another."

"I'll tell you something, Mum. When I look at Him, He looks straight back at me, following me anywhere I go in my room. Sometimes I close my eyes and I can still see him—the halo, the long hair, the funny eyebrows, the eyes that are so big."

⁂

Flakes of soot from the forest fires were drifting down like confetti. The pieces hung in the air, looking silver before landing to leave long black streaks on the tiles.

Christopher leaned back and put his arms around the shoulders of Evelyn and Michael as they were seated at the table in the backyard. A hug worked every time; it sweetened the next act, which in this case was that he was deserting them to join his friends. "Thanks for the good food, but I don't think the gods are happy with us."

"I know. It's not nice to smell the forest and animals burning. But we always eat in the yard on your birthday."

"The government is lucky koalas don't vote." He paused, worrying how she was going to take what he was going to say next. "I've been thinking of volunteering. Fire and Rescue needs helpers around Canberra."

"That's too dangerous, the flames can shoot up seventy meters and the smoke suffocates. Besides, you shouldn't stretch yourself so thin. You're already organizing Amnesty and you tutor kids in Redfern."

"Mum, you're being overprotective. I'm eighteen, remember?"

"Of course, darling—actually, that's another thing. We've been meaning to talk to you. How do you feel about being baptized?"

That was another topic, and his friends were waiting. "Wow, that's out of the blue."

"Not for us. Now that you have turned eighteen ..."

"Here's to your birthday," Michael toasted with his wine. "But it's up to you. It's a long tradition that can connect you in a small way to your ancestors."

"I suspected you were crypto-Christians. All these icons everywhere. Do I need more evidence?"

"As Michael said, it's up to you." Evelyn ruffled his hair. "You are an adult now—as of today. We wanted to wait until you understood what it meant."

"Is everyone in the family baptized? Leanne too?"

His mother served him a slice of cake in a napkin to take with him. "Everyone in the family is."

"But how do you baptize an atheist? And besides, I'm too old to be stripped naked ..."

"You won't have to do that, you know, and, anyway, nobody asks babies if they believe, and you wouldn't have been too old for John the Baptist." She kissed him on the usual spot on the cheek. "Whatever you decide about the ritual," she added, "the important thing is you live your life with Christ's principles."

"So, that's why you've been telling me about those camels and sowers and Samaritans."

He was in a hurry. *If I agree,* he thought, *it will be a reverse birthday present. It will make them happy. Besides, Christians don't kill their apostates.*

"Perhaps," he said. "I could do a lot worse."

"We could have the ceremony on Ithaca, my grandfather's island," said Evelyn, looking pleased at his response. "At the old monastery. Kathryn and I were baptized there."

Evelyn continued, "In fact, your aunt could do the honors, if you wish."

She was making too many suggestions and it was getting late. He tossed his keys from hand to hand—this signal would be clear to them.

"I'll join the flock, if that'll make you happy," he said and kissed them goodbye. "Just don't expect to make a sheep out of me."

At the door he turned to wave to them. He saw his mother crying and Michael comforting her.

❧

Cypress, olive and palm trees grew within the perimeter wall of Kathara Monastery and outside it, much like in the rest of Ithaca, were oak and olive trees. Goats were scaling rocks to graze treetops and Spanish broom. To Christopher, the sound of their bells was the music of Ithaca—gentle as intermezzo on the stroll, a crescendo on the gallop.

Together with his mother and aunt, he entered the sprawling compound that straddled the mountain and took in vistas of two blue seas. A woman in black was applying whitewash on the steps, paintbrush in one hand, cigarette in the other. Evelyn caressed a basil plant thriving in a ceramic pot and raised her scented hand to Christopher's nose.

She explained the monastery had seen better days, when the island supported twenty thousand people, including a prosperous community of monks. Now the population was two thousand in winter, though double that in summer. As to the population of monks, he could see the last remaining one.

The day they arrived on the island, Christopher had helped clean the ancestral grave. Beach pebbles covered the earth, but weeds had fought their way through. While Evelyn and Kathryn were pulling out the weeds, he scrubbed the moss and dusted off the headstone to show more clearly the names of those resting there, the most recent one Evelyn and Kathryn's grandfather, their *papou*—his great-grandfather. On the following day, they had visited the acropolis of Ithaca and wandered down through the ruins of the presumed palace of Odysseus. The sun was hot, but there was a nice breeze at the spot the king had chosen for his palace.

Interlacing his arms with his mother and aunt, he now entered the chapel of the monastery. The scent of burning incense blended with the smell of melting wax and lemon-scented furniture polish. The ceiling was celestial blue sprinkled with gold stars. Looking down at him from the walls were life-sized icons of saints and martyrs painted in the Byzantine style. The main feature of the chapel was an icon of the Virgin Mary which, according to folklore, had been found in a rubbish dump. Christopher reflected on the euphemism, *nice name for something that was found in the rubbish*—"Kathara," the clean one.

The priest, a tall, heavy-set man, entered accompanied by the monk, who sharply rotated his hand with three extended figures, looking around and asking, "Baby?"

When Evelyn pointed at Christopher, the monk exclaimed, "Baby!"

On the priest's instructions, Christopher stripped down to his underpants and stood behind a makeshift font, a washtub. After some loud chanting, the priest blew air onto his face three times, vertically and horizontally in the form of the cross, blessing him each time.

The ritual progressed with the priest exorcising Christopher of Satan a few more times, Evelyn translating with the help of a pamphlet.

How did the priest know I am possessed by Satan? He was pleased with himself for coming up with something to tease his mother and aunt with later.

The priest then faced east, scooped up water with his cupped hand and poured it over Christopher's head, declaring, "Baptized is the servant of God, Χριστόφορος, in the name of the Father and of the Son and of the Holy Ghost, Amen." He poured more handfuls of water on Christopher before concluding with a drawn-out psalm.

He hung a golden cross around Christopher's neck, a gift from Kathryn, which had been passed down to her from their grandfather, saying, "Finally, I baptize a man not a child!"

Evelyn whispered in Christopher's ear, "This bathtub is not the Jordan River, but there is more to this than the holy man thinks."

"What do you mean?" he asked, wiping smudges of olive oil from his eyelids.

"Nothing. Nothing in particular. Just that it was Israel where it all started. He too was a man when baptized. Like you."

"What started? Who was like me?"

"Nobody. Nothing, really. Absolutely nothing …" She was biting her lip and fidgeting with her pamphlet. "Just that I realized how much I wanted a child when I was there. Even though until then I had not been quite aware of it."

❧

"I'm a Christian!" Christopher shouted from the top of the campanile, having run up the winding stairs of the slender three-story bell tower.

"Bring out the lions!" Evelyn shouted from below.

The campanile was balanced at the edge of a precipice. The same strong wind that buffeted him at the mountaintop whipped up white crests on the waves of the Mediterranean Sea, hundreds of meters below.

As though on canvas, before him lay the green island of Ithaca, blue skies above it, azure sea with white strokes around it, its coastline white from the froth of waves that came to meet it. He could see the red-roofed houses of the port of Vathy as if from an airplane cockpit. Vathy was built around the horseshoe shape of the harbor, in the middle of which, amongst the boats and small ships, a tiny island had surfaced, pine trees partly obscuring the church that crowned it.

His mother joined him on the campanile. "It's a beautiful thing you did today."

"It wasn't much, Evelyn. Just about everybody does it."

"But you're not everyone, my beautiful boy. Nothing could have pleased me more than having you here today."

"You always say I'm different, but you never say why. I know I wasn't conceived the conventional way, but there seems to be more to it."

"Well, I just meant you ..." She turned to look away.

"Why are you getting so emotional? You were like this at my birthday—I saw you when I was leaving."

"Come on," she said after a few moments. "I'll show you something." She pointed to the plateau opposite. "That's where the main town was in Ithaca during the Middle Ages. People couldn't live near the water because of the pirates."

"Poor pirates."

"Well done, Christopher. You have only just become a Christian and you already love the enemy."

"Only a sense of justice. Imagine them arriving here browbeaten and finding nobody to play with."

"Just as well they didn't find Odysseus, my beautiful boy, because his arrows would have found them."

"Amazing anachronism there, Evelyn. The only thing I would say is that this is what you'd expect of the arsonist who torched Troy."

"Wait a minute. Don't condemn everybody. We need our heroes. Heroism was the virtue of that age and Odysseus could not escape his destiny."

"Okay, okay, now. Don't get so defensive. Have your hero."

"My grandfather thought Odysseus regretted burning Troy."

"What good did that do for Troy?"

"Remember, I told you how in his poem "Ithaca," Cavafy uses Odysseus' journey as a metaphor? He wrote that you will not meet the Cyclopes unless you carry them in your soul. Unless your soul stands them in front of you." She paused. "Let me put it another way. Cyclopes do not exist; they are the figments of a tormented mind."

"But isn't it better to leave him a hero who slew real monsters? How is it edifying to Odysseus if the monsters are fake?"

"An Odysseus tormented by the burning of Troy and battling his internal monsters is more valiant. We all battle internal monsters. My grandfather actually wrote a poem that tries to explain why Odysseus saw Cyclopes."

In the unbearable pain of the soul,
You ask why—
Of gods and of men—
Why to ashes you turned,
The beautiful children of Troy?

Cyclopes surround you,

And you search for the harbor of Ithaca,

A harbor of ships and of souls,

Where never again they'll find you,

The cuckolded kings of Sparta.

"Evelyn, now, that sounds like post-traumatic stress, to say the least. And maybe it's not only Odysseus who is suffering it."

"The fire of Troy burned forever in the conscience of Odysseus. But, yes, we all suffer from the burning of a Troy."

"Fair enough for him—he was being destroyed by what he had destroyed. But you haven't burned Troy."

She leaned on his shoulder. "You know, you too may have to battle for your own destiny one day. Not with arrows, but with the courage of Odysseus."

"I've been meaning to ask you, Mum. What happened to Michael? I thought he was going to come with us."

"Well, yes, but plans changed. Things did not turn out as we'd hoped. What else can I tell you? He has friends, a friend that is … in Buenos Aires and he had to …"

"Keep going. Is this a lady friend? Is that what's upsetting you?"

"Actually, he has lost someone and now he's searching—we both are. Yes, a woman. But not exactly his friend … I can't exactly … We have lost contact with … and we are trying to …" She closed her eyes.

"Mum, please, whatever it is, you don't have to tell me. I don't want you to cry."

Chapter 7

MAUVE BLOOMS

We have run out of options, Evelyn thought.

The despondency on Michael's face only deepened her own. She grasped his hand. "Exactly the sort of thing María would have done."

"Yes," he said, "switch him from school to school to keep a step ahead of us."

He had just returned from Argentina where he had been systematically visiting schools. Besides the winters, now he was also visiting during the summers. They were worried about a flaw in their approach. María might have transferred the boy from a school Michael was about to visit to one he had already visited. It was so difficult to accept that luck was now the only thing they could rely on.

He walked across the living room and turned off the music. "Giving photos of Christopher just to the detectives was not enough."

"I should have listened to you, Michael. It was a mistake not to do a missing-persons campaign from the start. Anyway, now we have hope with Christopher. When he learns he has a brother, he will be our best help with social media."

"And we could go to Argentina again, darling. All of us. But how much do we tell him?"

"Michael, can you smell something?"

"What? Smell what?"

"Something burning."

He took a few sniffs. "Are you sure?"

She described a faint smell, reminiscent of forest fires or clothes burning. He could not smell anything in any room of the house or outside in the yard. When he pressed her, she admitted the smell had also appeared twice the previous week.

"Evelyn, we need to look into this immediately."

"What can I say? If one must fall ill, it might as well be next to Harvard Medical School, or next to Dr. Michael Adamec."

"I will call Dr. Matheson."

She could hear the urgency in his voice as he spoke to the neurosurgeon. She had wondered herself if something was amiss. All she could hope for now was that the unwelcome symptom would never return.

❦

Evelyn tried to read the faces of the others waiting for an MRI at Neuroscience Research Australia, trying to determine who was there just for a routine check, and who might have more worrying symptoms, like hers.

The MRI technician led her into a room empty but for a forbidding cylinder that towered above her. It looked like an airplane turbine. Evelyn lay on the stretcher and a technician positioned her head in a helmet-like coil. The instrument had a bore that accepted her body comfortably, but she still felt claustrophobic.

Heavy knocks came from all directions. Even with muffling headphones, it was jackhammers competing with submachine guns. *A tumor of the brain. Did I get infected?* She recalled the stubborn morning sickness. *Could it have something to do with getting DNA from His brain cells?* She closed her eyes. *No, no, I'm not thinking clearly.*

Enclosed within the magnet, her eyes firmly shut, she considered potential scenarios. The best she could hope for was low malignancy—a tumor that was operable. *How will Christopher cope without me?*

At least Michael would be there after she was gone. Though unconventional, they were a family. But not a whole family. There was someone missing—the other one. Those beautiful cells that divided in front of her eyes would now be another Christopher. *I'll probably never meet him, but Christopher might. They might find one another.*

She felt her body move in the opposite direction—out of the bore of the magnet that felt like a premature coffin.

The radiologist said that she was regarded as an urgent case and that he would send the images to the neurosurgeon immediately.

Just as she reached her laboratory, her phone rang displaying an unfamiliar number. "Ms. Evelyn Camilleri, I'm calling from Dr. Matheson's office regarding the MRI you had this morning. Is it possible for you to come now?"

She retraced her steps. This could be nothing good—it was now a matter of how bad. She jiggled her phone, torn over whether to call Michael or wait till she had the results.

She stopped in front of the hospital elevators. The names on the signboard floated before her eyes as she searched for Dr. Matheson's. Was this failure to focus a symptom too? *No, it can't be. I am just second-guessing my own body.*

After counting slowly back and forth to ten, her breathing became deep and even. The sense of calm was still with her when she arrived at the suite and introduced herself to the receptionist. The woman called her through immediately.

"You can go straight in," said the receptionist, indicating the door. *Was there a flicker of sympathy?*

Fear building up, she knocked lightly on the timber door. It looked unnecessarily wide. Dr. Matheson smiled briefly as he introduced himself and offered her a seat. On his desk was a photo of himself with a woman and two boys flying kites as colorful as the rainbow. Mounted on the wall opposite were lightboxes with black-and-white MR images.

"Evelyn, I know you're a scientist. I want you to look at this image." He pointed at one of the MRIs on the wall. "Can you see in the T1 signal a region of intensified brightness? It's in your right temporal lobe."

Something was disturbing about the shapes she was looking at. It was as though someone had used an orbital saw to take slabs of her head with the brain inside it, eyes, ears and nose hanging on the outside.

"Yes, I can see."

"Unfortunately," she heard him say, "it's a tumor."

So everything is coming to an end, she thought. *But how could it all end so soon?*

"Is it malignant?" she asked, haunted by the sound of her own voice.

The doctor looked again at the images and then sat next to her, placing his hands on his knees. "It looks invasive. The only way to find out for sure is to do a biopsy, but, in any case, it needs to be excised."

"Can you make a prognosis?"

"If the malignancy is low grade and we succeed with the excision, you can expect reasonable recovery. But I'm concerned by its size."

"If it is high grade, what are my chances? How much time do I have?"

"It's difficult to make predictions, but, if it's highly malignant, three to six months on average." He reached over and squeezed her hand. "I know this is very hard, Evelyn, but we need to focus on the most appropriate treatment."

"What do you think I should do?"

"I think the best option is to have it excised."

She looked again at the region of brightness of the T1 signal. *No hope,* she thought. *No hope.* "I've got to get my affairs in order," she heard herself say.

The doctor stood up with her. "We should call someone to accompany you home."

"Thank you, but I'll be okay. I live nearby."

For the first time she was eliciting sympathy from a person she had just met. But, at the same time, she still felt in control. In the lift, she looked at herself in the mirror as she would at someone who might give her courage.

The strength held until she was outside the building. Frightened and confused she walked through the hospital grounds. None of the passersby seemed as unlucky as she had just become—not even the young man stuck in a wheelchair. She wished she were like him. At least she would still have time with Christopher, and still have hope of finding her other son.

Fate had brought her punishment, but what was her crime? *Had cloning Him been hubris? No, bringing Christopher into this world was an act of love.*

She felt worse as she skirted the university on her way home. She had been singled out, condemned. Cars drove past her, cyclists whizzed past her, people walked past her, everyone immersed in their normal lives. *How do they go on without noticing the turmoil around them?* Yet, only a day earlier she had been just like them.

Part of her body had turned against her, killing her from within, stealing her life and hopes. Of course, she had noticed herself aging, her biology changing, her stamina declining. But she had plans that spanned the next five years, the next ten. She had responsibilities, grant obligations, employees, students. She had friends. She had family. She had Michael. She had her beautiful son. And beyond all this, she still had to find her missing child.

Three months would not be enough to see Christopher graduate; it would not be enough to see him find true love. Three months would not be enough for the things she had hoped—to watch him grow into himself, to realize the potential that was inside him. All her dreams of witnessing his life events were suddenly disappearing.

And there was no time for another trip to Argentina.

Three months. And what three months lay before her. Three months that would rob her of her independence, her dignity. Her mind. How much more humane if she were condemned to die by firing squad.

The doctor could not have made a mistake. The images were clear. It had to be true. She could walk no further. *I have to call my friend.*

"Michael, it's ..." Suddenly her voice would not come out.

"Where are you, my darling?"

"Almost home. I just ... I just needed to hear your voice."

"I'm coming now."

She continued walking without ending the connection, needing the reassurance of his presence. She could hear him leave his room, go out of the building and start the car.

Michael will take care of me. He will take care of our boy. He might even give Christopher his brother.

❦

She felt Michael's arms around her.

"Remember, this is only one opinion, Evelyn. All he has is images; he could be wrong. There's someone in Melbourne who's really good. We will fight this."

Sharing the burden brought her relief. "I'm worried how Christopher will take it."

"We don't have to worry him just yet, but of course he will know soon enough."

"So, you think there's still a chance?"

"Always, Evelyn. *Always*. There is even such a thing as spontaneous remission. What do you think miracles are?"

All she needed was a shadow of a chance and she would grab it with everything she had, but she was also preparing for the worst. "If I go, you'll look after him, won't you? And you will keep searching …"

"Our boy is everything to me too. You both are. And I promise you I will keep searching for our other one." He kissed her lips. "Besides you're not going anywhere."

"You know, Michael, I tried to live my life with Christ's principles. I've managed very little, but I now realize *you* have."

She brought his palm to her lips. Michael hugged her and in his embrace she closed her eyes.

Why did I deny to myself that I have loved this man all these years?

⚜

Infuriated by his last lecture, Christopher was striding home, muttering arguments under his breath.

The sixty-five richest people owned as much as the four billion poorest people combined. What about equality and justice? What happened to the principles of the Enlightenment? He enjoyed shocking all the girls in the cafeteria with the statistics, and now was eager to shock Evelyn too.

Opening the door, he saw his mother. She was on the sofa, her back resting against one of the arms, her feet in Michael's lap. He wondered why Michael was there that time of day. *Did I show up in the middle of something?*

Evelyn stood up, calling his name.

"Mum, are you feeling all right? You look pale …"

"Oh, Christopher, I wish I could spare you this."

"Why, Mum? What's wrong?"

"I had an MRI this morning."

"MRI … What for?"

"I've been smelling odors that weren't there. It's a symptom. Michael arranged for the appointment."

"A symptom of what?"

She stayed quiet and he looked at Michael, repeating, "Symptom of what?"

"I just got the results," she said. "They … they think it might be … a brain tumor."

Michael got up too. "There are many things that can go wrong with the brain and get better."

"Is it certain it's a tumor?"

"The surgeon thinks so, but we'll get a second opinion," said Michael.

"It's a diagnosis," said Evelyn. "Without a biopsy he can't tell if it's malignant."

"You and me, Christopher. Together we will look after your mother."

"We will," he said almost mechanically. "Yes, we will be together," he added more emphatically. He wondered whether he should ask, but in the end he did. "What happens if it's malignant?"

"They will remove my right temporal lobe."

Christopher felt the muscles of his body lose strength. "Remove it?"

"Yes," she said. "That part of the brain is not functioning now, anyway; I will not be any worse off after its removal." He saw her try to smile.

She came to him and pushed back the hair from his forehead before kissing him on his dimple. "And I'm not going to leave you so soon. I have unfinished business."

In her embrace, he placed his chin on her shoulder.

Behind her, through the glass doors, he could see the crepe myrtle. Its branches were bending down toward the ground, burdened by trusses of mauve blooms.

Book Two
JOSÉ

Chapter 8

TODO POR LA TIERRA

María Olfi picked up the dead bird with her gloved hand and buried it under a patch of grass next to a tree.

She returned with her broom and shovel to collect the rest—cigarette butts, discarded food and broken bottles that reeked of alcohol. If only someone would tell the crazy revelers it is the turn of the year and not the millennium they are celebrating …

She glanced up at the tall columns. It was humbling to work so close to La Catedral, but her back ached and it was a relief when her shift ended.

On the bus back to the small apartment in Barracas she shared with her mother, María was caught up in the same thoughts that had been troubling her all day. Should she risk her soul a second time? Could she hurt her heart again? The day before, the solicitor, Señor Guzmán, had contacted her. Another Australian couple, Miguel and Evelyn, was looking specifically for her. They were friends of the couple for whom she had done it before. The first time it was because her husband was ill and she had been desperate to find money for his treatment. Now, illness had struck her mother.

It is a sin to give birth to another woman's child. But is it not a greater sin to fail one's mother? There was no other way to pay for the healer.

The Church taught her to choose the lesser of two evils, though the way the Church ranked evil was confusing at times.

And now there was another thing to consider. The first time, she had not expected to love so much the child she had harbored in her womb. The separation was torture. Suddenly, there had been nobody to hold. Nobody to attend to. Nobody cried. Nobody wanted her milk. *How can I go through that pain again?*

María dug her thumbnail into her index finger to keep from crying on the bus. Alone; she was facing everything alone, despondent and humiliated. Her husband had abandoned her, disappearing on a night she was working a second job to clear his gambling debts. It had only been a few weeks, so if she accepted the surrogacy, people would think he was the father. She could give the baby to this Miguel and Evelyn, telling everyone she had put it up for adoption.

As the bus was arriving at her stop, she felt she was coming close to a decision.

❧

María ran her hand protectively over her abdomen.

She was kneeling on the padded board, one hand on the backrest of the pew in front, eyes shut in prayer. Six months had passed and, aside from some back pain, everything was going smoothly. But with each passing day her agony increased. *How is it fair,* she asked herself, *to give birth to two children and remain childless?*

She thought of the sad story behind the church—of a widow murdered by a lover blinded by jealousy. The widow's grieving parents had built the church. Marble statues of Felicitas Guerrero, the murdered mother, and her children towered above. *Perhaps there, in His Kingdom, I too will be reunited with my babies.*

In spite of the traditional healing paid for by the surrogacy money, her mother's days had come to an end two months earlier. From that moment, solitude became even more frightening. She had never been so lonely. Did she have to endure a lifetime of solitude—*or is the salvation inside me?*

Time was running out. In the quiet of the church, her mind was in turmoil. She had taken an oath on the Bible. But back then the child's heart was not beating in her womb.

For the last little while, she had felt certain it was a boy, no matter how much her friends at work said it had to be a girl because the baby rested high. The baby was the only person in the world who was hers.

She whispered to him now, as she had since the first time she felt him move. "How do I know these people will love you? The woman who will take you away from me hasn't carried you. You haven't shared her body. I don't know her. She doesn't know you. How can I give you to a stranger?" She took a breath and stroked her belly again. "You have all my love. But if I give you away, I will never know what happened to you… Perhaps I could go to Australia and help them bring you up.

"No, no, no, they wouldn't want me. It is the gift they want, not the giftwrap."

Eyes closed, she was murmuring when the baby gave her a big kick, startling her into opening them. In front of her was the main altar and above it the crucifix. She raised her eyes to Him—His arms extended out and up, blood dripping from wounds on His hands, feet and side. His head hung down as though He was looking at her. Angelic was His face even during the torment. "Give me peace, my Lord," she whispered. "Give me strength; give me wisdom; guide me, my Lord."

Just then, she heard wings flapping. A white dove had flown into the church. The bird swooped over her, then circled the dome before exiting through the open door, flying with precision and grace.

She recalled the Sermon on the Mount. "Look at the birds of the air; they do not sow or reap or store away in barns, and yet your heavenly Father feeds them." How many times had her mother repeated this in the face of uncertainty about their next loaf of bread? But these words were not only about food. These were words of hope told by the Lord to all in despair.

She rushed to the door, but the white bird was gone. It was nowhere to be seen.

The hope is inside me, she thought. *Why else would the Lord send me the sign of hope if not …*

⁊⁊

It was going to be a long bus ride, but she was not alone, her arms were cradling a baby.

She had been María Olfi before entering Maternidad Sardá, but as Martíta de Olmos she was now leaving the maternity hospital. She had changed her first name and taken her mother's maiden name to avoid detection.

As for the child, she could only have named him José after her late father, the only man who had ever shown her kindness. *These are the bonds that matter,* she thought—*parent and child. Husbands come and go, but my son will never abandon me.*

Still, everything would come to nothing if the Australians found her. The baby looked nothing like his father. Michael was blue eyed and blond. José had black eyes, black hair and olive skin. But of course the less he looked like his father, the more he must have taken after his mother. They could certainly identify him. The danger was extreme. *But if I manage to cross the Brazilian border, I will be able to breathe.*

The family from Curitiba had promised her work for a few years and after that she could return to Buenos Aires and put José in school. By then, her trail would have gone cold, unless the Australians were obsessed. But why would they spend years searching? They had only contributed a frozen embryo and some money; and money was obviously no problem for them.

Luck had been on her side—José had arrived almost a month early. She had hoped Señor Guzmán was not yet scouring the maternity wards. Just in case, she had given her old address for the hospital records.

Soon after the sign from the Lord at Santa Felicitas, she had quit her job with the municipal council and found work as cook and cleaner in private homes, accepting lower pay to stay hidden. It had hurt her to abandon her home in Barracas—her favorite corner where she read the Bible every evening, the room where she had nursed her mother to the end. But it would only have been a matter of time before the lawyer started looking for her, so she had severed contact with everyone.

She had told the other drifters at the ruined house where she had been staying for the last month that she would go to her sister in Peru after giving birth, and they should definitely not expect her back. Incredible it was, but these strangers cared more for her than her actual relatives. However, from now on, the last thing she would need was attention. She would have to live unnoticed—a shadow.

José was fast asleep, his black curls a contrast to his white blanket. "We have a big trip ahead of us," she said to the warm bundle in her arms. "But what matters is that you and I will be together, now and always."

For a moment she questioned whether she was really doing the right thing. Would her child have a better future in Australia with the rich, educated family?

No, no, no, came the answer from within. *Nobody could love José more than me. And love is more than all the riches.* "Love never fails," she said aloud.

Probably playing with his friends, thought Martíta as she was waking up. *Or could it be they found us?*

She had brought José back to Buenos Aires only a few months earlier and they were staying at a *conventillo,* a boarding house at the busy intersection of Calle Balcarce and Carlos Calvo in the San Telmo district. The residents were mainly elderly people without money and without hope, drug addicts and Peruvian migrants. In the crumbling building, missing windows had been replaced by corrugated iron and strips of mismatched fabric. Occasionally, sacks made do for drapes. The roof leaked, but luckily they were on the ground floor.

The Australians have found us. The frightening thought was gaining ground in her mind as she jumped out of the bed.

When they first moved to the *conventillo,* most tenants were still paying rent. Since then, neighbors had told her it was no longer necessary. They had all become squatters. The wealthy owner was not interested in the meager rent, preferring to let the building run down to avoid heritage objections to his redevelopment plans. On the bright side, there was water and someone had rigged it so there was free electricity. The common kitchens and bathrooms meant you knew everybody and the sorrows of life were shared, though the lack of anonymity was worrying.

They have come and stolen my boy, she thought again, dressing as fast as possible.

During the previous night, she had struggled to find sleep. Something had been troubling her, but she could not think what. Every now and then, a high-pitched whistling breath escaped José's nostrils as he slept next to her. Propping herself up onto her elbow, she had watched over her little boy. It was the middle of the night, but, even with thick drapes, light from the traffic entered the room. She could make out the features of his face, soft in repose. Lying back down to sleep, she had wrapped her arm around him. He had grown and was almost as tall as her, though he was so skinny she could count his ribs.

That is it, she had thought. *I've been giving him more food lately, but he is still too thin. Maybe he has worms or something. I have to take him to the doctor.*

The sun was out and well on its way by the time Martíta hurried into the yard looking around for José. *He never goes anywhere without telling me,* she thought. *They found him. They found him and they have taken him from me.*

She had been taking as many precautions as she could—changing her name, going to Brazil, her hair no longer short and blonde, but long and black. But what protection could that offer if there were detectives at her heels? She had forbidden her son to be in class photos with the other children. José did not look anything like Miguel, but, strangely, he did not look much like his mother either. Martíta had asked one of the children she was babysitting to search on the computer for all the Evelyns at The University of New South Wales in Sydney. There were twelve by that name and José did not resemble any of them. That was odd; either none of these was the right Evelyn or the father had a dark olive complexion—which ruled out Miguel.

In the yard, children were chasing after a ball in the dust, bare feet slapping the cobblestones in a drumroll. She stopped one of them. "Hola, have you seen José? Is he here?"

"He doesn't play with us anymore. He's always with Nina."

"Is she asking him for help?"

"Nina thinks he's her son," said the boy. "She's *loca*—crazy."

"You wouldn't say that about *your* grandmother, would you?"

"She's *loca* too," said the boy.

Martíta walked out onto the street and saw José coming toward her, holding Nina's hand.

"Hola, Mamá," he called out.

"Where have you been, *mi niño*?"

Still holding the woman's hand, he was quick to explain Nina wanted him to take her to Buenos Aires, so he walked her to the corner from where she could see the Obelisco. "But she always forgets," he said. "So, we have to keep going back. It doesn't matter how many times I tell her this *is* Buenos Aires; she has to see the Obelisco."

The old woman kept looking around her.

After taking Nina to her room, Martíta asked, "Have you been giving her your food too?"

He stared at the ground.

"But, *mi niño*, I bring her leftovers from the restaurants. I will talk to the priest at *la Iglesia*."

❦

José stood looking at the door. A radio was playing inside.

Curiosity piqued, he knocked. An old man opened the door—short, stout and balding, thick spectacles resting on the tip of his big nose. "This was Nina's room," said José.

"It *was*. It's Alberto's room now. And who are you, little friend?"

"I'm José."

"Were you Nina's friend?"

"Yes. I used to help her buy groceries—and find Buenos Aires."

"You're a good kid. Helping someone find Buenos Aires is not an easy thing. I heard she had dementia."

The old man's hair was sticking out over his ears. "Nina was nice," José finally said. "But she did not remember."

He looked around the room. It was nothing like before. The table was full of books and they were also spilling out of open boxes onto the floor. The walls were covered with posters—penguins marching across the ice, rainbow-colored fish sheltering inside colorful corals, and a big river branching into many small rivers as it emptied into an ocean. There was also a poster with little monkeys sitting on a rock, dwarfed by giraffes whose heads were as high as the treetops.

"Nature is pretty, eh?"

"That one is different." José pointed to a graph.

"Ah yes. The Keeling Curve and, in a way, it's about nature too. It shows the increase of carbon dioxide concentration in the atmosphere, but you are too young to understand."

"No, I'm not," said José, still looking at the graph.

"I will be giving a talk about it Wednesday next at the Humberto Primo Elementary."

"That's my school!"

"Ask your parents to bring you and they can explain things to you."

What a strange old man, José thought.

❧

José had been counting the days, reminding his mother to take that night off work.

Wednesday had arrived, but now he felt he was going to be out of place. This meeting was about something he had never heard of and where there would probably be no one his age. He had asked and found out that Alberto was a professor, a neuroscientist, but he didn't know what that meant.

It felt strange, too, coming to his school at night. He and his mother had just arrived at the forecourt with the two huge magnolia trees. Side by side, they entered the foyer. It was decorated with paintings by the pupils. He led his mother to the paintings done by two girls in his class. One was of some beavers balancing on a tree that had been swept away by a raging river. The next one showed the previously terrified beavers now blissfully dancing tango on the beach of a green island. "Look, Mamá, this one continues the story of the other one."

She smiled, but he knew her eyes were on another painting, the one he had done in black and gray—it was of himself and Nina having breakfast, sitting on a tablecloth, the branches of a magnolia tree shading them.

"If I kept giving Nina food she wouldn't have died."

"She was very old, *mi niño*, and had a weak heart. It was not from not eating. She was lucky you cared for her."

They climbed the staircase to the first floor and entered the hall. There, on the large timber stage, stood Alberto, wearing a white shirt, black jacket and red tie. He moved a vase with blue jacaranda flowers that was partly hiding him. Projected on the screen behind him was the title—*Todo por la Tierra. Todo por la Vida*—Everything for the Earth. Everything for Life.

José counted fifty-six people in the room, most of them old, but, to his surprise, there were some boys and girls too. He waved at his teacher from the previous year, as he and his mother sat in the front row.

"Stay still, José," Martíta said sharply. "It's not polite to fidget."

Realizing he had been turning his head left and right and tapping his fingers on his legs, he put his hands in his pockets. "Mamá, is there something wrong?"

"I shouldn't have brought you here; there may be bad people who want to harm you. Foreigners. Remember what I told you, don't ever follow a foreigner."

"Foreigners don't understand Castellano, Mamá. They wouldn't be here because—"

"Citizens of Argentina," Alberto said, looking at the audience. "There is an unholy race between invincible financial interests on who will first bring Nightfall. The chemical industry has released eighty thousand compounds and has toxified the planet from pole to pole. The nuclear industry enables dictators with no loftier ethics than those of crocodiles to acquire nuclear weapons. The fossil-fuel industry has purchased the political process and is resetting the climate thermostat three to five degrees Celsius higher this century and seventeen to twenty-four degrees higher by the end of the millennium.

"And just in case these grim reapers fail to extinguish life, scientists are planning the *coup de grâce*—geoengineering. They want to 'dim the planet'—to reduce the sunlight that reaches Earth. In an insane effort to countermand global warming, they will damage the ozone layer with sulfur dioxide. Worse still, they provide governments with the greatest argument for inaction—that scientists can cool the Earth should the need arise."

Usually José understood everything his teachers said, but Alberto was using new words without explaining them. It was a relief when the professor pointed to the graph he recognized from the poster, the Keeling Curve, which in the end was not that difficult to understand.

Alberto then projected another graph with red, green, blue and black bars. "Here is the scariest thing of all—the corporations have reserves of petrol, gas and coal which, if burned, will produce five times the amount of carbon dioxide needed to take us over two degrees Celsius of warming this century. If ever there was fool's gold! They will sell us their reserves and we will burn the fossil fuels, making the atmosphere inhospitable to humans. Unless we destroy the corporations.

"But we will fail to destroy them because they have money to convince enough of us of the greatest lie ever told—that there is no consensus among scientists that human activity is heating the Earth."

The professor was looking directly at the audience as everyone listened quietly. "Obedience to the law is a hallmark of civilized society, affording protection for the weak and security for all. However, we are not obliged to obey laws drafted by the fossil-fuel industry to safeguard itself while wrecking the planet. On the contrary, we are morally obliged to disobey them."

"Look straight ahead," his mother ordered after José had turned to look at a girl his age who had come with her father to also sit in the front row.

"It is time for our organization to act. TodoPorLaTierra must lead an environmental revolution against the doomsday machine—the economy."

José did not know what the "doomsday machine" was, but figured it had to be something serious because the room had gone dead quiet.

"A patriot believes his country is right because he is born in it. An *earthiot* places life above all else. I urge you to become earthiots and assist humans and our fellow creatures to live the life due to them. It's time. It's time for us to say—*Todo por la Tierra y Todo por la Vida.* Everything for the Earth and Everything for Life.

"And I will leave you with the last sentence of Darwin's *On the Origin of Species*. It speaks of 'endless forms most beautiful.' Please let us not make them extinct. 'There is grandeur in this view of life … whilst this planet has gone cycling on according to the fixed law of gravity, from so simple a beginning endless forms most beautiful and most wonderful have been, and are being, evolved.'"

José stood up to clap, seeing some others were doing it, repeating inside him, *Todo por la Tierra y Todo por la Vida.*

His mother pulled him down, telling him he could applaud from his seat and he was not to look back at the audience. Alberto moved in front of the lectern and asked for questions.

An old man cleared his throat. "Alberto, you are suggesting the destruction of civilization. If we follow you, won't they simply paint us as terrorists?"

"Us destroying civilization?" asked Alberto. "It is the opposite. This civilization is destroying us. The terrorists are those who are turning the atmosphere into a soup of simmering toxins. Without our consent, they are subjecting us to a gigantic geophysical experiment— an ice-free world with feverish temperatures. If this is not bad enough, because of overpopulation and travel we present the microbial world a unitary body of humans—all humanity in a petri dish ready for decimation by a virus."

"But Professor, nobody wants to go back to the Dark Ages," said a woman. "Ask anybody here."

Slowly José turned to look at the woman who asked the question; quickly his mother turned him back.

"I never said we should go back to the Dark Ages." Alberto took a sip from the glass of water on the lectern. "We must go back much further."

"But how do you destroy the doomsday machine, Professor?" asked a woman who looked as old as Nina.

"*Compañera,* among the most efficient ways to reduce greenhouse gas emissions is to destroy the airport towers, car factories and oil installations."

There were murmurs in the audience. José leaned forward in his seat. Something about what the professor was saying didn't seem right. "Alberto, if we do that—" he said and immediately his mother tried to stop him from talking. However, he had already attracted the professor's attention and he continued, "If we do that, they will put us in jail and then build them again."

"And we will get out of jail and keep fighting, my little friend." Alberto took another sip of water. "In revolutionary times, people are forced to take sides and an environmental movement can rise out of the rust and rottenness of the present system. I can't be certain of what an environmental revolution will bring. I can only be certain of what its absence will bring. Extinction."

José glanced at the others sitting in the front row. Some were looking at Alberto, but others were staring at him. *Maybe I said the wrong thing,* he thought.

❧

It was a mistake to have come here, Martíta thought. *They do not have to be foreigners. They could be locals, and they definitely have my photo.*

What good had it done to take José to the front, after he had brought everyone's attention to himself with his comment? The best she could do was keep him facing forward as the room emptied. She asked him to help put the chairs in order.

Alberto approached them, jacaranda flowers in hand. "Hola, José. *Mucho Gusto, Señora, y muchas gracias* for your kind help. These are for you."

"*Encantada.* I'm Martíta. *Muchas gracias.*" They kissed each other on the cheek. "My son liked your talk very much."

The three of them walked out into the cold breeze, Martíta pressing the flowers to her chest and holding José around the shoulders.

Alberto walked beside José. "Little friend, brave of you to say something. Did you understand much?"

"Some things," José replied. "But I want to ask—"

"What do you say first?" Martíta interrupted.

"Can I please ask something?" On receiving a nod, he continued, "Why isn't everyone working to make the Keeling Curve come down again? To stop the carbon dioxide curve that's going up and up."

"They say we can't protect the environment because it will hurt the economy. Have you heard anything more insane? But even if governments wanted to ban cars, they would have to fight the automobile industry, the petrol companies, the pension funds, the banks and, ah, of course, the drivers."

"But there are things we can do without fighting anybody," said José.

"Unfortunately, nothing is won without a fight. Do you have something in mind?"

"We cut down trees for Christmas. Can't we *plant* trees instead?"

"That would be a start. If we estimate three hundred million Christian families cutting Christmas trees, your proposal would result in an annual gain of six hundred million trees. But much, much more is needed."

"Alberto, if the police put you in jail for marijuana, why can't they put you in jail for damaging the environment?"

"How do you know about marijuana, José?" asked Martíta.

"Some kids in the *conventillo* have pots with—"

"Have you smoked it?" She stopped walking. "José, do you know what you are talking about? Marijuana is an illegal drug."

Has he swallowed his tongue? Martíta wondered. *Why is he looking at Alberto?*

"Okay," said the professor. "It's not the end of the world if you smoke a joint. But there is something you need to know. Marijuana can bring about illnesses of the brain. You have a good brain. *You* should be the king in your skull-sized kingdom. Not the marijuana."

"Did you hear what the professor said?"

They started walking again. Alberto touched José's nose with his finger. "I sometimes give public talks on drugs," he said. "I talk about their effects on the brain. However, my next talk is about overpopulation. You were caught out by your question about marijuana, but it shows you are inquisitive. What do you think? Will you come to the next meeting, if your mother has no concerns of course?"

Martíta looked at Alberto over José's head. How could she not have concerns about her son listening to talk of revolution? But then again, she thought, *del dicho al hecho hay mucho trecho*—word to deed is a long distance. Besides, the professor could help José stay away from drugs. "Yes," she said. "I'll make sure he comes."

"Thank you, Mamá," shouted José.

But what if the Australians find him? she asked herself.

In any case, she could not keep him in a cage. Indeed, if the professor took him to meetings it would be better because her face was known to the Australians. "You are an educated man, Professor, and José can learn from you."

"I would like to ask something, please, Alberto. Can science help us?"

"It's supposed to, my little friend. But there's no sign of it. Science and technology are ruining humanity." The professor sighed. "I can see the writing on the tombstone, 'Homo sapiens: Intelligence made them extinct.'"

Chapter 9

THE END OF EDEN

José's mind went back to one of the discussion points in the talk. "Alberto, remember the man who coughs just before he asks a question?"

"How can anyone forget him, my little friend?"

"He asked something about having the liberty to use his car."

The two of them were walking home along Avenida 9 de Julio after the evening's forum where Alberto had explained the aims of TodoPorLaTierra. The city shone red, yellow, blue and green, a sea of traffic lights and flickering neon signs.

"'Liberty to wolves means death to sheep,' to answer you with the words of a philosopher. And I bet you're clever enough to figure out who the sheep are." He pointed to the statue of Don Quixote on the green median strip. "Here is my hero. He attempted the impossible."

José looked at the knight who was emerging from the rock, riding an exhausted horse, but still pointing his sword in defiance of something or somebody, or everybody.

"Look over there, Alberto; you can be like your hero. You can free all those animals." José pointed to tethered helium balloons held by a street vendor—seals, ducks, lions and dinosaurs. "I could free them with my slingshot, but they might not make it out alive."

Alberto chuckled. "That's it—dream of shattering the chains. But I shouldn't have shown you how to make a slingshot. There were enough broken windows in the *conventillo* already and your mother—"

"Wasn't that man at your talk tonight?" José interrupted.

Alberto looked at the man and quickly steered José across to the service road, weaving between slowly moving cars.

"Be that as it may," he said, once they reached the opposite sidewalk, "for Don Quixote the enemy was the windmills. For us it's the polluting factories we want to destroy, and the windmills we welcome. You know, my little friend, San Telmo can be proud. It had the first windmill in Buenos Aires."

"No, no, no. Why destroy the factories when they can make bicycles?"

At the intersection with Avenida Independencia they joined a crowd of pedestrians waiting for the green light. Alberto kept glancing at the people around them. José looked to see if he could spot anybody else from the talk, but he was also looking at the traffic. A continuous stream of cars passed in front of him. Little clouds bloomed out of their exhaust pipes—small pipes, large pipes, double pipes, quadruple pipes, all of them filling the atmosphere with exhausts. He could smell the fumes and even taste the bitterness on his tongue. "We have to make the people listen," he said. "After they hear us, they will unite with us. We need to put our bicycles on Avenida 9 de Julio to stop the traffic. Then we can tell them. No violence, we just need the people united."

"Little friend, what you are describing has a name. It's called 'passive resistance.' It has been tried. You will place yourself at the tender mercy of the corporations. They have the money. They have the influence. They buy politicians and brainwash the public. Last year in Copenhagen, each country actually fought for the right to pollute more than the others. If ever there was anything 'rotten in the State of Denmark' …"

⁂

One for each apostle.

"There are twelve columns," said José, as they stood at the corner of San Martín and Rivadavia facing La Catedral.

"And you are twelve years old. It all matches, my little friend."

It was one of the Sundays that Martíta worked and Alberto had taken José to mass, which had just ended. They were walking in Plaza de Mayo toward Casa Rosada, the rose-colored palace. The sun had risen above Pirámide, a monument with the image of the sun engraved on it and surmounted by the statue of a woman bearing a shield and a spear.

The flock of pigeons in front of them parted to allow passage.

"You know, Alberto, I don't understand how God can allow this evil. Like how He can let so many people kill each other in so many wars."

"It's a mystery to anyone who believes. But let me tell you what troubles me. Religions sometimes cause wars. They are not helping the environment either because they are against family planning—without family planning we get overpopulation."

"But Alberto, if you are a Christian, then you have to care for the environment. Isn't that the same as caring for future people?"

"The correct term for what you are describing is 'intergenerational justice.' My little friend, your brain keeps surprising me. It's not in your nature to follow a revolutionary path. Neither would I want you to contemplate it at your age. I believe, however, that when you get older—"

A police car screeched to a halt just in front of them. The pigeons took to the air and everyone turned to look. Two policemen leaped out, wrestled a man to the ground, dragged him into their car and left as fast as they came, this time with lights flashing and sirens blaring.

People in the plaza stood frozen until the car disappeared. José felt Alberto's hold on him loosen as they started walking again.

"That was scary," said José, but Alberto remained silent until they were opposite Casa Rosada. A flag was flying on top of the presidential palace and another, much larger, on a flagpole next to them.

"José, I want you to understand something. As much enthusiasm as there is inside you, so much has deserted me. My wings have been burned by constant disappointment. And you have to understand that sooner or later I'll be gone."

"No, Alberto. What do you mean? I want you to stay with us. I'll look after you. Always."

"That is the nicest thing anyone has said to me. But, José, I need to prepare you in case things do not go well."

"Things will go well. More people come to the TodoPorLaTierra meetings now."

"And this is the problem. As long as I was fringe entertainment, nobody bothered."

"But you haven't done anything."

"I wouldn't quite say that. The farmers and the multinational companies suspect us of sabotage in the Jujuy Province."

"Did we do that?"

"Let us say they think we did."

❧

The hall was filling up. It was nearly three years since Jose had first gone there to hear Alberto. He had learned a lot since that first meeting, but he still didn't feel he was ready to speak. "Alberto, you know everything. I'm not ready; I don't know enough."

"*Más sabe el diablo por viejo que por diablo*—the devil knows more for being old, than for being the devil. So much for me; as for you, you know enough, my tall-little friend. Relax and do as we said."

Every time he looked over his shoulder at the growing audience, José felt butterflies in his stomach. The crowd was flowing in all directions, filling the hall with chatter. In his stomach, the butterflies were now flapping their wings.

The stage in the old school hall was about a meter above the floor. José stood up and looked back.

A collective sigh of relief went up as he managed not to fall after tripping on the first step of the stairs. It was good the professor was at the other side of the room, preoccupied with guiding latecomers to empty seats.

He saw Alberto nod to him. José took a deep breath and did exactly what the professor had told him—imagined he was speaking only to him.

"This is the story of a tragedy," he began. "An Eden found and an Eden lost." He raised his voice when he saw Alberto put his hands around his ears. "It all began in Quebec, on a branch of the St. Lawrence River. There lived the beavers, hard workers who had felled over a thousand trees and produced a huge dam that blocked the river. One day, things went horribly wrong. The water pressure burst the dam, washing away the trees as easily as matchsticks.

"The last tree added to the dam had twenty beavers, ten males and ten females, clinging to it for dear life. On it they drifted for five days and five nights as they were swept away from land, far from their birthplace. Sleepless and exhausted, they thought death was near. As if by miracle, the tree was washed onto the shore of a tiny island paradise, green and leafy, crystal-clear water running down its mountain slopes.

"The beavers could see they would have to give up their wasteful ways because of how small the island was. They scrambled onto the land, kissed the ground and made a promise to preserve the environment forever, so it could preserve their children and grandchildren forever."

José looked at the people. Other than a man and a woman who giggled as they whispered, and some children sliding in and out of chairs, everyone was quiet and still. Feeling less anxious, he continued, "Given there were ten couples, they carved ten percent of the island into equal one-percent plots. No one could sell their plot and become poor. They left the remaining ninety percent of the island for everyone and called it 'The Commons.' In The Commons, the beavers found their food—tree branches, seeds, nuts and little creatures.

"The beavers got many things right, but, unfortunately, not everything. Giving each couple a plot of land was great for the first lot of beavers. But with grandmothers having babies at the same time as daughters and granddaughters, the plots had to be divided in half again and again.

"There was one beaver who saw the problem and wrote the book *The Beaver Bomb*. He said each pair of beavers should only have two children and, in turn, each of the two children another two and so on. This way the population would increase, but stabilize when deaths equaled births. The other beavers read the book, only to ignore it.

"While it lasted, the beavers enjoyed themselves at all-night parties, dancing tango and salsa. They were dancing on their graves.

"Overpopulation would have been enough to ruin the beavers, but something else happened first—'The Tragedy of The Commons.' Beavers looked after their own land, but didn't care about The Commons. The fools used as much of The Commons as possible for their own benefit. Each family was only supposed to take one kilo of food per day. Unfortunately, one family decided to take another kilo to satisfy its hoarding instinct. This family doubled its benefit, but the damage to The Commons was spread to everyone and, as a result, this family suffered only one-tenth of the damage it caused. It's like gaining ten pesos and paying only one in cost, leaving this family with a net profit of nine pesos.

Soon, other families did the same and, before long, The Commons didn't have enough seeds for seedlings to grow and replace the old trees. Eventually, the forest died, the soil was washed away, and the island paradise became just a rock that could only support the bones of the beavers, who had died from starvation."

José took such a deep breath that he almost coughed. He cleared his throat and turned to his last page.

"And so it was, each family pursuing its self-interest ruined the island for everyone. This was the end of Eden. It was the end of their science. It was the end of their art. It was the end of their children's stories. It was the end of them."

José slowly raised his head and looked at the people. They were all silent. He was certain nobody liked his story.

After sustained applause, a schoolgirl stood up. "Can I ask something? About science. Couldn't scientists get us to other planets?"

"I think that's science fiction," responded José. "If we can't protect this atmosphere, how can we create and protect atmospheres on other planets?"

An elderly man who always asked a question and was never satisfied with the answers slowly stood up. José clenched his fists in anticipation of what was to come.

"So, you told us the problem, José. What would an intelligent species do in this case?" And before José had a chance to respond, the man continued. "Just for argument's sake, assume Alberto is wrong and we are not mischievous monkeys with Stone Age emotions who climbed further than they could cope."

"We need to want other things,' José replied. "Not ever richer, but ever better. Imagine bicycles on Avenida 9 de Julio, children on skateboards, people walking and singing. Imagine gardens on Corrientes, rowboats on Río de la Plata, zeppelins in the skies of Buenos Aires."

He walked down the steps, though he would have preferred to leap over them and get quickly to Alberto. But people kept stopping him along the way, shaking his hand or slapping him on the back.

"Bravo, my little friend," said Alberto. "Perhaps I should stop calling you 'little' now that you are taller than me." He grabbed José by the shoulders. "You are already so clever and yet your brain will not attain connectional maturity for another six years."

"I forgot to tell that girl what you said—that 'good planets are hard to come by.'"

"Don't worry; you have earned your ticket for tomorrow."

José had put on the same white shirt and green pants he had worn when Boca Juniors had last won, hoping it would bring them luck. They would need it—today they were playing at El Monumental, enemy territory.

Alberto led him to their seats behind a goal area, at the horseshoe, a place full of singing and dancing River Plate supporters. "Don't you show that scarf, José. They will use it to hang you."

Surrounded by people in red and white, José quickly hid the blue-and-yellow scarf Martíta had knitted him. He stood on his seat to see the field. Looking longingly across at the sea of blue and yellow on the other side of the stadium, he wished he were old enough to watch from the Boca Junior stands alone. From where they were, he would just have to clap and scream in his heart.

"I feel it in my bones, José. The River will win. We cannot lose at home."

"*Gallinas* should not count their chickens before they hatch," replied José, using the derogatory nickname for Alberto's team—chickens, for cowardice.

"You are clever, my little friend, but that's not going to help Boca Juniors."

"If I'm clever, why don't you listen to me?"

"I always listen to you."

"Not when I tell you to stop talking about violence."

"What's the matter with you, José? You have a complex about violence."

"Alberto, even if violence was good, you wouldn't be good at it."

"You are underestimating me, my little friend. I can shut down a few factories and liberate a patch of the sky. Something like that," he said, pointing to the fireworks that had illuminated the sky. "And let me tell you about your approach. If you turn the other cheek, they will slap that one too."

The crowd on the other side erupted as Boca Juniors entered the stadium through a long, white tunnel. People stood up, waved their hands, sang, whistled, and lit fireworks.

"Besides," Alberto continued, "I am not proposing violence against people. It's the machines that need to be destroyed. The machines that destroy everything—the air, the land, the trees, the oceans. They unhinge the climate. This is protecting life not—"

There was uproar at the entry of River Plate. Red-and-white flags were flying, confetti in red and white rained down on them, balloons were taking off and the stadium was vibrating.

José shouted into Alberto's ear over the noise, "It'd be nice if we had this much excitement at the TodoPorLaTierra meetings."

Alberto smiled at him, but then the whistle blew for the start of the game and there was no time for smiles.

It could have been anyone's game. With one minute left in regulation time, the score was tied one all. José held his breath as

Riquelme moved with the ball from midfield. "Ah," he screamed, more inside than out, as the striker was brought down just outside the box. It was going to be a free kick. He looked up at the clock—Boca Juniors still had a chance.

River Plate built a wall of players, an impenetrable barrier that totally obscured the net. The goal seemed so small, the keeper so big. José could not see how the ball could get inside the net. The ball left Riquelme's foot at high speed, but it looked as though it was going way out. Then, in mid-course, it curved around the wall of players and flew toward the goal. It still seemed too wide. It smashed into the side post, but then hit the ground on the net side of the white line. José jumped up, only to stand still again, pretending to be upset.

He couldn't suppress a smile as they walked out of the stadium, the illuminated scoreboard still in his eyes. He thought he could tell who supported which team by reading the faces of the crowd. "Thank you for taking me. That was the best thing I have ever seen in my whole life."

"Good, my little friend. Now let me return to what we were saying with a football analogy. It will be as hard to convert climate skeptics as to make you a River Plate supporter."

"But Alberto, we *have* to try. If they see the truth, they will change for sure. Some things are getting better."

"You're distracted by cosmetic changes, José. Look, even here, on this strip they've exiled nature, they've planted a dozen trees. Small improvements happen, but they're swamped by catastrophic changes. My little friend, people will not see the truth and they will not change. I want to blow up the slaughterhouse, not delay our surrender."

"Don't blow things up. You will see, people will change."

"Change I've seen, but look at the direction. We didn't abandon our cars for bicycles—the Chinese abandoned their bicycles for cars. Throughout my life, I've walked in solitude. Back in the '60s people would not listen to me. Now that the Arctic Ocean ice is collapsing, I have the evidence."

He moved his hand as though to dismiss something. "What can I tell you? I had a nightmare the other night. I was on a plane that was about to crash. Strangely, the whole world was on that plane too. I kept repeating, 'Don't crash it. It's a pity to lose it.' But nobody was listening to me, my little friend. Heavy as a tombstone is people's indifference."

"*I* am listening to you."

"You are, and I know you will not remain idle. You may not believe in violence," Alberto said while searching for something in his coat pocket, "but take this Swiss Army knife and learn how to use it. You never know when you might need it."

⁂

Martíta was folding the laundry before José's return from school, when she heard a knock on the door and Alberto calling her.

She motioned him inside and offered him water. He looked exhausted, shoulders sagging, gait unsteady. She clasped his hands and, looking at him, noticed the blue bands that circled the brown irises of his eyes. "Is everything all right, Professor?"

"Martíta, I want to discuss something with you."

She pointed to the sofa, but he remained standing.

"They are after me. I might have to go into hiding quickly. I would like to give you the password for my safe box. I want you to have access to my money."

She picked up a towel from the washing basket. *This is dangerous,* she thought. *What if the police start searching for me? They already have my photo.*

"I want you to give José a better life," he continued.

She grasped his hands again, shaking her head. "I can't do it, Professor."

"José deserves to get out of the *conventillo*. He will flourish in a good school."

"Still, I cannot take your money. You will find a way back to us and you will need it."

"Listen to me, Martíta. This boy ... You understand, he is the son I never had. Let me help him while I can. Use the money to get this gem of a boy out of this place. Not even the air here is fit to breathe."

⁂

José was becoming increasingly worried.

Alberto was late picking him up for the monthly meeting of TodoPorLaTierra and there had been no response when he knocked on his door earlier.

Tense as a wound-up spring, he was sitting at the edge of the bed he shared with his mother. It was impossible to sit at his little table and read, or even to think of anything else. The setting sun shone through the window and onto the wall where all his school clothes and Martíta's dresses hung from the curtain rod.

He knelt on the faded red rug that covered the cement floor and, looking up at the statue of the Virgin Mary and baby Jesus, began praying.

He rushed to the door when he heard Martíta's familiar tread. "Mamá, Alberto hasn't come."

"*Mi niño*, I'm so sorry; I don't have good news. The police came. They searched the room of the professor."

"No, no. Not the police! Is he okay?"

"I hope so. They are saying he is a terrorist."

"Have they put him in jail?"

"I heard they've arrested some TodoPorLaTierras, but the professor is missing. He's probably gone underground."

"Where underground?"

"He didn't tell me and if we look for him, they'll follow us." She stroked his head. "He told me if he left Buenos Aires, he would leave you his books. I don't want you to see his room. I'll go and get them."

"Mamá, please, can I come? I have to come."

"Okay, *mi niño*, but don't get upset. Bad things have happened in that room. May God be with him."

As his mother opened the door, José saw the bed tipped over, mattress slit open, yellow foam stuffing scattered everywhere. The cupboards were smashed and clothes thrown on the floor, along with everything from the desk. The posters were torn from walls and the framed photograph of Alberto's parents that had hung above the bed was on the ground in pieces.

José began collecting things, trying to put them back together.

"It's not safe here, José. The police will come back. They'll think the professor has returned. They might even be watching the room now from across the street. Let's get the books and go."

"Mamá, I have to take the photo. I know it's the only one of his family. He will want it when he comes back."

"Wait. Let me get the glass shards out first."

Back in their room, José dusted off the books and started ordering them by author under their bed, all the while worrying that Alberto might be hurt. Many of the books had notes written by Alberto. Among the books were *The Population Bomb*, *The Third Chimpanzee*, *Requiem for a Species* and *The Rat Brain in Stereotaxic Coordinates*. As he began leafing through *The Population Bomb*, he suddenly recalled what Alberto had said to him that Sunday morning in Plaza de Mayo.

"Mamá, the companies will kill him. They will blame him for everything and kill him."

"Don't worry, José, they caught the others, but not him. The professor will outsmart them."

José nodded, but deep down he worried he would never see Alberto again. He covered his face with his hands. He felt his mother's arms pull him down to sit on the bed.

"Is he going to come back, Mamá?"

"*Mi niño*, it is hard for you. I'll miss Alberto too, but I hope he doesn't come here again because the police will put him in jail."

His mind went to something Alberto had said in his last lecture. "The time has come to refuse the 'gift' of the fossil-fuel industry—the carbon dioxide sarcophagus it is placing over our heads. As the whiff of extinction becomes stronger, I exhort you not to patience and pusillanimity, but to resistance and revolution."

"Why, Mamá? That's so unfair ... so unfair. The only thing Alberto wanted was to save us from extinction."

Chapter 10

MAGNIFICENT MARMOSET

José could only see a few familiar faces. It had been nearly six years since Alberto's disappearance. Might he show up from somewhere? If only for a minute, just so he could see that the bicycles had taken over Avenida 9 de Julio. The people had responded. The factories didn't have to be destroyed, but could remain open and make bicycles. The professor's goals could be achieved peacefully.

Cyclists milled around Plaza de la República, ringing bells, taking selfies, chatting, calling out to friends. They were in racing gear, high school uniforms and T-shirts with company logos. Children wearing colorful helmets sat on the back of their parents' bicycles. Even the Siga La Vaca restaurant chain was taking part this warm spring day.

For his eighteenth birthday, José's friends were giving him the best possible present—their participation in his demonstration. He had advertised through environmental forums, cycling clubs and even Alzheimer's disease support sites. Though his friends had warned him not to expect more than fifty people, there were over one hundred and fifty cyclists already, and the crowd was still growing. It had been a struggle to organize the rally, but José was not doing it only for himself, but also for the man who had been like a father to him.

The protesters paraded their banners, moving along with the regular foot traffic across the intersection. At every change of lights, they crossed the nine southbound lanes of the eighteen-lane Avenida 9 de Julio, holding placards and calling out "The Chain Sets You Free," "Cycle to Save the Planet," "Cycling Delays Dementia."

A number of pedestrians had gathered too, friends of the cyclists, as well as the curious. José looked at each of them in case he recognized the balding head, the thick glasses resting on the big nose, or at least someone from TodoPorLaTierra so he could ask for news of the professor.

Once the stragglers arrived at the plaza, the protesters took up the southbound lanes of the Avenida next to the Obelisco. Their destination was Plaza Constitución, two and a half kilometers south. Slowly they spun their wheels down 9 de Julio, the sounds of bells and voices in the air.

He felt free. José was on his old bike with its orange cyclist's flag. How liberating it was to ride in the middle of the road, no longer languishing at the margins, at risk of being collected by opening doors of parked cars.

Banked up behind the cyclists, cars with revving engines were honking horns and, as the fumes and noise got stronger, José grew apprehensive. The drivers had the option of using alternative routes, but some were determined to harass the demonstrators. When a group of cyclists reacted by stopping and blocking several lanes, others joined them until, standing shoulder to shoulder, they totally blocked the southbound lanes.

José rode back to the blockade. "*Por favor, amigos*, we want to change their minds, not to upset them. Remember the de-escalation technique—start moving and put the bicycles between you and the cars."

A man with shaven head and powerful tattooed arms jumped out of his car cursing at the cyclists closest to him. "You have nothing better to do, *carajo*. I have to go home and feed my children."

"Señor," said José, "this is not only for us, but for your children too."

"*Quién mierda te crees que sos*—what shit you think you are—to tell me what is good for my family?"

"We are a public interest group, Señor. We don't want to take anything from you. This is a protest against pollution of the atmosphere."

"*Hijo de puta*—son of a prostitute, you're wasting my time. *Te voy a hacer pelota cuando te agarre*—I will make a ball of you when I catch you. I know who you are. You're the one with the *trolo* flag."

"Oh, ignore him, José. Don't engage with him," a woman called out as they all started riding again.

The warm sun and the light breeze were not enough to erase the insult. Perhaps the professor was right after all. Some minds might change with the rally, but not in favor of cycling. *Is this the way to save the environment? Is there any way to save the environment?*

The cyclists reached Plaza Constitución and some stopped for drinks handed out by José's co-organizers. The team joined hands in the middle of a circle and raised them high, shouting slogans. It was agreed José would write up the story and update the blog while others would work the social media.

José returned to Plaza de la República, folded the banners and placed them in his backpack before heading home, taking Calle Santiago del Estero. He stopped behind cars held up at the lights of the intersection with Calle Moreno. "It was beyond our dreams," he recalled one of the co-organizers saying. *Maybe the professor will see news of the demonstration. Perhaps he was somewhere near me.*

As he was waiting at the lights, one foot on the ground, he sensed someone approach. In front of him a shadow grew larger. A punch on the shoulder threw him to the ground, the grit of the asphalt now hard against his cheek. All was murky as he lay on the road and above him a dark shape loomed. He heard his bicycle being smashed. José had rolled into the fetal position when he felt the full impact of a kick to his groin.

He heard a man shout, "*Te dige, hijo de mil putas*—I told you, son of a thousand prostitutes."

⁊⅄

"*Ayuda*," Lorena called out searching for help. "*Ayuda*, someone has attacked this boy. Help please, help!" she shouted with all her strength as she rushed to him.

She had been riding a short distance behind and recognized the orange triangular flag of the cyclist who had organized the rally. She cycled between cars and threw her own bike on the road to stop the traffic. Drivers honked their horns and some got out to help.

The boy tried to get up, but fell back to the ground. She checked him over. His breathing was labored but steady. He was opening his eyes halfway and blinking slowly. There was a bleeding cut on his cheek.

Pedestrians and drivers helped her load him, semi-conscious, into a car. She directed the driver to the nearest hospital from the back seat where she sat cradling his head and applying pressure to his cheek to stem the bleeding.

He partly opened his eyes. "Where're we going?" he asked.

"It's okay. You're safe now. Just rest."

"Who are you? Where—"

"I'm Lorena and we're taking you to hospital. Somebody attacked you, but you're safe now."

He nodded and closed his eyes. She had removed his helmet and was stroking his jet-black curly hair. His head rested on her lap, his broad shoulders pressing against her thigh. She kept staring at his face—long eyelashes, straight nose, small mouth, pointed chin. A dimple appeared on his left cheek every time he spoke.

"Who are you?" he asked again. "Where ... where're we going?"

"I'm Lorena. You've been assaulted, but you should be okay. Please look at me."

As he stared at her, she checked his pupils. She felt relieved to see they were properly constricted, though she had struggled to find their border because his irises were also black.

"Do you feel nauseous, dizzy?"

"Everything hurts. Where're we going?"

"I told you, but you don't remember. We're taking you to hospital. What's your name?"

"José."

"Do you know what the date is?"

"It's my birthday."

"I hope the rest of your birthday is better. What's the number to call your parents?"

"Number?" He hesitated as though searching for the number, but then said, "She doesn't have a phone."

"Give me your address and I'll send my friend Silvia to get her."

"No, my mother ... She'll be upset. Where're we going?"

"To the hospital. We'll be there soon. Now, listen. Tell me the last thing you remember."

"At the lights," he said barely audibly.

"Which lights? Do you remember which lights?"

"Santiago del Estero ... Was it a car?"

"A man attacked you. But it's good you're remembering things up to that point. You should be okay."

She kept talking to him, trying to keep him awake. Minutes later they arrived at the entrance of the hospital. José was placed on a stretcher and wheeled into Emergency with Lorena beside him holding his hand.

"He is concussed. Anterograde amnesia," she explained to the registrar on duty.

"And who are you?" he asked.

"I'm Lorena. I'm a medical student."

The doctor looked tired. "Does he have retrograde amnesia too?"

"He remembers things up to when he was attacked. So, if there is any retrograde amnesia, it should only be a few seconds. It may all be post-traumatic."

With torchlight, the doctor tested José's pupil reflex. "Good. Now, focus on my nose and tell me which finger moves," he instructed with arms extended.

Nodding at José's reactions, the doctor ran another test. "Grasp my fingers and squeeze them as hard as you can."

Lorena watched in silence.

The doctor turned to look at her. "Did he vomit?"

"No," they both answered.

"You wouldn't remember even if you did," said the doctor with a half-smile as he took José's blood pressure. "Your vital signs are good. Now, I need to assess the other injuries." He sharply pulled the curtain closed.

Lorena moved away, but could still hear the doctor talking. "What happened to you? This needs ice."

At least she could help with that. The curtain was still closed when she returned from the nurses' station with an ice pack. She hung back, but then went closer when the doctor mentioned her name.

"I don't know any Lorena," said José.

"You don't remember her. She is the medical student who brought you to Emergency."

José started saying something, but the doctor spoke over him. "Okay, your testicles are swollen and the penile shaft is badly bruised. We'll wait and see if catheterization is needed." Opening the curtain, he murmured, "I'll get a nurse."

Lorena moved forward, handing him the ice pack.

"You've been a great help, Señorita," the doctor said as he disappeared behind the curtain. "He is applying it himself, but could you supervise?" he said when he re-emerged. "Just keep reminding him to take it off when it gets too cold. Call me if there is a problem voiding the bladder." As he walked out, he added, "He has to remain in hospital even if consolidation of memory returns. It's concussion."

"I'll take care of everything, Doctor."

José was propped up on a pile of pillows, a plaster covering his facial wound. "We should tell your mother you're here," she said, touching him on the arm. "Can you give me your address so I can let her know?"

"Are you the nurse?"

"No, I'm Lorena. I was there when you were attacked and I brought you here."

"You are really nice to me. But tell me, it wasn't at the rally. The last thing I remember was waiting at the intersection of Moreno and Santiago del Estero."

She thought his voice was firmer. "No, I was at the rally too." She sat at the edge of his bed. "It was at the intersection. It was the driver who shouted at us. I recognized him from his tattoos."

"My mother's address," he said suddenly, "Humberto Primo 1569 Apartment 3. She is Martíta."

"Wait. Just wait. You remembered to answer my question! Do you remember my name?"

"Lorena."

"Oh, thank God, your memory has returned," she said, giving him a quick hug.

"But I don't remember how I got here."

"That's because you were concussed. You had post-traumatic amnesia. But it's over now."

"Thank you for staying with me. Are the others okay?"

"Everyone is fine. I'll notify the police and describe the man who hit you. I wouldn't be surprised if he has a criminal record."

"Please don't do anything like that."

"Why not? He'll bash more people."

"He is a victim too, a victim of his past, just like I am a victim of his anger."

Lorena could not believe what she had just heard.

"If we didn't know better," José continued, "we would be like him. And if he knew what we know, he would be with us."

"As you like," she said. "But I think he's the luckier of the two of you."

❧

Lorena had never walked alone in San Telmo. Just as well it was still light.

The day before, she had been stuck at university, unable to visit José. As she approached the partly subterranean Apartment 3, she thought of the penthouse she lived in and the light that streamed in through the bay windows.

"Hola, you must be Martíta," she said to the short, robust woman who answered the door. "I'm Lorena. I came to—"

Martíta squeezed her against her chest as though she would never let go. "*Gracias, gracias, mi ángel.*"

Still holding each other, they walked down the few steps into the apartment, straight into a small room that served as both kitchen and living area. A sink, a gas stove, a sofa and a cupboard surrounded a table covered with yellow plastic. The whole apartment was not much bigger than her room.

Martíta pointed to the door on the right. After knocking, Lorena slowly turned the doorknob and entered. José was sitting up in a single bed working on an old laptop, piles of books and articles around him.

The room was as dimly lit as she had expected, its small window partly blocked by the footpath.

"Lorena, you're here!"

"I was afraid you wouldn't remember my name."

"I've been rehearsing it," he said, suppressing a smile.

"Don't get up. You need to rest."

"I hope this is not something for me," he said. "*I* owe *you* favors."

"I passed by this organic fruit shop on the way and I couldn't resist these strawberries. Look, they'll help you get better."

"That's so nice of you," he said and motioned for her to sit at the end of the bed.

On the wall opposite, within arm's reach, were old posters, torn and patched together—penguins, giraffes and monkeys. There was also a graph showing the rise of carbon dioxide in the atmosphere.

"I can see you like animals."

"I do, but most of these posters aren't really mine. They belong to the professor who lived in the *conventillo*. Alberto was a man who … he was like a father to me."

He had become emotional, but she thought his face had good color. "Was the professor a biologist?"

"Kind of. He was a neuroscientist. We lost contact with him nearly six years ago."

"Did he teach you things about the brain?"

"He actually knew the human brain better than anyone in the world and he had concerns about its limits. He said the brain is far more *stupido* than we give it credit."

"That's a bit harsh, isn't it?"

José moved the books and articles out of the way. "Alberto was always saying harsh things. I remember when a lady told him we only use ten percent of our brain. He told her the idea was a sophistry—it may appear true, but it's false."

This boy is beautiful; this boy is clever, Lorena thought. *And someone goes and hits him …*

"So, José, the professor was putting down the organ he spent his life studying!"

"He claimed the brain has leftover reptilian parts—from snakes. They give us Stone Age emotions, unsuitable for handling our space-age technology."

"The professor taught you well."

"I could talk for hours about the things he taught me, but I'm afraid I'd bore you to death."

She changed position, placing a hand on the other side of the bed so she could look at him directly. "Remember, I told you I'm studying medicine. I'm always interested when it comes to the brain."

"Well, what can I tell you first? The professor was worried the brain is not suitable for the environment it has created. His point was that the hoarding instinct that helped us survive the savannas is now ravaging the biosphere." He took a breath and looked at the ceiling. "Yes," he continued, "I remember one time he told me the dinosaurs had a greater chance of surviving the asteroid, than we our avarice."

"And did you agree with him?"

"I told him the brain made people see slavery was immoral, and it will make them see damaging the environment is just as immoral."

"You were a smart kid, José."

"The professor taught me things; he helped me think. We disagreed, but also there was nobody I—" He stopped and turned his head.

She touched his hand.

A few moments passed before she heard his voice again, "Now, I go to meetings, demonstrations, hoping I will see him again."

"He left all of sudden; is that what happened?"

José nodded, but it looked as if it was difficult for him to say more.

They shared the fruit. She noticed he had stopped eating the strawberries. He told her he was going to share them with his friends who had brought him *flan con dulce de leche* earlier.

"I can see you're popular. Do you study with your friends?"

"With some of them. Others just live in the building."

She could not stop staring at him. "What do you study?"

"Oh, I'm in the last year of high school. If I'm lucky, next year I'll join you."

He is still in high school, she thought. *This will never work.*

⁊

José looked out of the window, catching a glimpse of the sky beyond the moving legs of the pedestrians.

The clouds, so ominous at midday, had morphed from steely gray to friendly white. That was a relief. He could not afford a taxi and it would be terrible if Lorena got wet on their first date—*no, not a date,* he corrected himself. *Just a movie.*

He looked at himself in the mirror. The best that could be said was he was clean and neat in faded blue jeans, which Martíta had insisted on pressing, and a blue checkered shirt over a white T-shirt. He could hardly wait to see Lorena's face and hear her voice again. Nothing would make him happier, yet he had never felt so anxious. Patting down his hair, he turned to leave, but swung around to look at himself again before going into the kitchen.

"*Mi niño,* you are adorable," said Martíta.

"That's what *you* think, Mamá." He sat next to her on the sofa. She had their family Bible open on her lap. At mass that morning he had been caught up in his plans for the evening. He didn't even know what color flower to get Lorena. Should it be red? Should it be white? *What is the right color to say "I like you," without scaring her off?*

At least for the moment he could concentrate on the Bible. "What is it this week, Mamá?"

"Ecclesiastes 9:11," she said, smoothing the page. "Listen:

The race is not to the swift, nor the battle to the strong, neither yet bread to the wise nor yet riches to men of understanding nor yet favor to men of skill; but time and chance happeneth to them all.

"Are you trying to tell me something?"

"Only that those who get to know you cannot but love you. It will go well tonight and if it doesn't, it will still be the will of the Lord."

He rested his chin on his palm while she continued reading. The words, their rhythm, their hidden meaning settled his nerves, but he still kept checking the time.

❧

Finally there was a knock.

He jumped off the sofa and rushed to the door. Lorena wore a light pink dress. José knew he was staring, but could not help himself.

"*Que Dios los bendiga*—God bless you," said Martíta, after hugging them both.

They were going to see a rerun of *Throne of Gaia*, but the movie was the last thing on José's mind. He wondered whether to take Lorena's hand as they were walking to the cinema. Was it too soon? Something like that required more courage than he had. Perhaps she thought he was only interested in her environmentalism, nothing more. How wrong that would be! Since the hospital, he could hardly think of anything but her. Her face appeared on the page of the book he was reading and, when he turned the page, her face was on the next one too.

Should I offer her my jacket? Although it was well into spring, the evening was cool. But she seemed warm enough in her cardigan. In her tall heels, her lips were nearly even with his. *Should I kiss her now?*

But how could he do that when he didn't even dare hold her hand? Strands of her hair curled and fell across her eyes, partly obscuring them. He wanted to push it back so he could see her entire face.

As he was lost in these thoughts, she asked, "Do you remember seeing it for the first time?"

After a second he realized she meant the movie. "Yes I do. Alberto took me to see it. I was so naive; I believed the whole world would wake up. But yet again, he was right."

"From what you have told me, he was very cynical. Shouldn't he have been giving you hope?"

"He wanted to prepare me for disappointment. In fact, he read to me from the Meditations of Marcus Aurelius: 'Begin each day by telling yourself: today I shall be meeting with interference, ingratitude, insolence, disloyalty, ill-will, and selfishness ... due to the offender's ignorance of what is good and evil.'"

"I can see you have high expectations of me," said Lorena.

"No, no, no. I just wanted you to know what to expect of *me*."

"Your words make me forget you're still in high school."

"I just memorized what the emperor said. Parrots do it too."

"Well, I think your brain is better than the parrot's."

"You know, birds have first-class brains; they just don't have good public relations. See? I'm using the professor's words again."

"Tell me something else the professor said about the brain."

"He thought love was bred in the brain. He wrote an article 'Darling I love you ... from the bottom of my brain.' In an interview, a woman journalist asked the professor, 'Are you insisting the heart has nothing to do with love?' He replied, 'If in a heart transplant I receive *your* heart, I will not fall in love with your husband.' He even designed a Valentine's Day card with brains instead of hearts."

With Lorena walking next to him, engaging with him, laughing with him, he felt weightless.

"What else did he teach you?"

"Alberto often talked about the impasse with overpopulation. He wanted to see a reduction in reproduction, so the Earth can keep supporting human life."

"I totally agree with that," she said. "I've been involved in family planning."

José thought he had overdone it with heavy discussion on their first date, but she seemed to like it. "Really, Lorena. Do you think we can change things? Sometimes I lose hope."

"I believe we can. And I like that you're so idealistic. People are changing. I mean, think of how many came to your bicycle rally. We need to keep doing that sort of thing."

"We *should*, Lorena. I've been thinking, public transport is an urgent issue. I read the government is going to dispose of what's left of the tramway infrastructure."

"I heard that too. We could start a web petition and hold a demonstration."

"I don't know that I could get anything together before it's too late."

"Maybe not you, but *we* can. I threw a fundraising party for family planning a few months ago and we made nearly twelve thousand pesos. And guess what? I put the whole thing together in three weeks."

"Wow, Lorena, your brain must be entirely frontal lobes."

"That'd better be a compliment—we haven't done neuroscience yet."

"Let me get the tickets and we can talk further."

It was going better than he had hoped. She said she liked him, or at least she liked his idealism. The important thing is she liked something about him. Maybe he did have a chance. She was stunning and smart, and an environmentalist. What more could one ask for? *But what if she's just interested in the environment, and not me? Maybe she can't imagine dating me.* He was plucking petals from daisies.

They walked in just as the trailers began, choosing seats at the back of the almost empty cinema. As they sank back into their seats, their arms touched lightly over the armrest. He could sense the warmth of her body through their clothing. He concentrated on her *moreno* skin. So beautiful. As lights flashed on the screen he could see every single one of her eyelashes. Her neck was long like that of a swan, her black hair curling out at her shoulders. She turned to look at him with her enormous brown eyes.

He was surprised to hear himself say, "You remind me of a marmoset," and quickly added, "I love those little monkeys."

"They are wild animals, José," she said, her eyes still looking directly into his. "I think you like to live dangerously."

"Can I ask you something?" She gave him an encouraging look. "There's only this skinny little armrest between us; it would be much easier if I held your hand…"

He saw the hesitation, but then felt her hand in his.

"But you're two years younger than me," she said.

"Yes, but Romeo was even younger."

"And look what happened to him."

"That's because Juliet was thirteen—and you're *not* thirteen."

"Oh, you know how to get out of trouble."

I am not quite out of trouble yet, he thought. In his other hand he was holding a carnation, gently to avoid crushing its petals. Should he offer it to her now? What if she wouldn't accept it? Worse, what if she walked out on him? *But if she agreed to hold my hand, she will tolerate receiving a flower.* The color was really the problem, but it was rather dark and she might not notice.

"A carnation," Lorena whispered when he placed it in her hand. "A fragrant red carnation," she said as she brought it to her lips.

※

She felt she had glided all the way to Avenida Callao.

The pink walls, bay windows, wrought-iron balconies and arched doorways of her home had never seemed so pretty. He had given her a flower, and he had held her hand throughout the movie. This was everything. She kissed the surprised doorman and walked up into her apartment humming a tango melody.

"Hola, Mamá."

"You seem happy, Lorena. Is there a reason?"

"I shouldn't be. I just saw a film about the environment that was so depressing."

"It can't be the film then."

"All right, since you want to know. Remember the boy who was attacked?"

"What about him?"

"He is doing much better. I saw it with him."

"Lorena, you shouldn't go to San Telmo; it's not safe for you there." She exhaled. "You did your good deed; now leave those people alone."

"Mamá, you have no idea. The boy is brilliant and he has an amazing heart."

"I'm just reminding you, the last thing we want is for you to get involved with somebody from San Telmo."

"You don't even know him, Mamá."

"And it certainly wouldn't be a good idea to bring him here."

"That's not fair."

"It's only logical," said her mother. "He doesn't belong here."

"What about your crook friends? Do they belong here?"

"Don't speak to me like that," she shouted. "When you get out of this phase, you'll understand, but until then don't let people see you with him. And don't catch something nasty from this boy."

"I don't care what your snobbish friends think. Let them find out."

"Little girl, without your father's money you wouldn't have been able to buy this boy's love. That's for sure."

"I only bought him a box of strawberries. I simply wanted to …" Lorena turned her back and headed to her room. *And even if it were true,* she thought, *how could she say that to me?*

⁂

Every time he read *Intergenerational Injustice*, José found hundreds of mistakes, in expression and logic.

Engrossed in his own manuscript, he had not moved from the kitchen table for hours. Martíta had long gone to bed, midnight showed the clock of the laptop Lorena had salvaged from a university asset disposal to replace his old one. He ran the edge of the blanket over the screen, wiping away specks of dust. Even with a blanket over his shoulders, he was cold.

As he was filling the hot water bottle for his feet, he heard a key enter the lock. He nearly scalded himself as he hurried to get to the door. He kissed Lorena. *How could her lips be so soft.* Breaking away, he hooked her hair behind her ears and looked into her eyes. "Magnificent Marmoset, you arrived and so has the best moment of the day. Let me massage your tango pains away."

"You're a true *caballero*," she said as she stretched out on the sofa, kicking off her shoes. "It was standing room only at the festival."

"Is a 'true *caballero*' allowed to ask how many men fell into your arms tonight?" He put the question while massaging her legs.

"Look at it another way—after tango, it's only you."

"I admire *tangueros* for their self-control."

"You're exaggerating, José. Only the upper part of the body is in contact. We resist the advancing *tanguero* as we retreat." She extended her hand and arrested his as it was massaging above her knee.

"I'm an advancing *tanguero* too, Marmoset."

"That's why I resist and retreat."

He kissed her. "So," he said, "what's actually true? Do people dance tango to express themselves artistically or to meet partners?"

"The first reason is beautiful, but I am afraid the second is true."

"In you, Magnificent Marmoset, I find truth *and* beauty."

"Come on," she said, as she got up and balanced on her toes, "let's do the best *tanguero* embrace ever."

⁂

José counted every one of them.

Fifty-one protesters had braved martial law. The junta that had taken control of Argentina on New Year's Day was mopping up pockets of resistance, dissention of any kind becoming increasingly dangerous. Having failed to prevent the alienation of the tramway assets, the Asociación Amigos del Tranvía took its chances and was holding a protest at the workshops. Cheering and waving colorful banners, a defiant crowd had gathered at the forecourt of the workshops the dictatorship had recently condemned for demolition.

Stepping up onto a ladder, José spoke to the motley group of tram enthusiasts and environmentalists at the rally. "Buenos Aires was the City of Trams and it can be again," he began. "The tramway workshops are of heritage value and much else besides. They can be the stabling facility for a future light-rail system that can provide a permanent solution to some of the city's traffic, parking and air pollution problems."

"Save the tramway workshops!" someone shouted and the crowd echoed.

"By condemning the tramway workshops," José continued, "the government is destroying part of our heritage and part of our future. It is condemning us to a toxic atmosphere and—"

He caught Lorena's glance and looked over at the wire-mesh fence. Two of the protesters had scaled it to erect a banner, "Light Rail. Not Freeways." Others lit fireworks. The police, who had been quietly intimidating the demonstrators, now stepped forward in formation, batons at the ready.

Hastily the protesters dispersed, but not before taking photographs to send to sympathetic journalists.

"The battle is lost," said José. "And, I'm afraid, the war too." He felt Lorena's hand tighten around his.

There, in the empty street, as they carried their ladder, he wished he had never said that.

❧

"It is politics besting science."

Lorena had just announced to the students assembled in a lecture room of the medical school that their petition had come to a dead end. The so-called minister of the environment and sustainable development had written to say the government had no population policy. Only one line on that, with the rest of the letter rambling on about how they had improved this, that and the other, but nothing of relevance.

When a first-year student asked her for some background to the petition, she responded that in medicine it was impossible to ignore the impact of climate change on health. *The Lancet* had published article after article on the topic, yet the warnings were being ignored.

Even as vector-borne diseases became endemic in previously safe areas, the link between sustainability and health was being denied—denied in government rhetoric, denied in their policy, denied by their inaction.

She saw the incredulous look of the people near her and took out her tablet. "Our petition was signed by the overwhelming majority of medical undergraduates."

> We ask the Chamber that Argentina works with other nations to attain a decrease in the per capita adverse environmental impact and to advance social and health interventions that support transition to a smaller, sustainable world population.

One of the boys spoke as he raised his hand. "Why should we have expected anything better? The National Congress is nothing but a rubber stamp of the junta—"

"Never mind that," interjected a girl. "We were looking for a deputy to present the petition even before the junta took over. But in catholic Argentina, no one would even meet with us."

"Okay," said another girl. "We were defeated with the petition. But defeat is a good place to begin—it can motivate you like nothing else."

"Then I should have all the motivation in the world," said Lorena. "We were just defeated on the light rail too. The government demolished the tramway workshops. *Amigas y amigos*, have we reached the end of the road?"

"It's the beginning of the road," said a girl.

Lorena looked at those assembled in front of her. They were idealists committed to the cause. However, was there any point in pursuing this cause now that the military controlled everything? What if the junta trained its guns on them? *This country has done that to its people before.*

Half a century earlier, another junta had massacred medical students. Mothers still cried for their sons and daughters. Fathers still laid flowers on unknown graves. *What is worse, to be killed by the junta or to live in silence as human life fades?*

Chapter 11

THE MERCY OF THE PIRANHAS

José stuffed loaves of bread, bags of dried beans, and fresh fruit and vegetables into a coffin.

Before nailing down the lid, he assessed its overall weight—it had to be realistically close to what it would weigh with a body in it. He had told Lorena to expect delivery of many more coffins to the medical school than those bringing cadavers for dissection in anatomy tutorials—the extras filled with food.

It was the evening of the 5th of March. Some days earlier, medical students, joined by students from other faculties, had barricaded themselves inside the medical school building using wood from construction sites. Lorena, as one of the organizers, remained there at nights.

José jogged around the building to the park in front to check the activity of the police. A recently erected barricade prevented anyone from entering or leaving. Transferring cadavers was legitimate, but he did not want to attract attention and, for the moment, this looked impossible.

He used a disposable phone to call his helper, the maxi taxi driver awaiting his signal to transfer the coffin. "I'm sorry, Señor, I must cancel the pizza delivery. It seems we are going to cook at home tonight."

By 9 pm a large crowd of supporters had gathered, held back by the police barricade. Two police officers in full riot gear stopped and searched him. They were wearing bulletproof vests and helmets with their visors lifted. Gas masks hung loose below their chins, batons, guns and canisters dangled from their belts. Their shields were leaning on the park wall. While they were frisking José, his hands extended, he looked over their shoulders. He could see about fifty police officers, who at that moment were parting to allow three military vehicles to approach the university building, vehicles presumably full of soldiers.

When they let him go, he took up a spot in the park directly opposite the building entrance. Large banners with green lettering were strung from the statues that adorned the entrance: "Liberty, Air, Land, Water," "NO to Overpopulation: We are the Asteroid *AND* the Dinosaurs," "Save the Earth from Us," "The Scientists Were Wrong: It's Much Worse."

He wished he were inside with Lorena, regretting having capitulated when she insisted they needed him on the outside to send in provisions. Now he feared for her and the rest of the besieged.

The students were broadcasting through speakers hung from the doors of the medical building. They seemed in good spirits as they took turns inviting people to the theater of the absurd they were about to stage.

Lorena's voice came over the speakers, mock interviewing another student. "Señor," she said, "you want to use geoengineering to protect the planet from overheating. Isn't this ironic if you are denying global warming is happening in the first place?"

A male voice rang out, "Señorita, we don't want to protect the planet; it's our sponsors we want to protect—the coal industry. Geoengineering may not work for the Earth, but it will work for us. It will buy us time to sell more coal regardless of global warming."

"Señor, you make Dr. Strangelove look rational," said Lorena. "Let me try my luck with someone else. You, Señor, can you give me a moment of your time? You represent the petroleum industry. Is it true you want proof beyond reasonable doubt that the planet will be destroyed before you stop drilling it?"

"No, no, no, Señorita. We demand absolute proof the planet is *gone* before we do anything that harms the petroleum industry."

"I have fallen into a nest of nature lovers," cried Lorena. "Let me try this economist. Señor, here's a simple question. Should we save the planet or the economy?"

The crowd had been drawn in. "The economy! The economy!" it chanted.

"The people have spoken, Señorita," answered a male voice. "We must save the economy. We have no interest in saving this unproductive expanse of mountains and swamps, poisonous snakes and disgusting cockroaches."

"Ah, men are a lost cause," she said. "Let me try this lady politician. Señora, what would you prefer, family planning or eighty million unwanted pregnancies every year?"

"But the Pope uses prophylactics and doesn't make any pregnancies!" protested a female voice.

Though consumed by worry, José could not hold back a smile, the same as that spread on the faces in the crowd around him.

⁂

"The tanks are coming! The tanks are coming!"

There was rumbling outside. Through the haze of sleep, Lorena had taken it for thunder. But then the screams made it clear exactly what it was.

The wake-up call she dreaded had come. Startled students rushed to the windows. Lorena ran downstairs and pressed her face against a window in the room next to the outer foyer. She could see the tanks, but could not make out their guns. Soon she realized why—they were aimed at her.

People were being chased off the streets, and the area cordoned off, as tanks and soldiers formed an impenetrable line. The trees and the church in the park formed the immediate backdrop to the tanks. Beyond the park, she could faintly make out the neoclassical building of the Faculty of Economic Sciences, the statue on its roof holding aloft the Argentinian flag as it furled and unfurled in the breeze. Suddenly light flooded the entire entrance to the Faculty of Medicine. Using her hand as visor, she looked at the troops encircling the entranceway—the slick black of their rifles.

We are done for, she thought.

Her phone rang. "Surrender, Lorena! *Te van a atacar a vos*—they are going to attack you!" her mother screamed. "*Rendite*—surrender!"

"The tanks are here, Mamá."

"*Rendite*, Lorena. *Por favor, rendite!*"

"Why would they attack us? We are unarmed."

Her mother kept shouting for her to surrender.

"*Tengo miedo*—I am frightened. Mamá. I love you. Tell Papá I love him."

Lorena ran into the outer foyer shouting, "Go! Go—go out the back!"

Some students followed her from the front rooms into the two foyers. They ran toward the loading dock at the back, but were met by returning students yelling it was sealed.

A siren drowned all other sounds. An ambulance must have arrived at the steps in front of the doors. Lorena turned to the boy next to her. "Did someone call an ambulance?" He frowned, and, as he did, she realized. "Oh, no! No!" she cried. "Don't let them in."

The shouts of the students guarding the entrance clashed with the shouts of students who were urging them to let the paramedics in.

But it was already too late. One of the "paramedics" lobbed a tear-gas grenade over the heads of students and into the outer foyer.

A student grabbed the grenade and threw it back out of the building. They managed to push the huge metal door closed, but they still had to deal with the noxious gas cloud inside. They slammed the doors shut between the two foyers to confine the tear-gas. Lorena's eyes shut, tears forcing their way through her eyelids. Nose running, throat burning, dizzy and hardly able to see and breathe, she made for the PC2 lab, the designated meeting place.

The lab was full of coughing and arguing students. Gathering her breath, Lorena pushed her way to the front of the room and climbed onto a bench. "Listen. Listen. *Please* lis—" she cried, but she gagged on tear gas and panic. *Where are you?* she thought. *Why didn't I let you come inside? Together we might have found a way.*

A moment later her voice came back. "Their orders are to attack us. We're going to die if we resist, but we can fight again if we surrender now. We have a lot more battles to fight."

Through the cacophony, she heard, "They'll attack us even if we surrender."

"No," someone shouted back. "Not if we come out singing *El Himno!*"

She recognized him. He had been the flag-bearer for Argentina at the last Pan American Games. There was silence until he shouted, "*Vamonos*—let's go!" A group followed him as he ran through the foyers.

Lorena edged toward the window in the room alongside the outer foyer. The student had already stepped out from the protection of the building. He held his white shirt above his head, and was waving it from side to side. She held her breath as he faced the tanks. On his body, illuminated by floodlights, she could make out his rotator cuff muscles, deltoids and anterior pectorals. The army held fire.

It all seemed as though it had happened before and it could not possibly happen in any other way. Some students, girls and boys, joined him and, their arms linked, they sang:

Oíd, mortales, el grito sagrado:	Hear, mortals, the sacred cry:
¡Libertad, libertad, libertad!	"Freedom! Freedom! Freedom!"
Oíd el ruido de rotas cadenas,	Hear the noise of broken chains,
ved en trono a la noble igualdad … .	See the noble Equality enthroned … .
Ya su trono dignísimo abrieron	The United Provinces of the South
las Provincias Unidas del Sud	Their most honorable throne have opened.
y los libres del mundo responden:	And the free ones of the world reply:
Al gran pueblo argentino, ¡Salud!	"The grand Argentine people, we salute!"

The last lyrics of the anthem faded. Lorena released the breath she was holding.

A huge blast sent a vibration rushing through her body. She jumped back. Glass, marble fragments and broken masonry cascaded down around her.

As the air started to clear, she took a step forward. No trace remained of the students who sang the anthem.

High-explosive shells had smashed the wooden barricade. Now she was looking at five broken statues, which just before had stood proud above the entrances. They had taken the banners down with them. Moments later, the last statue toppled, smashing itself on the steps.

The next barrage hit the south door of the building, the main access. The thick metal door roared as it fell, dragging down its supporting frame and leaving the building unprotected. With the outside door gone, the shells penetrated the glass-paneled doors that separated the two foyers. She saw metal frames buckle and all glass panels shatter.

There was no distinction between fixtures and students. They crouched low with hands above their heads, but this was little protection from debris raining down on them.

Lorena sought refuge under a desk, her eyes on the blond and brown marble that was arranged in a geometric pattern on the floor.

The street was quiet. All the commotion was now inside.

Looking out through the gaping doorway, she thought of trying to escape, but instead she ran to the inner foyer to help, her shoes crunching glass on the bloodied marble floor. Students who moments earlier had been running and yelling were now strewn over the ground. *Who is unconscious and who is dead?* They all looked like the broken statues.

Able-bodied students dragged the injured away from the crumbling partition between the two foyers, coughing as they breathed in the lingering tear-gas. They cleared an area for triage, carrying those still breathing there and placing a finger on the neck of others in search of a pulse.

Lorena went to assist a boy she recognized from lectures. He was bleeding from shrapnel wounds to his chest. As she applied pressure to the area, warm, sticky blood oozed between her fingers. Its acrid, metallic smell made her gag. Cries of help and cries of pain blended with shouts of first aid instructions.

Then the building was plunged into darkness.

Like rats in a panic, students deserted the foyers. "Forgive me; I'm sorry ... I'm really sorry," she said to the boy, stepping backward, then turning and rushing up a flight of stairs, groping for an unlocked lab. Around her, students using torches from their phones searched for a place that could save their lives. They sought safety in toxic cabinets, corrosive cabinets, fume-hoods, cold rooms, electron microscope rooms. Leaving the door open to give the impression the lab was empty, Lorena hid under a bench in the space between two filing cabinets.

A little later, the lights came back on, to be followed by rifle shots coming from all directions. There were cries of students being arrested. She smelled xylene and alcohol. *The building could explode.*

She held her breath when she saw the boots of a policeman at the doorway. He left. As her father would have said, time was moving as slowly as snails on a Sunday stroll.

She had taken only a few breaths before the policeman returned, this time entering the room. His feet came closer, then his face appeared before her as he bent down to look at her. "Here's our girl," he said with a grin.

He poked Lorena out of her hiding place with his rifle, then handcuffed her before shoving her out of the door toward his partner. The second man, shorter and fatter than the first, put a pistol to her face, spun her around and pushed her down the staircase, the muzzle of the gun knocking against her head.

They stepped over bodies, fellow students, blood congealing on their faces. The boy she had tried to help had his mouth open in a frozen scream, his red blood spilled on the blond marble.

The foyer had the smell of a slaughterhouse.

Convinced she was being marched to her own death, there was no time to think of him. She was too frightened to even beg for mercy and could hardly navigate the doorway as she was pushed out of the building at gunpoint.

Vans full of captured students were moving north on Calle Paraguay. On the floor of a van crammed with other female students, Lorena heard a gasp in her ear, "They're killing us. They're killing us."

⁊⊱

That must be her father.

José had been in the morgue for a while before noticing a tall man standing at the opposite side of the big hall; he was clutching a bunch of white tissues, occasionally bringing them to his face.

Heart racing, legs hardly supporting him, José walked between two rows of autopsy tables with corpses. He held a suitcase in one hand and a drum full of water in the other.

The man embraced him as soon as he heard his name. "I thought you might be José." He let go, only to embrace him again, kissing him on the cheek. "I'm frightened they will throw me out even before I have a chance to search."

"No, Señor Scremin, I have a plan."

"And I'm frightened to look. Under one of these sheets … There is a chance … My boy, I cannot, I cannot do it."

"I've checked all but the row against the wall," said José. "Each time she is not here … each time she is not under the sheets, we have one more hope."

Without talking, they continued looking at one another.

"But, Señor Scremin, we must not lose time. I found other students and I took photos of them. The students tend to be the ones in the zipper bags."

"Our children in zipper bags …"

José explained his plan. If someone asked them, they would say they were from El Departamento de Anatomía de Universidad de Buenos Aires—Professor Alberto de Robertis and his assistant, José de Olmos, looking for suitable cadavers for their work. José showed Lorena's father the drum full of water, ostensibly formalin for fixation of the tissue, the immersed cotton wool to assist in maintaining the shape of the brain. If they were asked their requirements, Señor Scremin would say sudden death in the age bracket eighteen to sixty, with no history of neurologic or psychiatric disorders. They were searching for a normal brain for comparison with their dementia cases. José reassured Lorena's father the morgue staff were upset about the killing of the students, only wanting a credible excuse to allow them to search.

"One more hope," José repeated. "Every time she is not here, we have one more hope."

With Señor Scremin holding on to his arm, he went to the row against the wall and began lifting one sheet and then the next.

In the heart there was only one hope—not to find the one they were searching for.

❧

How many days have I been here?

Lorena could recall the three nights in the cardboard box and something like ten or more in the cell. She should have kept count. Perhaps they would tell her the date—it was not a state secret.

All was quiet. Was the dreadful dawn approaching? She could not tell the time by hunger either, that being a constant. She was given meager portions of boiled potatoes, chicken anuses and whatever was left after the soldiers and officers had eaten. There was, however, a dispensation. After she fainted twice, the doctor who had come to examine her diagnosed hypoglycemic crises and recommended chocolate rations.

Aside from the brief relief from hunger chocolates provided, their wrappings became the paper for her jail diary. The pen she had stolen from her interrogator, when he demanded she write where her friends were hiding, slipping it under the insole of her boot. It was in her boot too where she hid her small diary. She wrote nothing dangerous, just notes on her daily routine.

Tiny though it was, her cell provided an opportunity to walk, something impossible in the cardboard box they had kept her in for those first three nights. And, being warmer, she no longer had to deal with the interrogator offering blankets in exchange for sexual favors. Even the damp and mold were easier to tolerate. The stone walls were painted a gray that seemed to drown any light coming from the small barred window.

The previous day she had been collecting tree branches in the yard, pressing them into bundles as ordered, for use in the sole stove of the building. There, among the sticks, was a plastic cup that she brought back to her cell. She was allowed only three bathroom visits per day and bodily needs became torture at times.

Had everyone abandoned her? José? Her parents? They couldn't have. But where were they? Maybe the police had declared her dead.

Is there nobody searching for me? Have they already held my funeral? An empty coffin. The flowers white. The choir singing off key. Which photo did they put on the coffin? The one with the red skirt from the holidays is not good. My mother would have picked that one, but my mouth is twisted.

Into her mind came the boy she had left behind, that day when every life seemed to hang by a thread. Could she have saved him had she stayed? How did his parents learn of his death? Did they know she had tried, and that she was sorry? *What difference would it make, now that their boy was dead?*

She could be certain of nothing, especially the wisdom of starting the protest.

Lorena could hear birds outside. Morning. Soon the sky began to lighten, the signal that, once again, she would face her interrogator. Sure enough, she could hear the footsteps of the guards approaching her cell.

The interrogator handed her a blank sheet of paper and, as he had day after day, told her to write what she knew about the students involved in the protest. Before, she had refused to write anything at all, but now she started writing whatever fiction she could think of, anything to gain a little peace, to ward off the constant harassment.

Her interrogator unbuttoned his shirt, revealing a scar on his abdomen. "You did this to me. You gave me these ulcers."

Tightly curled, graying hair covered his expansive belly. "That had nothing to do with me. Anyway, it looks like a gallbladder incision."

"Don't talk back to me."

"Come on, I want you to make me feel a little better. You can tell me what it is that turns you on. What gets you going when you have sex with the other environmentalist vermin?"

Lorena put her head down, trying to ignore him. Her hair, filthy and greasy, hung in front of her face. He pulled up her chin, forcing her to look at him. She could smell tobacco and rotten teeth. His demands were never-ending. Most of all, he wanted to know what excited her when she had sex.

"I am a prisoner, not a prostitute."

"You are what I want you to be. You Earth-idiots have fewer rights than the *putas* anyway."

"One day we will be free and then *you* will have to answer."

"Our cemetery already has a few *putas* who said these things."

"The torturers of the Dirty War had to face justice."

"A sweet *puta* should shut her mouth and open her legs. Just answer the question."

Lorena wanted the bizarre interrogation to end. Looking down, she saw her boots, which now had no straps. "I like them to wear boots with straps."

The inquisitor dashed outside. "I tell you what turns her on ..."

༚

The shouts of the tormentors and the screams of the tormented seemed to come from inside her cell, there being no masking noise from revving motorcycles that morning.

A few days had passed since the degrading interrogation. It was almost noon, but there was no let-up in the torture of the others.

In the middle of the commotion, Lorena found herself being escorted outdoors and made to stand facing a wooden shack. All she could think was that they were going to execute her. *I refused to betray the others and now I am useless to them.* She had a fleeting urge to start giving names, to betray everyone, to betray José. Anything so she might be spared. She literally bit her tongue to keep the words from spilling out.

She was now close to the shack, a crumbling structure made of scrap timber, mostly plyboard, without even a door. A soldier pointed at the opening. "Go," he said. "You have five minutes."

"Five minutes for what?"

She entered it with hesitation, but smiled inside when she saw the water pipe. After God knows how long without washing, she had been dreaming of a shower. Her hair, lank and oily, was matted with knots impossible to comb out with her fingers. It felt like filth had embedded itself under her skin. Her terror subsided to be replaced by shame when she realized four soldiers were going to watch her undress.

Fighting to feel detached, she undressed. Her skin crawling under the stare of the soldiers, she turned her back on them and stepped under the flow of cold water. Without soap, she was reduced to scraping the dirt off with her nails, leaving a crisscross of red tracks over her body. There was no floor in the shack and quickly the ground turned to mud, and as the rest of her body got cleaner, her feet got dirtier.

She ran her fingers through her wet hair, trying to untangle it. A soldier whistled at her and she stopped showering, afraid standing naked for long would be misunderstood. Having no towel, she wrung out her hair and shook the water from her body. Every bit of her skin was rough with goose bumps. Still wet, she quickly stepped back into her dirty clothes.

As she was led away from the relative shelter of the shack, the wind made her gasp. Teeth chattering, she was taken to a different area of the prison, to a small room guarded by a single soldier sitting in the corner near the entrance. On the other side of the room there was a table and three chairs. She sat in one of them, shivering, rubbing her arms and legs with her hands to regain warmth.

"Why am I here?" she asked the soldier. "What's happening?"

The others would call her *puta* and Earth-idiot. He did not react, not even to acknowledge he heard her.

She had been allowed to shower. Why? Were they just cleaning her so they could violate her body before killing her? *Am I being allowed a trial? Are they transferring me? How will José ever find me?*

Lorena had no idea how much time had passed, only that she had stopped shivering and her hair was almost dry. A new soldier entered the room, looked her over and left without saying a word. Her arms and legs were restless. From dreadful death to sweet release the possibilities were endless. All she could do was wait.

"You have visitors," said the soldier near the entrance, startling her.

She had begun thinking of him as a gargoyle—ugly, immovable and unresponsive. "Who? Who is coming?"

As though he had returned to stone, no response came. Had he even heard her? Lorena was too elated to be concerned with him. She was going to have visitors—news from the outside world.

A dark voice rose up within her. *These people are devious.* What if he said this to make her more manageable?

Jumping at even the smallest sound, she waited. Hoping the guard's words were true, she imagined José walking through the door. Any moment now, he would stroll in, call her "Magnificent Marmoset," and take her out of this place forever.

⁂

When the door finally opened, all she could see was the figure of the soldier who had checked on her earlier. He blocked the entire doorway and she could not make out who was behind him. Her heart rose to her throat. He stepped inside, holding the door open for—

"Papá, Mamá!" she cried.

She ran to her father, who wrapped his arms around her. It felt safe in his embrace. Her mother clung to them both.

Lorena felt ashamed for a moment—she had not even considered the possibility *they* might be the visitors; now she was elated.

"Keep your distance," the soldier ordered. "You on one side of the table and the visitors on the other."

"*Mi hija hermosa*—my beautiful daughter!" Her father reached his hand across the table to grasp hers. "What have they done to you?"

"No contact," said the soldier, who was now standing over them, the gun by his side unholstered.

Slowly her father withdrew his hand. "We love you, Lorena."

Her mother had also sat opposite. "This cake was in one piece, but they cut it up because of security—"

"Why didn't he come with you?"

Her parents did not respond. She felt the hair on the back of her neck stand up. "Where is he? Why isn't he here?" she asked.

"He managed to get this visit through Amnesty," her father replied. "But he is now missing; he hasn't been seen for days."

As her father said this, back turned to the soldiers, he pulled down on his lower eyelid with his index finger. This was his signal whenever he wanted to cancel out something her mother was saying. "Missing" did not mean killed by the junta. *He is alive,* she thought. *He must be hiding.*

"I can't believe we've lost him. How can I live without him?" she said as convincingly as she could, raising a finger to her face herself, so her words would in turn be discounted. Of course, in hiding, José was hardly out of danger with an army after him, but at least he was alive.

"Do you know how the others are? The other ones who were arrested."

"No one is telling us anything. We didn't even know where you were until a week ago. The first place I went to look for you was ..."

He stopped.

"The morgue," said her mother.

Lorena covered her mouth with her hand.

He extended his hand to caress her bruised cheek. "This must be tender and your skin feels so dry. Does it hurt when I touch?"

"This is the first human touch, Papá."

"*Mi hija hermosa*, why have they done this to you?"

"They are asking me about the others. But they're the ones who know the truth. We are either in prison or dead. I have no information. Papá, you have lost so much weight."

"They don't know how mistaken they are, *mi hija*. You are the daughter of an officer who fought for Argentina; who was injured in the Malvinas. Our family is loyal to our country. They are holding you by mistake." She knew why he was shouting all these things. "I have spoken with the Archbishop," he continued, voice trembling. "José was in contact with Amnesty before he disappeared. It's a mistake you are here. We will bring you home soon." He held her chin up and now she was looking into his brown eyes, the color of her own. "Do not cry, *mi hija*; you will be home soon."

She nodded to him and tried to smile. "Did José come to see you before he disappeared?"

"He did," said her father. "And he sent you apples and strawberries, but they are not allowed here. He also wrote you a note, which they kept. What can you see from your cell? Or is there no window?"

"There is a window with bars. I can see a brick wall and the green roof of a house. And the sky. Did you read what he wrote?"

Her mother leaned backward. "*He* is all you ask about. That nasty *vagabundo* who got you into this mess."

"No, Mamá, of course I want to know how you are too. Of course I do."

"How do you think we are? Because of his *diabólicas* ideas, you have shamed us and now—"

"That's not true."

"Your poor papá, *Dios lo ayude*—God help him. He is suffering so much; it's straining his heart. We are in disgrace. Why did you have to help that boy?"

"That's not fair. You have to understand. I am here because of *my* ideas. It is not José's fault."

"It's all his fault. This is the thanks he gives our family—ingratitude for grace."

"If not for him you wouldn't even be visiting me now. I am responsible for what I did. We were doing the right thing."

"How could it be the right thing if you end up here? Our only child in prison like a common *puta*."

"You know, Mamá, that's what the guards call me too."

Her parents did not speak and she continued, "If that's how you feel, why did you even come?"

Her father extended a hand to caress her hair. "We came because we love you, Lorena. No matter what you did, you are our daughter and we love you." His touch, his voice, his words were soft. "We are not alone. My friends in the army will help us," she heard him say.

The soldier who brought them in came close. "*Señora y Señor*, it is time for you to leave."

Lost in the argument with her mother, Lorena had forgotten she was a prisoner. Reality struck her. Her parents would return home, but she to her cell. Precious time had been wasted arguing. *What if I never see them again?* "Mamá, I am sorry. Papá, I will be home soon."

"*Mi hija hermosa*, be strong, be patient. You're our only family. When we take you out of here, you will dance tango again, and in the best dresses, and in the best shoes. I'll buy them for you."

The visit was so short. When did that door open? When did it close? Please God, keep José *alive even if I never see him again.*

❧

"We cannot go armed," said José.

He was meeting with six medical students to plan a raid on a detention center holding students from the uprising. The group called itself "5 de Marzo," that being the date of the killing of the medical students.

"On the contrary," said the girl sitting next to him. "The *only* way we can go is armed."

He felt an impasse had been reached without their taking as much as the first step. How could he convince them not to adopt the methods of their oppressors? How could he show them there was another way? "By its nature," he said, "the detention center is actually vulnerable. The only thing we need do is to get one of the guards on side and persuade him to leave the cells unlocked. We can free our friends simply by—"

"They will be free and dead," interrupted another girl. "Unless we neutralize the guards first, they'll kill the prisoners and they'll kill us."

All the students spoke, one by one, and often more than one at the same time.

Be evil to correct evil? José was in despair. *Do I abandon my beliefs or do I abandon the effort to free the students? Lorena could be amongst them.*

The evening gave way to the night, and the night to the dawn, but no one was giving an inch. Since well before dawn, they were just repeating themselves.

Was he unreasonable to oppose the consensus? He had objected to the violence against the machines that Alberto had advocated, and was now objecting to violence against the guards when everyone else in 5 de Marzo wanted it. *Maybe Alberto was right—I have a complex against violence. But how do I get rid of it?*

José asked the others to let him try his way first and then, if he failed to free the prisoners, the others could go in with arms.

They did not agree, convinced that once the guards detected the plot, the detention center would be unapproachable. They decided to raid it two days later.

He knew he had little time before violence took more lives—lives of the guards and lives of the prisoners.

It would have been a hard dilemma in which to place anyone, let alone someone he only knew in passing, but he decided to speak to one of the guards at the detention center whom he had seen at mass. If the guard were a true Christian, he might not betray him. He might even risk his life to help the prisoners.

But it was not only *his* life the guard would place in jeopardy. The junta could exact revenge against his family too.

Is my plan anything more than changing the target of the gun?

⁂

The crumbled chocolate cake still rested on Lorena's bed three days later, a reminder of her parents' visit.

She would not eat it.

There had not been an interrogation since and she wondered if it was because of her father's influence. Perversely, without the interruption of interrogations, she had too much time to think and began to fear isolation would drive her mad.

She tried to imagine herself outside with José, just meeting him at the fresh fruit and vegetable markets like before. He would tell her again how difficult it would be to recognize her amongst the flowers. And she would laugh again.

She wanted them to be just normal people living normal lives, walking hand in hand, eating, singing, kissing. But then she remembered the bitter argument with her mother. It was clear that no matter what José did, her mother would never accept him. *As much I love mamá, he is my life.*

Voices in the corridor brought her back to the reality of her cell. She held her breath, but could not make out the words. Then she heard the key turn in the lock and the bolts being drawn. *Are they releasing me?*

Her father had told her to be strong and patient, but perhaps things had moved faster than expected. She followed the two soldiers. There was no shouting, no sarcasm, no abuse as they led her to the interrogator's office. This was not the usual routine. Her hopes were high.

The interrogator did not shout at her either. He sat motionless behind his big desk, a laptop open in front of him, trays holding documents on either side of it. On the shelf behind him was a small Argentinian flag, two blue horizontal stripes framing a white stripe with the image of the golden radiant sun.

"Good morning, pretty girl," said the interrogator.

In a soft voice he told her to undress. A shudder ran down her spine. *Will the soldiers dishonor the flag?* Her breath was short, her mouth dry. Her eyes skittered between the three men; she was a gazelle cornered by three hyenas. There was no place to hide; no escape. The two soldiers came close to her. She felt a hand move up her hip and along her waist. She slapped it away before it reached her breast.

The soldiers twisted her arms behind her back, immobilizing her before throwing her on the floor and pinning down her arms and legs. She tried to scream, but only managed to cry.

The interrogator approached and, with the help of the others, tore off her underpants. He unbuckled his belt and let his pants fall to the floor. "You are a pig," she said. "*Vergüenza nacional*—you are a national shame."

His head was close to her face, but she could not lift her head enough to bite him. She could smell his breath, even taste it. Utterly overpowered, she gathered all the sputum she had.

"*Puta de mierda*—shitty whore. And I left my boots on for you."

Lorena shut her eyes, waiting for the blow. In her darkness, she saw dancing stars. His elbow chipped one of her incisors and split her upper lip.

"*Monstruo grotesco*—grotesque monster," she whispered. Spitting out her tooth, she saw her blood hit his face.

"Cover the whore's mouth."

Someone gagged her. Her legs were forced apart and held open by the soldiers as he mounted her. Eventually, he collapsed on top of her, belly first.

She bit into the gag as she felt his trembling fat mass against her skin. He clambered off her, only to be replaced by the next one.

※

"THE JUNTA CANNOT CONQUER AN AMAZONA"

Lorena rubbed her eyes, but the writing in green letters was still there on the brick wall opposite her cell. She now realized the reason her father had asked what she could see from her window.

Two weeks had passed since her ordeal and for the first time a burst of energy flowed through her. José's message was fresh air entering her lungs. *He is alive and he taunts them. The junta is not invincible.* Perhaps a better day was coming. Perhaps they would free her. She would reclaim her life. *But my body? How can I ever reclaim my body?*

Her period was late. This could be due to stress and poor nutrition, *or perhaps …*

She banged the door with her fists, screaming for the guard. She was almost hoarse by the time he came. "Please, please, I need to see a doctor."

"Are you sick?"

"I might be pregnant."

"That's your problem. Don't make me come back here again."

She stared at the guard as he walked away. Just another snake in this pit. If only she had something to throw at him, to make him feel the pain they were inflicting on her. She looked again at the wall. The writing was what she and José were about. She tried to recall his touch, his scent, his voice, his humor. But the terror of possible pregnancy and HIV infection eliminated all other thoughts.

A bizarre image entered her mind. She was in a helicopter, her swollen belly as big as the interrogator's. Shackled in chains, her skeletonized legs were wasting away from AIDS. And who was the father of her fetus? Was it José or one of the monsters? The interrogator laughed as he opened the helicopter door. Instead of the sky, she saw an expanse of marble. She tried desperately to hold on to the doorframe as he was forcing her out. Further and further out.

※

I will keep going until they listen to me.

Lorena had been noting the days without food in her little diary, uncertain as to when she would no longer be lucid.

On the fourteenth day of her hunger strike, a little after dawn, a young man was let into her cell. He was in civilian clothes and carried a leather case.

Her chest tightened—*The doctor has come to kill me.*

"I'm Dr. Cuello, an intern at the Argerich Hospital," he said with an attempt at a smile.

She could feel her chest ease a little. "I know the hospital. I'm a medical student."

"Tell me what's happened to you."

"I might be pregnant."

"When were you last sexually active?"

She could not respond.

"You are upset," he said after a moment's silence. "Maybe you need to stop thinking about this for a little."

"They pack-raped me."

"I have to ask," he whispered. "Could it have happened before you were imprisoned?"

"I know exactly when it happened."

"I'm so sorry," said the doctor, squeezing her hand. "I'm very sorry."

She pulled her hand away. "Don't touch me."

"No, no. I'm here to help. You are frightened. I understand. Let's just talk."

He asked her name. She told him about her medical studies and became less tense. He then asked if she knew how to diagnose pregnancy.

"Human chorionic gonadotrophin in urine."

"Exactly," he said. "And you must know how to examine a patient's vitals."

"Blood pressure, pulse, respiratory rate, temperature."

"Lorena, will you let me do that now? Tell me if you are uncomfortable, anytime, okay?"

She nodded and allowed him to carry out the basic examination.

"The pulse is fine, but you shake when I touch you. Your sclera is too pale—anemia. You're too thin. You can't stay on hunger strike."

"It was the only way to see a doctor."

"They can't keep you here like this. Your tooth needs attention too."

He gave her a small jar and left the cell.

When he returned, he aspirated some urine with a pipette and placed several drops on the test strip.

While waiting for the result, he examined a wound on her arm that had collected pus. After flinching a few times, she remained still long enough for him to treat it.

Leaning over her arm as he was applying disinfectant, he spoke urgently, "If you are pregnant, better pretend it was a boyfriend. Whom do I notify?"

"José de Olmos," she whispered back. "Humberto Primo 1569, Apartment 3."

She saw a line of ants marching on her windowsill. Unimpeded by the bars, the ants were going in and out of the jail. Beyond the bars, the sun was shining for everyone, but her.

❦

"No, my child. I've asked you to the confessional so that *I* can tell you something. I know it is risky for you to come here, a risk for the rest of us too, but our Lorena is in danger. She is pregnant."

"She … She is … She's still alive! Who told you, Father?"

"Dr. Cuello. She is unwell, anemic and on hunger strike."

"Father, can I email Amnesty?"

"The doctor suggested you do so, but be careful how much you reveal. Other lives hang on this."

Quickly José tried to type his email, but slowly came the writing and it was laced with errors. He went over it multiple times.

Her jailers will likely exercise one of two options—either kill her now or kill her after she gives birth. You would certainly be aware of *los desaparecidos*, how entire classes of medical students disappeared during the Dirty War, how the military would keep a pregnant prisoner alive until she gave birth, appropriate her baby and …

He knew that Lorena's father, although unaware of the pregnancy, had approached Archbishop Aguayo, who had written to the President requesting leniency.

Surrounded by the wooden walls of the confessional, José was certain of only one thing—this time the Catholic Church was on the side of the angels …

Chapter 12

A MARBLE BABY

In a moment I will be outside these walls, Lorena thought as she followed the soldier to the gate. *But no matter how far I go, the jail will be there—at the end of every road.*

"My beautiful girl, José is waiting for us." Martíta enfolded her in her arms, then quickly stood back. "Let's hurry before they change their minds."

Holding hands, they rushed away from the gate.

"I insisted he should wait two blocks from here. The army and the police have been searching for him since the jail breakout."

"The jail breakout?"

"They freed three prisoners. A yacht took them to Montevideo. And you would be proud of your father and José. My beautiful daughter, I can't believe you're here."

Martíta told her how her father, when he met José at the morgue, put him in contact with a yacht owner sympathetic to the students, and how José managed to free the prisoners without anyone getting injured.

On turning the corner, Lorena saw José running toward her. Breathless, she stopped. His arms closed around her as she buried her face in his neck. *It has been so long without hearing the beat of another heart. And it is his.*

She breathed in the fragrance of his body. Her fingers curled tightly around the fabric of his shirt. It was her José.

"Magnificent Marmoset, it's over." He murmured the words against her hair. "You will be with us forever."

"I will, *mi amor*, I will."

She could feel the vibration of his voice as he continued, "Mum made empanadas to give you energy. Remember the fruit you brought me after the hospital?"

With an arm around her waist, he led her to the waiting taxi. Before getting in, he hugged her again and she heard him say, "I am sorry about this, but you really need to decide. Your father wants you; he is desperate to see you, but your mother …"

"Can I come home with you, please?"

José kissed her lips. "Home is not the one you know. Silvia is hiding me. We'll stay there for now."

"What if they are following us; what if they arrest you?"

"I've been watching. Nobody is following us. The junta is too busy with its internal conflicts now. It's about to collapse."

They all sat in the back and José gave the address to the driver. "We will soon be at our hiding place," he said to her. "And you can finally rest."

There was a tango waltz playing, the driver humming along. Lorena was about to cry. José leaned forward and asked him to turn it off.

"I'm so proud of my father," she said as they got out of the taxi. "But I know they won't approve."

He held her in his arms.

Martíta hugged her too. "We'll be here for you no matter what— no matter what you decide," she said. "I couldn't have loved you more if you were my daughter."

Maybe I will be able to put my past behind me, Lorena thought. *In all my misery, I could not have hoped for better arms to hold me.*

ꝫ⳥

Her own shouts woke her up early in the morning.

The sheets were tangled around her and she was struggling for air.

"Magnificent Marmoset," she heard José's voice. "What is it?"

"I dreamt I was still there. It seemed so real. Hold me, please."

"You're home with me. You're safe now. You too kept me safe. Remember? You're safe with me."

"Please, don't let them come for me ..."

"Nobody will come. Just close your eyes and remember our first date. Give me your hand, like that first time in the cinema. Let me hold you."

She found her breath, but images from the nightmare were still flickering before her eyes. "Tell me you won't leave me, please."

"I will hold your hand forever."

Her heart slowed down and her breathing became more even.

There was a smell of frying bacon. Silvia must have heard them and was preparing breakfast. Holding hands, they entered the kitchen. After hugging Silvia, she headed for the bathroom.

The night before, her friend had guided her there, to the tub already full with fragrant water. After helping Lorena take off her clothes, Silvia had become agitated on seeing the sores over her arms. When she asked if they hurt, Lorena had not answered, afraid she would cry if she revealed how the burns had been made. Silvia helped her into the bath, warm water coming up to her chin. She had felt the buoyancy and had breathed the sharp, sweet smell of lavender oil.

She had avoided looking in the mirror the day before, but now she examined herself. *What has become of me?* There was the broken incisor. Her bones protruded at the shoulders. Her breasts had become a little larger though, tiny pink stretch marks extending like a spider's web on their underside. Her nipples were a slightly darker shade of brown. Though small, the curve at her lower abdomen was visible. Running her hand across it, she could feel a definite bump.

When she returned to the kitchen, Silvia began serving the bacon and the vegetable omelet. "You look so much better today."

"I feel better."

José kissed her forehead, nose and lips, before leaving to attend a meeting of 5 de Marzo.

Silvia then sat next to her at the table. "Your father called me. He wants to come and take you home."

"No, not now. I know he is worried, but I'll speak to him when I'm ready."

"Are you sure that's what you want?"

"It's impossible for me otherwise, Silvia. If I don't do this, I will never leave that jail."

"Listen to me, Lorena, just for one minute please. José knew we would talk."

"José—I can't…"

"He asked me to tell you he will help you whatever you decide. If you decide to keep it, he would love it as much as he loves you; that's exactly what he told me."

"I can't do it. I just can't. You weren't there, Silvia. Rape is a horrible thing."

"I know. I'm so sorry … I can't imagine."

Lorena rubbed her temples. "I can't talk to José about it. I don't think I'll ever be able to."

"You can speak to me whenever you're ready. We used to tell each other everything."

"But how can I talk about something I can't even stand thinking about? I try to imagine it never happened. But then at night everything comes back. There is no floodgate I can close. No crack I can escape through."

⁂

How do I ask for forgiveness before committing the sin?

It made no sense, but this was exactly what Lorena had done earlier that afternoon when praying to the Virgin for mercy.

Now, a few hours later, walking on the poorly lit street, she felt that everyone knew what she was about to do; surely her swollen belly betrayed her. *Or is it only me who can see it?*

Next to her walked Martíta and Silvia, silent for the entire walk to the private clinic. There was no indication it was anything but a residence. She caught herself thinking this was just a routine visit and all that had passed had been a dream. Then a middle-aged man ushered them through a dark hallway to the brightly lit surgery at the back where the anesthetist was waiting.

"It's me; I am the one," explained Lorena, noticing the gynecologist's puzzled look.

She held Silvia's hand as the doctor examined her.

"You should've come earlier," he eventually said. "It's possible, but now there are greater risks and it could affect future pregnancies."

"You know the reason I must proceed, Doctor…"

"You are not a picture of health either," he said after finishing the examination.

He left the room to return in scrubs, carrying more for the others. He had sent his assistant home just before they arrived.

Lorena smelled something sweet as she breathed deeply through the mask the anesthetist was holding.

When she woke, she saw Silvia and Martíta leaning over her.

The doctor explained that he had had to remove a lot of tissue, that it would be difficult for her to conceive again. "But it's over," he said. "I'll let you know the HIV and hepatitis B results as soon as they're available."

It's over, Lorena repeated to herself. *But so is my hope for a child.*

"The body has ways of healing, my beautiful girl," said Martíta. "Time will heal everything."

Time, Lorena thought. *What is the use of time if the past finds new ways to torment the future?*

⁂

My beautiful Lorena. Her body has been abused twice.

José held Lorena gently as they walked into the bedroom. She lay on the bed, her head in his lap, while he caressed her hair. "How are you feeling, my Marmoset?" he asked.

"Terrible. But less of a prisoner," her voice just above a whisper.

How beautiful she is, he thought. *But how can I make her believe she is still beautiful? How can I make her feel free?*

She spoke again. "I knew I was not doing the right thing by the little life, but I thought I was doing the right thing by me. And now it turns out it might have been my last chance."

"We will always have each other and there are so many children to love. Children who need love. Amongst them we'll find our child."

She buried her face in his hands. "You would have been the best father in the world."

He kept caressing her.

"*Mi amor,*" she said, "what's going to happen to all the people still in jail?"

"5 de Marzo will make another attempt very soon. We will free as many as we can. In any case, the news is that the junta is on its last legs."

"And the doctor who diagnosed me? He was so gentle. I want us to find him."

"I didn't want to tell you earlier. Dr. Cuello disappeared. He let me know about you through a priest and even suggested I inform Amnesty. The military police must have suspected him."

"Has there been no news?"

"No. He was not one of the junta's doctors. Dr. Cuello was a good man. I feel terrible I exposed him to danger."

"This is horrible, José. If only he has managed to go into hiding. What he must have suffered. What about his parents? Does he have a wife, children?"

"I avoided contacting his relatives. It would have been even more dangerous for them."

"When will the bad news end? When will people stop running to hide from their death." She shook her head.

"Last night," she continued, "I dreamt I was in an explosion. Limbs were everywhere and in the middle of it I was giving birth ... I was giving birth to a marble baby."

Chapter 13

AT THE ÁRVORE VELHA

If only I could chase away her nightmares, José kept thinking while half-listening to the talks.

Even six months after being freed, Lorena was still having recurrent nightmares—giving birth to the same marble baby. She had not come with him, still uncomfortable with crowds, especially near strange men. And there were a few silent figures that evening, men José had never seen in previous meetings. The junta was losing its grip, but, as an insect that stings before its death, it was still a menace.

Before the talks, José had spoken with an elegant old lady seated next to him. They were at a fundraising dinner held by environmentalists under the guise of a church function at the Hotel Chile. Nearly a hundred people attended to raise funds to save the Magellan penguin of Patagonia. In a severe storm during the previous December, eighty percent of new chicks had died, exacerbating the effects of habitat loss on an already declining population.

When the formalities were over, the lady seated on his other side whispered to him that he was actually talking to Dr. Chichina Ferreyra, the first girlfriend of Che Guevara.

"Really? He is my hero. Do you think she'd mind if I asked her about Che?"

"Try her."

Perhaps this was not the safest time to bring up the name of his hero, but he turned to face Dr. Ferreyra. "Is it true you knew Che?"

"I knew Ernesto."

He noticed one of the strange men was glancing at them and led the doctor to the bar. "I admire him," he said once they had distanced themselves. "He risked his life for the public good. I smile in pain when I look at his poster on my wall."

"I don't know what exactly you admire in him. Before, you said you are for peaceful resistance. He was a violent man—he said, '*Uno, dos, tres, cuatro, muchos* Vietnam.'"

"There was violence, Dr. Ferreyra, but he took the side of the oppressed. The environmental movement needs people like him. Not for his use of violence, but for his commitment. Don't you think?"

"What I think he and his friend cared about was to see their names written in history. They made our local dictators suppress us even more." She reached over to adjust the collar of his shirt. "You see, sometimes it's hard to know the difference between a hero and someone on an ego trip."

"I've read there were many people upset at Guevara's assassination; there were even church services."

"Church services for Ernesto? Bah, *qué tontería*—what nonsense! He told me if Christ walked on the Earth now, he would squash Him like this ..." She gestured with her thumb as if squashing an ant.

"And yet, Christ and Guevara had similar ideals, though different methods."

"Ernesto wasn't a nice man, José. He abandoned his wife."

I am not getting anywhere this way, he thought and asked, "Did it hurt you when they killed him?"

Chichina looked at him as though to read the motive behind his provocative question. Eventually she said, "Yes, it did." She glanced at her watch. "Stay back and I will show you something."

José accepted eagerly.

"But let me ask you something too, young man. You're Catholic, aren't you? Some Germans stayed in the Nazi Party to reform it, but eventually even they gave up. Isn't it time for you to leave a church that discriminates against women and promotes overpopulation with its ban on protection in sex?"

"Look at it this way, Dr. Ferreyra. This function is under the auspices of the Church." He excused himself to farewell some people.

After nearly everyone else had gone, Chichina approached him. "How are you now?"

"Still with the Nazis," he replied as he indicated a table.

She reached across the table to caress his face and then opened a small envelope to show him photos of his hero—photos never published. One of them showed Che and Chichina sitting on the ground at the forecourt of a building drinking *mate*. Another showed him riding a motorcycle during his famous tour of South America, where he was radicalized. Che had written on the front of the photo, "To my followers in Argentina."

"I showed them to you," said Chichina, "so you can see Ernesto was simply a man, just like you; not a hero, not an idol, not Che."

⁊⁊

It was a small achievement—a letter published in *Página/12*.

But for José it was an important step, his first letter in a major newspaper, and it came on the heels of victory—the overthrow of tyranny. The medical students were freed; the political prisoners were freed; the exiles were coming home. He felt pride in Argentina. The mothers, the fathers, the sons and the daughters would be together for Christmas. Together they would welcome the new year.

Holding hands, he and Lorena arrived at the bar where Silvia was waiting for them with Marcello, a psychology student. Marcello sported a bald head, having shaved his afro to raise funds for research into post-traumatic stress disorder in released prisoners. His mixed African–Italian descent had granted him dark skin and contrasting blue eyes.

No sooner did they order than Marcello pulled out his phone. "Let me read you this famous letter," he said. 'How can it be that Israelis and Palestinians still bomb each other while humanity falters and fades? What is the meaning of the works of Aristotle, Newton and Einstein when intelligence extinguishes itself? The recent disappearance of Pacific islands under the waves shows the sinking of the Earth to be more than a metaphor and—'"

"Not so loud," whispered Lorena, tightly holding on to José.

"Nobody is spying on us, beloved friend," said Marcello. "It's just a matter of extinguishing your conditioned fear, as your psychologist would have told you. Keep close to us in all places and there will be fear extinction before you know it."

"Marcello, if you were as good an environmentalist as you are a psychologist, you'd be perfect," said Silvia.

Marcello cut two white flowers from the creeping jasmine and gave them to the girls, who simultaneously kissed him on the cheek. "For your love, I would scuttle skepticism."

"Look, look, señoritas," said José, "skepticism has metastasized from coal-mining executives to psychology students."

"It's nice to see you pugnacious, *mi amor*, but please not so loud."

José stroked her hair and bent to whisper in her ear, "Magnificent Marmoset, we're safe now. The junta is in trouble. Let me hold you tight. I want you to feel safe."

"But, Marcello," said Silvia, "if we don't know the consequences of what we are doing, we shouldn't do it."

"Sublime Silvia," said Marcello, "using fear instead of rational arguments to force behavioral change is precisely what religious fundamentalists do. As a skeptic, I demand proof."

"Fine then," José replied. "Let's reverse the burden of proof. Prove to me that burning fossil fuels will not unhinge the climate."

Silvia came up with counter arguments until Marcello raised his hands in mock surrender. "Okay, I give up. It's times like these I wish we had more sycophants and fewer environmentalists."

"And something else," said Lorena in hushed tones as she clung to José's arm. "This is not about models, but about what *has* happened. In the last five years Brazil has lost an area of forest three times the size of Switzerland."

"On the forest I'm with you, but I am not falling for the rest," said Marcello.

"Then, I have something for all of us," said José. "I've been meaning to tell you, but wanted to figure out some things first. Just think of this: the four of us organizing a Pan-American collective to protect the Amazon through peaceful resistance."

꩜

José nudged Marcello. "If Don Quixote tilted his sword at windmills which caused him no trouble, why shouldn't we put a spanner in the works of this company?"

Marcello was visiting José to do research for Resistência Pacifica, the organization they founded to network people concerned about the Amazon Rainforest. They were huddled over a computer at the kitchen table trying to obtain live images of the logging operation, but it was not possible.

"You've jumped up and down before on things that have proved fictitious. This time, though, you're chasing shadows of fleeting ghosts."

"They are damaging ghosts, *amigo* Marcello. The tour guide wouldn't lie. We have to find out what's happening south of Manaus."

"The only evidence we have is this report of a single tour guide. We can't mobilize Resistência Pacifica without solid evidence. Since we can't get satellite images, we have to go there."

"Of all people, you are the one who knows about post-traumatic stress disorder, Marcello. Lorena may not be strong enough for me to leave her."

"She is progressing well, but, yes, she might regress from worrying about you. You are a worry even in Buenos Aires."

"Let's talk to her." José put his phone on speaker. "Magnificent Marmoset, I'm here with Marcello. We can't confirm the tour guide's report. We need somebody on the ground to tell us what's happening south of Manaus."

Her voice came through clearly, "The Brazilians are the logical ones to ask and you speak Portuguese. Call them."

"Would you feel okay if Marcello and I went? You know, it'll be just for gathering information on what's going on."

"This is not Curitiba where you grew up, José. The Amazon is the most dangerous place in the world for environmentalists."

He took the phone off speaker and walked into his bedroom. "Magnificent Marmoset, it's just me now."

"José, what about me? I'm not sure I want you to go. This will be the first time we will be apart since ..."

"We've always said keeping the fight is keeping true to what brought us together. But we won't sacrifice your health for our convictions. In any case, we don't need to decide for weeks."

"I know it's the right thing for Resistência. I know this fight is important for us, but, *mi amor* ..."

Did I do the right thing to even ask? he reflected. *She has been through enough already.*

❧

José looked at the distant shore they had left behind and the distant shore they were sailing toward. Between the shores flowed the Amazon.

How difficult it is for love and this fight to co-exist, he thought. *Our love was born in this fight, but the fight could consume it. I should tell her all I feel for her as well as all I feel for this fight. Then it will be up to her to decide.*

"*Compañeros,*" called out Carlos, the law student who was their Brazilian contact. "Have you ever seen anything like this?" As they sailed downstream and across the river, there was a sharp change in the color of the water, one side dark, the other light, both reflecting the setting sun.

"It's Río Negro joining Río Solimões to give birth to the Amazon," continued Carlos. "The two rivers originate in different catchment areas of the Amazon Basin and have different temperature, different acidity and different color. Río Solimões carries more mud, yellow mud, and so it appears lighter. At Manaus, they run in parallel, their waters mixing hardly at all."

It seemed as though a knife had divided the rivers, except where eddies from the yellow river invaded the dark river to follow its flow, and the converse.

It was dusk by the time they arrived at the guesthouse, a hut with thatched walls and roof set in a clearing abutting the river and surrounded by towering jungle on the other sides. Run by a local family, it catered mostly for researchers and eco-tourists.

They were led to a small room with bunk beds, spartan but clean. Angelo, their tour guide, insisted they rest early, but José was drawn to the forest sounds. In the darkness, it felt as though the river was carrying him deeper and deeper into the heart of the jungle. The susurrus of the breeze through leaves was the background music that was punctuated by short sharp staccato calls, long cries and even whispers in the mystery of communication of the creatures of the dark.

☙

Birdcalls had replaced the polyphony of the night.

José began to get into the rhythm and started paying more attention to the tropical forest, which by now was all but drowning the track, forcing the four of them to follow each other's steps. He looked up. Just then they were passing by a palm tree with glossy green leaves and some ferns with pale young leaves and darker older ones. Sunrays unfiltered by the canopy bounced off some leaves, while filling others with light to make them glow. The shadows became darker as the light skirted branches and trunks in its impeded journey to the ground. Some tree trunks, straight and slender, were covered in thick green moss. These trunks supported the emergent trees that penetrated the united foliage of the canopy. Other trunks of older trees, wider than the span of his arms, played host to stag horns. Vines draped themselves over branches to dangle like curtains. For a moment, he wondered if he could swing through the forest from vine, to vine, to vine. Younger trees were awaiting their turn for their day in the sun. Growing on the bushes and on the ground were flowers—crimson, orange, bright yellow, some shaped like birds.

More than anywhere else he had been, this place spoke of God. *If only she were here with me. If we could live this moment together.* "How could anyone see this and not believe in the divine?" he said, hardly conscious he was saying it aloud. "Why would anyone want to harm this place?"

"For money, José," replied Marcello. "That's the short and the long answer."

After about three hours of solid uphill hiking, they heard the sound of falling water and soon enough they reached a creek with a small waterfall. For lunch, they sat around the cascade, on fallen trunks, soft from the brown moss that grew on them, fallen leaves, gold and yellow, at their feet.

After lunch, Angelo, machete in hand, guided them away from the track, moving for hours through dense forest. Blindly following him, they fought foliage and hidden roots until the hours of the day came to an end.

They set up a tent, the half-moon high above them. Around the campfire, Angelo told them stories of pumas, jaguars and alligators. He warned, if they heard a "tac-tac" sound it would not be from a branch breaking. "It will be a jaguar stalking you."

"Angelo, Carlos tells us you are descended from the Amanyé," said Marcello.

"That's right. My grandfather taught me about the forest when I was a child. During his time, the old life began to change. There are only a few of us now who still know these things, like where to find food, or how to find our way through the jungle."

"How do you feel about the flooding of the valley?" asked José.

"As you would if they put Buenos Aires under Río de la Plata."

"The principal problem is the dam," said Carlos, placing some more wood on the fire. "An added problem is the logging. They are not confining themselves to the area to be flooded. They are taking trees from far away."

"Surely you would have laws against that," said Marcello.

"So you would think. The problem is that the companies draft the laws that are supposed to regulate them."

"Timber theft happens all the time," Angelo added. "It's usually ranchers turning forest into pastureland, but this is different."

"Angelo, how far afield is TerraDyname cutting trees?" asked José.

"You'll see for yourself in the morning. When I first saw it, I felt nauseous. My grandfather told me many, many times that we must only take from the forest in ways that cannot be felt by the river." He shook his head. "This is the opposite. They're taking everything."

☙

The wind brought with it the smell of sawdust.

For as far as José could see there were felled trees. The hills were shaven. The valley was naked.

By late morning the four of them had reached a hill crowned by a large boulder. José had climbed the rock and from this vantage point he was now looking at the operation through binoculars. Before him was a large area completely denuded—all the trees were lying on the ground, except seedlings standing as infants watching over their parents' corpses. Trunks, being lighter in color, stood out against the deep green foliage. *This is the end of magic,* he thought.

Bright yellow machines confronted the remaining trees, their huge tires crushing low-lying vegetation. Though the machinery was massive, the tree line ahead dwarfed it. A procession of trucks full of tree trunks snaked its way to the river. On their backs they carried thick logs and thin logs, and all sizes in between. "This is the funeral of the forest," he said.

"I have to show you this," Angelo said, pointing at a huge tree beyond the logging operation. "The Árvore Velha."

José saw its crown, bright green and symmetrical, towering above neighboring trees. It easily reached thirty meters. "Of all the things we have seen, this is the most majestic," he said as they all stood looking at it.

A gunshot, followed by its echo, shattered the silence.

"Everyone down," shouted Angelo. More gunshots followed. "Let me find out where they are shooting from …"

It was not clear whether the shots had been aimed to frighten or to kill them.

"They are over at the equipment. We can only risk a few seconds to get some photos and footage."

To the sound of gunfire, Angelo used a high-resolution camera, while the others took photos and videos with their phones. "And now we go," he said, ushering them back into the forest.

José felt his heart pounding his chest. The horror of the crime against the forest continued to well up, until nothing else was in his mind.

The guide did not allow them to stop until they reached their campsite of the previous night.

As they sat down, Marcello opened his arms. "So many trees on the ground! So many machines!"

"The harvester speeds up the whole thing," explained Carlos, still panting. "The man in the cabin can use it to cut the tree at the base, cutting straight through the trunk. The other knives can delimb very quickly. With it, one man can chop down a huge number of trees. Those with the pincers at the front are grapple skidders. They're used to transport the trunks."

"The Árvore Velha—the Old Tree," Angelo recommenced his story, "my grandfather told me a *mogno* tree takes a few human lifetimes to grow, so you must think hard before you cut one. Those mahogany trees are almost extinct here because they have the best-quality wood for furniture. As you saw, the tree stands on the top of a small hill at the end of the valley. They've got to go through her to get to the next valley."

"So, if we stop them from cutting the Árvore Velha," said José, "we force them to build a new road to access the next valley. They will have to go around the mountain, or start again from the river."

"A new road will be expensive," said Marcello, "so, they won't hurry into it."

"If the Árvore Velha is lost, the next valley will be lost," said Angelo. "If you want me, I will guide your volunteers."

José saw a swarm of butterflies tightly bunched on the ground. With their vertical light green wings, they resembled sailing boats. Some were taking off, others were landing to join the cluster.

He thought even their conversation could disrupt the lives of these butterflies. If Resistência Pacifica made a stand, the protesters would be more vulnerable than the butterflies. Unarmed volunteers would be fighting a company with a budget bigger than that of some countries.

To his mind came Alberto. If the professor disappeared for some speeches in Buenos Aires, what would their fate be in the jungle? Starting this fight would not only mean total devotion, but also enormous risk.

His mind returned once more to Lorena. *Together we can fight for the forest, but only if she is able to. I should not step into this if she needs me near her. Even if she doesn't come here, she still lives inside me. And so does my mother. Each of us lives inside everyone else and the loss of one can only be the loss of the other.*

Book Three

CHRISTOPHER

Chapter 14

FAREWELL

I never told her how much I loved her.

Christopher looked beyond his mother's coffin, at the altar, which in the Greek Orthodox tradition no woman was allowed to approach.

The iconostasis, pierced by three arched doorways, was the most ornate wall in the church. Saints in jeweled robes and golden haloes stood in their private recesses, either killing wildlife or blessing anyone who turned their gaze at them. *There is no consolation to be found on this wall,* he thought.

Unwelcome memories of the last months swirled through his mind. That lunchtime he had come from the university, his mother telling him what she herself had learned hours earlier. The moment he heard the diagnosis after surgery—he was there when she was told a malignant cancer in her right temporal lobe had invaded her frontal and parietal lobes and spread to the other hemisphere—a butterfly glioma. "I've experienced one miracle," she had said, looking his way. "I might be lucky again."

It took a while to accept he was losing her. One morning, he had gone to the hospital earlier than usual. It was before visiting hours, but a nurse nodded to him to enter. He had quietly pulled aside the blue paper curtain surrounding Evelyn's bed. She was sound asleep, face slack, mouth half open. Her skin, smooth, almost translucent, was stretched thin over her bones. During his previous visits, she had always worn brightly colored scarves tied like turbans, claiming she could finally put them to use. For the first time the shaven head confronted him. The red-raw half-moon incision branded her for what she was—a brain cancer patient.

Placing the local newspaper and the latest copy of *Scientific American* on her table, he had sat in the visitor's chair. This close, he could smell her jasmine perfume under the disinfectant. He shut his eyes.

"You are early," she said.

Her voice had startled him. "I skipped rowing. I brought you the local rag and your magazine."

"I don't like you skipping training. Besides, it doesn't give me time to get ready."

"Mum, it's just me; you don't have to get dressed up or anything."

"I know that, my beautiful boy." She gently hit his hand. "But I like to." An attempt at a smile stretched her gaunt cheeks. "Tell you what. Go and get me an espresso from downstairs."

He had returned to find her looking bright, almost healthy, the way she usually did. The color of her turban, green that day, matched her eyes and brought out the pink on her cheeks. The blush on her face was not a promise she would get well. *Women wear make-up to enhance their looks,* he had thought, *but my mother to hide she is dying.*

"Do you remember when we cycled in the park, Mum?"

"And we will cycle again, my beautiful boy," she had replied. "And then, we will go to the backyard and roll down the slope. The whole length of it."

But as the weeks passed, she lost interest in everything, including him. Christopher felt he was speaking to himself when he talked to her about the news or about their neighbors. Sometimes he wondered if it was worth talking to her at all, but then would feel guilty. Her face, increasingly sallow, was no longer hidden under make-up. He doubted she could apply it, even if she wanted to. He had tried to encourage her to at least keep wearing a turban, but she didn't seem to notice when he would put one on her head. She didn't care about her appearance anymore. But *he* cared. He wanted her to want to look her best. To be the Evelyn he knew.

On one of his visits, Dr. Matheson had asked her if he could borrow Christopher for a few minutes. She nodded listlessly and the doctor led him into the hallway.

"How are you coping?"

"It's like it's not her anymore." Christopher looked away, throat tight. "It's as if it's not my mum in that bed."

"I'm sorry," the doctor had said. "The areas involved with attention, motivation and planning are being invaded by branches of the tumor that weren't excised."

"Is there anything I can do?"

"The best thing you can do is what you're doing now—keep visiting, be there for her." A nurse had interrupted them briefly. "And another thing," he continued. "You will find she'll increasingly fail to notice things to her left. It's the classic contralateral sensory neglect following right parietal lobe lesions. For this reason, it would help if you placed yourself to her right. Sit on her right."

"I was thinking, Dr. Matheson, do you know of something that could encourage her? To give her motivation to want to get better." As he was formulating the question he was already guessing the answer.

"I'm afraid there's nothing more we can do," the doctor had said. "In the brain there are neurons responsible for motivation; if they're lost, so is motivation. There's no magic. There is no ghostly substance that transcends neurons."

He had returned to his mother and tried to make her smile by recounting incidents from his childhood. The only thing he managed was to get her to say a few words.

At lunch, she ignored food on her left and started eating it only when he rotated her plate. Mixed were his emotions—distress that his mother did not notice the food on half her plate and momentary satisfaction when he helped her to find it.

Until late in her illness she kept mentioning the trip they planned for Israel, but then came the day when she would only say one word; the same word again and again.

Later he had talked about it with Michael, who was quick with an explanation. "If there are lesions in Broca's area, patients show poverty of speech. At times, one and only one word is left to them. Broca's area is in the opposite hemisphere to the one originally affected, but this is a butterfly glioma."

As he was escorting Christopher to the door, Michael had asked, "What was the word?"

"It's sad. Only one word, and it has nothing to do with her life. I mean, she has no brother."

"The word?"

"Brother. She keeps repeating it. Brother."

Michael had said nothing.

Christopher had tried to get his mother's attention by using the same word himself. It was the only time she became excited. She would look at him as though waiting for the moment he would say it again. He had wondered whether she was trying to say "father" and got confused, but when he used the word "father" she did not react.

Like a ball left to bounce on its own, her response became weaker and weaker until she showed no reaction at all.

On the first of March, he had tried to show her his photos from the rowing competition. She said nothing and kept staring to her right, away from the images.

He had also brought her lychees, her favorite fruit. "They are the last of the season," he had said. "Here, I'll peel one for you. The pips are really small." He squeezed her hand. "Mum, please, please say something."

He felt a squeeze in response. "Is there anything you would like me to do for you?" She was unresponsive, gazing to her right. "Squeeze my hand for 'yes.'"

There was no response. He wondered if the first squeeze had been a reflex. "Listen to me, Mum; it's our game. If you hear me, squeeze my hand."

Nothing was left. The pride, the determination, the independence were gone. Her spirit was gone. Only the familiar body remained, and it was dependent on nurses for even basic functions.

Within two weeks, a stroke had sent her into a brief coma … and then it was only a short time until this moment—this moment when Christopher was standing listening to the priest sing, "And this is the promise that He hath promised us. Even eternal life."

At her request, the icon of Christ that had hung above her bed ever since he could remember had been placed over her chest. Now it was going to disintegrate with her. Eternal life was promised to those already dead. It would have been simpler to spare the living. *Would it be a relief if I could believe we would meet again?*

No, he thought. *Her death would hurt me just as much.*

He glanced at Michael, who was standing next to him, and remembered a scene that he witnessed when Evelyn was first admitted to hospital, her speech not yet impaired. He had gone to visit, but, through a slit in the curtain, he saw Michael was already there, sitting quietly. Not wanting to interrupt what seemed to be silent communication between them, he had stayed quiet himself, staring at the corridor wall on which a green balloon made into a smiling face was hanging. Smaller balloons in red, mauve and blue surrounded it.

"I love you Michael," her voice ended the silence. "I have loved you from the start. You are part of all my happy memories. I have been stupid all this time. Afraid to commit. We had all this time together, you and I. Time enough for you to tell me you loved me. Time enough for me to say it back to you."

There was silence behind the curtain until Evelyn spoke again. "Michael, will you ever forgive me?"

He heard the sound of a kiss and Michael's voice, "There is nothing to forgive. I always knew you loved me. That's why I stayed. And it's not too late; it's not too late to tell me."

But it had been.

Christopher was brought back to the present by a gentle touch from Michael. He took the hand of the man who always stood by his mother, hoping his fingers would transmit what he felt.

It dawned on him that despite all these years of thinking of Michael as his father, he had never called him "Dad." It wasn't that different from Evelyn, who had been unable to acknowledge her love until it was too late.

Such had been his surprise at his mother's confession, that he asked about it next time he saw Dr. Matheson.

"Many of my patients react to their diagnosis in a similar way," said the doctor. "They want to surround themselves with their loved ones and are prepared to acknowledge feelings they might have kept hidden for a lifetime."

Despite the explanation, Christopher was still puzzled. His mother had made the mistake of a her life. There was no reason for her to have hidden her love. The other explanation the doctor had offered also seemed tenuous—the two brain hemispheres could elaborate different conscious states; the tumor in her right hemisphere may have disinhibited, set free, love harbored by her left.

How different life could have been, he thought. He would have had a father, and Evelyn and Michael would have had each other. It was sad. It was sad for both of them—Evelyn, who never understood the love she felt, and Michael, to whom it had always been denied.

He remembered something she had said when she was first admitted to hospital. She told him to go to Michael if one day life challenged him more than he could bear. She had then quickly moved on to another topic and never mentioned it again.

The priest made the gold thurible swing like a pendulum, giving off round puffs of fragrant smoke at each reversal. The sound from the small bells reminded him of the goats of Ithaca, when he and Evelyn dueled over the ethics of King Odysseus. The sound also reminded him of the wind chimes in their backyard. When he was little, his mother had taught him a mixed-up alphabet where every letter stood for a different one. There was a reward when he got ten right in a row—they would roll down the grass of the sloping backyard in a tight embrace, dizzy from turning and turning and turning.

꒰

As Evelyn was being lowered into the grave, Christopher felt his chest tighten.

Buried with her were the memories only the two of them shared. It had been months since his phone had rung displaying Evelyn's photo, and now it never would. He would never again hear the words "my beautiful boy" and he would never again call out "Mum."

Michael handed him a red rose to throw onto the coffin and then recited a poem by Callimachus of Alexandria, from ancient times.

The news you were gone, Heraclitus, brought me to tears.
I remembered how many twilights we had worn out together,
Talking the sun to his rest. And now, I suppose,

You are nothing but dust, old friend, in your home far away.
But your nightingales are singing, too quick for the touch
Even of death who robs us of everything.

It was his turn to read a poem from Cavafy of Alexandria of modern times, a poet his mother liked.

Ideal and beloved voices of those who died ...
At times in our dreams they speak.
At times in thought the brain hears them.
And their sound for a moment brings back the first poetry of our life,
Like music of the night that fades in the distance.

The two of them threw the first handfuls of earth.

As Christopher stepped away, his aunt followed, holding on to his arm.

He cast his eyes over the crowd, picking out Swan, Monique, Vicki and Jess. Evelyn had welcomed all his girlfriends, but she had been concerned about the quick turnover. No sooner did he develop an interest in someone, than he lost it. She knew when he left a girl his heart was broken too, but he could not help himself.

"Love, like schizophrenia," she had said, "needs to be present for at least six months before it can be diagnosed. What have I done to make you yield so to temptation?"

"Why can't I like more than one girl, if I can like more than one song, more than one sport, more than one book?" he had replied. "It's hard to get the balance right. I'm not so sure *you* did."

"I got it wrong the other way," she had said. "All the more reason I'd like to see you get it right."

"What do you mean, Mum?"

"I wasn't able to move from love to love. But instability can also be a problem."

"When I find a girl who stimulates me physically and mentally, then it'll be forever."

"Fine, but until then don't make love first and ask questions later."

He knew his mother was right; if only he could act rationally when it came to attractive girls.

Michael indicated it was time to go. Swan approached and interlaced her fingers with his. He saw the sympathy in her eyes, but it didn't touch him. He gave her a quick smile, his face becoming somber again at the thought of going back to the house to which Evelyn would never return.

Aunt Kathryn had already arrived and was coordinating the wake. His only task was to stand in the living room and accept sympathy as people approached him in an unending stream. He should have been grateful for the stories they recounted of his mother, but instead it felt as if the house was being invaded.

One minute he would feel calm and the next overcome by sadness. Sorrow came in unpredictable waves. He wanted to be alone, to let go of the pretense that he was coping.

It was after midnight by the time everyone left, and, with Swan gone too, he was alone. Almost immediately, he regretted letting her go. Their relationship had not been going well, but now he felt lost in his own home, amongst furniture and paintings drained of charm.

He put on Debussy and sat at the dresser next to Evelyn's bed, idly touching things she kept there—reading glasses, copies of *Scientific American*, novels. Framed photographs showed the two of them on his first trip to the zoo, and with Michael at his high school graduation. At the back of the dresser was a large pink shell he had found on the beach when he was little. He had given it to her to hold her jewelry. A single amber earring rested in it, its partner having been lost; there was now no reason to search for it.

She would have added a photo from my university graduation, he thought. He stared hard at the photos, trying to remember her as she had been, rather than the image of the last few months that was stuck in his mind. She had been the perfect mother. *If only I had been a better son.*

He had flouted her rules, always being eager to challenge her, behaving as though the more he strayed from her, the stronger his personality would be. And it had been so difficult to admit he was measuring himself the wrong way.

Neither had he been good enough to the only father he had known. One incident he regretted the most. He had tried Michael's patience on those early Saturday mornings when going to rowing practice, while at the same time Michael was teaching him to drive. Christopher would not get up until it was too late to make the stretch session. Eventually, Michael had tried to apply some discipline and warned next time he would give him only one wake-up call.

The following Saturday, Christopher got that call and then heard the clatter of Michael making coffee and Evelyn shuffling into the kitchen. He had put the pillow over his head, but could still hear their muffled voices and the squeaking of chairs.

Evelyn asked if he had woken Christopher up and Michael explained the new rule.

"Oh, give him another chance."

"No, Evelyn. No other chance. That's not how life works."

Bloody Michael, he remembered thinking. *This isn't life; it's about getting a bit more sleep.* He had laid on his back fuming before hoisting himself out of bed and going straight to the car without speaking to anybody, slamming doors for good measure. He had driven to McDonald's, but would not speak, even as Michael paid for breakfast.

"Why aren't you talking to me, Christopher?"

"I don't like your attitude," he had replied.

At least in this case he could still make amends. If Michael and Evelyn had gotten their act together, he would have been Michael's son. He never felt any other way. Nobody could have been a better father, gentler or more affectionate. His desire to find his biological father took nothing away from what he felt for Michael.

He ran his finger over Evelyn's leather-bound Bible on the bedside table. It was dusty. Taking a tissue, he wiped the book clean. His mother was the last person to have touched it.

His gaze drifted to the darker patch of cream on the wall behind her bed. This was where her icon had hung all those years, the one that was now with her. She had told him the depiction of Him with fair hair and blue eyes was Westerners making Him look like them. In fact, Jesus would have had black hair and dark eyes just like his own.

He picked up the photo she used as a bookmark and smiled down at the cheeky, gapped-tooth image of his six-year-old self. It was marking Matthew Chapter 1. He remembered the day she took it. There was love in the smile he gave his mother. When she took that photo, did Evelyn know how much her little boy loved her?

I was too slow and she left too soon.

Exhausted, he lay on her bed, wrapping himself in her blankets. Even though his mother had not slept in it for months, it still held a lingering scent of her.

⁊⁊

I won't need them in Jerusalem or Rome, but they will be vital in the Amazon.

Christopher tossed his hiking boots into the suitcase. He had dovetailed the holiday with the commencement of his work with TerraDyname in Brazil.

Evelyn had planned the holiday before her illness and, besides themselves, they had included Monique, his girlfriend at the time. "I want us to see the places where lived the kindest man the world has known," Evelyn had said. "I hope you don't complicate things and break up with Monique."

As Evelyn's illness progressed, she became even more insistent and anxious about him still going on the trip. On some days, it would be the only thing she would talk about. He even thought the brain tumor had made her compulsive. It was not that she had forgotten she had mentioned it; it was that she was compelled to say it.

He placed books, camera and other heavy items on the left, near the wheels, and dumped his clothes on the right.

Things did get complicated. He would be traveling alone. Not only had he broken up with Monique, but also with Swan after that.

The break-up with Swan was awkward. It was his fault; he had slipped back into his normal pattern—quick enthusiasm, abrupt boredom. Without fail, just on three months into a relationship, love would be lost. To make matters worse, the more Swan had felt him distancing himself, the tighter she had tried to hold on, literally holding him tighter.

He threw a bunch of cords and adaptors for electronic equipment into the suitcase. Different places had different languages, different cultures—and different wall sockets.

Problems with his relationship with Swan had come to a head a few days earlier while they were visiting the Jenolan Caves in the Blue Mountains. There, from the beginning, the poor chemistry between them was evident and he became convinced more than ever of the impasse. They had gone to the caves with two friends who were attempting to reconcile after a break-up. Christopher had been tuning in and out of the conversation. From the moment of entering the caves he felt unwell. "I'll go outside for some fresh air," he had said. "Meet me at the exit. Take your time."

Swan kept holding his hand, offering to accompany him.

"No, please enjoy it. You wanted so much to come; I'll wait for you outside."

Hastily, he had returned to the entrance. He was sweating and his breathing was fast and shallow. Although not claustrophobic, he had panicked as soon as they had gone below ground. It had been suffocating inside. He felt entombed.

As he paced back and forth near the entrance, his breathing slowed, but his palms were still clammy and his chest tight.

His phone vibrated—"U ok? Want me to come out?"

The message had left him feeling only more confined. She was cloying, always touching his arms, his hands, his hair. She was forcing him to play boyfriend when he wanted to do anything but. It was as though a veil had been lifted and suddenly her body, her habits, her mannerisms, her voice, none of her qualities was desirable. All he had adored in her before was now objectionable.

He lifted some of his clothes to put a Staminade bottle with the heavy items on the left of the suitcase, inside a boot.

When their friends had dropped them off back in Sydney, Christopher caught the sympathetic glance that passed from the other girl to Swan, and he felt yet another stab of guilt.

"Swan, we need to talk," he had said as they were walking through Martin Place to take the light rail toward the university.

"Look, Christopher—"

"I have to tell you. I don't know where our relationship is going." She did not speak and he continued, "I think we need to go our separate ways."

She said nothing just then, as though she couldn't believe what she had heard. As they kept walking, he heard her voice. "I knew it. I knew it was risky loving you."

"Swan, I can't say anything else. I'm sorry. Simply, I'm sorry."

"Look," she said after a while, "maybe you're depressed; it's so soon … We might save our relationship if we give it time."

"I'm not depressed. It's not because of my loss. It's because I can't promise you something I won't be able to carry through."

As he rubbed her back, he had felt the tension in her shoulders. He thought for a moment of saying he would stay and try to make things work. But even with the hurt he had caused so evident before him, he sensed freedom was near.

After closing his suitcase, he swung it off his bed onto the floor and rolled it to the door.

The sound of the wheels stayed in his mind in the silence that followed. The rest of the house was dark and no sound was coming from anywhere—no fingers on the keyboard, no music, no TV. At this time, Evelyn would have been preparing their dinner while watching the news. He sat on his bed, elbows resting on his knees, head in his hands. This was the house he was going to leave behind. After the trip, to its silence he would return.

The very trip without his mother seemed meaningless, but she had insisted he go. *Why had she been so adamant? Could it be something more?* She had gone to Israel before he was born. Had she set the stage for him to discover his father? *Otherwise, why Israel?*

He got up and walked to the corner where the didgeridoo rested beneath a poster of his favorite Aboriginal band. Black and red sections succeeded each other on the surface of the hollow log, kept apart by white bands and rings of black and red dots. He sat on the floor and started breathing into the tube.

The last thing he had heard Swan say as she was going away was, "I don't know why I still love you. You don't deserve it."

Chapter 15

JERUSALEM

A golden cross rose from the blue dome of the Church of the Holy Sepulcher at Golgotha.

It was the Wednesday of Orthodox Holy Week and Christopher had joined a tour group. The Israeli guide stopped in the forecourt, in sight of the arched doorway and the interior of the church beyond. Also in sight was an armed Israeli soldier on a rooftop. *Just as well we don't have many holy cities,* he thought.

The smell of incense was unsettling, reminding him of his mother's funeral. The guide explained the crucifixion would have taken place approximately where the crucifix now stood inside the church. This was the conclusion of Saint Helena, the mother of Emperor Constantine, who visited Jerusalem in AD 325. "Although the exact position of the cross might not be the one indicated," said the guide, "it could not have been more distant than ten meters from that point." *My mother would have wanted the evidence,* he thought.

People in the group spoke Spanish, Italian, French, English and various Asian languages, but the guide talked only in English and Spanish. How would a Jewish woman present the supposedly miraculous events associated with Jesus—as facts or fiction?

She spoke a bit more before letting them walk into the church, where they filed past the crucifix on the stage over the presumed point of crucifixion. Christ's effigy on the cross was a two-dimensional cutout, in accordance with the Greek Orthodox prohibition of statues. Above the icon, on the vertical beam of the cross, was the infamous sarcasm—"INRI." The ground around the cross was covered with panes of glass and was lit to reveal the ancient rocks at the peak of Golgotha. Elsewhere, quivering candle flames sent shadows dancing across the walls.

Christopher got as close as he could to the image. Nails pierced Christ's palms, the weight of His body dragging His arms down. His feet were crossed over one another and pinioned to the wood by a single nail. Blood dripped from the wound in His chest. On His head was the Crown of Thorns, surmounted by an ornate metal halo resembling rays of the sun.

"Close your eyes." He spun around. It was Sarah, one of the two women with whom he had struck up a conversation earlier.

"Close your eyes," she repeated.

He turned back and looked at Christ's closed eyes before closing his own.

"Imagine it," Sarah continued. "The sun burning your chest. The crowd taunting you, mocking you, feeding off your pain. The hard wood biting into your spine. Imagine the nails boring through your palms, tearing your flesh, breaking your bones. Imagine the thirst."

In the silence that followed, eyes still shut, he could almost feel the assault.

"Your name means 'bearer of Christ,'" she said, touching his hand.

His mother had told him that. As soon as he had started talking, he had asked her, "I know I am Christopher, but how did you know?" She told him she had named him that way because she loved Christ.

He thought of telling Sarah, but then decided that was something too intimate to share with a stranger.

The guide gathered the group and led it to the Holy Canopy. "Below this small chapel is thought to be the tomb of Jesus," she said. "It is a cave, one of many inside this church. It is believed Jesus was buried in one of these, if he were buried within the walls of the Old City. Unfortunately, there is no way of knowing which one.

"It was also from this point," she said, pointing to the ground, "that Jesus is said to have ascended to Heaven, leaving no mortal remains."

"Were you meditating before?" asked Natalie, the other girl he had met, one of the French ladies in the group. "I saw you with your eyes closed."

He stepped back to look at her. "I guess so. Sarah made me reflect. She speaks so eloquently about the Passion."

"And what do you think?"

"His martyrdom. It's not as if Jesus was a criminal. All he did was talk of love."

"That is not what the Romans perceived," said Natalie. "For them it was the stopping of the rebellion. The execution was political."

"Execution all right," said Christopher. "As to the rebellion, Natalie, His pacifism was hardly menacing the Empire. Their conscience perhaps." They were separated as a group of students passed between them. When reunited, he continued, "And look at the sarcasm—the mocking INRI sign. 'Iēsus Nazarēnus, Rēx Iūdaeōrum—Jesus of Nazareth, King of the Jews.' There you are."

The guide had said they drew lots on His clothes. All Christopher could think of was his mother's clothes tumbled on the floor of her bedroom. He had not managed to put them away. It seemed now so remiss of him not to have done such a simple thing.

❦

Could one of them be my father?

Around Christopher, men were bowing to the wall that rose some twenty meters above him. The Wailing Wall was made of large stone blocks, some brilliant white, others charcoal, with shades of sand and cream in between. A pilgrim was stuffing a piece of paper between the stones, pushing it hard because the crevices were overflowing with notes; he then turned to face the bright blue sky, his hands by his temples, his eyes shut.

Young boys, accompanied by their elders, marched to the beat of drums. Men stood at lecterns, as though to give speeches. Some seemed to be traditional Hasidic Jews—black fedoras atop long side-curls.

Earlier, as they approached the vast expanse of concrete in front of the Wall, the men had been segregated from the women in the group. Now they were reunited and the group started making its way through the Arab sector of East Jerusalem, heading to the Jewish Quarter. Above their heads, clothes were hung out to dry on lines strung between buildings. The shops were so full of produce that it spilled out onto the footpath. Stands with finely crafted metals abutted stands with gaudy plastic toys, jewelry and sacks of spices and dried fruit. The latest electronic goods competed for space with piles of oriental carpets whose soft blues, pinks and greens were offset by the strong hues of the kilim rugs that hung on the walls.

Men sat at small tables inside coffee shops, and outside at benches drenched by the afternoon sun. Clouds of smoke billowed out each time they took the brass narghile pipes out of their mouths and exhaled, the scent of apple-flavored tobacco mingling with the aroma of strong Arabic coffee spiced with cardamom.

"Is this still the Arab Quarter?" Christopher asked the guide, as the group moved away from the shops.

"It is the Jewish Quarter now," she replied.

"It is the Arab Quarter!" shouted a shopkeeper.

"These neighbors do not love one another," Natalie whispered to him.

"Christ's teachings probably have no bearing here," Christopher whispered back. "The stuff about 'love your enemy.'"

"But is Christ going to love His enemies on the Day of Judgment?" she asked.

"You're referring to the prophesies in the Book of Revelation."

"Yes, and to be truthful, Christopher, I prefer the gods spare us the floods, the famine and the sword and give us sex, drugs and rock 'n' roll."

"Poetic you are, Natalie, but I don't think Christ would have sent the horsemen of the Apocalypse to make men slay one another." He spoke again after a moment. "I know what you'd say—He wouldn't need to. They do it on their own."

⁂

There was something familiar about the boys walking down the steps of Via Dolorosa.

Tall, skinny, with black hair, dark eyes and olive skin, to Christopher it seemed like he had seen them before.

Sarah caught his gaze and glanced back and forth between him and the boys. "You know, I've noticed from the start, you could pass for a local. If you spoke Arabic, we could have used you to do the haggling."

Sarah's hair was riotous, curls escaping from clips and ties to form stray ringlets about her face.

"I fit everywhere, even here," he said. "But look, this via is not as solemn as you might have thought, Sarah."

The two of them were walking along the bustling street while the rest of the group was scattered behind them. Fishmongers displayed glistening seafood in tubs filled with melting ice, red mullet lay next to silver bream, snake-like eels next to small yellow fish with blue-and-red stripes.

Further along, they were confronted by the sight and smell of meat. A blowfly buzzed around buckets of red and yellow offal. His stomach turned as he looked into the eyes of a dead calf. *What makes some of us salivate ...*

Via Dolorosa was a long, winding alley with steps that scaled the height of Golgotha. It was the route Jesus had followed from the palace of Pontius Pilate to His crucifixion. Above the shops, and occasionally over Via Dolorosa, were living quarters. Scattered among the shops were the Stations of the Cross. Station III was commemorated by a sculpture affixed to a wall—Jesus falling to the ground for the first time, the cross weighing down on Him.

The present rhythm of life in the Via was disconnected from the human drama its name acknowledged. Now life was going on as though nothing dramatic had ever happened there.

Among a group of beggars sitting on the steps of the Via was a young man playing with the top of his head. A large segment of his skull was as soft as a baby's fontanel. He was pressing it into his brain and releasing it, oblivious to his surroundings.

Christopher asked Sarah to wait. As he approached, the young man looked at him with vacant eyes.

Sarah approached too, giving money to all the beggars there, who by now had hands extended. "I wonder if they are genuine or this is their second job," she said.

Does it matter? Christopher thought.

As he gazed at Via Dolorosa, he felt the same sadness he had felt at Golgotha. If ever there were someone who didn't deserve this fate. Why did He attract so much hatred?

Recalling Sarah's comment on his resemblance to the locals, he wondered again whether it was Israel where Evelyn met the man she had kept hidden all her life. As a child, he had searched in vain through his mother's old photo albums for a man who looked like him. He had found an album marked "Israel Jan 1997" with an inordinate number of photographs of the desert and a skeleton in various stages of being assembled.

The dates did not match for him to have been conceived in January. He did not push Evelyn on something she clearly preferred not to speak about. Neither did he want to ask Michael for fear of offending him.

Michael cared for me all my life—nobody could have been a better father. And who really is the father? The one who contributes a sperm, or the one who brings you up? I have to give up this quest.

❧

The more he tried to dismiss the idea, the more he found himself focusing on it.

Why did they hide my father from me? Why did he want to remain hidden?

Could there have been some sort of disgrace? An illicit affair? Something that neither his mother nor Michael would want him to know? Could they have been concealing a rape? It would stand to reason not to want him to know of a father like that. But all was speculation. Not a single clue.

Seated at the back of the taxi, Christopher could see the mountain range ahead, bald but for grasses and the occasional tree. In the distance, the color of the mountains was a faint blue.

Evelyn had arranged for a day trip to HaSolelim, a kibbutz near Nazareth. Evian, the exchange student who had stayed with them in Sydney, had put her in contact with his father, a founding member of the kibbutz.

The road passed through cultivated areas and meadows full of red and yellow poppies in among long stretches of rocky ground. Irrigation, the driver told him, was via long hoses with holes that provided drops of water directly to the roots of the plants. Taking the turnoff for HaSolelim, the taxi arrived at the swimming pool and parking lot at the outskirts of the village. Cars not being allowed in, he walked to the square.

Loni and Elva, Evian's parents, welcomed him. Loni was tall, like his son, and perhaps he too had been slim in his youth. Elva, on the other hand, was just as skinny as he remembered his childhood friend, and had the same green eyes and full lips.

"We have never forgotten the kindness your mother showed Evian," said Loni. "We are sorry we never had the chance to meet her."

"Evian told us so much about you," said Elva. "You were the cleverest child he had met."

"We had fun together. He is in America now, right?"

"Both our children are there." Elva took him by the arm. "But you must be tired. Let's have something refreshing at this café."

The café was shaded by a large cypress tree. Couches and mismatched armchairs surrounded scarred timber tables, the long counter fridge displaying baklava and cakes.

After ordering, Loni and Elva explained HaSolelim was once a different place. They had come there when they were young, back in the late '50s. The kibbutz was dedicated to mutual help and social justice then, but now young people depart in search of affluence. There was sadness in their voices at the lost dream.

Christopher recalled his lecturers in economics going over Marxist theory. At the time, he had thought Marxism was ultimately the only system that made sense. Soon he realized the drive for affluence afflicted even those committed to social justice. *Who would turn down a bigger house, a better car?*

"What you did here," he said, "is similar to what Christ and Marx had in mind."

❧

Perhaps there in the hills, amongst the cypress trees, might still lie the secret of why Nazareth produced a rebel who challenged authority from the Pharisees to the Romans.

They had left the kibbutz and gone for dinner at an Arab restaurant in nearby Nazareth. While he waited for Loni to park the car, Christopher closed his eyes, bringing to mind the features of the face in the Byzantine icon above his bed—arched eyebrows, serene eyes, elongated nose. When he was little and had high fever, the icon came to life. In his delirium, it grew larger than his room, yet somehow it fit inside it.

Now, as Christopher stood surrounded by mountains, he was in the very place where the man in the icon had grown up. Possibly the old olive tree with the huge trunk at the side of the road was a sapling then. With eyes still closed, he wondered what he would say to Him, and what He would say to him, had they met. As a child, in his imagination, he had come up with a body to go with the face in the icon—a man wearing a tunic and sandals, walking briskly, as if on a mission. All he had to do now was to bring the image to the present location with surrounds as they might have been in ancient times. He mentally replaced the asphalt with cobblestones, leaving the olive and cypress trees to stand where they were, just shrinking them to saplings.

Christopher could see that the stones He stepped on as He came toward him spelled out the word "vengeance." But as He walked over them, they changed position and no longer spelled "vengeance," but other words that lifted Christopher's spirit.

"Christopher, are you all right?" asked Elva.

He opened his eyes, realizing his hand was extended as if reaching out to the man who had just vanished from his mind. He looked around to orient himself. "I'm okay," he answered. The image he had conjured was still vivid, though the surroundings were the same as before.

She took his hand. "Oh, my dear; it's too soon. You're still grieving for your mother."

Over dinner, he participated in conversation on autopilot. It was as though everything was happening at a distance. He barely tasted the food he ate.

When they walked out of the restaurant he hung back and closed his eyes, hoping the image would return. Nothing happened.

His hosts were waiting for him, so he jogged to catch up. Might they know something? There was nothing to lose. "Did my mother ... do you know if my mother had any friends in Israel?"

Loni gestured to show empty hands. "Not that we know of."

They were his only contacts. There were no clues—nothing to hold on to. *I am trying too hard. Mum has given the only explanation there is and I have to accept what she said. There is nothing more to this.*

⁂

At the head of the procession in the Church of the Holy Sepulcher, two altar boys were walking backwards, while swinging incense burners that filled the air with a sweet, musky smell.

The fragrance again reminded Christopher of his mother's funeral. He tried to clear his mind of thoughts of Evelyn, but they returned unbidden. On the one hand, he did not want to forget anything about her, but, on the other, he did not want the memories to be intrusive.

Having returned to Jerusalem, Christopher had squeezed into the church for the Good Friday service. In contrast to other churches, the effigy of Christ was not unnailed from the cross. Instead, a fabric the size of a tablecloth with His image embroidered on it was showered with rose petals. Tenderly held from each corner by priests, it was slowly carried down the eighteen steps from Golgotha to the main part of the church.

When he was little, he had told Evelyn he wanted to watch *South Park* rather than go to the Good Friday service. Her response, "You have to obey me because I made you." Later he had realized how important Good Friday was to Evelyn and Michael. On Good Fridays they were both sad. It was the one day of the year he always stayed with them because he felt he was needed. It seemed they lived a contradiction—atheism with the worship of Christ. And for some reason, they clung to him on that day.

Next in the procession came pairs of boys holding lanterns with candles, crosses with candelabras and gold disks symbolizing the sun. The fabric with the image was placed on a marble base over which hung nine ornate lanterns. It was the re-enactment of the anointing of the body by the women. The fabric was then carried to the entrance of the Holy Tomb.

The choir sang hymns that reminded Christopher of music his mother played. Evelyn had taught him the lyrics of her favorite.

Ω γλυκύ μου έαρ, γλυκύτατόν μου τέκνον, που έδυ σου το κάλλος;
Oh, my sweet spring, my sweetest child, the sunset of thy beauty
I behold.

He had scorned the effusiveness of it, but she had said it was beautiful, especially in Greek. It was a metaphor, she said, and it was the lament of a mother who had two sons. "Well, some claim Mary actually had another son," he recalled her saying when he asked.

The fabric was interred in the Holy Tomb. An orthodox priest told him it would stay there until light from the tomb was sent to the four corners of the world, just prior to the Resurrection.

Outside the church, people were cupping their palms to shield the flames of their candles, attempting to keep the "holy light" for as long as possible. Candlelight illuminated faces from below, reversing the usual facial shadows. Many candles were extinguished by the wind, to be relit by strangers with an exchange of wishes.

He felt a presence near him and looked back. There was nobody. He turned right around. An old woman approached him. She wore a black scarf and was singing from a pamphlet. Her candle had dripped wax that hooked on the paper cup surrounding it. She reached his candle with hers to relight it. Her face was as wrinkled as the bark of the old olive tree in Nazareth. She looked serene. *Perhaps Jesus brings her peace.*

Alone once more, he thought of the sacrifice of a life for justice. The world now was preoccupied with business, not benevolence. He used to think he needed to gain financial independence before helping others, but now he was beginning to wonder. *I might get the money and lose my soul.*

Evelyn had told him the parable of the rich man, the camel and the eye of the needle. He conceded economists were unlikely heroes, but argued they could contribute to social progress, not least in the provision of food, shelter, safety, health and education.

One day she had asked him to explain his motivation for his choice of profession, but then mercifully had said that one of the most difficult things to understand is your own motivation. "I know only some of the reasons behind the most important decisions of my life."

On his way back to his hotel in East Jerusalem, Christopher passed a sleeping German Shepherd that bore an eerie resemblance to his old dog Olive. He recalled the question his mother had posed to him when he was still in primary school. "Imagine standing on the deck of a ship holding a cup of poison in one hand and Olive in the other. It's too windy and you can't hold on to both. You have to let go of one of them, and the one you drop will fall into the ocean. The poison will kill all the fish and hundreds of millions of people will starve to death. Which one do you let go of? The poison or Olive?"

"Can Olive swim?" he had asked.

"No, no, she'll drown."

"I'll hold on to Olive," he had replied, feeling ashamed.

"That's the natural response, Christopher, but is it the moral one?"

He looked down at the cobblestones and the image of the man with the Byzantine eyes came to mind. *What He would have told me is that I am far from the right path.*

Just then every path he had taken seemed problematic. With the trip to Jerusalem coming to a close, he still had no sense of its meaning. There was nothing to indicate Evelyn had organized it so he could find his father. Maybe she wanted him to find Christ—a way to connect with His philosophy, the suffering and the redemption. *After all, wasn't that what my baptism was about?*

"The journey is important and not the destination" was the central point in the poem by Cavafy. *But what if things are actually what they seem?* Christopher wondered. *The destination would then be important and not the journey.*

Odysseus had a destination—Ithaca, wife, son, even a father waiting for him there.

Chapter 16

ROME

Who is this José de Olmos?

Christopher had been informed that the mastermind of the resistance to the construction of the dam on the Amazon was this Argentinian environmentalist. The file provided by TerraDyname contained information about his police record, but offered no explanation as to why he had left home to get involved in Brazil. He had no social media presence, though there were links to Resistência Pacifica's pages. No photos of him came up, except one that had his name in the legend. It was taken from a distance and showed a group of protesters perched like birds in a tree.

To negotiate successfully, Christopher had to understand this man's motivation. The construction of an environmentally friendly energy source was at stake, and, with it, the ability to lift hundreds of thousands of Brazilians out of poverty. Why was de Olmos so opposed to it?

While waiting for his flight at the Ben Gurion Airport, he perused the homepage of Resistência Pacifica. The heading read, "Our Forests, Our Lives—Stop the Desecration." He trawled through the website to familiarize himself with the group that was obstructing the construction of the dam. The centerpiece of the homepage was a photo of a river meandering through forest that had been logged, in part also burned.

> **Rivers and rainforests sustain life.** Half of the Amazon Rainforest will be lost by 2025. The ancient FOREST will be ancient history if we do not ACT NOW. Resistência Pacifica is peacefully resisting TerraDyname's monstrous mega dam at Terra da Árvore Velha (The Land of the Old Tree). Unite to resist the logging and damming of this precious source of life and inspiration.

The page offered the experiences of those who had completed their "tour of duty," as well as a forum discussing the principles, logistics and effective methods to frustrate TerraDyname. Recent footage taken at the Árvore Velha was included, protesters standing between trees and heavy machinery. *Not as I imagined it, but that is their take,* Christopher thought. *Maybe they have even doctored the images.*

In the search field of the site he typed "de Olmos" and downloaded an article written by him.

Is the Brain the Right "Size"?

> Puzzled we stand before nature, surprised by our own existence, dazzled by our space-age technology, and unaware of our Stone Age emotions.

> The task of creating a sustainable society may prove elusive due to the large-scale behavioral modification required and the limited intellectual, motivational and emotional capacities of our brains.

> Despite the apparently large morphological and behavioral gulf between the humans and the great apes, analysis of the DNA shows the humans to be more closely related to the chimpanzees than the

chimpanzees to the gorillas. It is so proximal, you can have a blood transfusion from a chimpanzee if you are the right blood group.

Anatomically, the human brain should be considered a branch of an evolutionary tree of brains, a tree that also features the brains of the fish, the reptiles and the birds.

This de Olmos is presenting himself as a philosopher and environmental warrior, thought Christopher. *No doubt he will see me as just another suit.*

A marginal structural superiority is the rationale for the human hubris. Never since Narcissus fell in love with the reflection of his face in a river has there been such adoration of a bodily organ as there is now of the brain. And never with less justification.

Without considering the severe limitations which evolution has placed on the brain, we dare to play God with the Earth. In an insane effort to countermand global warming we are contemplating geoengineering to dim the sun so that we can burn even more fossil fuels. This is the *coup de grâce* to the dying humanity.

At least de Olmos is original, Christopher thought. *Nobody else has attacked the brain. But how do you negotiate with someone like that?*
   The title of the next chapter read, "Is the only Sustainable Society one of Hunter-gatherers without Fire?"
   What does de Olmos want? To give up fire? To return to pre-Promethean times? His ideas do not come from any textbook in economics.
   From what Christopher had read, it was not clear what academic discipline de Olmos was following; his thinking was an amalgam of ethics, neuroscience, ecology and theology.
   I have to hand it to the guy—he has a coherent rationale, convoluted though it is. My own position is not as pure, but it doesn't require

sacrificing everything. Hydroelectric dams deliver major community benefits. And what could be more environmentally friendly?

Maybe this de Olmos knows something I don't. One thing is certain— one of us is deluded.

❦

Purple bougainvillea adorned his path, but there was no bounce in Christopher's step as he climbed the Scalinata of Piazza di Spagna and walked through the gardens of the Villa Borghese. Anxiety about his involvement with TerraDyname had gripped him.

Earlier in the day he had checked in at the hotel Il Piccolo and was now going to meet Francesco, an Italian doctor he had met through Michael. He saw him approach accompanied by a tall woman, her luxuriant dark curls shining with a hint of red in the afternoon sun.

"This is my sister, Antonella," said Francesco after embracing him.

"*Mi piace*," said Christopher, his eyes fixed on her dancer-like frame.

"*Piacere, piacere*," corrected Francesco. "*Mi piace* means 'I like you.'"

"I like '*mi piace*' better," said Antonella.

"I know just enough Italian to get myself into trouble."

"My sister is an undergraduate in English literature," said Francesco. "You will have no trouble."

It's hard to see beyond the beauty, Christopher mused. Evelyn certainly had not sent him on this trip to find a girlfriend, though. *If I woke up next to this woman ... no, I have to look beyond the obvious. It can only be a digression from where I am going—wherever that might be.*

"You are an economist now, eh?" said Francesco. "And you will be working for TerraDyname? Remember when you told me the government must print more dollars and give them to the poor to end poverty?"

"I have a degree now, but it doesn't mean I have better ideas."

"Your mother adored you. What a beautiful woman she was."

"She had planned to come here ..."

"I am sorry, Christopher. It would have been double the pleasure if she had."

Once in Villa Borghese, they were surrounded by Greek, Roman and Renaissance art. A marble statue of Daphne, the beautiful fleeing nymph, showed her in the process of metamorphosing into a laurel tree to escape abduction by Apollo, the sun god.

As they left the Villa, Antonella linked arms with both men and they walked together through the park. He reminded himself Italians were warm; but he also kept thinking that giving way to temptation was not going to bring him peace. Most likely he would revert to his old ways. *I have a sense Rome may hold something. My mind needs to be clear.*

They went to Piazza di Spagna to take the tube. As much as the sights, it was the people in the Piazza who were the spectacle, milling around the fountain, sitting on the steps, some with arms around each other as they posed for photographs, their chatter rising to meet the noise of falling water.

He looked at the rock boat that was forever sinking inside the fountain. Evelyn had told him it symbolized the flooding of Rome centuries earlier. There was as much water inside the boat as around it.

Cars were weaving their way through the crowd down the one-way street that narrowed into the station tunnel. The three of them navigated idle horse-drawn carriages and stalls laden with toys and souvenirs, the air fragrant with the smell of chestnuts roasting on red glowing coals. Christopher noticed a group of Italian men staring at Antonella, their heads turning to follow her even after they passed by. He glanced at Francesco.

They surfaced from La Metropolitana as evening fell on the Eternal City. They sat in the outdoor section of Osteria di Agrippa, taking in the view of the columns of the Pantheon. "It is here," said

Antonella. "'Pantheon' means all gods. Do you think Hadrian was trying to include all religions?"

"No, I reckon he was trying to avoid the word Parthenon," said Christopher.

He tried to count the robust columns, but some were hidden by others. Nearly two millennia in the rain, nearly two millennia in the sun, the building had something of a ship that sailed proudly through the waves of time.

❦

"Magnificent Marmoset, it's going to be okay," said José, putting his arms around her. "They'll release us soon; they know about our conference."

Lorena had stopped screaming, but he wasn't sure she was registering what he was saying. Her face was white, her eyes skittering back and forth. "Lorena, I am here. We are together."

Fear was still in her eyes, but at least she was focusing on him.

"Lorena, pardon me. I drew police attention to us. I overreacted."

"It was not the police. It was the pamphlet—*the image.*"

"I didn't actually see the pamphlet, but I can guess," he whispered.

"José, forgive me for shouting before. I can't stay here any longer. There is too much marble all over this place. Tell me we'll be free."

"Definitely, they will release us soon. We have not hurt anyone and this is Italy."

Lorena now settled in his arms.

"Marmoset, there is man out there who looks exactly like me."

She did not respond. "Lorena," he said, pulling her even closer to him. "Did you hear what I said?"

"What man?" she asked.

"In the crowd, a short distance from the van as they closed the door. He looked just like me."

"No, I did not see him."

"It was really weird; it was as if I was looking at myself."

She nodded, but he could see she had not understood.

José thought of the man with the black curly hair and dark eyes.

He looked my height too. Did he see the resemblance? José asked himself. *He must have. He was looking straight at me.*

❦

Christopher kept looking back.

A scuffle had broken out near some display tables at the North Colonnade. As they walked away through the columns to reach St. Peter's Square, the shouts faded, overlaid by the hum of human voices and the running water of yet another fountain.

He caught up with Francesco and Antonella, who had stopped at the sight of St. Peter's Basilica. The church shone as it rose into the blue sky. Rows of white columns reached forward. His mother had told him to perceive them as welcoming arms.

"To the right of St. Peter's," said Antonella, "is the Vatican building, part of the Apostolic Palace. The Pope appears at the window of his papal study on the third floor at Christmas, Easter and every Sunday to bless the pilgrims. Last week was Easter and the square was full."

"Big piazza; it's hard to believe it can fill up," said Christopher while trying in vain to see what was happening at the other side of the colonnade.

"Come on, Francesco," said Antonella. "Let's take some photographs."

"Thanks. I'll catch up with you." Christopher jogged back through the colonnade. Two carabinieri were pulling a bearded man into a van, while a frantic girl was pulling him the other way. By the time he got closer, the police were pushing both of them into the van.

The girl, whose back was to him, kept screaming. He was certain the bearded man noticed him. In fact, he was looking only at Christopher until the van door closed behind him.

"What happened?" he asked somebody in the crowd.

"They said the pamphlets were unethical," said the man with a thick Irish accent.

Christopher asked for more information and was told a person from a religious group tried to give the couple a handout, something about condoms being evil. The girl gave it back to him and then the trouble started. She started yelling something about HIV and overpopulation. The religious man asked what kind of a Catholic she was. "Somebody shoved somebody and then the *carabinieri* showed up," said the man.

The crowd soon dispersed. Christopher picked up a fallen leaflet and headed toward St. Peter's.

❧

The gaze of the arrested man still in his mind, Christopher joined Francesco and Antonella to enter the Basilica from the north wing, visiting first Michelangelo's *La Pietà*.

He stared at the marble Mary and the marble Christ. Located behind glass, the mother was holding everything in her arms, and nothing. Her downcast eyes were examining what His enemies had done to His body.

She had a straight nose and a small pointed chin. Whatever she might have looked like in reality, Christopher thought, Michelangelo had rendered her beautiful.

One thing, though, she looked too youthful for a woman with a thirty-three-year-old son. Still supple, Christ's body yielded to her embrace. The stigmata of crucifixion and the wound on His side were understated. Neither the Madonna nor Christ betrayed the violence of the Passion.

In the nave of the church was a bronze statue of St. Peter. The Apostle of Christ was blessing people with his right hand, holding the keys to Paradise with his left. Christopher walked up and down the length of the nave, the features of the sidewalls unfolding in the periphery of his vision. He touched all columns within reach, at times stopping to listen to the choir in the central chapel of the Basilica.

Rays of the sun entered the nave through the dome windows, illuminating airborne dust particles that crossed their path. He approached the heart of the Basilica, the crypt holding the bones of St. Peter. It was in a sunken part of the church, behind a wall solemnized by Bernini's four twisting black columns.

"Sacretia" read the sign pointing to a partly open door off the left aisle. On entering, Christopher was met by a wall of marble on which were carved the names of the bishops of Rome, an uninterrupted regression line that went back to St. Peter—the very St. Peter whom Christ called the rock upon which the church would be built. Suddenly, history seemed tangible. The interval between then and now was brief. The list on the wall was a chain that connected him to the man upon whose birthday time was balanced as on a fulcrum.

On his way out of the Basilica, he stopped again at *La Pietà*. His mother had shown him photos of it. "And Christ was the hero to the end," she had said. "A flower that blossomed in a desert."

Two thousand years have passed and the desert has not seen another flower like it. For a moment, he was puzzled by his own thought. *Where did that come from? This place. It must be this place.*

❧

"You don't have to be religious to admire Christ," said Christopher when he met his friends outside the Basilica.

"Rome can be as good as Damascus," said Antonella. "I will take a photo with the colonnade in the background."

"I noticed you went twice to *La Pietà*," said Francesco.

"Who can blame me. This image has been burnt into human consciousness."

They ascended the dome to get a view of Rome. What was unexpected for Christopher was the views of the vast interior of the church on the way up and on the way down—red and black, silver and gold, and shades of blues, pinks and greens flowed over ceiling, walls and floor.

From the Basilica, they passed through the row of chambers that led to the Sistine Chapel, joining the river of people meandering through the art collection.

In the chapel, crowded among other paintings on the ceiling, was Michelangelo's image of God about to touch Adam's index finger to give life to man. *God would have made his job easier if he had made the woman first.*

Talking was not allowed in the Sistine Chapel, but there was a hum from shuffling feet and whispers, punctuated by *shsh* from inspectors trying to keep people quiet.

Filling the entire wall behind the altar was *The Last Judgment*, depicting the Second Coming; souls ascended or descended to their eternal destiny as judged by the Christ of the Apocalypse. *Would I ascend or descend that wall?* he asked himself. *If, of course, there were a soul inside me.*

He had no doubt where Evelyn's would be except for a minor obstacle—*non-believers need not apply.*

He had gone to the Vatican thirsty for symbolism and hard it was to drink from a fire hydrant.

❧

There was the aroma of freshly brewed coffee and the melody of Italian conversation.

Christopher had been looking forward to visiting the famous Antico Caffè Greco on Via Condotti. They were ushered through a number of crowded rooms to the back, where they were seated around a tiny marble-topped table. The walls were crammed with paintings, some monumental, some exquisitely small, old striped wallpaper visible in the gaps between.

"A guy and his girlfriend got arrested," said Christopher after the waiter left. "A fight with a stallholder handing out these leaflets." He pulled the pamphlet from his pocket. "A clash between two moralities. It's a sin to use condoms, and it's a sin not to—what of HIV and overpopulation."

Antonella flinched. The pamphlet showed a fetus in a glass jar, head disproportionately large, facial features distorted.

"You know, something strange happened. The man who was being arrested kept staring at me as I was approaching the van. I suppose he was hoping I'd help. I feel bad I didn't."

"And get arrested also?" asked Antonella.

"Look, this wasn't a brawl. They were protesting about an important issue."

"You know what, Christopher?" said Francesco. "You don't sound like a TerraDyname-sort-of guy. Economists are not supposed to be so sensitive."

"I was thinking I might be able to do some good through a big corporation, and this thing today has given me an idea. They have asked me to come up with proposals to end the stalemate with the construction of the dam in Brazil. I could suggest some of the profits from the project be donated for family planning, HIV, or pandemic preparedness."

"I think you might end up with a dam but no pandemic money."

"Francesco, if he does not try, he definitely will not succeed," said Antonella. "We all need romantic ideals."

"I know I sound like an undergraduate advising the vice chancellor, but I'll take my chances."

"I am with you," said Francesco. "Just be careful. Do not trust their word."

"Is there anything for Brazil in this project?" asked Antonella.

"Cheap electricity to develop its northern states, employment, spawning of industries. But I know what you're getting at. The company will come out very well, with rights to revenue from electricity and water, in addition to timber rights in the area to be flooded."

"I do not know about this dam in particular," said Francesco, "but, generally, dams need roads and the roads bring fires. You are talking of ecosystems being converted to cattle ranches and mines."

"I have read indigenous groups are opposed to damming the Amazon," said Antonella.

"They have a point," said Francesco. "Aside from what I said before, dams block fish and turtle migration, and water released from the turbines is oxygen poor. So downstream river stretches become inhospitable for some fish species."

"I have read what the environmentalists say too," said Christopher. "And some things make sense. But something I find hard to believe is their claim the hydroelectric dam will provide a permanent source of methane that would enhance global warming. They argue this is because soft vegetation grows rapidly in the drawdown zone, only to decompose under anaerobic conditions on the bottom of the reservoir when the water level rises. I don't know if they are exaggerating. They even claim the carbon dioxide contribution of the dam for the first ten years would exceed that of the city of São Paulo."

"So," said Antonella. "Whom do you believe in the end?"

❦

With the time for the teleconference approaching, Christopher paced his hotel room gathering his thoughts.

At the last moment, he read aloud the synopsis of the briefing pack, freshening up on the terms and arguments. He joined the meeting and his computer screen split into three windows, populated by the participants.

"Hello. Sorry, Nathan, we're keeping you up," began the man who had introduced himself as James Howard, the Chief Financial Officer. "So, our aim today is to brief our negotiator for the Amazon and discuss the standoff. Welcome on board, Christopher, I trust you've read the brief. Any questions, comments?"

Christopher had been prepared to discuss things with Nathan from the Sydney office—the person who had hired him—not the Chief Financial Officer. Howard's involvement signaled the stalemate was of major concern to the company. Christopher didn't know how to address this person who was now looking squarely at him through his blue-tinted lenses.

"Thank you, Mr. Howard," he said belatedly. "I can see the problem we have with Resistência Pacifica. They've attracted international attention and made us look hostile to the environment. I'm in Rome and it's a topic of conversation even here."

"This Argentinian firebrand, José de Olmos, is garnering too much public sympathy," said Nathan. "That's why we've selected you, Christopher. You are young too, eloquent and likeable. You will be our positive face for the public."

"But I need a positive story to present," said Christopher. "We're at a disadvantage. Logging and damming the Amazon isn't popular, even if it is for hydroelectric power."

"New recruits with high marks and extraordinary ideas," said Howard. "What's more positive than green development, Christopher?"

He cleared his throat. "What are you suggesting? Remember, we're accountable to our shareholders."

My warm welcome was brief, Christopher reflected as he took a deep breath. "Mr. Howard, some commentators have argued the Amazon belongs to the world."

"You've swallowed the propaganda, Christopher. The Brazilians object to the implied loss of sovereignty. Their president castigated the Europeans for destroying ninety-nine percent of *their* original forests and having the audacity to point at Brazil with fingers dripping oil. For the benefit of both of you, Australians can't point the finger either. Australia is the largest exporter of coal and its exports stoke the fires that burn it."

"The president wins the argument, but Brazil is not our only client. We need the Europeans and—"

"Listen," Howard interrupted, tilting his head down and looking over his glasses. "Legally we have the right to build this dam. We are operating within the law of the country. Also, we have the right to harvest the area to be flooded. What the hell are the trees going to do underwater anyway?"

"Yes, Mr. Howard. But what about the roads? We might be able to reduce the proposed network and save ourselves some costs too. The environmentalists oppose—"

"Don't lose sleep over what they oppose. But, if we can find a formula to save money by building fewer roads, we can satisfy them on this. We are not inflexible; right, Nathan?"

"In flexibility, we are the cognitive equivalent of rubber bands, James. But let me backtrack and say that it is only through hydroelectric power we can avoid a two-degree increase in temperature and ecocide. A two-degree increase in temperature relative to pre-industrial times, for example, will eliminate corals in the Great Barrier Reef and elsewhere. Not to mention that it will convert the Amazon forest into a savanna."

Christopher thought of abandoning his plan for philanthropy after the catastrophic introduction. But on the other hand, this was likely to be his only chance and he would not forgive himself if he did not take it. "There's one other thing," he finally said. "We can make the project more appealing. Some sort of philanthropic work would bring public acceptance."

"And what exactly do you mean by philanthropic work?" asked Howard.

"We could give six percent of the profits to some major cause. I suggest either family planning or pandemic preparedness. These areas are underfunded and this money can make a difference. And it will appeal to the public."

Howard leaned forward, his face now filling most of the screen. "Six percent! Christopher, the board will take a dim view of any effort to turn TerraDyname into a charity."

�

The conference call had been over for hours, except in Christopher's head.

What can I offer the environmentalists if the board ignores me? His degree, his internship, they had prepared him for exactly this, but did he have it in him to keep going if the company were not prepared to compromise?

His eyes fell on the document saved to his desktop. Between preparing for the briefing and sightseeing, he still had not finished reading the de Olmos article and scrolled to where he had left off.

> **Injustice infinite.** Like Kronos, the god of time who devoured his own children, the present generation will deliver its own progeny to extinction through the untold suffering of a terrestrial inferno—an increase in temperature of 3 to 6 degrees Celsius this century and 17 to 24 degrees by the end of the millennium.

The adverse environmental impact can be simplified in the equation Impact = Population x Affluence x Technologies. The impact can be reduced if we reduce our reproduction, or our affluence or our polluting technologies. The flamboyance of the rich is not compatible either with survival or justice.

The next section was titled "Pangenocide" and presented the moral grounds for the argument that future generations should be stakeholders in all current decisions that might make them extinct. Christopher eventually reached the last page.

Our morality "bypass" must be attributed to the functioning of the brain, as can be inferred from the study of brain damage. Damage to the frontal lobes results in erosion of foresight, diminished concern for the future, disinhibition and perseveration in unprofitable paths. We are the frontal lobe patients.

Finally, returning to the question posed in the title of this article, of whether the brain is the right "size," the humans are trapped in an evolutionary vise. If the brain were "smaller," less clever and incapable of language, it would not have produced the science and technology that today threaten existence. If the brain were "larger," it might have comprehended the problem, even solved it.

The conclusion is inescapable: The brain is just not the right "size."

Then what is the bloody point? thought Christopher. *What can we do if our brain is not the right "size?" I suppose de Olmos is trying to say, "Know thyself?" Make people aware of their cognitive and emotional limitations. Obviously, he has not heard of green development.* Denmark doubled its economy and decreased its carbon footprint. This de Olmos should have taken a course in economics.

The screen saver activated—a picture taken at Maroubra Beach two years earlier. Evelyn was standing between him and Michael, in the background the rocky escarpment separated the green headlands from the blue Pacific.

He bent forward to see the details. His mother was staring right into the lens, looking healthy and happy. He wondered whose side she would be on—the shareholders' or this Argentinian extremist's. He wasn't sure he wanted the answer.

⁂

"The twins had been left in the forest to die, but were rescued by a wolf who suckled them back to health …"

Christopher was listening, as Antonella was telling told him the myth of the founding of Rome while driving along Via Apia to the catacombs.

She described how the twins Romulus and Remus, fostered by shepherds, grew to be strong leaders. Discovering their royal blood, they avenged the injustice against their father and restored him to the throne. After deciding to found their own city, they fell out, unable to agree on the site. They dueled and Romulus murdered his brother and named the city Roma, after himself. To appease the resentful ghost of Remus, Romulus was forced to institute a festival for the dead, the Lemuria.

Christopher followed Antonella to the entrance. They had the Catacombs of St. Callixtus almost to themselves. Going back to the second century, these were some of the oldest, with sixteen pontiffs buried there.

The last time he had been underground was at the Jenolan Caves, where he found himself fleeing for the exit. Today he was without the feeling something was stealing his breath; today he was visiting the roots of Christianity, and he was looking for an "entrance."

To wherever it might take me.

On surfacing, he spotted the church around the corner from their point of arrival and strolled toward its blue door to wait for Antonella. Towering above him were white pillars, all the more brilliant against the cream background of the walls. Tilting his head, he read the inscription above the threshold—*Domine Quo Vadis*—Lord where are you going?

His footsteps echoed through the church, so he softened his tread. In the center of the church there was a marble slab with two footprints and words carved around the perimeter. He stared at them, lost in the waxy gray-white of the stone.

He felt the presence of someone near him and, recalling what had happened in Israel, he willed the image of the man from Nazareth to reappear. He turned around slowly.

"You seem much absorbed," said Antonella.

He looked at her and gave a brief smile.

He heard her say the footprints represented the miraculous sign of His presence. "Supposedly, this place is where Jesus came to St. Peter, who had fled Rome to avoid martyrdom. Peter asked Jesus exactly what the sign says."

"'Lord, where are you going?'" said Christopher. That is what he would have asked too, of the Lord and of himself.

He felt far from every destination, unguided and uncertain and as hollow as the catacombs.

❧

"Don't go!" Christopher called out.

The room was dark. He sat up, groping around him frantically. "Where is she? Where is she?" he whispered. His panting eased as he realized the marketplace was no longer there; his mother was not there; this was his hotel in Rome.

He reached for his phone on the bedside table. It was only 2 am. His flight was early in the morning, but, as he lay his head back down on the pillow, he realized sleep was not possible. He tried to swallow the panic, but it rose like bile in his throat.

Even minutes later, the images remained strong. He had dreamt he was standing in a marketplace, just like the ones he had visited in Jerusalem. People were bustling around him, bargaining loudly with hucksters, the smell of sweat and spices filling the air. He was dressed in rags, the rough fabric itchy against his skin. His legs ached from standing all day, the hot sun burning his forehead. He was hungry and wishing his wares were something edible. On a red cloth spread on the ground and in his open palms he displayed his merchandise—rusty nails. People would take them, tossing him silver coins in return. He scrabbled along the ground to retrieve the fallen silver pieces and stuff them in his pockets. Soon his pockets bulged and his clothes weighed him down—down into the soil and the dust. He couldn't leave until he had sold all the rusty nails. But there appeared to be no end to them. Suddenly, his pockets seemed to erupt in an explosive cloud. Silver coins sparkled in the dust as they rolled away in every direction. He crawled on his hands and knees, picking them up and putting them hurriedly back in his pockets, but no sooner had he put them in, than they fell out again. Passersby picked up stray coins, kicking dust into his eyes.

As he looked up, through the dust he saw the figure of a familiar woman. She turned slowly to face him and he forgot about the coins, mesmerized by this brown-haired lady. He murmured her name, waving his hands though they were full of coins and rusty nails. She did not acknowledge him. He repeated her name, louder each time. On the third time she looked down at his hands and shook her head before disappearing into the crowd. He tried to follow, running after her, pushing people aside and shouting, "Don't go ... Don't go," until his own voice woke him up.

Christopher went to the bathroom and poured himself a glass of water. He looked at his reflection; his eyes were rimmed with dark circles, his skin pale. He sipped slowly from the glass. The image of his mother from the dream was fading, but not her reproach.

He tried to remember what she looked like in real life, but only scattered elements came to him—the location of her freckles, the crinkle of her eyes when she smiled. He stared harder in the mirror hoping to catch something of his mother in his features. As a child, he had played the game of comparing their reflections. Now as then, he could find little resemblance.

He remembered a colleague of Evelyn's approaching him at the wake as he was standing in the living room looking out at the garden. The crepe myrtle tree was in autumn flame—a conflagration of red, yellow, orange and purple. She had touched him lightly on the shoulder. He had the awkward moment of failed recognition and even now he could not recall her name. She was a tall Chinese woman dressed in a severely cut, dark-blue pantsuit, hair dyed brown and pulled back in a braid. In slightly accented English, she had spoken about his mother's contribution to genetics—how her work with genetic markers of childhood cancer had opened up a new field of research into specifically targeted treatments. Her voice was low and emotional as she concluded, "I know, to you she was simply your mother. But to the rest of us, she was an inspiring scientist. Her work is a legacy you can be proud of."

It was too soon to think of his own legacy. Still, if he were to die next month, this project would be it—a project with question marks all over it. What if TerraDyname refused to make concessions? Resignation would then be the only option. He would be branded as the bleeding heart, but on the other hand he could return to his normal, predictable life. He could go back to university, back to his friends and maybe even sort things out with Swan. *It would be so much easier—none of this constant agonizing.*

He tried to remember why he had broken it off with her, but only felt the dead weight of a departed love.

Turning off the light, he returned to bed and lay on his back, eyes wide open in the dark. In a few hours, he would be in the sky over Brazil. He thought of the giant statue of Christ the Redeemer in Rio de Janeiro—a symbol of redemption.

Will I redeem my soul or lose it with what I am about to do?

De Olmos could not possibly be correct.

"With hydroelectric power," he murmured, "Brazil can arrest the temperature rise that would convert the Amazon Rainforest into savanna.

"De Olmos is saving a tree and losing a forest."

Book Four

WHEN FLOWERS FALL

Chapter 17

THE TWO RIVERS

Unity they will achieve, Christopher thought, *but not here, not now.* Two rivers flowed powerfully in the same riverbed, one darker than the other, one colder than the other, one more acidic than the other. Their origin was different, but their destiny the same. Nothing prevented them from mixing and flow united. But mix they did not here at Manaus. Neither yielded. It was as though a glass wall separated Río Negro from Río Solimões.

He leaned over the stern of the boat that was taking him from Manaus to the construction site of the dam and watched the turbulence produced by the propeller. He put his hand into Río Solimões. The water was tepid.

He could feel the sun burn him wherever it hit exposed skin, and the humidity made matters worse. Loose-fitting white clothes protected his arms and legs from the sun and the mosquitoes. The clothes stuck to him.

The noise from the engine would have been enough to inhibit conversation with Oscar, the foreman who picked him up at the airport, but anxiety kept him from even trying.

Though not superstitious, he found himself dwelling on his dream with the coins and nails. Even two days later, the panic was still lying in wait. Had he been so focused on personal advancement that he overlooked problems with the hydroelectric dam? Was he about to betray people and his own conscience with this dam? But why couldn't his company's success coincide with the public good? In the end, who had priority—the local indigenous people, or the hundreds of thousands who would get electricity and jobs?

Why am I so conflicted? For every decision I make, there is a dissenting voice inside me. He remembered what Dr. Matheson had once said to him, "The mind is a parliament of opposing deputies." In his case, it was more like civil war.

Howard's zeal in stressing the environmental credentials of TerraDyname was now making him doubt them. Still, the CFO had informed him earlier that morning that the board had agreed to nearly everything he had asked for, and advised him to tell the protesters the scaling back of roads would come at a high price for TerraDyname, gains from reduced construction being far outweighed by increased transport costs. Howard had spoken of the need to end the stalemate within two weeks, otherwise the offer would be withdrawn. "We can't afford to lose more time with these extremists," he had said.

"I understand, Mr. Howard," Christopher had replied. "But I hope, if it looks like I'm nearing agreement, the board will give me a few days' grace."

"I can't speak for the board. Try to get there in time. As for the philanthropy, it's five percent for pandemic preparedness, and for direct use in Brazil. You know, it's a political decision. Still a hell of a lot of money."

"Now we have a strong offer to make."

"Good luck, Christopher. And remember, we're the ones providing clean base-load energy. *We* are the environmentalists. *We* help the people of this country. And the industries our power will support will employ one hundred and fifty thousand people. This is power to the people."

Howard did not say it in as many words, but it was clear nobody was irreplaceable and if Christopher failed, there would be someone else to take his place or they would go ahead, protesters or not. Perhaps Francesco and Antonella were right about these corporations. The jobs might be in things like aluminum smelters that harm the ecosystem. The money might be given as bribes dressed up as pandemic preparedness.

As the boat was crossing the two rivers, he became more optimistic about the concessions. The benefits to the community should out-weigh the shortcomings. Meanwhile, he had an offer that should appeal to de Olmos. For whatever reason, the board had indeed agreed to restrict the road network and, in addition, a major donation would now support a worthy cause that could save people in this country. He would present de Olmos with the data, now including the tangible social benefits. *What more could this guy want? Abandon clean energy?*

He looked up and saw some huts on the opposite shore. Now, as the boat veered and began heading toward them, doubts again occupied his mind.

Earlier, in Manaus, Oscar had said, "We can visit. Good for the families. Okay for you? Good for their morale and you see how they live."

He had led him to a white four-wheel drive, sides emblazoned with the TerraDyname's logo—a green globe interlaced with the letters "TD." The driver took his suitcase and opened the door for him.

The wide roads and heritage buildings gave way to lanes cluttered with clapboard-pole houses built from plywood and corrugated iron. TV satellite dishes rose like mushrooms from rooftops, the monotony of gray broken by lines bearing brightly colored clothes hanging like Tibetan prayer flags.

"The *favelas*—here the families live," Oscar had said as they were getting out of the car.

Christopher had nodded he understood the word "slums" and the reality. He could smell the foul odor from a pile of torn garbage bags by the roadside. On a mural, a bodiless hand rose from a lake. Heading toward the hand was a red car, and all were under the threatening gaze of a hawk. A black cat walked lazily in front of Christopher, leaping up with a high-pitched yowl as a barking dog rushed at it.

An elderly woman in a red skirt and yellow top, her long hair in a braid, grinned on receiving money from the driver. Oscar explained it was to "protect" the car.

The workers' families had been waiting in the square around a communal pump. Barefoot children, wearing an assortment of ill-fitting clothes, many in faded soccer jerseys, shouted as they chased each other. Young girls stood straight backed, their hair in neat plaits, their simple cotton dresses sparkling clean. They had made an effort for his arrival. If only he could meet their expectations.

Suddenly one of the older women had come up to Christopher and grasped his hand, crying as she talked rapidly. Oscar approached, but Christopher gestured to him to let her stay. She wiped her tears with the back of her hand and spoke quickly.

Oscar interpreted, "Her husband works for TerraDyname. She says they are all hungry here, you know. No pay, no food, because the *ecologistas* help the trees. The men can't work. But who helps the people? Children are hungry, *Senhor*. We don't know what to do; you must do. Men must work."

"How many men?" Christopher had asked. "How much money does one family need for two weeks?"

"Forty men," answered Oscar. "The *bolsa família* of the government is enough for four in the family for one month—one thousand one hundred reais."

Christopher had made a quick calculation. At the going exchange rate, for two weeks it meant eleven thousand dollars. "I will cover this," he said.

He had held the woman's hands, bending to see her face. "Please, don't worry. The children will have enough for two weeks and hopefully by then your husbands will be able to send money again."

The boat had crossed both rivers and he was now walking next to Oscar on the floating pier, a wooden pontoon that rose and fell with the water.

As Christopher stepped on the wet sand, he thought again of the little boys at Manaus. They looked thin and malnourished. *In Sydney, in Jerusalem, in Manaus, nowhere is there an effective social net.*

While he had been speaking to the distressed woman at the *favelas*, the boys had crowded around him, tugging at his sleeves and repeating "*Futebol, Senhor.*" They broke away after he nodded in agreement, quickly forming two teams and kicking the threadbare ball between them, goals marked out with items of clothing at either end.

He and Oscar had joined opposing sides. Oscar surprised him with his agility, but that was nothing compared to the grace of the boys. Christopher stopped to take a breath and roll up his sleeves, his shirt sticking to him from humidity and sweat. He looked at the boys. Even the youngest competed with commitment.

"*Falta!*" Christopher's teammates had yelled, and he with them, as a boy on the other team tackled their striker. Oscar mimicked a referee, whistling sharply and pretending to pull a card from his pocket. The offending boy helped the striker up. The striker was around nine, his matted hair sticking up in every direction. His grazed knee was trickling a line of blood, but he was entirely focusing on lining up the penalty shot. Christopher had cheered with his side when the ball went between the presumed goal posts, as Oscar and his team stood helpless.

The duress under which the families were living was clear, but surely the blame was misdirected. The problem lay with the distribution of wealth. *You cannot blame the environmentalists for the favelas in Brazil.*

Advancing now on the opposite shore, they plowed through the gently sloping intertidal area for about five hundred meters before reaching ground unaffected by high tide. Christopher looked back. Silently before him flowed the two rivers that made up the Amazon, the largest body of water in the world by volume and the backbone of the Amazon Rainforest.

The people are lacking essentials and this development is needed, he thought. *But will the dam provoke a giant that must not be disturbed?*

⁂

Not even birdcalls interrupted the silence of the jungle.

Christopher was walking behind Oscar on the track to the base camp. The Amazon of his childhood dreams teemed with animals— the shadow of a jaguar, the rustling of grass from a slithering anaconda. But in reality, animals were good at hiding and had ample opportunity to do so in the exuberant vegetation.

Sun-seeking trees joined their crowns to form a tall canopy, while ferns and other shade-loving species provided a second tier. At a lookout, he was able to view the canopy from above. It was a fine-grain mosaic of shades of green, gaps appearing where creeks ran or trees had fallen.

As one of the supply routes for the project, the track was well trodden, but everywhere the forest was trying to reclaim it. Low branches and tree roots that grew horizontally required vigilance.

None too soon, they arrived at the base—a large clearing about the size of a football oval. At the center was a shipping container surrounded by tents with their flaps lifted. One man was playing a guitar, while around him others were smoking, playing cards or doing nothing. Washing was thrown over tree branches.

Oscar introduced Christopher to the other supervisors. Vitor, a heavyset man with short neck and sloping shoulders, shook his hand energetically. "Hey, boss. Be welcome. Sweating, *né*? Very hot here," he said, pointing his finger at the ground. "Not like home, *né*?

"We finish with this wait," he added, throwing his arms in the air. "We want to do. We want to start. You must to show the *ecologistas*," he said, clenching his fist to make his biceps bulge.

Christopher kept looking at the man, trying to formulate a response that would navigate between gaining time and keeping the workers on side. He saw Vitor's lips form a thin line below his moustache. "We stopped in Manaus and I saw some of your families. I understand your frustration," he said and waited for Oscar to translate.

The men cried, "sim!"

"Sim," Christopher shouted back to them. "Yes, your children need you back at work and I have come to try to make this happen. I have concessions to offer Resistência Pacifica."

A collective growl arose from the men at the mention of the ecologists.

"But I need your help too," he continued. "If we lose public support, we risk the entire project. I know you have been patient for a long time."

"*Longo, longo*," they roared back once they heard the words from Oscar's lips.

"Too long, yes. But I ask you to wait for just a little longer."

He and Oscar walked away, but not before leaving his computer on slide show to present the photos he had taken of their families—the boys playing soccer, the neatly dressed girls, the wives, the elderly. One after the other, the men cheered when one of their family members showed up on the screen.

Christopher had asked for a briefing on the standoff at the Árvore Velha. As Oscar opened the door of the shipping container, the heat captured inside the metal walls washed over them. The desks were cluttered with laptops, printers, folders, fans, and even garbage bins. Maps and satellite images covered the walls. Two cockroaches scurried to another hideout when Oscar moved a chair.

"Where are the environmentalists?" he asked after Oscar grabbed a folder and they headed toward a tent.

"A camp about two kilometers far," said Oscar, waving his hand dismissively to his left. "But they stop our work at the Árvore Velha, a grand *mogno* tree. You name it the mahogany, I think. They make rotation. About six of them come, but the Argentinian is at the tree since he come back," he said shaking his head. "Sometimes he is the only one. For them is picnic. For us is no picnic."

"Do the protesters climb trees?"

"*Sim.* When we start again, they climb trees, it is suicide."

"Oscar, we don't want to make martyrs out of them. They will be the heroes and we the villains."

"You the boss," Oscar said, throwing up his hands. "But you are new. They are bad people. The foreigners turn our Indians against us. *Our* Indians."

"I saw something on the internet. Resistência Pacifica posted film of indigenous people with painted bodies protesting with spears and bows and arrows."

"Boss, it is all *teatro*. The foreigners *agitar* the tribes." Oscar made a stirring motion with his index finger. "They promise the tribes more compensation, more reais," he said rubbing his fingers together. "To make protestation for the cameras. When the cameras go, the Indians wash the paint, put on the Nike shorts and the Havaianas and play *futebol* with us."

"Who brings supplies to the protesters? The food."

"Protesters who come bring the food. From many places. This woman in Argentina organize, *la Amazona*. This is what they name her. His girlfriend. She is very, very good. *Inteligente*."

"So, who is the mastermind?" asked Christopher, pointing to his own head. "The girlfriend or de Olmos?"

"I do not know." Oscar waited while they ducked under the tent entrance. "Maybe de Olmos. It is embarrassment for us, boss. Some time ago we had not enough food. The *ecologistas* gave food and some of our men eat it. It cannot happen again. Is bad. Show very weak."

"Are supplies okay now?"

"Now *sim*. I told to the men not to eat no food from the *ecologistas*. Next time they use *venero*."

"Poison! Are they violent?" asked Christopher.

"No, no violent. But José de Olmos is a *maluco*—crazy. He does not want us to cut down not one tree."

"Have you met him?"

"No, but two workers met him and he brainwash them," Oscar said, rotating his index finger in the air above his head. "The workers left. He can infect our men with crazy ideas."

"Oscar, have you ever thought de Olmos might be right?"

Oscar looked puzzled, then chuckled and slapped Christopher on the back as if to congratulate him on the joke. "Boss, he wants us to give up everything, the cars, the airplanes, the electricity."

※

De Olmos would turn off the light at the end of the tunnel to save on electricity, Christopher reflected.

To refuse giving up a single tree meant he had conviction, but he was also irrational. How could one negotiate with a person like that? *Maybe it would help if I cast the issue in global terms. Or should I stress the benefits to Brazil?*

As Christopher was mulling over his approach late in the evening, a message arrived from the TerraDyname team with an image showing one person guarding the tree, along with de Olmos' number. He was eager to put the company's concessions on the table, but, at the same time, he was apprehensive any misstep could waste the one chance he had.

He took a big breath and selected the number, worrying his call might not be answered since it was from an unknown number.

"*Buenas tardes.* Is this José de Olmos?"

"*Sí.*"

"My name is Christopher Camilleri. I am from TerraDyname. I have come here to negotiate with Resistência Pacifica." There was no response. "My aim," he continued, "is to reach a compromise that will satisfy both sides."

"There is nothing to negotiate."

"But if we can't do that, we won't find a solution," said Christopher.

"The solution is you cancel the dam." José spoke slowly and clearly, with a Spanish accent.

"Please, listen to me." Christopher stepped out of his tent into the relative cool of the evening. "I read one of your articles and I think I understand what you are fighting for. Our aims are not so different."

"The aim of Resistência Pacifica is one only. We will not accept anything that damages the forest."

"I would like to state from the outset, this project will follow world's best practice. Beyond that, I have been able to extract concessions. Some of your concerns are addressed and TerraDyname can still undertake its work."

"You do not have work legitimate here."

"Brazil needs clean energy, José. On that I presume we agree. There are some environmental costs to the dam, but look at the benefits—clean, cheap, *renewable* energy."

"The forest captures the carbon dioxide. What you will do is cut it and inundate it. You will burden Brazil with an unbearable loan and leave behind a floor of sand instead of the forest."

Christopher heard the buzz of a mosquito. He should have been inoculated against yellow fever before coming to this part of the Amazon. "With respect, José, that's not true. By replacing coal, the hydroelectric dam eliminates not just carbon dioxide emissions, but sulfur dioxide, mercury and nitric oxide too. No other renewable can provide electricity for Brazil the way this dam will."

"You have wounded the Amazon. I do not trust TerraDyname. Look what you do in India and China."

Christopher did not know much about these other projects. De Olmos could easily score points now. "As it concerns the Amazon," he finally said, "perhaps we have not fully explained what we are planning. It will cause minimal environmental disturbance, but bring major community benefit. We are giving electricity—"

The mosquito returned and Christopher waved the hand holding the telephone. "As I was saying, we are giving northern Brazilian states electricity and employment, improving their quality of life to approach standards enjoyed elsewhere in South America." He continued in virtually the same breath, for fear de Olmos might stop listening. "And I can now inform you that, as part of our talks, TerraDyname will contribute some of the profits to social development. Up to five percent will be donated for pandemic preparedness right here in Brazil."

"Do not say you have concerns about the Brazilians. The people are losing their homes because of you."

"Our contract provides for this. We have joined the State of Amazonas to relocate affected communities to what in fact will be better accommodation."

"They do not want to relocate; they want their way of life."

"José, if we think rationally, we should be able to bridge what divides us. I know Resistência Pacifica opposes road construction. TerraDyname will reduce the proposed road network. This would minimize adverse impact."

"Your company is maximizing the impact, not minimizing. And even if there is no road, the problem is the dam itself. When you damage the forest, you deprive future generations of the right to life."

Christopher stayed silent; in his mind came the intemperate thoughts he had read in that article.

"You are responsible to the company," de Olmos continued. "But you are also a citizen of the Earth. Look in front and beyond the immediate profit. Children will continue to come to life after we die. They are the stakeholders and you must not ignore their rights."

"Reducing the suffering of the living," said Christopher, "should not be thought inferior to protecting the rights of the unborn."

"You have made a better deal than Faust. For the money, you are not selling your soul to *al diablo*. You are selling the lives of the unborn."

"José, if you and I come to an agreement, everyone gains. If not, within two weeks the company will proceed without any concessions. I don't need your answer now. I only ask you to hear me out."

"I hear you. And I conclude you cannot have seen what your company does here. Because if you had seen, you would know you are committing crimes against the nature. If you come with me, you will lose your innocence immediately."

"You are right. It's my first day and I haven't seen the forest. I will come and you can show me. Tomorrow. I can come tomorrow morning, if you wish."

There was silence. He wondered if de Olmos had changed his mind and wanted nothing to do with him. Meanwhile, the tents around him were quiet too. The men had stopped their conversation. But how could they understand anything with their limited English? *Is the name "de Olmos" enough to make them hold their breath as I am holding mine now?*

Suddenly, a clear voice filled his ear. "Resistência Pacifica will not allow you to damage the greatest expression of life on Earth. Nevertheless, I will meet you at the Árvore Velha. *Buenas noches.*"

᠅

José fell asleep with the conversation still reverberating in his head.

Could there be some truth in what the negotiator was saying? Most likely, this man was using an environmental concern as a pretext to exploit the environment. On the other hand, it is possible that ...

Two condors were flying majestically over the forest. Their pitch-black capes tapered into feathers that spread like outstretched fingers. The sky was bright and clear, the sun catching their white collars. Beneath them, a lush green canopy continued endlessly in every direction, bound only by a shimmering distant ocean. Effortlessly they soared on gusts of wind, losing height during the lull, only to rise again on the next gust. Piercing through clouds into clear skies, they flew over the forest until the ocean waves glittered beneath them. Without hesitation, they continued over the open sea. It was timeless, distance measured not in units, but by the wind against your eyes and in stretches of coastline that crept in and out of view. The two birds cruised seamlessly together, sometimes one ahead and then the other, crisscrossing above and below each other, holding each other's talons when in aerial cartwheels. Without signal, they veered back overland. They flew over forest, over snow-capped mountains and

over glacier-filled valleys. But then, as they started following the trail
of a mighty river, they turned and looked at each other. They could
now do nothing but fight. Razor-sharp talons and dagger-like beaks
gouged each other's eyes out as they were both falling from the sky.
One tried to flee, desperately flapping its wings to escape the other's
grip, fighting against gravity, against its fellow, against time.

José woke with a jump, as though he had been in free fall and
had hit the rocks of the Earth. It was 4 am. He knew sleep would
not return.

Christopher was watching two young samurai warriors fight to the
death. He could almost feel the weight of the metal armor of one of
the warriors and the unsoftened contact of the heavy bronze helmet.
Their long swords glinted in the sun as they sliced the air. With every
blow, Christopher could feel the sword vibrating in the warrior's grip.
His opponent parried, but his elevated arm revealed a chink in the
armor. He took advantage and swung mightily, finding his mark. The
wounded adversary staggered and fell to his knees, hands clasping
the gushing wound. The victorious samurai moved in front of the
vanquished one and carefully rested the tip of his sword on the neck,
against his exposed flesh between helmet and breastplate. There would
be no mercy. He sank it in, the sword gliding through soft tissue, the
weight of the man now heavy on the hilt. He kicked him off, freeing
the sword. The dying man fell onto his back, eyes wide open. The
victor forced his long sword again through his opponent, this time
through the abdomen and into the dry earth below. Where the sword
stabbed the Earth, a fountain sprang up. The trickle from the fountain
became a raging river. Not the trees, not the boulders, not the
victorious samurai could stem the river. Weighed down by his armor,

the victor could not float, he could not swim, he was meters below the surface, with no breath left in him.

Christopher was drowning. He woke up gasping for air. Slowly his breathing returned to its rhythm. He lay in bed, and, with eyes open, waited for the dawn.

Chapter 18

SUNSET AT DAWN

He saw birds flying up to the canopy, making way at his advance. At first light, Christopher had taken the jungle path to the Árvore Velha. The morning was relatively cool, leaves dripping dew onto moist ground. A black tarantula, its massive body covered in barbed hair, sat next to its nest on a large rolled leaf. Christopher gave it a wide berth, staring at it until he was at a safe distance.

He called when he was a few hundred meters from the Árvore Velha.

"*Usted me decepcionó*—you disappoint me," came the answer.

"What do you mean, José? What happened?"

"The betrayal of life happened. And you need to decide if you will remain part of the betrayal."

Christopher stopped walking and leaned against a tree trunk which was covered by soft moss. *Has TerraDyname moved beyond its remit? What haven't they told me?* he wondered.

"José, I don't understand why you say that. Our ultimate aim is the same. Hydroelectricity is one of the ways to protect the planet."

"The planet can do without your protection. You are exploiting it. Do you want us to unite with you and find forests pristine to inundate?"

"There is no need for sarcasm. I'm coming to meet you to find a mutually acceptable solution. We are producing green energy and I have extracted concessions. Major concessions."

"*Le vendiste tu alma al diablo?*—have you sold your soul to the devil? You are offering sophistry for syllogism and *egoísmo* for *altruismo*."

Christopher did not respond. Something had turned de Olmos against him. Or had he got it wrong when he thought negotiation was possible with someone like him? Now it was becoming personal, and *his* decisions and character were under attack. This could lead only to impasse. "José, I too respect the forest, not least because it has reservoirs of diseases past and diseases future. It is when the forest is damaged that pathogens produce pandemics. Hydroelectric dams help stabilize the climate and will protect the forest."

After a few moments' silence José spoke. "Pardon me. I am too severe. Perhaps we agree on the principles. Our argument is over the actions we should take…"

"Let's have that argument. Give us time. I want to hear you and you to hear me."

"Let's have that argument, Christopher, but remember, in the end it is binary—we flood or not flood the forest," said José.

"We are minutes away from each other, José. We can discuss this face to face."

"You will not convince me to flood the forest. But perhaps I can convince you to work with me to reconcile humans with the nature. To end the war on the nature." He paused.

"This forest is ours," José continued. "Join me. Unite with me to—"

Christopher recoiled and distanced the phone from his ear, but the deafening sound of an explosion now reached him directly, coming from the jungle straight in front of him.

The ground shook under his feet.

Then the echo of the explosion arrived from behind him.

He put the phone back to his ear only to catch something shouted in Spanish followed by a series of crashes. It was as if a tree had fallen, taking others with it.

Holding the phone to his ear, Christopher started running toward the explosion.

He hoped de Olmos might still be listening. He stopped. "José, José, can you hear me? Can you hear me, please?" The connection was still open, but there was no response. *Perhaps it's an accident. Or could it be sabotage?* He heard a thud as though the Argentinian's phone was dropped.

He called Oscar. "What has happened? Where are you?"

"Boss, I just found. It was him, Vitor, he did the explosion."

"What? de Olmos might have been killed."

"*Nao.* No killed. Just scared."

"What did you do? You knew I was going to meet him."

Christopher started running again toward the Árvore Velha. He swiped at overhanging leaves and branches along the track, scratching his hands on sharp spikes. Trees kept grabbing his clothes. On a short downhill stretch he picked up speed, but he stumbled on a root and fell chest-first on a rock. He could not breathe. Tears stung his eyes and he felt soft, gritty mud work its way into scratches on his palms.

His breath returned in a few seconds. He pushed himself up and started running again. A cloud wafting like remnants of fireworks reached him, bringing the smell of exploded powder.

He could now see the mahogany tree lying on the ground, having crushed adjacent vegetation. It had left a tear in the green dome in the shape of a keyhole, through which a flood of light reached the ground. He had a flashback of the light through the cupola of St. Peter's. He lowered his gaze. The Árvore Velha had no branches for about twenty meters from its roots, but then issued a symmetric crown, now smashed on one side like a fallen umbrella.

He reached the tree. Banners in different languages were still clinging to fallen branches. On the other side, roots that had previously snaked through the earth were now pointing at the sky. Behind the roots he could see scattered trees, but beyond them there was nothing.

"José," he called again and again as he ducked under the foliage and climbed onto the crown and over some banners. It was green everywhere—the foliage of the Árvore Velha, adjacent trees, and ruined ferns and climbers beneath.

He dialed José's number and heard the phone ring at the other side of the crown. He rushed toward the sound. The legs of a man protruded from under the foliage. The brown trunk of a tree fern was on top of him, itself crushed by a branch of the Árvore Velha. "José, I am here!" he shouted. "It's Christopher."

There was no answer. The body lay motionless. He shifted the outer parts of the fern leaves to get at their base. He could see José's black hair.

Pulling with all his strength, he managed to get the trunk off José's body. It looked hopeless. The tree fern had crushed the man. His face was covered in blood and the red color was spreading over his blue shirt, presumably from wounds to the chest.

Christopher leaned over him. "I've got to stop the bleeding, José." He applied pressure to the surface ballooning with blood, but most of the blood was actually coming from a neck wound.

He heard a phone ring.

José was trying to say something. There was blood frothing at the corners of his mouth. Christopher leaned over, his ear now close to José's face.

The dying man murmured, "I ... I failed."

"Help is coming. You can pull through, José."

"I failed. Tell ... Tell them ... I am content is only me. Tell my mother ... Ask her to pardon me."

"I'll tell them, José. Just keep breathing."

"Tell *mi* Lorena ... Tell her today I met a small ... a small marmoset ... I talked ... I talked to the marmoset and it talked to me ..." His voice faltered.

Christopher lifted his head to look at the man's face. He saw the lips tremble. As José struggled to speak, a dimple formed on his left cheek.

"It asked me to thank her ... For its home she tried to save. Tell Lo ... *mi, mi* Lo ..."

As Christopher continued applying pressure to the neck wound, he remembered Evelyn's words, "Make sure the blood circulates around the body." He started cardiopulmonary resuscitation, but, with every compression he made with his united palms, more blood oozed out of the wound.

He checked for signs of breathing. There were none—the chest was not rising and there was no airflow from the nose or mouth. The sound of José's breathing was now only in Christopher's head, the echo of a sound now gone.

The bleeding seemed to ease off; he maintained the compressions, humming the rhyme his mother had taught him to stay in time, "Row, row, row your boat gently down the stream ..." But even after many minutes there was still no breathing.

Suddenly, the smell of blood filled his nostrils. Frantically he kept pressing, panting with exertion and mumbling the childhood rhyme. Was he fast enough and strong enough, or maybe too fast or too strong. It was hopeless, but he kept trying. José's motionless eyes were staring at the sky; the pupils were large. He checked for a pulse—there was none. He could not stop. José could come back.

Bleeding had nearly stopped. Could he have lost all his blood? *I have blood, but how do I give it to him?*

There had been no pulse in José's body, no heartbeat, no breathing for over an hour. His pupils remained fully dilated.

Every time Christopher tried to close the eyelids, they opened again and dead, dilated eyes stared back at him. He could see the irises were black. *How do I give him rest?*

José's face was covered in blood. Terrifying as it was, Christopher could not stop looking at it. He had to find a way to wash off the blood. In the smashed tent, along with sleeping bags and food, he found a crate with bottles of water. With one hand he poured the water over José's face, and with the other he washed it.

He used voice command to call Oscar. "Why aren't you here yet? De Olmos is dead."

"We come and we bring—"

Christopher understood none of what Oscar kept saying. With José's face largely free of blood, he could now see the deep-set eyes, the long eyelashes, the strong eyebrows, the straight nose and the black wavy hair that matched the beard. He recalled the dimple on José's left cheek and touched his own cheek, forcing himself to smile. He could not feel his dimple, but he knew it was there, on the right cheek. It was as though his own face were reflected in José's—a mirror-image reversal.

In Jerusalem people look like me. In Rome people stare at me. In South America people look like me. What is going on? It must be some kind of delusion.

Thick drops of rain started to fall. He looked at the sky through the tear in the canopy. Clouds had set in. His heart pounded against the wall of his chest; his mouth was dry. He knew he was confused, but didn't know what to do. This had to be a nightmare—the murder, the vanishing pulse, the resemblance. Isn't this what the poem his mother told him was all about? "You will not meet the Cyclopes unless you carry them in your soul. Unless your soul stands them in front of you." *If ever there were monsters … I am surrounded by Cyclopes and they must all be in my imagination, exactly as Evelyn said. This is all too bizarre.*

He pinched himself to wake up. But this was not a dream.

He looked at the face before him once again, his mind racing through memories in search of an explanation. There was a resemblance between him and de Olmos. *Maybe I am seeing things. After all, the dimple is on the opposite side.*

De Olmos' body was distorted because the land under it was not flat. Christopher dragged it to level ground. His white shirt was now sticking to his skin in places where blood had soaked the fabric, especially on the middle of his chest where José's head had rested while straightening the body.

He sat next to the dead man and for a long time he stared at the roots of the Árvore Velha. They were massive, but broken and torn from the Earth that had harbored them.

⁂

The afterimage of dilated eyes was still with him and the smell of blood still in his nostrils when Christopher stood up and walked toward the emptiness beyond the trees.

Suddenly, he found himself at the edge of the logged area. Nothing was left standing in front of him—not in the valley, not on the slopes, not on the mountaintops. None of the satellite images had prepared him for this. For the first time, he saw what his company was doing to the forest.

It was relentless removal of all the trees, logging was not confined to the area to be inundated. There had been no thought spared for the forest. Feeling he was about to lose control, he sat down, cradling his head in his hands. Drops of rain were still hitting his head and shoulders. *What have I done? The environmentalists were right. It was a gross error to—*

A soft but sustained rustling sound interrupted his thoughts. It came from a bush near the body. He ran back, his mind on predators that might have smelled the blood. He knelt and put his hand on the forehead of the dead man. The body was still warm.

He again thought there was a resemblance. *Could we be related? Could my own father be Argentinian? Could we even have the same father? It's impossible to think straight.*

If they could do this to José, what else are they capable of? What if all the evidence disappeared and himself along with it? He took photos of José, of the two of them, of the fallen tree, and the clearfelling of the forest, and uploaded them onto his blog, scheduling release in two days.

Christopher heard Oscar calling him. He shouted back, "Oscar, I told you, José is dead. We need to get the police here by helicopter."

Oscar walked up, accompanied by two workers who took off their hats when they saw the body. "Is better not the police, boss."

"This is a murder. We need the police *now*."

"The police have no helicopter."

"They can borrow a helicopter from the army. We'll pay for that." Oscar looked at the two men. "We have guards."

"This is a matter for the police, not the guards."

Finally Oscar made the call.

"Tell them it's urgent. A man has been killed. We'll transmit them the coordinates. They can land at the camp." Christopher stopped suddenly and looked at Oscar, trying to decipher his words. Was he calling the police? Or would a group of paramilitaries arrive to dispose of two bodies?

José's phone rang again. Picking it up from the mud, Christopher said, "This is José's phone."

A male voice responded, "*Que?*"

"Are you from Resistência Pacifica? Is everyone there safe?"

"We are all here. Where is José?"

"I am from TerraDyname."

"Where is José?"

"I am sorry … Just this moment I am—"

"Why you have the phone of José?"

"I am really sorry. José … José is dead. It was—"

"What you say?"

"José … José died in the explosion."

"*Asesino!*"

"No, I tried to help. Please listen—"

His family would call me the same, he thought as he stared at the silent phone. *His family … de Olmos asked me to tell them his last words.*

Christopher refused to return with Oscar to the camp to wait for the police. He felt weak, but knew he had to guard the body against predators and more.

The phone rang again, this time displaying the name "Marmoset." A vignette at the side showed a brunette with long hair. The call was canceled before he had a chance to answer. *Perhaps it's for the best I missed the call. Right now I can't find the right words.*

Lying down on the leaf-covered ground, he looked up. The clouds were shifting, revealing patches of blue sky. He recalled the logged valley. His company was committing crimes—the forest on the mountains was gone. And now this—a man who tried to protect it has been destroyed.

Soon the place began to feel eerie. He was alone next to the body of a man who had died in his arms and who looked like him. How could all this have happened?

Who was José?

Who is my father?

❧

The rain had long stopped, but water was still dripping down from the canopy, trickling through his hair and down his cheeks. The forest would not recover. Erosion would carry the soil to the Atlantic Ocean.

An image of Evelyn came to Christopher's mind—Evelyn the scientist this time, the geneticist in the white coat, as he had seen her countless times in her lab. He recalled the test-tube shakers; the ones on the benches tilted from one side to the other, and then back again like a seesaw. There was a shaker inside a refrigerator, visible through the glass door; it went around and around in the same direction. He remembered the high-pitched sound of the centrifuge spinning at over one hundred thousand revolutions per minute. Evelyn examined the DNA of everything, from drosophila to mice trying to find an answer to—

It struck him—*DNA is the answer*.

He emptied a water bottle and placed some of the coagulated blood from José's neck into it. Tightening the cap, he went to the fallen tent, where he found a small sack to put the bottle in.

The protesters could not be far. Oscar had said their camp was about two kilometers away. They probably called because they heard the explosion. Perhaps they feared for their own safety. Or, maybe, they would come to claim the body.

He crossed the dead man's hands one over the other, keeping his own hand on them while trying again to close the eyes.

He looked at the banners on the fallen tree as they flapped in the breeze. "Let the River Run Free," read one of them. He heard distant footsteps.

Finally, two policemen and the two guards arrived without Oscar. The police wore Ray-Ban sunglasses and carried assault rifles. They seemed unconcerned, almost jovial. The younger man was overweight and the walk had taken its toll. He was soaked in sweat and rain and, when he took off his cap, his hair remained stuck to his forehead.

"Christopher Camilleri," he said, holding out his hand, his voice echoing in his left ear—it must have had air trapped in it. "I am the liaison officer. I was on the phone to the man when the crime was committed and came immediately to the scene."

"We know the accident happen here this morning," the younger man responded. "We talk to Oscar."

"This was no accident." Christopher turned away from the men and gazed at the fallen tree, trying to regain his composure.

"Yes, yes, we investigate now."

"Vitor should be arrested. This is an assassination."

The guards came closer when Vitor's name was mentioned.

"No conclusions," said the young policeman. "The *polícia* must to look at the big picture to find who is involved. We have our procedures." He put on his hat again. "The dead man is Argentinian. The Argentinian consulate needs to learn this."

The police consulted each other and then went to the body. The younger one pulled out his phone and took pictures. They were glancing at Christopher too. *Are they also seeing the resemblance?*

"A tree was killed," said the younger policeman. "Kill a tree, you go to jail in Brazil. But they may have permission. A man died too. Yes, we will investigate Vitor and the others."

The older policeman gave the nod to the two guards to load José's body onto a stretcher. Walking behind them, Christopher kept looking at the track beneath his feet and at José's arm that hung off the stretcher. It was rigid and slightly bent at the elbow, but at the shoulder it bent much more, as though the bones there had vanished.

This was what he was looking at all the way to the base camp, while the same words kept coming to his mind, "I talked to the marmoset and it talked to me … It asked me to thank her … for its home she tried to save."

Chapter 19

NO ES JOSÉ

A *re my steps leaving an accusing trail?*
Christopher was pacing the departure lounge at Manaus Airport, his flight to São Paulo having been delayed. It was only twenty minutes, but he worried he might miss his connection to Buenos Aires.

At the camp earlier, as he was bundling his bloodstained clothes into a separate compartment of his suitcase, he had heard the helicopter engine start. There had been ice in Oscar's eyes as they said goodbye. Christopher had not told him he was leaving Brazil and perhaps Oscar assumed he was going to stay in Manaus. It was hard to know who was guilty and who was innocent.

He had given his statement at the Manaus police station, reliving for them how he had come upon the ruined man under the uprooted tree. They confirmed Vitor would be taken into custody. He was given José's address, possibly because he asked politely, possibly because they were used to doing favors for TerraDyname.

After meeting with the police, he had delivered the blood sample to the Instituto Nacional de Pesquisas da Amazônia. He filled out a form with his details and a nurse took blood for the DNA comparison. As he left, the receptionist smiled and wished him "*bom dia.*" It reminded him of what his mother had noticed after her diagnosis—everyone going about their normal lives, while hers was falling apart. He had the same feeling now—ahead, for everyone else, was the prospect of a "good day."

The taxi driver had understood his rush and delivered him in time for check-in, pointless now that there was a delay. He could not block the memory of the events of a few hours before. He saw the arm again hanging from the stretcher, the bones missing.

Until the moment he had seen the legs protruding from the canopy, he had hoped a furious José would appear, berating him for the loss of the tree. Then the final realization—his hands searching for a pulse no longer there.

In his nostrils was again the smell of blood and on his tongue the salty, metallic taste of gunpowder.

Any minute now, he expected accusing fingers pointing at him. He had not controlled the workers. His speech the day before must have infuriated Vitor. That was probably when he decided. Or was he paid to do it?

If I had left a bit earlier in the morning …

How long would it take for the news to break? He checked his phone for headlines, but there was no mention yet; possibly it would not rate as anything more than local news. At some point, *his* world would know. Michael would know, Swan, his friends, everyone. Nothing he did from now on could remove this shadow.

I must call Michael. But how do I tell him about the worst moment in my life? How do I explain why I feel this way?

❦

Buildings, roads, trees and neon signs were quickly passing by.

Sitting at the back of the taxi, Christopher contemplated checking the news again. There were missed calls from Oscar and the Chief

Financial Officer. He vacillated. As if on cue, the phone vibrated, displaying the name "Howard." He did not want them to think he was hiding. He had nothing to hide.

"Christopher, I heard about the accident."

"It was no accident, Mr. Howard; you know it. I don't want to be part of this anymore."

"You got it all wrong, Christopher. You need to stay in Manaus and handle things."

"No. Not me. You need to realize what you're doing. Your employee killed a man. Consider this my resignation. And I suggest—"

The phone went silent, but Howard was no doubt already spreading the word. Christopher could guess the conversation ...

"*Mr. President, Christopher Camilleri has turned against us. This boy has the loyalty of a snake, but none of its charms.*"

"*We have two options, James. Get rid of him, or arrange for an insurrection—we can hire some guerilleros to attack us. Compensation is in our contract. In any case, with the kind of presidents we have here in this country and in Brazil, we have little to fear.*"

Christopher's legs were twitching with agitation as he stared at the buildings flanking the grand avenue the taxi was following.

Suddenly, the name of the street seemed familiar. But not only the *name* "Avenida 9 de Julio," the avenue itself, the multiple service roads and the median strip started reminding him of something too. The sorry horse rider with the sword looked familiar, as did the stately building on the right, and the tall white obelisk. It seemed as though he was extracting an image of the street from a distant dream. *What else can it be but déjà vu?*

However, the sense of familiarity kept recurring every time he looked out of the windows.

When the taxi took an unfamiliar side street, his mind went to the dream he had in Rome. The nightmare with the coins and the rusty nails was only a few days earlier and yet an age separated him from the person he had been then—so naive and arrogant.

He should never have walked blindly into this. His mother was surprised he chose economics. She was no longer there to consult when the offer came from the company. He was lured, seduced by the promise. *They liked my ideas, they praised me, they offered me the world and I never asked the price.*

He was flogging himself over a past he had no power to change. But what else could he do when he knew he was responsible for what happened? He did not protect José. He did not resist these people.

Having concentrated so much on getting to Buenos Aires, he had no idea what to say now. As he was following the progress of the taxi on his phone, he wondered what could be said that wouldn't make matters worse. What should his first words to José's mother be? He had to take responsibility. *I have come to apologize to you for failing to keep your son safe.* He wouldn't blame her if she refused to see him. He was imposing himself on her. She would want to be with her loved ones. That was how it had been for him after Evelyn's death—wanting to hold and be held by someone close.

The taxi came to a halt. He checked his watch—ten minutes to midnight. Too late to visit, but he had to try. Seeing the driver nod to indicate it was the right address, Christopher passed through the entranceway into a courtyard that provided access to a group of apartments. Weeds, some in flower, were growing on roof tiles and in cracks on walls. On the outside of the building and inside the courtyard there was graffiti, large, spray-painted letters that glistened in the low light.

He reached Apartment number 3. The door was in need of paint and bore traces of posters that had been stuck on it. He thought he heard someone crying inside.

His heart was racing as never before. He waited for it to slow down before knocking.

❧

"*Entre*," a female voice answered.

The door was unlocked. As he pushed it open, Christopher saw two women in black looking at him and sitting on a sofa as though frozen. The room was dimly lit and he could not decipher the look on their faces. They were next to each other holding hands.

As he took the first step down into the apartment, the younger woman jumped up, threw her arms into the air and ran to him. Before he had a chance to say anything, the girl was hugging and kissing him. The older woman rushed to him as well. They were both crying and shouting, "*Mi Dios, mi Dios*, José, José."

"I am not … No, no." He tried to pull back. "I am not José. No José …"

The women kept embracing him, refusing to let go. In all the confusion, he kept asking them if they spoke English. They seemed not to hear him. "I'm sorry. I'm not José. Sorry, I am *not* José. I am really sorry." They were holding him by his arms, his neck, his torso.

Abruptly, the girl recoiled. "*No es* José," she murmured.

The older woman was still embracing him until the younger one grabbed her, shouting "*No es* José! *No es* José! *No es* José."

The older woman let go, but then grabbed his hand. She stared up at him. "*¿Sos vos José? ¿Donde está mi José?*"

He felt her grip weaken.

The girl asked him in English, "Who are you?"

"I am Christopher, Christopher Camilleri. I am here to apologize. I am so sorry. I failed to protect José. I am so sorry."

"Why *you*?" she asked. "Why *you* protect José?"

"I worked for TerraDyname. I was there when he died. I was there."

The older woman pulled him toward the sofa, sitting next to him and not releasing his hand. Her eyes were searching his.

She was examining the rest of his face, her other hand softly stroking his.

"We believed for this minute he is alive," said the girl. "But it is not real. It is not real." Both women were crying.

He looked around the room. On the table with the yellow tablecloth was a photo. It showed José without his beard. And on the walls too, on the pinboard and elsewhere, there were photos of José at different ages—photos that could pass as his own. *There has to be a link. We have to be connected. How else could a mother mistake her son?*

But it was dark, easy to make a mistake. After all, there was no resemblance he could detect between himself and the older woman. *José's last wish,* he reminded himself. *This is the reason I am here.*

With his hand still in the mother's, he started telling them what happened. "It was right after dawn ... I was talking with José on the phone when I heard an explosion ..." Every time he approached a detail about the death, he tried to omit it. "José was still alive when I arrived." He was speaking slowly, mainly addressing the girl, whom he recognized as the marmoset and realized was Lorena. She was nodding at each sentence before translating. "Mrs. de Olmos, José asked me to tell you he failed, but he was content there was no one else with him. He asked you to pardon him."

The mother covered her face with her hands. He looked at the girl and tried to continue, but could not. *How do I tell the girl that he used his last breath to honor her?*

Placing his hand on José's mother's back, he felt the tremor in her body. He bent his head and waited until his own tears stopped.

Recovering his voice, he looked at the girl again. "José's last words were for you. You must be Lorena."

She was motionless. Then she very slowly knelt on the floor and buried her face in the mother's chest. The mother cried out, "*Ellos mataron a mi muchacho. ¿Por qué mataron a mi niño?*"

Lorena stood up. "Martíta ask why they slaughter my son?" giving him a withering look.

"I tried to find out … but I don't know," he replied. "I really don't know."

"Your company is the monster." She averted her face as though she could not stand looking at him. Within moments, she was staring at him again. "*Why* you look like José? You tell to me why. Why you look like José?"

"I don't know. I've been asking myself that too. I am sorry, I just don't know." With the women silent, he continued, "I know I have caused you pain. But I had to come. He told me. I had to find you and tell you."

"If you really want, you could protect him." The girl was looking at him, straight in the eyes. "Nothing you did. Nothing. And you have the *arrogancia* to come …"

She stopped talking, but kept looking at him. Her gestures became wild, her arm poised as if to hit him.

The woman grabbed both of them by the hand. "*Lorena, pará. Hay cosas que vos no sabés. Mañana te cuento.*"

Lorena's arm sank down to cover her face. She sat hunched on the sofa, crying and whispering "José." Martíta stroked Lorena's head as her own tears flowed unchecked.

Abruptly, the girl stood up. "What did José tell to you?"

Trying to maintain his voice, he slowly repeated José's last words.

Lorena folded at the waist as though someone had punched her in the stomach. She straightened her body, only to fold in two again.

He took a step toward her, but Martíta had already enclosed her in her arms.

I am an intruder, he thought as he watched them. *There is no place for me in this grief.* He stood up. *I have imposed myself on them long enough.*

But then he heard, "Wait. Martíta will say to us things tomorrow." Barely audibly, Lorena continued, "Maybe you are a good person because you visit us."

Martíta reached out and pulled him down to sit beside her, holding his hand while also embracing Lorena. The compressor of the refrigerator had been on all this time, but he became aware of it only now, when it switched off.

They sat in the silence. The women's eyes were incessantly on him, but he knew they were seeing José. And what of the bloodstained clothes? *If they see them, it will open a new wound. A new focus of pain. The violent death will become clear.* José had not peacefully passed away; he had been murdered.

As though reading his thoughts, Lorena asked, "José was in pain? He has wounds?"

Christopher took a breath. His answer would be remembered forever. "He was calm. He was focused on the message he was sending you."

He noticed her big brown eyes. He knew that what the women needed and what he needed was distance and clear thinking. He had to leave to process what had happened and then decide whether to trouble the women again. "Thank you for opening your door to me," he said while standing up. "I know I have upset you and I am really sorry."

Martíta squeezed his hand and said through Lorena, "No, my son, the misery of the life comes and God put us together to support one the other. We want you at our side."

He did not know what to say and before he had a chance to think of an answer, Lorena spoke rapidly, "*Él no es inocente. Estás segura de que querés que se quede con nosotros?*"

Martíta then said. "*Está bien que se quede. Nuestras familias están conectadas. Honramos a José al aceptar a este muchacho.*"

"Martíta says she wants you to stay here. She honors José by accepting you. You sleep in the room of José."

The mother of the dead man opened her door to me and now she is offering me …

Martíta stood up and gave him a long embrace. Slowly she released him and kissed him on the cheek.

Then Lorena opened the door to José's room. She dithered, then also kissed him on the cheek.

In English mixed with Spanish, he heard her say, "This night will never have a dawn," or at least this was what he thought he heard.

Chapter 20

A SINGULARITY

It sounded as though somebody had been stabbed.

Christopher was awakened by a long, keening cry from the other room. *Was it Martíta?*

He got dressed, made the bed and took a step toward the door. He stood there worrying how they would react when they saw him come out of José's room. Martíta had said by accepting him she honored José. But for her to need to justify keeping him there, Lorena must have objected. Perhaps Martíta knew the answer he was looking for.

He could only hope Martíta's welcome would not evaporate. He wanted to be there for José's funeral. But then what sort of reception would he get? There was so much to learn about José and their possible connection. The DNA results were expected soon and surely they would provide the answer.

The night before, he had undressed by the light of the small lamp above the bed, barely taking in his surroundings. Now he could see there was just enough space to walk past the bed and reach the small desk at the window, the window itself being half-blocked by the road, which must have been raised after the building was constructed.

As he moved toward the door, he heard more crying, but stopped and sat on the bed.

On the wall abutting the long side of the bed, there was a poster of Che Guevara, its epigraph exulting victory, "*Hasta la victoria, siempre.*" On the wall opposite were faded and torn posters—a flock of penguins walking on Antarctic ice, coral reefs, giraffes and monkeys. He recognized the Keeling Curve, 2006 the most recent year plotted.

On the desk and stacked neatly under it were books in Spanish, Portuguese, English and German, many dealing with the environment and development. Christopher ran his fingers along the spines, looking for familiar titles. He nearly smiled when he came across English editions he had read himself—*Development as Freedom, Economics and the Environment* and *The Algebra of Infinite Justice.* Standing out because of its size was *The Rat Brain in Stereotaxic Coordinates,* a book he had seen in his mother's lab, in fact written by someone at their university. On a pile of books at the side of the desk was a Swiss Army knife, its signature white cross on its red surface; the scissor tool was extended, but the blade, screwdriver, can opener and the other tools were stowed away.

In contrast to the neat stacks of books, spread across the desk next to the laptop were bundles of papers, mostly printed pages, some in manila folders as though they were book chapters. *Intergenerational Injustice* was written in English across the front of one of the folders. "Dedicated to the earthiot Alberto De Robertis for his ardent affection for the environment."

He pondered the word "earthiot," while he flipped through the documents. A blue folder contained text and graphics depicting the evolution of the brain. Some of the paragraphs seemed identical to those in the article he had read on the web a few days earlier. A handwritten Post-it note was stuck on the folder, presumably for later inclusion.

A paradox. Some scientists endeavor to increase the life expectancy from 82 years (in the West) to 150. Meanwhile, other scientists estimate the life expectancy of the planetary systems that support civilization to be approximately 100 years.

José's tight, slanted handwriting was similar to his own, but with differences in the cursives of the "g" and "y." Christopher replaced the documents where he had found them. He would ask for permission to photograph the note, to have something in José's writing.

There was another burst of crying outside. As he was looking at the door, the phone vibrated in his pocket.

"DNA extracted from the two blood samples is identical. Samples lack viral remnants …"

He stopped reading. The answer was in the first sentence.

Something vague but positive was being born inside him. He had found a brother. José was his identical twin.

He was my brother.

But what was the use of this knowledge if the only thing he managed to share with José was two brief conversations—adversarial ones at that? Nothing could make up for the years lost, the years never granted. *The end has come without as much as a beginning.*

He remembered his impressions the night before José's murder— he was a formidable opponent. He might have been an extremist, but he was intelligent, eloquent and insightful. And he had been right, after all. He was a noble brother.

Christopher shut his eyes. Everywhere his mind turned, there was emptiness. Instead of answers, the questions were multiplying. One question was more compelling than the others—was this the connection Michael had in Buenos Aires, the missing "friend"?

Michael had visited there every winter, and not just winter. *But why wasn't I ever told? If José had been in my life, I would have been different too and none of this would have happened.*

No, perhaps that's not right. I am who I am.

Whatever his mother and Michael did, it must have been for good reason. They had given him everything and if they hid something ... *But why hide a brother?*

He looked at his phone and read beyond the first sentence. "Samples lack viral remnants sensitive to the noto-test, suggesting they belong to donors whose parents have not lived for at least 1,800 years. To speak with a counselor ..."

He reread the text several times, increasingly perplexed.

"We are confused also," replied the woman on the phone. "In answer to your question, we can confirm the samples possess identical DNA and are of Mediterranean descent. But there was an atypical finding. A singularity. The Mediterranean people possess remnants of viral DNA from a pandemic in that area at approximately AD 200. Because the people living then were infected, their descendants are carriers. The two blood samples do not possess the remnants. We therefore infer the samples came from individuals whose ancestors have not lived for at least 1,800 years. But this cannot be."

"This is ... this is obviously impossible. Can you redo the test?"

"We have redone the test. This result is a singularity; we reran the analysis. One of the samples was provided by you, correct?"

Christopher kept holding the phone. In his mind revolved maps of the Mediterranean—the Strait of Gibraltar, the speck that is Malta, the boot-like Italy, the extended fingers of the Peloponnese, the duck-like Cyprus, the Nile snaking through most of Africa to empty in Alexandria.

"*Senhor,*" he heard as in a dream. "*Senhor,* are you still hearing me?"

"Yes, yes, I'm just trying to make sense of it. Indeed, it is from me. Is it definite, this finding?"

"In genetics there is no definite, but is most likely. You may visit us ..."

Is this the reason they hid my brother? How could it be true and how is everything connected?

Surely the rest of this was some sort of mistake, but the identical twin aspect had to be real—José's mother and girlfriend confirmed it in the most painful way. *I can't think clearly. I have to concentrate on José's death. One disaster at a time.*

After thanking the counselor, he took the two steps to the door and waited. Somewhere there had to have been a mistake. Maybe the lab had faulty equipment and could not detect the viral particles; Manaus is not Melbourne. It made no sense. *How can you be certain something does not exist?*

Maybe Martíta knew the secret. Was this why she asked him to stay? The only other person he could ask was Michael. This must be why his mother had told him to go to him if life challenged him more than he could bear.

Without any warning, a word came to mind. He had been repeating it all this time, but now it took on a totally different meaning. It was the one and only word that animated his mother during her last days.

Brother.

⁂

With his head resting on the door, Christopher waited until he heard movements.

He came out quietly. Lorena was standing at the stove, her back to him, the smell of frying mushrooms in the air.

"Good morning, Lorena," he said as softly as he could.

As she turned and saw him, she dropped the carton of milk she was holding. She stood staring at him, tears in her big brown eyes.

"Can I help?"

As if a spell had been broken, she drew her eyes away and stooped to pick up the carton.

"Lorena ..."

She gazed up at him.

"The same you look," she said eventually. "The same." Crossing the short distance between them, she nearly took him in her arms, only to push him away.

He could feel her eyes on him as he stared at the white streaks forming on the floor. She stepped back and fell heavily onto the sofa.

He quickly cleaned up and then went to turn off the flame. The oil had started spitting and the skin of the mushrooms had crusted.

Lorena went to Martíta's room, then emerged holding hands with her. Martíta gave him a tight embrace and brought him to sit at the table, her calloused hand holding his. "*Gracias,* Lorena," he heard her say. "*Sos demasiado buena conmigo. Vos tenés que mantenerte fuerte. Ahora les voy a decir cómo tuve a José. Hace veinte años Miguel y Evelyn me pidieron que fuese madre por alquiler de su hijo.*"

There, amongst the Spanish words, Christopher heard the name of his mother and what could only be "Michael" in Spanish.

"Martíta gave birth to José after Miguel and Evelyn asked her to be the surrogate," Lorena translated. She then said, "Pardon, Martíta feels bad she kept the baby. I think she must not feel bad. I will tell to her she is the mother of the boy I will love *eternamente.*"

He looked at the two women. They were hugging each other, talking and crying. Martíta was neatly dressed, the collar of her blouse without a crease, her black hair coiled into a chignon and pinned into place. Her lined face and short stature contrasted with Lorena's. It was humbling to think this woman, passionate and forgiving, had given birth to his brother and was therefore his family.

My family, he reflected. *Can you call "family" a person you never knew? Is family something deeper, even beyond one's knowledge of it?*

With Lorena translating, Martíta spoke of her dilemma about whether to keep the child, of the dove in the church, of the years in Brazil, of Alberto, the passionate professor in the *conventillo* who changed José's life, of her constant fear "the Australians" would steal José.

She took Christopher's hand and looked into his eyes. He knew what was happening—*She cannot help but see her son in me.*

It was his turn to tell them something about what he had just learned. "Once I saw the resemblance, I requested a DNA test and the laboratory contacted me with the results this morning." He felt something soft brush against his leg. It was the cat with the black, white and yellow fur. He had seen her the night before, but today she did not avoid him. She brushed herself on his leg once more and he bent to stroke her. "They found that José and I are genetically identical. He was my identical twin."

"Identical twin!" repeated Lorena. "*Gemelos idénticos.*"

Martíta stood up and spoke quickly, holding Lorena's hands, at times lifting them to her chest.

Lorena then faced him. "Martíta said Miguel did not tell to her he had a child. When were you born?"

"I was born on December 14, 1997."

"Miguel came here soon after you were born," Martíta told him through Lorena. "I felt more worse because I thought I kept the only child of them."

"They didn't tell me they had tried to give me a sibling either."

Martíta sat next to him and rested her head on his shoulder. "I lost my son and you lost your brother," she said, pulling him closer to her. "It is my fault. I took the oath on the Bible to give the baby. The God punished me because I kept José."

Christopher squeezed her hand. *This mother could blame me,* he thought. *She could blame so many others.* "Mrs. de Olmos," he said, trying to keep a steady voice. "You gave José life. You are responsible for his life. This has nothing to do with keeping José."

She asked about Michael and Evelyn.

He told them of his mother's death. After Lorena translated, Martíta kissed him on the cheek and asked him to stay with them. He kissed her back and thanked her.

"Excuse me," he said as he took the phone out of his pocket and headed to José's room. "I need to tell someone who has the right to know."

❧

Christopher hesitated after hearing Michael so happy to receive his call.

"Something has happened," he finally said. "Somebody was killed yesterday in an explosion. He was about my age."

"What happened? Was it an accident?"

"No, it was all planned. But there's more. The dead man looked very much ... he looked exactly like me."

There was silence. "Michael, can you hear me? Are you okay?"

Still no response from Michael.

"Please speak to me."

"How ... how did he die?"

"He was assassinated; by a Brazilian worker. But TerraDyname is covering it up."

"Do you know ... Christopher ... Did he suffer?"

"I was there at his last moments. He was peaceful in spite of mortal wounds. I can't forget his eyes."

The seconds passed, until Christopher whispered, "But why didn't you tell me?"

"My poor boy. How could it ... How could it all come to this?" Christopher could now hear him crying.

"Do me this favor, Michael, please. If you're standing, please sit down."

"I'm sorry, Christopher. It's unbearable. I can't believe we've lost him forever. Are you certain he looked exactly like you?"

"Yes, he did. He was identical to me."

"He was our other son."

"I had a brother and you never told me!"

"Where are you now?"

"In Buenos Aires. In his home. In José's room."

"Is that what she named the baby? Have you found María Olfi?"

"Martíta de Olmos. I'm at her apartment. She mentioned you and Mum."

"She changed her name. I looked for them every year in Buenos Aires, in Cordoba, in Rosario, in Lima and so many other places. Are you sure … of course you're sure. It can't …" He stopped talking.

Christopher heard crying and, after a brief silence, Michael's voice again, "It's a strange thing to say, but my only solace is that my darling Evelyn is not with us."

"Michael, there's something else. I can't understand the DNA results. I got them today—the samples were from José and me. There was something about missing virus particles and having no immediate ancestors for at least 1,800 years. What is this?"

"Christopher, my son, you will have to cross that bridge too … Your mother left something for you. Please come home as soon as you can. You have to read her letter."

He sat on the bed, his gaze frozen on the phone in his palm. Then, as though following a decision already made, he accessed the internet to remove the pictures from his blog.

My brother should live in the memory of those who loved him. As they knew him. As they remember him.

❦

Why hide a brother? Christopher thought again as he emerged from José's room.

Martíta and Lorena were in animated conversation, with Martíta often looking at him and Lorena not at all.

Finally, Lorena said, "Martíta want you come to see the archbishop to do arrangements for the funeral."

Realizing he needed to shave, he went to the bathroom. He unbuttoned his shirt so as not to soil it, and saw in the mirror the small wound from his fall on the rock.

It was clear Martíta wanted him to stay with them. Being José's brother was enough to secure him a place in her home, but such abrupt intimacy, combined with the atmosphere of mourning and the barrier of language, made him ill at ease. He did not want to overstay his welcome, but at the same time he was eager to learn more about his brother.

He dried his face on the soft blue towel and entered the living room. Martíta and Lorena were standing together, holding his bloodied shirt.

"Blood of whom?" Lorena asked. "Martíta takes your clothes for wash and find this. The blood of whom?"

He stayed silent.

"The blood is *your* blood, Martíta thinks."

Christopher only needed to say one word or shake his head. He did neither.

The women spread the shirt on the sofa. They started doing up the buttons, one of them from the top, the other from the bottom, talking quickly to each other.

The bloodstain from José's head was on each side of the vertical row of buttons at the midline.

The women continued talking, slowly now and without touching the spread-out shirt.

Lorena stretched her hand to tug at his sleeve, her eyes dazed. "No," she said. "It is *not* the blood of José."

"I am sorry, Lorena … I'm sorry …"

The women fell to their knees and wailed.

※

It was not until the afternoon of the following day that Christopher said "*Hasta luego*," repeating the words he heard Lorena say to Martíta as they left for the cathedral.

She was taking long, smooth strides, at times creating a distance between them. The greater distance between them, though, was the silence. She remained silent even as they waited for the lights at intersections. He had stopped taking in the city surrounds, absorbed by the awkwardness between them.

The first thing he was able to focus on was the façade of La Catedral, the Doric columns reminding him of the portico of the Pantheon. Here too was a triangular frieze, this time adorned by depictions of Jesus and the apostles.

On entering the cathedral, the marble archways reminded him of St. Peter's Basilica. He caught a glimpse of the altar in the distance— Christ on the cross and above Him a much larger idol of Mary.

As linear and angular the architecture of the cathedral was on the outside, so full of arches was the interior. After passing through many archways, Lorena led him to a bench in a quiet alcove, presumably near the offices. They had walked on a mosaic floor and, now, under their feet were green climbers with pink flowers framed by brown rectangles.

As he sat next to Lorena, Christopher thought of his mother. He reflected that although he had entered churches a few times since her death, merely being in a place of worship had not helped ease his grief. What had helped was talking about her with Michael.

He turned toward Lorena. "If it is not difficult for you … I mean, if it is not upsetting, can you please tell me something about José?"

She looked at him as though the ghost before her had spoken. *This must be exactly what I look like to her, except in this case the body is here and the spirit is missing.*

It took her so long to respond that he assumed she had chosen to ignore him. But then, "Because you are his brother, I must to tell," came her voice unexpectedly steady and clear. "José had a big heart. He forgave everyone." After a pause she added, "We met when he was attacked after the rally of the bicycles he organized. I was on the bicycle and I saw … I found him semiconscious in the Calle Santiago del Estero, on *el asfalto.*"

She brushed her hair behind her ear, in what seemed to be an effort to fill in time until she had control of her voice again. "A driver helped me," she finally said. "We took him to the hospital." She was looking at the floor, her voice a whisper. "He forgave his assailant. His words I remember forever. 'If we didn't know better, we would be like him, and if he knew what we know, he would be with us.'" She stopped.

"He would forgive you too."

"I cannot forgive myself."

"José said the greatest enemy is inside us. He believed more people are tormented by their own brain than by their tormentors." She had previously turned to look at him, but now she averted her head.

I have not seen her smile, Christopher realized. *I probably never will.* What lay ahead was the funeral and then his departure. This was the picture he would carry with him of his brother's love. Just then she made eye contact, but said nothing.

"I read some of his *Intergenerational Injustice* this morning," he said, while they waited for the archbishop. "The neuroscience was a surprise. I thought he hadn't started university."

"He had an old mentor. He was the neuroscientist Professor Alberto De Robertis, who was also an environmentalist. The professor was disappeared seven years ago by the police. They attacked his organization, TodoPorLaTierra, Everything for the Earth."

"I saw the dedication in José's manuscript."

"He loved Alberto. He felt he lost his father," she said as the priest arrived.

They stood up. Christopher noticed the man's inquisitive look. Lorena introduced him as José's brother, before proceeding to converse rapidly in Spanish. The priest blessed them as he left.

"He says the archbishop will meet us soon and will be at the funeral."

"That is a real honor … Was José very involved with the Church?" he asked when they sat down again.

"José was fighting both sides. Inside the Church for things like equality, but also the atheists to make them see via prism different.

"In one of his blogs he asked the difference between Mussolini, Hitler and Stalin in the one side, and the Florence Nightingale, Marie Curie and the Saint Teresa in the other side."

"Ordination, I guess," said Christopher. "Women cannot be ordained."

"Nobody gave the answer you give." He thought he saw a brief tension on her lips.

Lorena continued in a low voice, without looking at him. Maybe she didn't really want him there and was trying not to be hostile. Then again, she had sat very close to him and her body was angled toward him, their legs occasionally touching. *She is definitely conflicted, tolerating me, but at the same time wanting to avoid me. At least she is talking to me now.*

Suddenly, the stained-glass window behind her burst into color; a cloud must have moved out of the face of the sun. "You are Christian environmentalists," he said. "That's the right name for you and José, isn't it?"

"*Exactamente.* And some of the time we have conflict because we are both."

"Can you give me an example?"

"It happened just before. The archbishop sent us to the *Vaticano* to speak in the meeting on the Church and the Environment. Something bad happened.

"Did you go to the Vatican?"

"We had organized many discussions here and the archbishop—"

"Lorena, what happened there?"

"Someone gave to me the pamphlet against condoms and against the control of the birth. It had a picture terrible. One fetus. One fetus."

"A deformed fetus in a jar!" Christopher jumped up. His mind raced back to the bearded man with the piercing eyes and the frantic girl trying to free him in the tug-of-war with the *carabinieri.*

She jumped up too. "*Sí*, why you know?"

"I saw you; I was at the colonnade."

"You was at the colonnade?"

"I saw the commotion and the Italian police arrest a couple, a man with a beard and ..."

"Yes, you saw José and me!"

"No," he said. "Why didn't I meet him at the Vatican instead? It all happened in a moment. If I were closer ..."

"José told me he saw one man who looked like him, much, much like him."

"I thought José was looking at me intensely, but I could not see his face well."

"I do not know all," said Lorena. "But how could José notice the similarity in the commotion if not for a connection deeper?"

"I think he was just extremely perceptive. I must admit I felt for the man who was being arrested and I was angry with myself for not helping."

She held his hand. "When you first came, I could only think of you as …" She paused, and then—"I see now your pain is *exactamente* like ours."

⁊⁊

So near … I was so near him in Rome. If only I had met him there.

Christopher's thoughts kept vacillating throughout the night, between the scene at the Vatican and what Lorena had said about José forgiving his assailant.

He tried to squeeze from memory more details of his brother. He had seen him for a total of a few seconds. Could he recall more of the scene of the arrest? Of José's urgent look at him? He kept thinking too about José's forgiveness of the man who had assaulted him after the bicycle rally—the reasons behind the forgiveness.

As the night advanced, Christopher's mind increasingly went to the man who had caused him the greatest sorrow—Vitor.

Once, his mother, prone as she was to lecturing, had used the rocks on the seashore in a metaphor. Some of the boulders were weathered smooth and were easy to walk on barefoot. Some were weathered sharp, ready to lacerate any foot that stepped on them. "We praise not the smooth rocks and blame not the sharp ones," she had said. "Experience too shapes the genetic material each of us is granted. There is no freedom. There is no praise. There is no blame. We are just genes sculpted by experience."

Another time, she said much the same thing, but seemed to reflect on her own life. "We are the puppets of our genes and experiences. If only we could abandon our undesirable desires, our obsessions, our compulsions, our unrequited love. The puppet is free only in as much as it loves its strings."

He could understand genes and experience were responsible for behavior and Vitor must be forgiven. *But could* I *really forgive Vitor?*

He imagined a possible encounter between José and Vitor. José would have tried to get Vitor on side as he had done with himself and with the workers whom he "demoralized" according to Oscar. Vitor would have perceived José's argument as a luxury of the elite, far from his own raw reality. Then came the violence, only to end in remorse for having taken José's life. *And now ... now it is too late for everyone.*

Dawn found him sitting at the kitchen table, at times looking at his brother's photo, at times at Lorena. She was asleep on the sofa, seemingly calm, though now and then her facial muscles contracted. The cat too was asleep next to her, bodies curled the same way. He was holding the framed photo in his hands when he heard her soft voice.

"Good morning," he responded. "How are you?"

"I slept little. And you?"

"I've been thinking of what you said about my brother—the reason he gave for forgiving his assailant."

She nodded, rubbing her eyes.

"I don't want to overstep," he continued, "but would it upset you if I went to Manaus prison?"

She buried her face in the cushion. "I go with you," she mumbled. "We go after the funeral."

I am doing it for Vitor, he thought. *And I am doing it to see if I can free myself of hate.*

Chapter 21

EL ÚLTIMO ADIOS

C hristopher stepped aside to let a cyclist pass.
By the time the cortege started moving, the cyclists had gathered at the front, some with black triangular flags replacing the usual vibrant orange. They led the procession as it slowly advanced east on Avenida San Juan and, on approaching intersections, some riders peeled off, sped up and blocked traffic.

Between him and the cyclists was the coffin, resting on a carriage drawn by a white horse. To his right walked Martíta and Lorena and to his left Silvia, Lorena's friend, all dressed in black. Behind them were the church choir and the other mourners.

As they were advancing, Lorena turned around and asked the choir leader, "*Por favor, pueden cantar el* Ave María *para mí.*"

"*Ave María* is sung at the weddings," Silvia said to Christopher, looking puzzled. "Typic of when the father walks in the church with the bride."

After a brief silence, the melody filled the air, "*Ave María eres la madre del amor …*"

Martíta stopped abruptly and, with her, the procession behind them marched to a halt. She embraced Lorena. "*Voss siempre serás mi hija.*"

"You always will be my daughter," translated Silvia.

The closer they came to Iglesia de San Pedro Telmo, the louder Christopher heard the bell toll in the left tower, each sound a stab in the heart.

The church was squeezed between a residential block and a museum, its ocher wall pierced by a rectangular window featuring a cross fashioned from blue stained glass. In recesses above and on either side of the window were three small statues. The black wrought-iron fence was hung with wreaths. The carriage advanced to just beyond the church entrance.

The coffin was carried into the church to the mellow sound of the organ playing Mozart's Requiem. Christopher followed Martíta and Lorena down the aisle toward the altar, where a semicircular marble colonnade cordoned off half a dozen pews at the front. Silvia sat immediately behind Christopher, alongside other close friends of José.

The coffin was in the aisle, next to Martíta. It was made of bamboo woven in a lattice of alternating shades of green and tan. Tearing his eyes away from it, Christopher looked over his shoulder at the stream of mourners entering the church. Many of them were about his age, but there were also the elderly and the infirm, with walking sticks and wheelchairs. He quickly turned to face forward, unable to cope with their scrutiny. *Were they all accusing stares?*

"Some of the old people come from the *conventillo* where José lived when he was child," said Silvia, leaning toward him.

The moment he turned back to face her he noticed a very old man, poorly dressed, short and bald, his long beard white as bleached bone. He was supported by two younger, but equally unkempt, men. *Would I have looked twice at these men? What would my life have been like had I been born in the slums?*

If he had faced adversity, he might have had José's commitment. On the other hand, not everyone from the slums became a José de

Olmos. Indeed, just about nobody did.

It must have been something unique about him—perhaps the influence of the "passionate professor."

While the words of the archbishop echoed through the church, Christopher tried to take in his surroundings, anything but the coffin to which his eyes kept returning. In an alcove on the curved wall behind the altar was a porcelain crucifix, illuminated from the back. In another alcove above it was a life-sized idol of the Virgin holding a naked baby Jesus, similarly illuminated. Her olive-green garment was adorned with gold trimmings and over her head was a luminous pallium. Higher still, just below the cavernous ceiling, was a black, wrought-iron cornice with the phrase *Honor et Gloria Soli a Deo*.

"Honor and Glory Only to God," Silvia explained, observing his gaze.

Only occasional words and phrases from the service were comprehensible to Christopher.

Archbishop Aguayo moved close to the coffin. "And let light perpetual shine upon him," he said and then turned his eyes to the elderly woman in the front pew.

Christopher had been told that Dr. Chichina Ferreyra was going to give the eulogy. Unsteadily she walked to the coffin, placing her hand on it before turning to face the congregation. A small pearl brooch adorned her black suit. "*Honor y gloria a José*" were her first words.

Even without Silvia's translation, Christopher understood that Ferreyra had borrowed the phrase from the wrought-iron cornice above her head, twisting it to praise José. She was a link between a revolutionary of the previous century and a young member of the Latin American environmental movement of this one.

There was to have been no other eulogy, but unexpectedly Martíta stood up and walked to the coffin. She stared at it for a few moments that stretched in the silence. Silvia brought her lips close to Christopher's ear and translated.

A spring night I gave birth to you,
An autumn dawn I lose you.
In the autumn you loved, my son,
To climb the tallest trees,
And with your eyes to milk the rays of the sun.

You were good. The sweetness was inside you,
The violets of the garden and all the graces of the sky.
Grace from your grace you gave, my son,
Life from your life.

As Martíta returned, Lorena stood up to hold her. She then took the three steps to the coffin.

She ran her hand over it. Posture straight as a candle, brow furrowed, corners of the mouth downturned, she took out of her bosom a flower, a red carnation, to rest it on the coffin. Her voice was a soft whisper.

"My love, this is for you," Silvia translated. "All the Sundays. All my Sundays were reflected in your smile."

Knowing all eyes would follow Lorena to their pew, Christopher was sure his fate was for those same eyes to see him as responsible for the assassination. He just wanted to pay respect to his brother and leave.

Yet, after the service, he received the same passionate sympathy as the mother and the girlfriend of his brother.

Today I am burying the son my mother never saw. The brother I never knew.

❧

As the coffin was carried out of the church, the old man with the long white beard reached out to touch it.

Tears blurred his vision. "It is my little friend," he murmured. "It can't be him. It should be *me* inside that coffin, dead, dead for him ... In his place it should be—"

"Let's go, old man. You're confused. Let's go," said one of his friends.

"Where are we going?" asked the old man. "Who is in there? Who? Who died?"

"I told you they are burying José."

"Tell me anything else, please. Not this. *Not* my little friend."

"Okay now. Don't get so upset. Maybe it's another José they're burying. We go now."

The old man looked up at the pulpit. It was gold and white. Its sides not affixed to the pillar depicted apostles in relief—Bibles in their hands, lions at their feet. But the pulpit itself was totally empty. There was no one in it. There was no meaning in anything. "I think I know this place," said the old man. "This is not good at all. Something horrible has happened here. Can't you see? This is the end of me."

But then, in his sea of confusion, an island of lucidity appeared. He saw a tall boy with black curly hair step forward to carry the coffin. This boy was much taller. In all those years he himself was in jail, the boy had kept growing and become tall and handsome. How strong his "little friend" was now.

The old man struggled away from his friends and rushed to the tall boy. "I know you. I know you from that little," he said. "You are *mine, mine*. They have made a mistake! They must learn their mistake—My little friend is alive!" he shouted as he grabbed the boy's arm.

"They must not hear us," in hushed tones he then spoke. "They must not hear us. They told me I cannot say anything. My little friend, only you and I know this. Only you and I."

One of his friends caught up with him. "Stop it. Stop it, old man. This boy is holding the coffin! Let him go."

He covered his mouth with his hand. "I cannot talk to you anymore, my little friend," he whispered. "On pain, on pain of death.

"They told me they will kill you if I ever talked to you. Keep the flame inside you, my little friend. Now I return to the shadows."

"Stop bothering the boy," said his friend. "It's late. We need to hurry if we are going to get to the garbage bins before they empty them. Come. Watch out now. There is a step here.

"Poor thing. You can't remember, you can't think ... Alberto, you can't even see anymore."

❧

Six young men from Resistência Pacifica were carrying the coffin on their shoulders.

Just before exiting the church, one of them turned around and signaled to Christopher to take his place.

"*No le de el honor. Él es de la compañía,*" said another pallbearer. Christopher did not understand the words, but he understood their purpose. He hesitated, but then accepted the honor when the man insisted.

Some of the weight of his brother was now on his shoulder. Without warning, the old man with the white beard grabbed him, momentarily weakening his grip on the coffin. He spoke to him in Spanish, at times shouting, at times whispering, before being led away by one of his companions. Shaken, Christopher watched him until the crowd closed between them.

People opened umbrellas as Iglesia de San Pedro Telmo emptied into Calle Humberto Primo. Branches of the two old magnolia trees at the school opposite arched over the street and the church forecourt, providing partial shelter from the mist-like rain.

Christopher counted eight steps from the elevated forecourt to the street. Slowly they carried José down the steps to the hearse. In the middle of Calle Humberto Primo were tram tracks, which abruptly ended at the level of the church, an unused, forgotten terminus.

Lorena caught up with him. "You see the tracks," she said. "We fight for the trams to return. This also was one of his dreams."

He looked at Lorena and nodded without speaking. He had just become aware of the cobblestones under his shoes.

He was a passive observer of his thoughts as they brought him the image of the man with the Byzantine eyes and the words He might have told him if He were near, "I am the nightingale caught in your plane's turbine. The fish that lost its home in your dam. I am the flooded tree."

The image disappeared as fast as it had come and with it ended the internal whispers. Raindrops washed his face and the only thing he could see now was the hearse awaiting his brother's coffin.

All around him and inside him, the sounds seemed to mingle.

On the way to the cemetery, they stopped at the intersection of Calle Balcarce and Carlos Calvo where the *conventillo* once stood, and then outside José's last residence, the residence that now hosted Christopher, before following Avenida Corrientes directly to the Chacarita Cemetery, where all but the prosperous were buried, as Silvia had explained.

By the time they arrived, the rain had stopped, but a sky full of clouds resembled a caved-in ceiling. The air smelled of rain and freshly dug earth.

The coffin was placed on two planks of wood that straddled the grave. The undertakers suspended it by pulling the straps taut under it and removing the wood.

"*Mi niño, mi niño, mi vida, no me dejé*—my child, my child, my life, don't leave me," painfully clearly he heard the mother's cry as the coffin was lowered into the earth.

The pallbearer who had given his place to Christopher stepped forward and gave each of them a rose, red as the blood that pulses through the body, before throwing into the grave a wreath made from branches of the Árvore Velha. "*Adios, compañero*," the man said. "*En nombre de la tierra por la que luchaste a la cual ahora retornás, adios.*" He then repeated it in Portuguese.

"Farewell comrade. In the name of the Earth, for which you fought," Silvia translated, then paused for a long while. "And to which you now return."

The rose in Christopher's hand had no thorns, its smooth, flexible stem issuing a single leaf. He looked closely at the leaf. It had serrations all around and was deep green on the upper surface and light green underneath. Leading directly from the stem was the midrib, issuing veins, like the tributaries of a giant river.

He knew what to do with the flower; the same as with the one Michael had given him.

As he let his flower fall, he noticed Lorena bringing hers to her lips before extending her hands over the grave.

During the trip back, he kept hearing what Martíta had said when, after a long wait, she let her flower fall: "*Mi último adios*—my last goodbye."

❦

A framed photograph stood in the middle of the dining table between two vases of white flowers, the same photo that was there the night Christopher arrived.

"*Noviembre 2018*," he read on the margin. It was from José's graduation, before he grew his beard. It was illuminated by three large candles.

Christopher was introduced to those at the wake he had not already met. Carlos was the first contact of Resistência Pacifica in Brazil and the pallbearer who had relinquished his place. Marcello was the pallbearer who had objected; he was José's closest friend and something in his voice suggested this was the man who called soon after the murder.

As they sat around the table, to his left was Archbishop Aguayo and to his right was Silvia and then Michelle, José's English teacher. He could hope for translation.

"So much light turned to darkness," said the archbishop after blessing the meal. "We are gathered here because we have lost the dearest person to us, because we will not have his indomitable spirit, because the one who brought the best angels out of our hearts is with us no longer."

As the archbishop spoke, he focused his eyes on one person at a time, going around the table as though addressing his remarks directly to that person. "But we also thank God because He gave him to us for these years. José fearlessly faced down the forces that threaten to negate life. Now that he has left this world, we wonder how someone like him was one of us," the archbishop concluded, his eyes on Christopher.

Nobody spoke until Martíta said, "Thank you, Father. Fate has woven the most unlucky thread into my life."

The archbishop held her hand. "This is a test of faith for all of us left behind. Little comfort it is to know, but our people say, '*A quien Dios ama, le llama*—God calls the one he loves.'"

The Spanish rhyme Silvia just translated was still in Christopher's ears when he heard Marcello say, "*El diablo gobierna el mundo. Dios hace lo que puede.*"

"The devil governs the world. God does what He can," Silvia translated and all conversation ceased.

It was painfully clear to Christopher who the "*diablo*" in that room was according to Marcello, and it was a relief when Michelle picked up José's photograph and turned toward him saying, "This is a beautiful picture. You look the same."

Christopher noticed the resentment on Marcello's face at the comment. "We spoke on the phone," he said. "But I never saw him until all was lost."

He felt the archbishop's arm on his shoulder. "I want to tell you I have in common your pain. I want to say more that no life can be thought lost if it has lifted the conscience of so many to that which is so noble. When …"

The archbishop kept speaking and Silvia kept translating, but the words were now blurred because Christopher could not stop glancing across at Martíta, the mother without her child.

While still seated, Marcello put his arm around Lorena and pulled her into him. "You weren't there. He was chained to a tree in front of the Árvore Velha when he told us a story. He told us to imagine a little indigenous child who always climbed the mahogany tree to see the stars. Imagine then the child growing old and forgetting everything, everything except the moments on the branches of this tree. So, the tree was the only thing that reminded her that once she was a child, simply a child. José told us he had met a woman who was this child and her tree was the Obelisco de Buenos Aires."

"The name of that woman was Nina," said Martíta. "To her he was devoted … I lit a candle …"—she was trying to regain her voice—"a candle every day he was in the Amazon—both trips. I knew it was too dangerous for all of you."

"José *knew* what he did," said Lorena. "He explained the dangers to the volunteers and took the greatest risk himself." She paused. "But Martíta, you will not be alone. I will be at your side. Always."

Christopher saw there were still a lot of vegetable empanadas and, soon enough, Martíta urged her guests to help themselves.

"I'm sorry for the little kids," said Silvia. "He used to tell them stories, different to each one."

"What sort of stories, Silvia?" asked Christopher.

"Allegories with a message or just jokes. He one time asked a boy eating a sandwich of chicken, 'Do you like the chicken?' The boy nodded and José replied, 'Aren't you lucky the chicken doesn't like you?'"

Silvia attempted to continue, but her voice had deserted her. She got up and left the table. Lorena soon followed.

The archbishop stood up to embrace both girls. "My children, a better day will come. Have faith."

They all remained quiet until Lorena whispered, "You know, he was writing his *Intergenerational Injustice*, or *Injustice Infinite*, as he sometimes called his book. One day he said to me, 'I have written a hundred thousand words and still haven't written a phrase like, "To be or not to be." My words are weak.' I feel that way too," continued Lorena. "This is exactly what I feel now."

⁊⁊

"*Triste vivo yo*—I live in sadness," Christopher heard Lorena say.

It ended the silence that had descended after all visitors had left and Martíta had withdrawn to her room. He could see her lower lip quiver, her eyebrows knit together.

He dried the last glass and sat with her at the table. "Nothing could have been more unfair to him, to you, to Martíta. Words are not enough. His life was more powerful than any words."

Seeing she was still in distress, he brought her a glass of water. Her head was averted, but then she turned and looked at him. The candles behind him were now throwing light onto Lorena's eyes, making her irises expand. "You have such big brown eyes," he said.

"José loved my eyes. He called me 'Marmoset,' it is the small monkey with the big eyes." She paused and again looked away. "Your brother liked my competences too. He did the theory and I did the tactics." A hint of a smile formed on her lips. "José said I was his 'frontal lobes' for my good planning. But ... I do not know *why* I say these things to you."

He felt a needle touch his heart. "We can remain silent," he rushed to say. "The last thing I want is to make you feel uncomfortable."

"Sorry, I must not be angry. I am not." She seemed to be searching for the right words. "In the jail, there was a window in my cell. One day I saw his letters on the wall opposite, 'The junta cannot conquer an *Amazona.*'"

"I admire him and I admire you, Lorena."

"Him, maybe. I am ... I am empty," she said, pointing at her sternum. "Vain and José knew. He loved me, but he molested me because—"

"Teased you."

"Yes, 'teased' me, because I want to be the best at everything and the most beautiful." She took a breath and continued, "He said I would leave him if he said Mona Lisa had a nice smile. And he liked to tease me when I decorated myself." She stroked her hair. "To go to the festival of tango."

A long pause followed and Christopher imagined scenes from the lives of these two people.

Lorena brought her chair closer to him. "You found something about us. How about you?"

"I studied commerce and economics and—"

"Can I say something? José would not have liked your economics. He said economists who support the corporations of the world are the followers of Faust."

"Well, I'm afraid he told me that directly," he replied, sensing his own bitter smile.

"But you are not *only* an economist. Correct? Tell me about *you* more."

"I just started working for TerraDyname and I thought I had extracted some concessions from them. At least they promised to—"

"No, no. I want something about your life. How were you when you were child?"

"I always lived in Sydney. My mother raised me with Michael. They never married. I don't know my biological father—that left a big gap. I am trying to find him. Michael, of course, has been—"

"But Michael *is* the father of you."

"Michael has been more than a father to me, but he is not my biological father."

"I am confused," she said, bringing her hands to her temples. "I believed the husband of Martíta was the father of José. But then she told us she was the surrogate. So I believed Miguel was the father of José."

"When I was little, Evelyn told me it was sperm from an unknown donor. I have already spoken to Michael and I'll find out more when I return to Sydney. I love Michael, but I have this need in the back of my mind to find my paternal origins, to know that part of me. My mother was a big part of my life, and now that she is gone …"

"Your mother. Your mother is the biological mother of José. Tell me something about her."

"Evelyn had a scientific mind, but I only thought of her as my mum. It wasn't until after she died I came to appreciate her as a scientist."

The cat with the three colors brushed her flank and tail against him. He bent down and stroked her soft fur. On her tail, black and white bands made a zebra pattern. "To me," he continued, "she was always tender, sometimes odd, sometimes funny, always my mum. She was crazy about safety. When I was little, if I started crossing the road without looking both ways, she would grab me and bring me back to the curb to start again. Even when there was no car. Always systematic and focused on her aim."

"I want to see her. You have photographs?"

He had taken this journey through the photos a number of times in the last few weeks. This time he just chose his favorite, a close-up of Evelyn.

"She looks not like you," she said as they huddled over the screen of his mobile. "I cannot see the similarity. You must to look like your father. Biological father. But she was very pretty."

"Michael is handsome too and he has the softest heart. He's an obstetrician—delivered me, actually. We spent a lot of time together when I was little. One of the games we played was what he called 'strip the metaphor.' He would hug me and say, 'Scratch my back and I'll scratch yours.' He would send me to pick oranges from our tree saying, 'I can always rely on you to pick the low-hanging fruit.'"

In the silence that followed his words, Christopher thought of Lorena's bond with his brother—how it would feel to experience this love.

But if he asked her anything personal, he risked offending her. Eventually, he worked up the courage to ask what she thought love was.

"Love is what I had with José," she said without hesitation.

They said nothing more for a moment.

"And you?" she then asked. "What you think?"

"I think love is as overwhelming by its presence as by its absence."

He saw her extend her neck and he moved to the side so her gaze could go beyond him, to the photograph that stood between the candles.

He heard her say, "Love lives when flowers fall."

❧

I have to tell Christopher.

Lorena stood still under the arched doorway of the rose-colored Manaus jail. They had just gotten out of the taxi, but she could not take another step.

"I cannot forgive Vitor," she said. "He took the heart out of my chest."

"You don't need to, Lorena. It's more than enough you came."

She looked at him. His expression of concern was so much like José's.

"I have to ask forgiveness from you and Martíta," he continued. "I should never have been involved with TerraDyname. You can wait for me outside here, or would you prefer to go back to the hotel?"

His voice, his expression, the dimple on his cheek, it was all the same—a ghost assuming flesh and bone was in front of her eyes. She expected him at any moment now to call her "Magnificent Marmoset."

"Speak to them," she told Christopher as they approached the guards.

He looked at her quizzically.

"Pardon me, I got you confused ... You lost your brother also," she said as they continued walking. "But you are *lucky* you did not know him. You do not know what you lost."

At the reception, she used her basic knowledge of Portuguese to obtain the pass to visit Vitor and was informed his wife and children were there to see him too."

The children cannot be guilty, she thought, *but the mother ...*

She saw a woman with three girls. The mother was cradling a baby, while holding hands with the eldest, the middle sister completing the chain. They were walking around in the small visitors room. The mother seemed to have indigenous ancestry, her rust-colored hair collected into a bun held in place by a long stick visible from the front.

Christopher took an envelope out of his wallet. "Please give this to her. It is to assist now that Vitor cannot work."

What if this is hush money from the company? Lorena worried. *But it can't be,* she thought. *This is* his *initiative. He would never have given me such money.*

She wrapped the envelope in her silk scarf and went over to the mother, connecting first with the older children by patting their heads. She spoke in Portuguese and then explained to Christopher when he walked up to them that she had told the woman they were José's family. The mother was speechless, unable to comprehend what was happening. "We try to do what we can for our families," Lorena continued. "Sometimes, the evil finds us."

After a moment, the wife said, "Vitor did not want harm. He wanted work. I am sorry; I beg for forgiveness."

"I have come to tell your husband I forgive him," said Christopher through Lorena while the woman nodded.

"Can I hold your baby?" Lorena asked.

After a brief hesitation, the mother handed her the child. Lorena rocked her gently in her arms. Turning to face Christopher she said, "I will never have a baby. Not with my love. Not with anyone."

She saw sadness cross his face as he stared at the ground.

The little girls were clinging to their mother, glancing at Christopher and hiding their faces.

He crouched in front of them and said, "You look sweet, even when you are hiding your faces."

Lorena translated for the children, then turned back to the mother. "Now the times are difficult for you." She glanced at Christopher. "The brother of José likes to help." She handed her the money wrapped in her scarf.

"Your forgiveness is already … I cannot have this," she said, pushing the gift back.

"Please accept it. It will mean much to Christopher, if you do."

The woman looked at Christopher, who took the package from Lorena and put it into her hands.

When the chimes rang for the start of visiting hour, Lorena knew she had to give the baby back to the mother. She hesitated for a moment, surprising herself. *It is the first time I do not feel babies are made of marble.*

⁊⁊

"Lorena, you are unsteady." Christopher caught her as she stumbled while following the guard in the tunnel leading to the cells.

"It is the memories," she said, placing a hand on the wall. "Bad memories."

He stopped. "Let's turn back now."

"No, I will be well."

As they continued on, he kept hold of her arm.

The further down they went, the darker it became and the smell became stronger, a combination of decomposing food, excrement and sweat. He handed her a tissue to hold over her nose and mouth.

The guard stopped in front of window 22, where Vitor stood some distance behind a pane of glass with a hole cut in it. There was no privacy—other prisoners also had visitors.

Vitor was in prison uniform—an orange sleeveless T-shirt and baggy shorts. There were manacles around his wrists and ankles, his tightly muscled arms hanging limp at his sides.

Christopher felt light-headed and, for a moment, he thought Lorena had grasped his hand to support him, until he noticed how pale she had become.

"Your brother," said Vitor, looking at Christopher and then shaking his head and looking away. "My wife said." He looked at Christopher again. "Your brother."

"Yes," said Lorena. "And I … I am the girlfriend of José."

Christopher felt Lorena tighten her grip on his hand.

Vitor looked at her, then back at Christopher. He opened his mouth, but then closed it again, as though what he held inside him was not ready to come out.

"Sorry, very sorry," he finally said in a whisper. "My family was …"

Christopher looked at the man in chains. *Can I really do it? Can I be the person who does something like this?*

A little later they asked the guard to escort them out. Even after they reached the outdoors, he could still hear the echo of his last words in the jail.

"My brother would have forgiven you. And I … I am sorry for your suffering now."

❧

"You need time to focus on your grief," said Christopher as they sat in the back of the taxi taking them to the airport. "I will not trouble you anymore."

She answered a few moments later. "No, you can return to us." After a pause, without looking at him she added, "I must to tell, now I see something of José inside you and—" She stopped again. "Pardon me very much," she said. "This is the second time today. I am sorry about before. It reminded me of my jail."

He thought of taking her hand, but her fingers were interlaced in her lap. "It is important for me you came today, but if I had known it would bring back memories, I would not have wanted you to come."

"You could not know. My country last year was living a second 'Dirty War.' This time the junta attacked the environmentalists because they were stopping the deforestation."

She continued, "There is forest little left in Argentina, but the jungles and savannas remaining were cleared so the American companies plant the soy *transgénica*. Just to feed the cows. The companies show the nature no mercy."

Sensing she had more to say, he stayed silent.

"The government was ruthless *equalmente*. They attacked us at the Facultad de Medicina de la Universidad de Buenos Aires when we made the protestation for freedom, for the environment and contra the overpopulation. The tanks came. They killed the students. They arrested others. I was tortured …"

Christopher struggled to align his impressions of who he had imagined *la Amazona* to be with what Lorena was telling him now. She had every right to be angry with life. She had been tortured in the body and in mind and now her love was dead. *I would stay with her,* he thought, *if only she wanted me to.* But the only thing he said to her was, "Lorena, I'm sorry. I did not know."

"Maybe you heard about *Las Madres de Plaza de Mayo*—the Mothers of the Plaza de Mayo," she said as she suddenly took his hand in hers.

She probably intended nothing more than to attract his attention, but at least it ended his dilemma.

"They united to find their missing children," she continued. "Children that became disappeared by the government in the 'Dirty War.' Every Thursday for five decades they meet in the Plaza."

She stopped, as they passed a stately building with arched doorways and large verandas. Surrounded by colonnades, it stood as a relic of the flamboyance of the rubber boom of Manaus.

"They wear white scarves. Each mother had embroidered there the name of her missing child. More mothers joined when their children became disappeared by the new junta. The old junta killed three mothers. The new junta told to the soldiers to kill all *Las Madres de Plaza de Mayo*."

"But I heard the soldiers mutinied."

"Yes. For the people of Argentina it was a moment of pride national."

"Lorena, Argentina can be proud of you. I hope the wounds heal."

Her eyebrows came together and furrowed her forehead. She looked just as she had at the funeral. "They will," she said softly. "They will heal for all of us. But not for him."

"Not for him," Christopher repeated. "One half of us will always be missing."

It was time to tell her. "They expect a big demonstration tomorrow at the site José died. I didn't want to trouble you before with this. I have been in contact with Carlos. After I leave you at the airport, I will join them at the Árvore Velha."

Chapter 22

A CODE REUSED

As the plane commenced its descent into Sydney, Christopher was gripped by fear of what would be revealed. There could be nothing good in what Michael was going to tell him. *Surely all this secrecy has been to protect me from some terrible truth.*

For a moment he was back in the forest, in the middle of the demonstration of the environmentalists. The multicolored flags, some with his brother's face printed on them, the slogans, the pulse of the protest had signaled a new beginning for the fight in the Amazon. There was the comradeship of the demonstrators, especially toward him. They had wanted him to be at the front and center of their activities. He had felt they considered him one of them and he felt increasingly certain he belonged nowhere else.

The approach to the airport offered views of the central business district, Darling Harbour and the Balmain peninsula. The Parramatta River branched into bays and then into smaller coves, like fractals. In the distance to the east, the suburb of Manly was visible astride the North Head at the entrance to the harbor.

He could feel her lips on his as he replayed their farewell at the airport. Just before Lorena went through the barrier, she had stood on her toes to kiss him. He had bent toward her, but did not turn his head to offer his cheek. To his surprise, she did not turn her head either. Lightly, briefly, their lips touched.

A few days earlier, when he was saying farewell to Martíta, she had placed her hand on his chest then pointed to herself, gesturing for him to return. This is what he wanted too—to sit and talk with the woman who had given birth to José, to hear stories about the brother he lost the moment he met him.

But he also hoped for something else—equally important. He knew he wanted to be with Lorena.

The rising sun made the waves that lapped the Opera House glitter, the building itself now resembling a cluster of mainsails. However, it was its northern aspect that stayed in his mind. It always reminded him of the mask of a science fiction hero his mother had given him when he was a child.

He followed the other passengers into the white aerobridge taking them to the terminal, a reminder of the long tunnel that led to the painful encounter in the Manaus prison. It had only been an interval of about an hour between the jail visit and the farewell kiss.

What did the kiss actually mean?

It had probably nothing to do with him—not with his beliefs, not with his character. His appearance, his resemblance to José, must have triggered her affection. He was an impostor, who for a moment had stolen the throne.

His mind leaped from event to event unpredictably. At the best of times he could not predict what his next thought was going to be and this was never more evident than now.

Some things made no sense at all. Why did TerraDyname hire him in the first place if their plan was to eliminate José? There, in the river of people reaching the terminal, unanswerable questions kept surfacing. *Did I do the wrong thing by not throwing out my shirt with José's blood?*

The taxi to Michael's house took him past Maroubra Beach, where his mother used to take him to boogie-board. The sea was violent, water billowing over the rocks as waves smashed onto them. A seagull soared above, making a number of seemingly aimless maneuvers before drifting with the wind.

The Pacific was still blue, the sand was still golden, the headlands were still green—the terrain kept its identity, but what of his?

❦

I live for the moments Christopher walks through this door, but this time ... I will cause him pain.

Michael was standing on the threshold looking in the direction from which the taxi would come, wondering what to tell Christopher about all that had passed.

Should he tell him of the love that enveloped him and Evelyn, of the love they lost, of the love they found again? Should he tell him how it all started—the ossuary and the discovery of the remains? The little flower Evelyn found near the ossuary would certainly be unimportant to Christopher. But it was important for her.

Should he tell him how they agonized over the wisdom of cloning? His lingering doubts on the authenticity of the skeleton and her unshaken belief? He certainly could not tell him about something that not even Evelyn knew—of his sudden affection for the cuckoo. His urge to emulate the bird's reproductive practices and fertilize Evelyn's ova with his own sperm.

It was the most important decision of his life—whose DNA to use for Evelyn's pregnancy. As it turned out, how could he have loved anyone more than Christopher? *My life has meaning because of him.*

Certainly he had to tell him of their anxiety about possible complications with the unprecedented pregnancy and, before then, how Evelyn had accidentally divided the embryo, creating two distinct lives.

He had to tell him of Evelyn's passion for science, of her vision to correct an injustice—what she perceived to be the greatest injustice of all time. And of her dream to see Christopher succeed in whatever he chose to do.

There was the moment when he held the baby boy in his hands and rested him in the arms of the woman he loved. It was the moment of their lives. Then there was the first look Christopher gave his mother—as though he recognized her, as though he knew her face.

But he also had to speak of the other embryo and how their dreams for his twin brother were shattered. Of the hope that became despair. There was that night, so many years ago, when they watched Christopher sleep, holding hands in silence till dawn.

He would not have to tell him what was going to become obvious after reading the letter—what Good Fridays meant, the monastery of Ithaca, Jerusalem and Rome.

If, however, the letter did not cover parts of their history, he had to be ready to explain, to tell him about the ancient scroll, the sign on the cross, the golden bangle with the initials—the milestones of their lives.

Is he strong enough to carry this burden or will I harm the one I love? How much to tell and how much ...

❧

Christopher hugged Michael before they entered the house.

He placed his suitcase at the front entrance next to the coat rack that was covered in bits and pieces as always. Hanging below the hats, umbrellas and jackets was a key suspended from a silver chain. It was the key to the house Christopher had shared with his mother.

Gone was the living room clutter that had accumulated during Evelyn's illness, when Michael neglected all else to focus on her. There were no longer piles of laundry on the armchairs or stacks of documents on the antique writing desk. The old couch was now covered with the batik sarong his mother had given Michael when she left the house for the hospital. On it she had embroidered, "For a Life with You."

"The kettle's on," Michael called from the kitchen.

"A cup of tea would be nice, thank you."

Weak sunlight was falling on the drawings Christopher had done as a child. There was no wall in the living room without a picture of him, either alone or with his mother and Michael. Though only mid-autumn, the gas fireplace was on, countering the chill of the Antarctic wind.

He sat down in his usual green wingback chair near the fire and removed from the coffee table a thick book—*The Human Nervous System.*

He could see through the open doorway into Michael's kitchen. The man he always thought of as his father, and who was about to reveal to him the secret of his life, was slowly stirring sugar into two teacups.

"Michael …" he started and trailed off, apprehensive of what he was about to hear.

"There you are, my boy."

Christopher took the steaming mug, wrapping his fingers around it for warmth.

Michael sat in the maroon wingback chair opposite. "You know, I always wondered if somehow you and our lost boy would ever meet. I knew he wasn't destined for obscurity and believed he would reveal himself to us someday. But I never … I never imagined it could come to this."

"Martíta told me about the surrogacy. Why didn't you ever tell me?"

"Your mother and I, we just wanted what we thought was best for you." Michael spoke softly, laboriously. "We thought a lot before deciding, but always had doubts."

"I understand when I was little, but keeping it secret even after Mum got sick?" He paused. "I had a brother—an identical twin. Why go to Israel when I could've gone to Buenos Aires?"

Michael remained silent, his eyes seemingly fixed on the steam rising from his own cup.

"What an irony," Christopher continued. "The trip Mum arranged actually brought me near ... I was so close to him in Rome. Michael, it's incredible; I was next to him. I didn't recognize him because he had a beard. But he looked at me as though he *knew* me, and his girlfriend later told me he was convinced I looked just like him."

Something like a bitter smile formed on Michael's lips.

"And at the same time," Christopher continued, "think how often you would have come close to him on your trips to Argentina. It was as though we were trying to hold something that always slipped our grasp."

"In the first years, I went there with your mother. We took you, but you were too little to remember."

"So, that's why 9 de Julio seemed familiar. I remembered it!"

"It would be amazing if you retained a memory. You were only eighteen months old the last time we took you. Later, I went alone every winter during the school term. I tried summers too. I searched for them but found no trace. I thought if he were to be found, I would've found him by now ...

"My boy, I want you to understand what a dilemma it was for us. If we gave you the knowledge, we would have given you the hope. It might have been worse to give you hope for a brother who was not alive—"

"But Michael …"

"We were working with probabilities. We didn't even know if María had given birth to the baby. You said she named him José, right?"

Christopher saw Michael's lips move without sound, as though he was trying to recall the times he had come across that name in his searches.

"We knew the date of conception. I talked to obstetricians, to anyone I could."

"I just keep thinking that if I knew about this, I would have gone to Argentina. I might have found him. I might not have joined TerraDyname. We lost our chance. We missed out, Michael. Both of us. All of us missed out."

"I understand how you feel. Over the years your mother and I despaired as our prospects of finding him were vanishing. We wanted our other child and we wanted you to grow up with your brother."

Between the occasional sips of tea, Michael spoke of his trips to Buenos Aires. He talked of the first visit when he transported the embryo and met Martíta, called María. He talked about all that followed, when their efforts to find the mother and the baby proved fruitless, their hopes increasingly left to luck.

In turn, Christopher talked about TerraDyname, the assassination and the cover-up, the lies and the ruination of the forest. He spoke of José, his formidable arguments, their moments together—moments which were to be José's last. He spoke of José's final words to Lorena, and of noticing the resemblance, including the dimple on the cheek. He spoke about the women holding in their hands his shirt with José's blood on it.

"But that thing about the ancient DNA; it has to be some sort of mistake, right? We can't descend from people that far back. It is not possible."

Michael did not respond. In the fireplace, the yellow–blue flames were dancing, but suddenly it felt cold in the room.

"My hope was to protect you from this forever," Michael finally said. "But now I need to tell you. This is why your mother wanted you to go to Israel … What do I tell you first? We were … we didn't know and we did what we thought was best … I am confusing you. I'm sorry. It will be better to read your mother's letter, to learn this from your mother's own words."

With Christopher following, Michael went to the antique desk and unlocked the small drawer on the right. He took out a tube and from it extracted a rolled document, which he placed into Christopher's hands, cupping them as though to ensure safe transfer.

The document had a red wax seal on it, with the inscription "From me to you." Michael's words rang loud in his head and he wondered for a moment whether it would be better to leave the document sealed. There could be nothing good under the red seal. *The singularity is our DNA.* Evelyn was a geneticist.

Did she alter my DNA? Am I chimeric—part human, part something else?

Maybe the flames were the best place for it. In his imagination, the flames were already melting the red wax over the singed pages. All he would then have to do is acknowledge to Michael that he considered him his father. He would tell him that he loved him, just as his mother had acknowledged her love in the end. He could open the avenues of his future himself, unburdened by the shadows of the past.

But, how do I destroy the last thing my mother left for me? And uncertainty might be more tormenting than the truth.

He broke the seal. He stood motionless, frozen. Moments later, as he was unfurling the paper, the letters started to reveal themselves, each taking hold of his consciousness as though without his consent, following a path laid down in childhood. It was written in their secret alphabet.

My sweetest spring,

As in a relay race, parents grant life to their offspring, keeping our species immortal. This sequence was not precisely so in our case. You are my beautiful child, but not only.

For you to have broken the seal means events in your life have made answers to your questions about your origins imperative. The first thing I want to reveal to you is that you have a brother, a monozygotic twin. I hope your twin, whatever his name, has given María, his mother, as much happiness as you to me. The two of you were one cluster of cells when I accidentally divided you.

May it be a beautiful day when fortune reunites you.

I can imagine your bewilderment at discovering this and your disappointment in me for not having told you. However, your origin is extremely complex and I had decided you should only find out if you had to.

If you have found your brother, you may wish to read the rest of this letter with him.

My beautiful boy, please tell this to the son I never knew. My dream was to raise the two of you together.

I hope his destiny holds love and purpose. I have no ill feelings toward María. I understand fully the bond she must have formed with your twin and why she refused to honor her contract. Even though she gave birth to him, your brother was not her biological child, and, as I reveal to you now, neither were you mine.

Before you learn of your ancestry, let me share this one last thing.

Nothing in life has made me happier than raising you. I was gathering the rays of the sun to make a rainbow.

"Christopher, you've gone pale. Do sit down." He heard Michael's words, but far louder were his mother's—

East of Masada, in the Judean Desert, I found ...

He did not answer Michael; he had reached the armchair, but remained standing. His eyes had moved on to the following lines, where Evelyn revealed the origin of the DNA.

Like lightning, the image from Nazareth came into his mind. It looked Byzantine—not like him at all. His mother couldn't be right.

Or perhaps it was his vision that was not right. That vision was based on the icon in his room. *How can I judge what is real and what is fantasy? Can anything be validated?*

He felt Michael's hands gently push him onto the chair. He read on.

... here I must also admit to a major personal weakness. As a student, I fell in love with the wrong person and was unable to progress even when I met the most beautiful man of my life, Michael. Sometimes, the idol is more attractive than reality. In this way, my love for Jesus was a way of keeping love in my life. He could never disappoint me. He was so distant, so obscure that my own thoughts could complete my idol.

I told no one of my fear of life bereft of love. This burden should not have been Michael's, should not have been yours. I did not want you to feel a stranger, an incidental outcome because this is not true. The truth is I discovered love when I first held you in my arms. What I wished most was to allow you to be your best self, to blossom like the desert flowers after the rain.

Christopher kept reading the unknown story of his life.

… My son, no one can be certain. Certainty is elusive. What I can attest to is your intelligence and compassion. If your twin is similarly gifted, this will be additional evidence, but never proof.

Now the secret is yours.

Even from distance, may my love protect you both. You are my children.

With love eternal,
Evelyn

He kept holding onto the paper, trying to reread it. Unable to concentrate, he allowed it to roll back up into a tight scroll.

Nothing could erase what he had just learned. The world as he knew it was over.

Michael took the two steps that separated them and pulled him up into his chest.

"It is not possible," Christopher murmured. "It can't be true."

Taking a step back, Michael looked at him. "The science is true—the cloning happened. As for the rest, that was her hypothesis. She always believed it."

"Did you believe it, Michael?"

"Christopher, what matters now is your own judgment. I loved your mother. As years passed, I loved her beliefs and dreams too."

"Did you ever think of telling me?"

"Evelyn had the final word on this, and I agreed. At first, you were too little to understand something so complex. We postponed it until you became an adolescent, and then until you became an adult, but even then we did not find the right moment. The years passed. Something you hold inside you for so long, in the end, it becomes a secret."

"So many things about me are dark secrets. My origin. My twin. And look what all this secrecy brought us."

They sank back down into the armchairs, Michael repositioning his next to Christopher's.

"Instead of searching for a brother who was real, I was searching for a father who wasn't. There was no father, right? I was not conceived, not even adopted. I was not brought into this world. I was constructed."

"No, no, my son. Your mother carried you for eight months. On her breast she nurtured you. We raised you in our arms. We loved every smile you gave us, every step you took, every word you said. All of our years together were true. *Nothing* was constructed."

"How is it fair for me to be reading this letter when she isn't here to answer my questions?"

Michael remained silent. Christopher felt he was losing control. "How can I find out who I am?" he continued. "*What* I am. Am I one of her experiments?"

As though through a kaleidoscope that transforms everything, he saw fleeting moments of his childhood. Everything seemed different now, even his own name. When did she decide to call him Christopher? Before extracting the DNA? During pregnancy?

After sitting next to each other in silence for some time, Christopher looked up and saw tears in Michael's half-closed eyes. *I can't stress him anymore.*

Yet, there was a question that was increasingly occupying his mind. "Tell me, Michael, why do you think she did it?"

"It was her love for Christ. She had this dream of bringing Him back."

Well, that didn't turn out right, Christopher thought.

"Did she love Him like a nun?"

"No, not like a nun. She was never religious. She didn't believe in anything metaphysical. She considered Him one of us. But, yes, she always admired Him."

"I know she loved you, Michael."

"Yes," he said, slowly nodding in agreement. "She told me at the beginning and at the end."

It's not entirely their fault. They tried the best they could. But did they not think of what it would do to me?

Christopher leaned over and held Michael. The time had come to reveal feelings he had kept secret until then, to tell him a word long overdue.

"Father," he said to him, perhaps for the first time in his life.

It was a beautiful word.

Time passed as they talked of their life with Evelyn, especially the childhood years. Christopher got up to bring water for both of them. "So, she didn't do it just to see if she could; right, Michael?"

"There usually are many motives behind our actions. I can be certain of one thing—Evelyn was a scientist when she began; she was a mother when she finished."

"Do you mean her motives changed over time?

"More that she had different motives even at the same time. But her love for you was above all else."

"Mum told me it was hard to figure out our own motivation."

"Perhaps at the beginning she wanted to correct an injustice, what she thought was the greatest injustice. But after she gave birth to you, all she wanted was to be your mother. Nothing else mattered once you were born. A single event in the life of a person can focus their motives, perhaps even confine everything to one motive. Her motive was you. If I could speak of a second desire, it was to find your brother."

"How like José, Michael. He too wanted to correct an injustice, what he called 'the injustice infinite'—this generation creating the conditions for the extinction of its progeny."

Though it had seemed things inside him might settle, Christopher felt the previous turbulence overwhelm him again. "But tell me, Michael, how can I know all these things about myself and still feel I am Christopher? I am someone else. Not who I thought I was."

"You are our Christopher."

"I can't get my mind around this."

"Look at you and José, how differently your lives developed. Even identical twins are different individuals, independent personalities."

"You mean, it's our environment?"

"Yes, the environment has an equally important role as the genetic code. It's the factor that can change everything."

The album with the photos from Israel came to mind and he asked Michael about them.

"Yes," he confirmed, "she photographed everything at the find."

"When I was little, I looked through her albums trying to find someone who looked like me. I don't look like anybody. And later, when I realized how important the trip to Israel was for Mum, I thought I would find a link there."

"She wanted you to visit the places where Christ lived and to form your own bond with Him."

The flames in the fireplace were repeating the steps of their dance. "To whom do I belong, Michael? Wait. If I am cloned, not only do I not have a father, I don't even have a mother."

"It is not just biology that determines where we belong. We belong to one another. You are everything I have." Michael stood up. "Let's walk to where your mother used to take you when you were little."

❧

The first lightning strikes were so far out at sea that Christopher could not hear their thunder. They became more frequent, audible and increasingly louder.

The two of them were walking the few hundred meters downhill to the northern end of Maroubra Beach. There was a strong onshore breeze, patches of blue sky appearing and disappearing between rapidly shifting storm clouds. The surfers, resembling seals in their dark wetsuits, were now scurrying toward the beach café, running low to the ground for fear of lightning.

As quickly as the sky had become heavy, so quickly did it allow light to come from where the firmament met the sea.

Walking along the promenade, Michael spoke of Evelyn's discovery and what followed. On their fourth lap of the beachfront, he brought his story to an end. Christopher stopped and looked at the water's edge. Each new wave was replacing its predecessor as it expired on the sand. "There is no end to this," he said.

"There is the end we determine. And there is the new beginning we choose."

"Michael, I don't think I can find closure."

"Nobody is invulnerable in life, my son; even Achilles had his heel. Things will get better. We have lost one of you. Please don't put yourself at risk."

"No, not me, Michael. There is no risk with me. I'm the defective embryo—the one from which she aspirated the cells. Nobody would bother to get rid of me."

"No, no. Don't think that way."

They started walking again. "That's not how it works," Michael added. "Embryonic cells are pluripotent—any cell can become anything and, as it happened then, you can even divide an embryo in two. Your genetic endowment was identical, like two drops of water." He stopped walking and reached out to Christopher, holding him back. "You are forgetting you are the boy who set up the Amnesty branch, who taught those children." With his hand on Christopher's shoulder, he continued, "These are compassionate acts. They are political acts."

"But who is the person who did these things? I can't but reconsider everything about myself. Michael, who am I?"

"You are the person who gave meaning to our lives. Our lives are interwoven as much as lives can be. You gave us the happiest moments, the happiest days, the happiest years. You and nobody else. You are a unique individual. No matter where you came from, no matter how you were born."

Michael kissed Christopher on the forehead. They embraced each other before continuing their walk.

"We didn't have you in the usual way, but it was with all the love we could give."

"There's no point in blaming Mum. But was she so ambitious, so idealistic to want to bring back Christ? How extreme! What a risk to her own health!"

"Your mother was ambitious in everything she tried. And an idealist. She was not an applied scientist, but a pure, basic scientist. You know her work forms a platform for the development of treatments of childhood cancer. As a scientist, she reached far. She tried to do the same as a mother, to reach beyond any limit."

"So, what does that make Him to me? Father? Brother?"

"Don't think of it that way. It will get you nowhere. Your mother is she who gave birth to you and your father he who raised you. Evelyn will always be your mother and I am, and always will be, your father.

The waves continued coming to the shore in their eternal rhythm. He thought of the flames in the fireplace. It would have been so much simpler if he had thrown the letter into the fire.

But I cannot disown my past.

۶

After returning to Michael's house, Christopher stepped alone into the backyard, closing the door behind him.

By now the sky was clear. The paperbark tree was familiar. The southerly wind was familiar. As different as he was feeling inside, he could recognize all that connected him with his past and their emotional importance to him.

The tree listed as it yielded to the wind. Pieces of bark were strewn all over the buffalo grass, next to snapped twigs. The swing his mother had made for him from a blue ship-mooring rope dangled from the tree, dancing in every direction. There was a knot at the free end of the rope where he used to sit when they swung him. Michael would push him and Evelyn would stand guard in case he lost his grip.

Christopher's mind transported him to his own house, where he thought the ghost of Evelyn might appear as he mentally visited each room. Etched in his memory were images of her sitting at her desk marking papers, lying on the couch, chatting on the phone in her firm, but serene, voice, the white cord hanging like a necklace.

Finally, his mind took him to his room. The icon was still hanging above his bed, the eyes still following him. It looked the same as it had always done since he could remember. But now it meant something else. It was a symbol of his mother's secret life and the mystery of his origin. On the other hand, nothing proved the hypothesis. It might all be false, a case of mistaken identity. But to Evelyn, it was all true. Michael made it clear—she believed her hypothesis to the end.

He asked Michael to join him in the backyard.

"Are you going to meet Swan tonight?" Michael asked a little while later.

The question brought him out of his reverie. "We broke up before I left. My fault as usual."

"One thing I learned from life, Christopher, is that it's nobody's fault. Nobody owes us love. Nobody. But if it happens, it's the only indestructible thing. Not even death can rob us of it."

He thought of another love that had survived death—a love that lives when flowers fall.

❧

Hardly a moment passed without thinking of his mother's letter. It was out of this world.

What if I am the failed part of this experiment? But, no. How could you call a "failed experiment" the countless times we rolled in the backyard, hugging each other, turning, and turning, and turning?

Memories of Evelyn's illness followed him like a shadow as he crossed the hospital grounds on his way home with his takeaway dinner.

He felt some relief when he left the hospital behind, but the thought of his house weighed on him. How could he find peace at home when everything would look different through the prism of the secret? He was not certain whom he could trust—or, for that matter, who would believe him. The idea would be taken as a colossal delusion.

Letting himself into the house, he walked straight to his room and lay down on the bed, still clothed. He did nothing, not even eat the takeaway; he just stared at the ceiling.

Rousing himself after a few minutes, he opened PubMed on his internet browser. Cloning would have to work similarly in humans as in other animals. In the search field he typed, "Cloning procedures mammals."

After a while he started to comprehend the general scheme. He and José came from the one egg Evelyn contributed after replacing her nuclear DNA with the ancient DNA. All their genes were the same and came from the ancient person who was buried in the desert—all, except the tiny fraction that came from Evelyn's mitochondrial DNA, from outside the nucleus of her egg. Barring this small maternal contribution, the ancient person had exactly the same DNA as he and José.

So then, what is my relationship with the ancient man?

Not that of father and child. Fathers share only half of their DNA with their children. Only identical twins share all their genes. It was not quite right, but identical twins was the best term to describe him and the ancient man.

They were born to different mothers. They were born in different millennia.

However, they were made from the same DNA. The very same molecule that produced the one, produced the other.

I am the identical twin of the ancient man, and so was José.

As monozygotic twins that spring from the same cell, he and José shared the same DNA sequence that was produced 2,000 years earlier for one, and only one, use. For one, and only one, person.

The unique molecule was borrowed.

Evelyn had violated its uniqueness, reusing it to produce two new people.

Mother, what a secret you kept!

❧

"Silvia, I have to tell you what just happened to me."

"Is there a problem?"

"Christopher called."

"Ha, what did he want?"

"He's coming back next month. He wanted to apologize for the kiss. He said I could think of it as a mistake."

"And you?" asked Silvia.

"I told him I forgive that mistake." She waited for her friend's response, but there was silence. "Silvia? Are you there?"

"I'm here, just surprised. Do you think you're ready for this?"

"I know I shouldn't have said it. I feel I've ... Silvia, it's like I'm betraying ..."

"Lorena, you have been through so much already. You will get through. All of us are here for you."

"I know, Silvia, but this is so confusing. I can say this only to you—when I'm with him, it's like somehow José is still here."

"You really need to be sure you're ready for this."

"This is what I want too. But I don't know how to get rid of my confusion. He looks like him, he thinks like him; sometimes it's like—"

"But it's *not* him."

"Nobody will ever be, Silvia. Nobody will ever replace José. And I know, deep down I know, I shouldn't use Christopher."

She paused as she tried to untangle the thoughts in her head. All seemed confusing and conflicting. "But there is so much in him that *is* like José. After the wake and in Brazil, we talked for hours about everything. I wanted to know him more. And I found things. The same things. Maybe I'm crazy. What if I'm just transferring to him things I feel for José?"

"I don't know, Lorena. I just don't know. Right now you are vulnerable. I think you need to slow things down."

"What do I do? There is no shadow where I can hide my pain."

"I know, my beautiful friend. Fortune has dealt you the best and the worst. But just promise me you'll wait until your emotions settle."

"Silvia, I'm afraid to say it, but it's true. Looking at his brother's face is the only thing that lessens my pain. Maybe I'm using him.

Maybe I'm deceiving myself too, but I can't help it. Inside me, hope is battling despair."

❧

Through the fixed glass pane above his window, Christopher could see the foliage of the Sydney blue gum and through the window proper he could see its trunk—patchy green, with areas of freshly exposed bark a brighter green than those weathered.

Head propped up on the pillow, he pulled the quilt over himself. As he stared at the borders between the patches, they swam under his gaze, blending into each other and staying out of focus.

He buried his face in the pillow and tried to think only of Lorena. He remembered the sympathy in her big brown eyes as she listened to him speaking of Evelyn. He thought about being close to her. The scent of her—not just floral, but darker, muskier.

He picked up the phone, only to drop it a moment later. He should not trouble her again. But she seemed pleased to talk to him the last time, even saying she forgave the "mistake." How quickly, how deeply he had come to love her mind and her body. But was it because of who she was, or was it to wash away his guilt? Everything was interconnected. There was no guarantee that through Lorena he was not trying to capture something of José, to connect with him.

Whatever the reason, every cell in my body wants her.

But for her, being with him would be a constant reminder—an open wound. *I should postpone the trip.*

He repeated the last thought, sensing the bittersweet temptation to call her—it could delay the next time he saw her, but he would hear her voice at this moment. He picked up the phone and readied himself to count the times it rang.

"Christopher, it is so nice to telephone."

It was answered on the second ring.

"I wanted to hear your voice."

"Well, yes ... Would you like to use the video?"

He could feel his heartbeat as he waited for her image to appear. "There you are, Lorena. I ... I wanted to check something with you. I'm thinking it might not be such a good idea for me to come back next month. I mean, you and Martíta may need some space. I could postpone it for a few months."

"Martíta asks about you."

"*Quiero verla, pero yo no quiero causarle ningún problema. Quiza debería quedarme en un hotel.*"

"*Eso,* since when you speak *Castellano?*"

"I've been learning from the internet."

"I can teach you this. And you are the brother of José. I do not feel it is correct for you to come to Argentina and sleep in the hotel. Martíta made the bed in the room of José. It is true ..." She paused. "The truth is I also want you to stay with us. I am very deep in my pain now. But I know speaking to you is good for me."

"*Muy bien, gracias,* Lorena."

"I told to some friends you said you will come."

"You did? And what did they say?"

"Marcello is not nice. He say the word 'fratricide.'"

How can I face them? Christopher thought. *How can I look at her again? She must be affected by how her friends see me.*

Lorena continued, "He said without you, José would be alive."

"And what do you think?"

"For me, is like part of José is still alive."

Chapter 23

THE SHORE OF RÍO DE LA PLATA

"José de Olmos"

Christopher read the name on the wooden cross.

A solitary sparrow scratching for grubs flew off on their approach. Greenery had not yet established a foothold on the grave. He could still smell freshly dug earth and, on coming closer, the fragrance of flowers recently placed there.

All the excitement he had felt on seeing Lorena waiting for him at the airport was now gone. He had kissed her on the cheek, saying, "See, I didn't make a mistake this time."

"I cannot forgive twice," she had said.

Her response had made him smile. But now, at the grave, he realized sadness would be behind any smile. His life, too, had been thrown into turmoil since José's death, since his return to Sydney, and his mother's letter. More and more, he felt the only place for him was there, in Buenos Aires, near Lorena and Martíta. *But I've been terrible in my relationships,* he thought. *Why would I think I know where I am going this time?*

But this is different; my feelings are different. If Lorena would give me a chance it would be forever. And if she didn't, it would still be forever.

There is no way I can get her out of my mind. Even if I wanted to, I cannot.

He saw her kneel on the grave and make the sign of the cross three times. She was clutching a small, round silver container with the Virgin Mary in relief on top. She took out the rosary beads and prayed on each of them, her lips moving silently.

After kissing the box, she poured water into the vase at the base of the cross. From her purse she pulled out a red carnation and placed it with the others. "A red carnation it was he gave to me the first time we went to the cinema."

There were many carnations in the vase. Some fresher than others. It seemed she brought him one every day. "Your love for him ..." said Christopher, "it is so beautiful and so sad to see."

"It is forever."

He did not speak and she continued. "The answer to what you asked me. I know it. Love is what never dies."

Christopher went closer to the cross.

Lorena stood up and took a step toward him. "*Dame tu mano. Vamonos ahora.*"

He grasped her extended hand and held it as they started walking toward the bicycles.

"I forgot to tell you," he said as they were about to ride. "At the funeral, an old man with a long white beard grabbed me by the sleeve as we were leaving the church. He was murmuring something in Spanish. He seemed frightened and confused."

"He might have been unwell here," she said pointing to her temple. "To many, José was like their son."

"I wish I had stopped and talked to him, but it was when I was holding the coffin. He wasn't alone, but he wanted me. He was clinging to me."

"He thought you are José."

"The professor," they both said and looked at each other. They returned to the grave and, sitting on the earth, talked about the professor and how they might search for him.

❧

A waxing moon was just rising from the water's edge, its light reflected on the surface of Río de la Plata. The city glowed on the horizon to the west, stealing the shine of the stars. After chaining their bicycles at the bank of the river, Christopher offered his hand and they began to walk.

"Buenos Aires is beautiful," he said.

"No person stops you from living here."

"Lorena, I would like to, very much so. But everything is happening so quickly and I'm not yet sure of my place. How would you feel if I were to live here?"

"Sometimes I transfer to you some of that I feel for him," she said, adding immediately, "but not often."

He could not believe how unpretentious she was. There was a lot he wanted to say, but something else had to come first. "Lorena, there is an important thing you need to know." He pointed to a bench. "Let's sit down here; please, come close."

"Here, I come close," she said as they sat on the bench. "Now, say it to me."

He put his arm around her waist and, after hesitating, she put her hand on his knee. The ripples on the river's surface softly came to rest on the shore. The moon had risen a little.

"It's about our origin, José's and mine. One thing is clear—we are identical twins."

"*Ciertamente.*"

"Yes, certainly," he said. "But there is more."

How do I tell her without making a monster of myself? And she is so religious! "To explain things, I need to tell you first something more about my mother. I told you she was a scientist. She was actually a geneticist." Feeling every word carried danger, he continued, "Her field was cloning. And this has to do with our origin. José and I," he paused to take a breath. "We were not conceived in the usual way."

"IVF?" she asked.

"Yes, but not only. It has to do with how she obtained the DNA that José and I share."

"How?"

"She extracted it from an organ of a person who lived long, long ago."

"You mean cloning?"

"Yes, Lorena. We were cloned from another human being. But there is something more."

"Cloned? Human cloning?"

"My mother left a sealed document for my eyes only. She wrote it in our secret alphabet. In it she explains our origin."

"Cloned from another human being is science fiction."

"I know it's hard to believe. It sounds impossible. And there is more."

He heard her repeat his last sentence as if an echo, surprise written on her face. He recalled her holding the rosary box, kissing it, pulling out the beads to pray on each one. *Perhaps this is not the right moment,* he thought. Immediately, though, he realized he might never manage to gather more courage than he had at that moment. "Lorena, look. The secret I am about to tell you is troubling and incredible. I'm not even sure I can believe it myself." She stayed quiet. "As I said, my mother extracted the DNA not from a living person, but from someone who died a long, long time ago. She discovered his remains in the Judean Desert."

"You mean Israel."

"Yes, they were in an ossuary buried in the earth. Besides the bones, there were other items, including a scroll written by people of that time."

"To clone she must to use a tissue preserved."

"Exactly. Amongst the remains was a preserved brain. Circumstantial evidence suggested to her the remains belonged …"

He took a deep breath before continuing. "They belonged to Jesus of Nazareth."

The color disappeared from her face. Her lips did not move.

In the long pause, Christopher kept looking at her.

"No, no, *Cristo* was resurrected!" she said. "No, no, no, this is not correct. Maybe you not understand. It would mean that …"

She did not complete her thought, but kept looking at him, switching her focus from one of his eyes to the other, until abruptly she grabbed him by the shoulders. "What if it's true? Nobody was like José. *Nobody.*" He could make out a few words amongst her whispers. "I have fear, I have fear."

He drew her against his chest and started stroking her hair.

"Nothing is certain, Lorena. It's only a possibility. I'm sorry to burden you, but if there were one person in whom I would confide …"

A couple with their child and a dog were walking past them. The dog had a small red ball in its mouth and was ducking away from the child, who was trying to grab it. If only *his* life could be this simple.

"You are not alone," she said shaking her head, as if trying to clear her mind. "Because you are with me."

"Lorena, I don't know if you have understood how precious you are to me."

He kept stroking her hair.

"José, *mi amor*, a clone of Him," she suddenly said. "It cannot be true."

"Let's assume we descend from someone who lived back then. Lorena, do you think it is possible to leave the past forever in the past?"

"We live this united. José is my life and you are his brother."

"*Gracias.* Nothing is more important to me than your acceptance."

She extended her hand to touch his face. "In you," she said, "I see not only the face of José."

※

It was as though he had negotiated a minefield.

Now the person with whom he had shared his secret was walking by his side on the bank of the river, their fingers interlaced. The one who mattered most and was directly affected by his mother's secret, not only did not reject him, but she wanted to assist him.

A chilly *pampero* wind started blowing in from the south. Lorena stopped and, leaning against the rail, looked out at the water. Christopher stood at her side, placing his arm around her shoulders. She pulled him behind her and now she was completely within his embrace.

With both arms around her waist, he held her tightly, resting his chin on her hair. She turned around and wrapped her arms around his neck. Their lips nearly touched.

"I know no one will replace José," he said. "Never and nobody. But there can be life after grief. I will wait for you." He tried to pull back, but she would not let him. He gently ran his hands up her back, reaching her neck, while she traced the outline of his nose, lips and chin with her finger. They remained motionless for a moment, then he started combing her long, straight hair with his fingers.

He placed his index finger on her lip line. She arrested it and brought it to her cheek.

Christopher leaned forward and kissed her on the forehead. Lorena stepped back, took his hand, and they resumed their walk on the shore of Río de la Plata.

※

What is it that we have experienced in the last few days? Christopher asked himself as he woke up.

Every morning when he opened the door of his brother's room, it was her he saw. Martíta left early for work, and Lorena would be standing in the kitchen preparing their breakfast. It reminded him of that first time, when she had dropped the milk.

So much had changed since then. How different her attitude was toward him. Still, all these changes could be misleading. He had not expressed these thoughts to her, afraid it would affect the delicate balance they had managed to find through conversation, through silence, through holding hands. After all, the things Lorena shared of her life with José and the things he shared of his life were enough to fill their days.

"*Buenos días,* Lorena. Sorry I got up so late."

"*Buenos días para ti.* Everything is nearly ready. You can put the things on the table."

They had spent the previous days touring with their bicycles, visiting the city and stopping at places she wanted to show him, including Avenida 9 de Julio where José had organized the bicycle rally, the place where once the old tramway workshops stood, the medical school on Calle Paraguay.

With the passage of time, he had become increasingly aware that Lorena's stories never strayed far from the events of the 5th of March, when the junta massacred medical students and imprisoned the survivors. That day was her first trauma, blaming herself for the

death of the students—a tragedy she subsequently connected with
José's death. During breakfast Christopher tried to gather the courage
for what he wanted to say.

"I thought of suggesting to you that we go somewhere," he said after
they had eaten. "I've been thinking of it all these days, but I'm not sure
you would really want to go there." He proposed they visit her prison.

After a while, she responded. "Perhaps it will help to overcome a
little the past—the culpability, *el tormento*."

It was as much as he could have hoped and he understood how
difficult it would have been for her to accept.

As they were leaving the house, he said, "Please promise me, if
you feel uncomfortable you will tell me." She nodded in agreement
and, holding hands, they started their walk.

ॐ

Where once the prison stood was now a small park, still under
construction. Christopher read the name at the entrance: *Parque de la
Liberta—Liberty Park.*

Lorena pointed with her finger. "In that location was the cardboard
box where they put me for the first three days."

She was shivering. "Do you feel cold?"

"Yes, I feel cold; you can please hold me?"

Christopher wrapped his arm around her. They walked slowly
without talking. When they arrived at the place she had pointed to, he
pulled out of his jacket four red roses—as many as her months in jail.

She looked at the flowers for a long while, then smelled them
before holding them against her chest.

They sat on a wooden bench in the shade of a small tree. Eventually
she began talking about some of the things that had happened to her
there. She told him of the morning she helped stem the nosebleed of

one of the guards. Searching the first aid cabinet, she unexpectedly found the ring they had taken from her—a gift from her grandmother. The guard did not let her take back her ring, but he did allow her to get warm at the wooden stove at the end of the corridor with the eight isolation cells.

"What motivated you and José to risk so much for the environment?" asked Christopher.

"Knowledge. I was second year of the university and José had knowledge of the environment because of the passionate professor."

"I've been thinking for a while of asking you about José's article on the Resistência Pacifica website. It was brilliant, but so pessimistic. Was he exaggerating about the brain not being the right 'size?'"

"He believed the humans will become extinct because of too much confidence in their brain," she said. "*La arrogancia colosal.*"

"Yes, his argument makes sense in the context of learning our limits—the limits of the brain. The 'know thyself.'"

"Alberto told to him the most dangerous things humans possess is not weapons nuclear, but a brain with remnants reptilian and emotions Paleolithic."

"I guess José didn't have faith science would solve our problems."

"Alberto explained to him the limits of science."

She changed her position and rested her head against his shoulder. "José showed me the video from when he was a child," she continued. "He gave a speech to the TodoPorLaTierra—Everything for the Earth, the organization of Alberto. He used a story about the animals to make a caricature of the behavior of the humans."

"Really? I use animal metaphors too."

"His stories of animals were about the environment, in *parodia* of what the people do to the planet."

"I admit mine were lighthearted." He noticed her questioning look. "Frivolous, meaningless."

"José could be *frívolo* too. He joked, especially about my many years of learning the tango. He said his next book will be *How to Learn Tango in Less than Twenty-Five Years*. For our última Christmas he made two electronic cards for *tangueros*, '*Que te abracen sólo aquellos a los que tú quieres abrazar*—may you be squeezed only by those you wish to squeeze' and '*Qué los ochos siempre sean para adelante*—may all your figure-8 steps be forward.'"

In the shade of the small tree, Lorena continued recounting her history with José. As Christopher listened, a thought was gaining ground. Almost without meaning to, he expressed it, "The two of you had love and purpose."

"I saw the blood of José. Did you hold him in your arms?"

꣠

"And you are not the clone of *el Cristo*," Christopher heard her say as they finished breakfast. "You are just the brother of José."

That was what he wanted to hear, though he knew she did not quite believe it. They talked about what the *Parque de la Liberta* would look like once completed. And always with tenderness, they talked about José and about each other's lives.

In his mind the fundamental question was, *Is this the beginning or the end of something?* He was only certain of one half of it. She was the woman he thought had only existed in his imagination. Perhaps he felt that way because he wanted to emulate José—to be like him even through the people he loved.

Hard as it was to decipher his motivation, it was easy to feel the world only had meaning next to her, in whatever way she might accept him.

Through fortune and misfortune, I am here looking at her, talking to her, holding her hand. There is only one thing, though, I cannot do—take the first step.

But the first step was unfolding before him, at that very moment. Lorena was gently pulling his hand, leading him to the sofa.

As if in a waking dream, he lay with her, encircling her body with his own, her back pressing into him as he cradled her head in the crook of his arm. She pulled a colorful blanket over them. Red flowers were in the center of green squares, which were separated from each other by lilac borders.

He ran his hand down her arm from her shoulder to her fingers and back again, his breath in synchrony with hers. Each moment, each movement had meaning.

He was in control of neither body nor mind, but knew that there were boundaries he could not cross before she did. The very things that drew them together could equally pull them apart as haunting memories and fears of betrayal hovered between them.

She turned around and looked at him, her lips close to his. In this dance of emotions, he felt compelled to follow her lead as their lips lightly touched. *This is everything,* he thought, as she curled into his body.

He started undoing the buttons of her blouse and she the buttons of his shirt.

He softly kissed her collarbone. His fingers brushed against the soft lace of her white bra. He slipped them under the strap to ease it off her shoulder.

Suddenly, she stopped him with her hand and backed away. "Pardon me," he heard her say. "I thought I could, but I cannot."

She straightened her blouse and rebuttoned it.

He kissed her on the forehead and then on the tip of her nose. "We will do only as you wish," he said. He sensed her relief as she rested her face against his chest.

He felt out of his depth, lost amongst the sea of reasons that might draw Lorena away—the most obvious his own face. He didn't just resemble José. He was his mirror image. Even worse, he was linked to the death of her love. There was no one worse with whom to betray José.

Beyond this, there was her horrific experience in jail. He could not imagine what memories intimate contact might trigger, and possibly she had never made love with José.

"What is you think?" she asked.

He had not realized he was being scrutinized. "About you, only you."

She turned onto her stomach and, half leaning on him, looked down at his face as though to see his answers more clearly. "What things about me?"

"Oh, many things. That you're the most beautiful, most intelligent, most unique girl I have met." He paused. "But, I'm afraid, Lorena, I'm not bringing you peace."

"I do not know what I want from you, but I know I want you near." She was leaning forward on her elbows now. Although dressed, the top buttons of her blouse were undone and he could see her bra. He traced the curve of her jaw with his fingers and then caressed her shoulder.

"I'm sorry, Lorena. Do you want me to stop?"

"Stop? No, I do not want you to stop."

He kissed her, starting at her forehead and slowly moving down to touch her lips with his, like the first time. She moved even closer. He pulled his head back and asked her to turn to the side so he could see her profile. *Nothing could be more beautiful.*

She took his hand from her shoulder and repositioned it over her heart.

He could count the beats, aware of the closeness of their bodies. But once again she drew away.

The intimate moment was gone.

"I do not know what is wrong with me," he heard her say.

He covered her with the blanket. He wanted to hold her, but, before even trying, she had found a nest in his embrace. "Let time pass, Lorena," he said.

"I do not think time will ever be enough. Christopher, do not worry more. You are near to me. I accept you. But my body does not follow. I believe it not possible to make love with you."

He wanted to say that he too was devastated by the loss of his brother, but he hoped time would heal the wounds. He wanted to ask her to take one step at a time, to place trust in what they could share. But he waited, sensing she had not finished what she wanted to say.

And then her voice put an end to the silence, "I want you to know this. I am damaged. I cannot ... probably I cannot give birth to a child."

Chapter 24

DEAD SEA SHORE

What could be worse than life without meaning?

In the border zone between sleep and wakefulness came the question that so often visited him since the events at the Árvore Velha.

Christopher had woken up confused, for a moment feeling as if he was still on his first trip to Israel. But then memories of recent events gripped him.

He suddenly felt nauseous as he was assailed by images of his brother dying beside the Árvore Velha. In the dim light, everywhere he looked—on the walls, the ceiling, the floor—the scenes played out before him.

He lay back on the bed and closed his eyes, but the images were still there. The memories were like a magnet, pulling him down to where he should not be.

I have to escape.

Pushing himself out of bed, he went to the window to open the curtains. The blinding light of the outside made the images fade. What lay ahead in Israel was clear. The question was—what after Israel?

His phone rang and for a second he smiled as he saw the name. "Lorena, it's 3 am for you."

"Christopher, you are well?"

"Are *you* all right? Did something happen?"

"No, I am worrying about you."

"That's sweet. Are you at Martíta's?"

"No, no, in my house."

"I will call you at the end of my day—at the beginning of yours."

Her voice lingered in his mind as he set his navigator for the Dead Sea shore. He wore his watch on the wrong wrist and stuck a note on the dashboard to his right, "I Drive on the Right."

The desert's dry air was rushing through the open window, pulling at his hair. His mind went to his mother and his brother, and then swung back to Lorena. Could he possibly seek a future with her beyond the shadows of the past?

I am not who I thought I was. Genetically, I am identical to the other two. This is something José never knew.

What if their true identity were revealed. The Christians would see José as the advent of the Second Coming. *As for me, they would probably see me as the Antichrist or at best a blasphemy.*

He could imagine a conversation between the president of TerraDyname and James Howard.

"So, how come there is a brother now, James?"

"Well, it's a paradox. How could someone from the slums of Buenos Aires have an identical twin in Sydney's elite and not even know about it."

"Genius James—everyone else can't tell identical twins apart and you can't see the similarity!"

On approaching the destination, he made a U-turn and parked on the shoulder of the road. He got out and took photos of Masada. The mountain was tall, naked and rugged. The security station was visible near the platform of the chairlift. *If only I had a few hours' grace from their scrutiny ...*

The sky was full of cotton-wool clouds and he did not have to contend with unfiltered sun. At thirty-three degrees Celsius, though, it was ten degrees above the pleasant temperature of Jerusalem. Some distance away, a large rock clustered together with a group of smaller ones. He started walking toward it.

I have to accept I am genetically identical to Him—it is just about the only truth I can hold on to. But Sydney is not Nazareth year zero.

His mother had said to him that much as different artists sculpt different statues from the same block of marble, different environments produce different characters, even in identical twins. *She must have had José and me in mind when she said that.*

No two people can be identical characters if they lived in different places, let alone in different epochs and in the wake of each other. And this is equally true of identical twins.

On the other hand, Buenos Aires is not Nazareth either. Yet, José forgave his assailant at the bicycle rally just as He forgave those who crucified Him.

The large rock had a vertical face. He braced his arm with his backpack and, like a rugby player approaching the forward line, tried to shift it with sharp jabs. It did not budge. Gripping the rock from below, he tried hauling it up.

When nothing happened, he took a deep breath and tried again, the tendons in his neck and arms as taut as piano strings, but to no avail. He took another deep breath and started again. Again nothing. He used the handle of the shovel as a lever. The stick bent. It bent some more and then came the awful sound of it breaking.

Turning around, he rested his back against the rock and used the power of his legs to push. The rock shifted. He pushed more. It began to tip. Arteries were pulsating in his temples and neck. Sweat was running down his forehead; his mouth was dry. He went to the car to get some water.

What could be worse than life without meaning, he kept repeating to himself as he walked toward the road. Back in the car, he quickly drank half a bottle of water, pouring the rest on his head.

Whoever I am, there is always a chance for a new life. If I choose a life with Lorena, I may be choosing love without sexual intimacy—she said as much. But how could that be worse than life without love?

He started walking back.

No, it is impossible to think of myself without considering my origin.

He started digging. The earth was loose, soft, but the sloping land made it fall back into the hole. But then, there was nothing there. He dug further and still found nothing. *Has someone stolen the ossuary?*

Evelyn and Michael could not have misled him. His mother's letter was clear. He sat on the rim of the pit he had dug. Confused, he double-checked the GPS and shook his head in disbelief. He was about twenty meters away from the correct coordinates.

Frustrated and relieved, he picked up his broken shovel and walked over to a spot in the desert with an undulating surface devoid of rocks.

Again he set to work, shoveling the soft earth. Finally, he uncovered two rocks. Rolling them away, he began shoveling through yet another layer of earth, until he reached a hard, smooth surface. Seconds later he was certain—the top of the ossuary was emerging from the depths of the pit.

He had to touch the things revealed in his mother's letter. *What's more, I have to give the bones the peace due to them.*

This was his origin and his destination.

As he was about to lift the lid and confront his past, his hands became weak.

He stopped and sat on one of the rocks. The desert was so quiet he could hear blood pulsating in his ears. In his ears too were Michael's words about the discovery of the skeleton, and in his eyes his mother's letter—the beautiful and the terrifying words of that letter.

He bent down and stroked the lid of the ossuary as though it were a living thing. The time had come. He used the shovel to prise it open.

The ossuary was full of bones. The skull, calvarium sawn off, sat on top, confronting him.

With his bare hands he removed the bones. There was the fractured rib, the piece of wood and the bangle that had once graced the wrist of a woman. He wiped away decades of dust to view the inscription—"MM."

He picked up the skull and reunited it with its calvarium. He started rotating it on his palm, inch by inch, breath by breath. *My hands can hold nothing more sacred.*

He looked around him. He was near the place where the Jews had made their last stand against the Roman Empire. In the late afternoon, the mountains to the west cast long shadows toward him. There was courage in those besieged at Masada. All but the last of them submitted their necks to the sword, the last one dying by falling on it.

They might be my ancestors. He shook his head. *No, they left no descendants and, besides, their DNA came decades after mine.*

However, the besieged may have known the man to whom he owed his existence.

He looked again at the bones and artifacts in the ossuary. All would become cinders by his own hand. The silence of the desert that had held the secret for so long would now absorb it forever. The secret would live only in him and the other two people who knew of it.

The desolate, forsaken place all around him was about to be engulfed by the night.

José was right, he thought. *The greatest tormentor is our brain.*

Who decides in the end? Is my mind just a sea of chemicals? But, even so, we are identical. We all have the same sea inside us. Why then should I not be like them?

"You are not alone because you are with me." The searchlight of consciousness stopped on Lorena's words.

It was becoming clear to him—he would find meaning only if he joined her to continue the fight for the forest, the fight against the "injustice infinite."

But before taking a step forward, he had to relegate the past to the past. History had to rest. To dust he would turn the bones that spoke the words his mother taught him.

His long search ended here, where it all began. There was *no* father. There were three brothers. Three identical brothers. And there were three mothers.

All was quiet on the outside and all was finally settled within. The sun had set in the Middle East, but a new day was beginning in the Amazon.

He texted Lorena. "A nightmare brought us together. May a dream unite us."

"Christopher, there is something that I must to tell you," came her response.

"Please, tell me."

"I will defeat my tormentors," she wrote. "Inside me, the heart of José will beat."

"They deserve to be defeated. José will always be inside you. If there were not enough reasons to love you …"

"You do not understand me," she replied.

He stared at the screen. Was he about to learn of the only thing that could lessen the pain of his brother's loss?

Soon after, yet another message arrived, "And if you understand, you may want not to come."

Within reach in front of him was a tiny yellow flower. Its beauty and fragrance to the world it offered for the taking. Were it not for the little flower, there would have been no color anywhere. How could this small plant blossom in such adversity?

"I will come," he answered. "Please, tell me hope is alive."

"Today I found," Lorena wrote. "A child. I will bring to the world a child."

The End

ACKNOWLEDGMENTS

My strongest thanks to my agent, George Karlov, for his belief that concepts presented in this book deserve to be heard at the time humanity is about to eliminate corals, simplify life in the oceans and burn the Amazon.

Marg Bowman, a brilliant editor, worked with enthusiasm, to the benefit of anyone who may read this novel.

Courtney Nicholls published this book with great care and speed and Debbie McInnes undertook its promotion with conviction and commitment.

Laksmi Govindasami, an intellectually gifted medical student, helped develop the idea into a book.

Kiriaki Orfanos, with affection for the ideas expressed in the book, and perfection as a character trait, turned my writing from science to literature.

Writers and friends Sue Woolfe, Ken Ross and Gordon Graham taught me how to penetrate a hero's character and portray his/her feelings and motivations.

Events from Melpo Lekatsa's resistance to the military dictatorship in Greece gave me a starting point for the development of one of the heroines of the novel.

My children, Alexi and Yvette Paxinos, as well as their partners, Portia Bridges and Cem Hizli, made suggestions and were companions on the journey, as was Elly Paxinos in the first years of writing.

I thank the writers/consultants who helped me: Nick Bleszynski, Mireille Juchau, Bryce Courtenay, Dimitri Tanoudis, Nicola O'Shea, Carlos Irineu, Rosie Scott, Michelle Moo, Barry Oakley, Emily Maguire, Thomas Voulgaris, Owen Lewis, Paul Watson and Irina Dunn.

ACKNOWLEDGMENTS

Friends in Argentina and Brazil contributed to the authenticity of the descriptions: Marta Graciela Garcia Lorea, Patricia Lillo, Silvia Olfi, Benedito Machado and Griselda Doroni.

Scientists advised me on points related to their specialties: Kris Barlow-Stewart, Shmulik Marco, Philip Fearnside, Richard Bryant, Dionisis Sikiotis, Bart Nuttin, Michael Bendon, Oscar Scremi, Phil Waite and Aphrodite Papaioannou.

Many good friends read the text and gave me their thoughts: Mariana Tsehos, Dora Chrysikou, Gulgun Sengul, Anne Wahl, Robyn Hutchinson, Sunali Lewis, Eleni Petridou, Martin Cohen, Wendy Searle, Christina Vasilatou, Maki Moraitis, Maria Panagiotakopoulou, Grace McDonald, Marie Foster, Charles Watson, Peter Birrell, Giannis Pylarinos, Diana Troiani, Sarah Bedford, Dorje Swallow, Con Castan, Joanne Tracey, Marcia Manning, Alexander Whillier, Petros Alexiou, Dimitra Bechlikoudi, Dimi Kahrila, Athena Kovatsi, Daniel Benitez, Katerina Aggelakopoulou, Vrasidas Karalis, Margaret Scott, Martin Cohen, Taso Germeni, Anna Stathopoulou, Pantofili Varvarigou, Voula Sakka, Angelos Vlahos, Natasa Fraggouli, Carolyn Crowther and Kristie Smith.

Chichina Ferreyra, a friend of Che Guevara, kindly allowed me to refer to our conversation, modified for the purposes of the book.

The lyrics of Giannis Ritsos inspired my own. From E.O. Wilson I borrowed the thought "Puzzled we stand before nature, surprised by our own existence …"; from Santiago Ramon y Cajal "… exchange protoplasmic kisses in an epic love journey" and from Holdren and Ehrlich the equation for environmental impact.

At a recent moment of dark levity, a friend asked me how my novel was going. I said, "Two decades and still not finished." Her encouragement: "My cousin's novel was published posthumously."

Photographs relevant to this novel from research trips to Israel, Greece, the Vatican, the Amazon and Bueno Aires can be found by clicking on the image of the red cover of the novel at https://www. neura.edu.au/staff/scientia-professor-george-paxinos-ao/

If you read the book and wish to communicate with me, please email g.paxinos@neura.edu.au with email title A River Divided.

BIOGRAPHY

George Paxinos studied at Berkeley, McGill and Yale and was a visiting scientist at Cambridge, Oxford, Karolinska, Stanford and UCLA. He is Scientia Professor of Medical Sciences at Neuroscience Research Australia and The University of New South Wales in Sydney.

He has identified and named more brain areas than anyone in history (94 nuclei) and published 57 books, his first, *The Rat Brain in Stereotaxic Coordinates*, being the most cited publication in neuroscience and, for decades, the third most cited book in all science of all time.

The first edition of his *Atlas of the Human Brain* received the Award for Excellence in Publishing in Medical Science from the Association of American Publishers, and the latest edition the British Medical Association Illustrated Book Award.

His atlases and concepts of brain organization are used by most scientists working on the relationship between the brain and cognition, emotion, motivation and thought, including neurologic or psychiatric diseases such as Alzheimer's and depression, or animal models of these diseases.

In recognition of Paxinos' contributions to psychology and neuroscience, he received the Alexander von Humboldt Award (2003) and the highest awards from both Australian national societies—the Distinguished Scientific Contribution Award of the Australian Psychological Society (2007) and the Distinguished Achievement Award of the Australasian Neuroscience Society (2015).

He was President of the Australian Neuroscience Society (2005–2006) and President of the International Brain Research Organization World Congress of Neuroscience (2004–2007).

Activism for the environment. In the 1980s and the 1990s, Paxinos was the principal advocate for the return of trams to Sydney, founding

The Light Rail Association, which aimed at reducing reliance on the car and consequent atmospheric pollution. Again, out of concern for the environment, Paxinos stood as a candidate for the Australian Cyclists Party in the 2015 New South Wales state elections.

Twenty-one years in the making, *A River Divided* is his first novel.